Esca...

H.M.S. Bulldog and
Growler Attack

PARHAM BAY

Escape to West

Antigua

ENGLISH HARBOR
1st Cruise
under French

2nd Encounter with
H.M.S. Bulldog

Miles
0 1 2 3 4 5

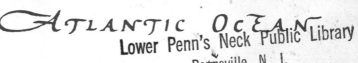

ATLANTIC OCEAN

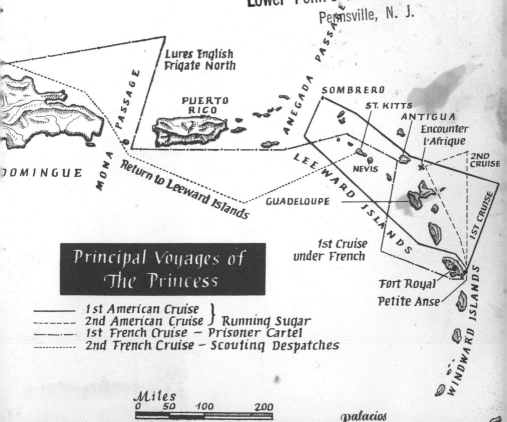

Lures English
Frigate North

PUERTO
RICO

ANEGADA PASSAGE

SOMBRERO

ST. KITTS

ANTIGUA
Encounter
l'Afrique

2ND
CRUISE

MONA PASSAGE

Return to Leeward Islands

NEVIS

LEEWARD ISLANDS

DOMINGUE

GUADELOUPE

1st Cruise
under French

1ST CRUISE

Fort Royal
Petite Anse

WINDWARD ISLANDS

Principal Voyages of
The Princess

———— 1st American Cruise ⎫
-------- 2nd American Cruise ⎬ Running Sugar
—·—·— 1st French Cruise — Prisoner Cartel
----------- 2nd French Cruise — Scouting Despatches

Miles
0 50 100 200

palacios

SEA ROAD TO YORKTOWN

By Harvey Haislip

SEA ROAD TO YORKTOWN
THE PRIZE MASTER
SAILOR NAMED JONES
PLAY (Broadway 1952)
THE LONG WATCH

HARVEY HAISLIP

SEA ROAD
TO YORKTOWN

Doubleday & Company, Inc., Garden City, New York, 1960

Fic

Hai

Library of Congress Catalog Card Number 60-13736
Copyright © 1960 by Harvey Haislip
All Rights Reserved
Printed in the United States of America
First Edition

2115

To my wife, GEORGIA,
*whose help on this and earlier novels and stories
has been my mainstay.*

"In any operation, and under all circumstances, a decisive naval superiority is to be considered as a fundamental principle, and the basis upon which every hope of success must ultimately depend."

GENERAL WASHINGTON TO THE COUNT
DE ROCHAMBEAU, WHEN PLANNING THE
CAMPAIGN THAT LED TO YORKTOWN.

LOG OF THE *PRINCESS*, PRIVATEER

FIRST PART

Begins clear and cool, and a fresh northeast trade.
Sailed Brest for Martinique.

MIDDLE PART

Begins hot and humid—hurricane season.
Sailed Leeward Islands under sealed orders.

LAST PART

Begins with squalls and heavy rain.
Action at St. Kitts.

FIRST PART

January–June, 1781.
Begins clear and cool, and a fresh northeast trade.
Sailed Brest for Martinique.

CHAPTER ONE

FRANCIS JOSEPH PAUL, the Count de Grasse, Chef d'Escadre des Armées Navales, Knight of St. John of Jerusalem, stepped from his twelve-oared barge onto the landing at Brest. He had commanded a division in the battle off Ushant in 1778; and again in the West Indies, off the Grenadines, in 1779; and later that same year he had fought on the American coast in D'Estaing's failure to take Savannah from the British. In 1780, under De Guichen, he had led a division in the great battle off Martinique. Now, in January 1781, his flagship had come to an anchor in the roadstead, one of forty ships still working in from sea. It was the first time in many months that M. de Grasse had trod anything more stable than a ship's deck.

The French fleet had fallen into disrepute. Victories had been few and, even when claimed, had not justified acclaim. French naval commanders had become expert at disengagement from fleet actions. To keep a fleet in being, rather than the destruction of enemy forces, had become the pattern.

M. de Grasse, accompanied by his *major d'escadre*, paused for a moment at the top of the landing stairs and let his eyes sweep the panorama of this great naval arsenal: the city climbing the hills above a medieval fortress-castle; tier upon tier of stone houses, cold and dure as the Breton coast on which they stood. Beyond the long masonry mole spread the dockyard: storehouses, sail lofts and rope walks, and a forest of masts rising from ships at the repair and victualing wharves. In the estuary, hulks lay in all stages of rigging or unrigging, and breaking up for salvage. Close to the mole the guard frigate lay anchored, her stern hauled up by a stout hawser so that her bows always pointed toward the entrance, ready to cast and sail if her presence should be required in the great outer bay, or in the seaward approaches to Brest.

The hills, to the Count's joy, were dark with citizens watching the fleet come in. Frenchmen, *le bon Dieu* be thanked, had not forgotten these storm-racked ships and weary men who had so long been the bastion of French interests afar in many seas. They had been recalled to Brest to refit and refresh themselves before launching new campaigns: the West Indies and the Indian Ocean, it was said.

And, although here in this armada were most of the great sea commanders of France: D'Estaing, De Guichen, Suffren, La Motte-Picquet, there was another rumor to be heard: when the combined fleet sailed again, the Count de Grasse, now a junior, would be in chief command.

In the closing years of the eighteenth century, when France, after supporting the American Colonies in ill-kept secret, had been brought to book by England, when ships were short-handed and badly found and the public treasury empty, command on a distant station would be no sinecure. It warmed the Count's heart to see these people on the hills. Their support would be needed if the fleet was to be kept strong.

As he and his *major d'escadre* strode along, handsome figures both, men stopped working to stare curiously, some doffed their hats: the usual stevedores and workmen found on a dockyard quay. Among them two strange individuals caught the Count's eye. They sat on a warping bitt, absorbed in the arriving ships. One, from his uniform, was an officer; the other, a common seaman; yet it was easily seen that they were friends. English, the Count assumed. Prisoners of war were granted considerable freedom, on parole of good behavior, while waiting transportation in exchange cartels.

The strangers slid down from the bitt, seeing the two French naval officers, and stood at attention, saluting. One was a boy, handsome, his face weathered to a golden tan, his fair hair, bleached by sun, drawn together on his nape and tied in a queue with an end of ribbon. A boy outstripping his clothes in his rapid growth to manhood, his bell-bottoms too high on his half-boots, his brass-buttoned cuffs creeping up to expose chilblained wrists. It warmed the Count, having left home himself when but eleven to become a Garde de Marine. Close to half a century ago, but he had not forgotten.

The boy's companion was a burly seaman, tough as weathered-oak—the kind a naval officer dreamed of having beside him when boarding enemy ships.

The Count returned the salute casually without breaking stride. But there was something about these two that called to him. He had been a prisoner in England after the battle off Finisterre. Then an *enseigne de vaisseau*, humiliated by defeat and capture, his loneliness had seemed unbearable. Now, thirty years later, his great heart remembering, he stopped and turned back.

"You are being treated well?" he inquired in labored English.

"We have just arrived in Brest, sir," the young officer replied.

"And you are to be exchanged, *n'est-ce pas?*"

"Oh, no, sir. We're not prisoners." Replying, the youth had slipped naturally into fluent French.

"But you speak my own tongue as well as I," M. de Grasse exclaimed. "Yet we are not compatriots, I'll swear."

"Permit me, sir." The boy made a courtly bow. "Midshipman Thomas Potter, United States Navy. And this is able seaman Reilly. We're old shipmates."

Reilly swept off his broad-brimmed shiny hat in an arc that made the ribbons stream. "Sarvant, Your Lordship."

The Count stifled an exclamation of surprise. "Is there an American man-of-war in the roadstead then?"

His *major d'escadre* replied. "If there is, monsieur, I do not know where. Every spot where a deep-draft ship can anchor is occupied by one of ours—or soon will be."

"We're not from a man-of-war, sir," Mr. Potter hurriedly explained. "The fact is, I'm not actually in the American Navy. But I was."

"An' wasn't the both of us, your honor?" Reilly exclaimed. "Wid that grand little fighting Scot, the Commodore hisself!"

"You fought with John Paul Jones?" the Count demanded, at once impressed.

"Yes, sir. Aboard *Ranger* and *Serapis* and *Alliance*. And after that, aboard a privateer in the Channel."

"And now?" M. de Grasse inquired.

"We have come from Dr. Franklin in Paris," Mr. Potter explained, "to settle the affairs of that privateer before she sails for the West Indies."

The Count had heard of the American minister's venture into privateering. Benjamin Franklin, by issuing commissions to American captains of French-owned, fast, small cruisers, had managed to keep a flow of British prisoners coming into France for exchange with American seamen in English prisons. There had been no great objection to this when France was carrying on a pretense of neutrality while secretly aiding the American Colonies; but now that open war had broken out, France needed English prisoners for her own account, and all her ships under her own flag directed by her own minister of marine, and all her seamen in French-flag ships.

"It is well for American privateers to move into West Indian waters," the Count said. "They have served their usefulness in the Channel and along the French coast. Besides, they will find plenty of activity in the Caribbees. The war will be decided there."

"Dr. Franklin thinks so too," the young American replied.

"I have served in the Antilles a long time," the Count said. "No doubt I shall serve there again, and we may renew this brief acquaintance. I am the Count de Grasse, and this is M. de Vaugirauld, my chief of staff."

The engaging personality of this tall, distinguished old sailor left Thomas Potter wide-eyed and speechless, but not able seaman Reilly.

"'Tis a fine grand fleet Your Lordship commands," he said.

"I command but one division," the Count corrected.

"May ye soon command the lot, sor, for 'tis me belief, an' many a grand seaman I've seen, no finer figger of a man iver trod a quarterdeck than your honor."

The remark, startling as it was, set the Count's shrewd eyes twinkling. "And I've never seen a finer figure of an able seaman," he replied.

"The saints presarve Your Lordship in battle, is the prayer of able seaman Reilly."

"And bring victory to America and France," the Count said, devoutly crossing himself. "If I encounter your Dr. Franklin at court in Versailles, where I go now to regain my health, I shall tell him of this meeting."

He bowed to terminate the conversation and, with his hand resting lightly on the arm of his *major d'escadre*, passed on.

CHAPTER TWO

THE DECISION to abandon the privateering venture had not been Dr. Franklin's, although on several occasions he had stated, with considerable warmth, that he was heartily tired of the sea and ships and the men who sailed them. Except for crossing the Atlantic as a passenger, he had had no previous experience in maritime affairs, and the problems of managing privateer captains, some of whom had been Irish smugglers and, consequently, English outlaws, were many and vexing. But since these fast ships brought in captured British seamen to be exchanged later for American prisoners, he would have continued their operations had not M. de Sartine, French minister of marine, requested him to recall the commissions he had issued. French-owned privateers under American captains would no longer be welcome in coastal harbors.

The captains thus stripped of their American authority could accept French commissions, in which case their operations would no longer concern Dr. Franklin; or they could find bases other than harbors along the French coast. Only one, Captain Jonathan Wilder of the *Princess Royal*, chose the latter course, his decision being helped by the suggestion of the French owners, cold to far-distant operations, that the ship's officers take their accumulated prize money in shares of the vessel. Thus they would become owners of the ship in which they served.

This transfer, and departure from Dr. Franklin's jurisdiction, would require completion of certain documents and records; and to act as his agent, the American minister had sent Midshipman Thomas Potter to the coast. The son of one of the old statesman's staff, young Potter had served for two years as a midshipman under John Paul Jones and had, in addition, made a privateering cruise aboard *Princess*. Not willingly, it was true, having been impressed on board, but none the less gainfully in both prize money and experience.

And since, before the cruise was out, Midshipman Potter had been sent as prize master of a captured ship, in which capacity he had shown himself unusually competent for one so young, Dr. Franklin was anxious to find other employment for him. There were now no American men-of-war in European waters to which the American minister could attach the young officer; he therefore used him, for the time, in his own service. On this mission, Thomas Potter had arrived in Brest, with his old shipmate and friend, Reilly, as he had explained to M. de Grasse.

When the Count and his *major d'escadre* had gone on their way along the quay, young Potter had climbed back to his seat of vantage on the warping bitt, while Reilly had seated himself comfortably on the boy's sea chest, his back against the bitt's upright. For a time they were silent, gripped by the scene in the harbor.

Division after division of ships stood in, squadron following squadron: frigates, two-deckers, and an occasional three-decker looming above the rest. As if to welcome them home, the sun broke through the slate roof of a January sky, bright shafts splashing the white royal ensigns surcharged with golden fleurs-de-lis.

Beyond the Goulet, through which the ships must pass one by one, the outer roadstead was alive with vessels, tacking back and forth, waiting their turn. Once a ship had cleared the narrow entrance, men, like ants, crawled out on yards to shorten sail and furl the storm-grayed canvas. With storerooms and magazines close to empty, and water butts in need of filling, the barnacled hulls rode high, their sides between wind and water streaked with the green of sea grass. Great, stocked anchors hung at the catheads, ready for dropping.

" 'Tis a grand thing to see," Reilly observed.

"What I'd like to know," the boy said, "is what's so important about the West Indies to need all these ships out there?"

" 'Tis the rum an' sugar an' spice to be had. There's no richer trade."

"You can't win a war on sugar and spice," the boy remarked.

"What else would it mean, if a country was to lose that trade an' the other take it?" Reilly asked. " 'Tis why the fleets don't get far away from it."

"But our war's in America," Tommy argued.

"Suppose now," Reilly answered patiently, "the French fleet was to sail to Ameriky to help win that war. Wouldn't the British gobble up the whole West Indies—sugar an' spice an' all? Rodney took Martinique, gone nearly twenty year, but when the final treaty was writ, France got the island back. 'Twas not to Admiral's likin', I don't misdoubt; he's back agin now, old, but hammerin' away to capture Martinique once more. 'Tis me belief he will, happen this fleet we're lookin' at doesn't get out there soon."

"You'll be back there soon, too," the boy said.

His remark brought a questioning glance into the old seaman's eyes; eyes gray-green, with deep crow's-feet at the corners from wind and sun and laughter.

"Aye," he answered. "But not cox'n of old Rodney's barge this cruise."

Reilly's hair had once been a flaming red but was faded now with sprinkled gray. Yet there was still the strength of a young man in his great arms and barrel chest.

These two had been shipmates for nearly three years; it seemed to young Potter he had known Reilly all his life. That would be the hard part of not sailing to the West Indies aboard *Princess*—good-by to Reilly. Reilly, who had taught him the seaman's way of lashing a hammock with seven marling hitches, no more, no less; and how to reeve a running bowline, and make a long splice, and fashion a double Matthew Walker knot. Reilly, with a steadying hand and good advice whenever there was trouble; who smelled of hemp and tar and rum, and got drunk too often, yet, even sober, would speak his mind to any man no matter what rank or station. Reilly, his head full of sailor's superstitions, believing that sea gods shaped a sailor's destiny and that when the sea got hold of you it never let you go.

It would be hard to part with Reilly.

"Ye'll not be shippin' out wid us, sor?" Reilly asked, as if reading his mind.

"When the documents are all signed and in order," he explained, "I must take them back to Dr. Franklin."

"God bless the ould gintleman wid his kites an' all," Reilly said, "but could ye not send thim to him by post, along wid a letter from yourself explainin' any matters?"

He could, of course, but there was more to it than that. "I told my parents I'd be coming home."

"If 'twas a promise, we'll say no more about it," Reilly assured him.

"It wasn't exactly a promise," the boy said. "I told them I'd be home, that's all."

"I don't misdoubt your father will be gettin' a job for ye behind a desk in the good doctor's office."

He didn't answer that, finding the thought of a desk job too distasteful to be considered even for a moment. Instead he asked, "Are you really a praying man, Reilly?"

"Me, sor?" Reilly sounded as if he thought the lad had lost his senses.

"You told M. de Grasse you'd pray the saints to preserve him," the boy reminded.

" 'Twas just a manner o' sphakin', sor. There's no stoppin' a cannon ball wid prayer."

"You might be moved to get out of its way, though."

"Prayin' is well enough for officers, sor," Reilly said. "A bunk to kneel forninst is wan thing, but a common sailor, now, wid naught but a hammick . . ."

"What's a 'hammick' got to do with it?"

" 'Tis no comfortable thing at all, kneelin' beside a hammick that's swingin' in a seaway, an' maybe get a clump on the head."

"It's not the kneeling," the boy told him. "It's what you feel and say." They prayed in his own home every morning after breakfast, before his father went to the office: mother and father and the three children kneeling beside their chairs.

" 'Tis not likely there's an angel in Heavin would cock an ear to anything I'd say," Reilly observed. "Wid me drinkin' an' cursin' an' all?"

"You're no worse than any other sailors."

"Whorin' an' all?"

"Doesn't everyone?"

It was not often that able seaman Reilly showed signs of discomfiture. He did now. In their daily life on shipboard he had not seen the changes. He had seen only a lad growing out of his jacket—which any blind man would see. And blind he had been, for there were other ways that lads grew. Was there any reason the nipper should be different from the rest?

"I misdoubt the folly of ithers will be an excuse whin defaulters are called to mast, come the end, to be told who goes aloft an' who below."

"Then you do believe in heaven!" the boy said jubilantly.

"Ach, an' did I iver say contrary? Hell, too. I learned me

catechism as a lad an' prayed regular at me dear mither's knee, whilst expectin' to feel me ould man's boot any minute, him comin' home each night in a fuddle, bad temper oozin' from his skin wid the whuskey."

"That's in your favor," the boy told him.

"Ye might mintion it to thim above, sor, since ye be a prayin' man."

Mr. Potter got down off the bitt, straightened his black neckerchief, and pulled down the cuffs of his jacket. "Here comes the captain!" he announced.

Jonathan Wilder, striding along the quay, was tall and rawboned, but the winds of the Channel had not yet blown the gray of Forton Prison from his sunken cheeks. He was a merchant sailor, yet there was the stamp of a man-of-war's quarterdeck about him in his double-breasted blue greatcoat, topped off by a tricorn, and a sword swinging against knee-britched legs. He was so intent on the harbor shipping that he failed to see the two who were waiting for him until he heard their greeting.

"Captain Wilder, sir!" Thomas Potter called, saluting.

"'Tis well I hope your honor finds hisself," Reilly said, with a touch of his hat brim. "Afther all thim bouts o' fever."

"Tol'able," Captain Wilder answered, halting his stride to observe them. "I hope you got your bellyful of English prisons."

"It wasn't bad, sir," young Potter replied. "Two days was all."

Two days! Captain Wilder had spent two years, much of the time manacled to the deck of a prison hulk or in the "Black Hole" at Forton Prison, the severe punishment meted out for attempting to escape. But after several futile tries he had made it and got across the Channel to France, where he had found seaman's work privateering.

"No use standing here in the wind," he said, shivering in his greatcoat although the sun was still shining. "Come aboard."

He strode off at once, briskly. Midshipman Potter picked up his quadrant case and hurried after him, stretching his legs to keep alongside. Reilly brought up the rear, his broad-brimmed hat cocked aslant by the boy's sea chest, balanced on one brawny shoulder. His own sea bag dangled from a hand big as a snatch block. Captain Wilder walked close to the edge of the quay and whistled between his teeth. The shrill call brought a boat from a recess in the masonry. It drew alongside the landing stairs.

Reilly took up a pair of oars to help the single occupant, and Captain Wilder took the tiller. Mr. Potter, having nothing to do, watched the ships coming to anchor.

Whitecaps were flecking the roadstead, and the farther the boat pulled from shore, the choppier the water became. "A good job I found a berth close in," Captain Wilder remarked, his eyes on a sleek Baltimore clipper. The flood tide was trimming her taut anchor cable with white lace, and the current, building up a little bow wave, made it look as if she were under way. The long narrow lines of her hull promised speed, the drag aft and the rake of her masts, along with the rise to her bows, meant handy maneuvering. Essentially a fore-and-after, she carried a square fore-topsail and topgallant, which would give her speed running free while, close-hauled, the fore-and-aft sails would hold her closer to the wind than any ship of the line or even frigate.

The port lids along her sides were painted black to match the hull, concealing the guns behind the bulwarks. But the lids could be dropped in seconds to let her long six-pounders run out, six on a side, to snatch the initial advantage of surprise from larger ships.

Captain Wilder swung the little boat in a wide arc under the privateer's counter. There was her name in bold letters across her stern: *"Princess."*

"Lookin' for the *Royal*, Mr. Potter?" the captain asked, as if reading the boy's mind. "Took it off—too much the sound o' kings an' queens. Plain *Princess* more suited to freedom's flag."

As the boat came alongside, men on deck stopped work to stare. A boy at the taffrail began to shout, "Don Tomas! Don Tomas!"

It was Angel, the Spanish cabin boy. He pointed to the boat

to attract the attention of the men on deck. "*Hombres!* Look you! It is Don Tomas! He has come back!"

The men congregated at the rail near the side ladder. They shouted greetings in several tongues. "Tommy!" and "Reilly!" they called to the boat. "We thought you had deserted us!"

An officer poked his head out the cuddy door, and, seeing them, came on deck and joined the men. He was tall and wore a short, sky-blue jacket with silver buttons. His black hair was queued with a ribbon and sun glinted on a golden loop in one ear.

"*Mon ami!*" he yelled. "It is you!" White teeth gleamed in a narrow, hawk-like face, dark as weathered mahogany.

Young Potter stood up in the boat, rocking it crazily in the current. "Gascoyne!"

"Sit down!" Wilder ordered. "You want to capsize us!"

There was good reason for the youngster's excitement: the last time he had seen Gascoyne, the French officer had been stretched out on the deckhouse roof, a bullet through his lungs. And since Gascoyne could not sail the fine prize they had just captured into port, and Captain Wilder had no remaining officer who could navigate, young Potter had gone as prize master of *Vixen.*

"Are you all well again?" he shouted to the handsome Frenchman.

"But of course!" Gascoyne replied.

"Just ask the girls ashore," someone yelled gleefully.

Meanwhile the boat was dancing in the current, sheering this way and that, and Reilly got out oars again. "Heave a boat line!" Captain Wilder yelled, spray glistening on his face. "You want I should catch my death while you welcome the prodigal?"

Reilly deftly caught the line and took a turn around the snubbing post and the men on deck hauled the boat close, to be hooked on. " 'Tis a grand homecomin' they've give ye, Mister Midshipman Potter," Reilly said.

As Thomas Potter followed the captain up the ship's side,

Gascoyne embraced him and he felt the play of firm, lithe muscles. Though he did not like the woman fragrance still clinging to the Frenchman's soft, striped jersey, he liked Gascoyne. No matter how many girls he might have ashore, aboard he was splendid.

"But it is good to see you, *mon ami!*" the Frenchman exclaimed in the charming English the boy remembered so well. "And that Irish *gamine?* Did things go well?"

Wasn't it just like Gascoyne? Because there had been a pretty girl on board the captured transport he had to make a romance of it!

"She got safely back to England, that's all I know."

"Nothing more, *mon ami?*" Clearly he had failed Gascoyne.

"Of course not!" But his cheeks were flaming, and one of the men called:

"She kissed him good-by at Portsmouth dock. We seen it."

They were crowding around him. Metzger, the square-jawed tough from New York who, after *Vixen* had been recaptured by an English frigate, had let his back be flogged to a bloody mess and still would not betray a shipmate. And Jacobs, another of the prize crew. And Booby, the giant West Indian black. They had all had a taste of prison after *Vixen* had been brought into Portsmouth. His friendship with these men had grown in the common experience of suffering and danger.

Metzger said, "Ain't we been wonderin' all along was Tommy coming back? And here he is!"

"Who be ye sphakin' of?" Reilly demanded.

"Tommy. Ain't that the little bugger's name?"

"It is, begod. But ye'll show more riverence sphakin' to an officer or ye'll feel the back o' me hand!"

"His girl she call him Tommy," Booby said in his soft slow way. "Seems like we could."

"Call me what you like," Tommy flared, "but if I hear another word about the girl there'll be trouble."

"There's still a word to be heard from me, sor, by your lave," Reilly persisted. "There'll be no callin' of you Tommy whin I'm around. Mister Tommy if they like, or Midshipman Tommy, the wan handle or the both; but niver widout."

Gascoyne laughed. "Splendid! Was it a nice kiss, Midshipman Tommy?"

What could you do with a man like that? Nothing, when it was Gascoyne. So Tommy hid his embarrassment by following Captain Wilder below.

They went through a door in the after end of the deckhouse, half above, half below decks, down three steps into a snug cuddy. He had often written up the log on the hinged shelf which ran along the starboard bulkhead, and worked out traverse sailings while Captain Wilder slept on the flag chest opposite, not wishing to be far away from the wheel. With the cuddy doors open and a mattress spread atop the chest, the captain could seen the helmsman's legs, and could check the ship's course on the telltale compass which swung in gimbals on the forward bulkhead—without so much as sticking his head into the weather.

Hooks on the bulkheads, wherever there was any space, accommodated tarpaulin hats and storm clothing, and a row of round portholes on each side furnished ventilation and light; but not light enough to penetrate the darkness at the foot of the companionway to the berth deck.

Down there Tommy found himself in a kind of gloomy twilight, even though the swinging oil lamp was lighted; but he knew that country well enough to get around in the blackest dark.

The sight of the familiar cabin, which ran the full width of the berth deck aft, made it seem more like a homecoming than even the warm greetings of the men: the sideboard with the usual clutter of crockery jammed into fiddles to prevent breakage when the ship became lively in a sea; the locker, used as a catch-all for odd gear; the low deck beams beneath which any but a short man must stoop or bump his head.

Sunlight, filtering down through the barred glass of the skylight above the table, struck amber shafts from a bottle of wine set out with glasses on the red-checked cloth. Gascoyne at once began pouring. "We must drink to our midshipman's return," he said gaily.

"I'm teetotal," Captain Wilder grumbled. "How many times must I tell ye?"

"Some day you may change your mind, *peut-être*," Gascoyne replied hopefully.

"You waste your time hopin'," Wilder growled.

Gascoyne raised his glass, and Tommy drank with him. But he felt a terrible hypocrite, knowing that he had not returned to stay.

"Angel will clean up your old room," Gascoyne told him.

There were four small cubicles forward of the cabin to accommodate the principal officers. Junior officers, and prize masters carried at the beginning of a voyage, were obliged to swing in hammocks in the passage outside those rooms.

"There's no hurry," Tommy said.

Gascoyne went around the table and stretched his long legs out on the transom-settee, glass in hand. The red-checkered cloth, the wine, and Gascoyne on the transom! The picture was complete.

"Suppose we get down to business!" Captain Wilder suggested.

He had stripped off his greatcoat and tunic, and sat at the table in a long-sleeved woolen undershirt that did not conceal the wasting of his big, bony frame. As he shuffled through a stack of papers, Tommy saw the livid rings on each wrist where the manacles had chafed.

"There's a deal o' things to be done afore we sail," the captain warned.

"We are attending, monsieur," Gascoyne said. He emptied his glass and set it down.

Captain Wilder thumbed through the papers, checking them against a letter. "All these here documents must be sent to Dr. Franklin, according to his instructions."

"That's why I've come," Tommy told him. "To see to it."

"Aye. 'Tis what the good doctor says in his letter. And, say

I, the sooner started, the sooner finished." He began checking his papers against Dr. Franklin's letter: "Smooth log; muster roll; list o' dead and missing; certificate of prize shares paid an' receipts for same; certificate that all debts for stores, equipment, or services is paid afore sailing." He fingered the graying stubble on his chin. "That's the stumblin' block right there," he said.

"There is trouble, *mon capitaine?*" Gascoyne inquired.

"I've paid all the men's claims, as this here certificate shows; and money's impounded to pay the dead and missing—their heirs or whatever. But there's no money to pay off this young feller an' the chandler too. So if he ain't willin' to come along as partner in the venture—there ain't funds to suffice."

"But of course he will come," Gascoyne said. His black eyes flashed. "To the West Indies! Where your Irish *gamine* is going."

"I hadn't planned to," Tommy replied.

"You will not go out to see that pretty girl?" Gascoyne asked, astounded. He turned to Captain Wilder. "She is charming— besides, her father is a milord, captain in the Royal Navy."

"Won't help us a mite gettin' this craft ready to sail," Wilder said, unmoved.

Gascoyne looked baffled. "You do not wish to see that pretty girl again? She will be waiting—I saw it in her eyes, even when she was kicking you." He paused to explain to Captain Wilder. "When we took her prisoner, she fought like a little hellcat. *Magnifique!* She will fiight, *mon ami,*" he assured Tommy, "but she will give in. You will see."

"When the papers are ready," Tommy said, with all the dignity he could muster, "I am going back to Paris."

"He goes to Paris," Gascoyne said, disheartened, "while she goes to the West Indies. Her father will be governor of Nevis."

"I thought we was gettin' down to business," Wilder grumbled.

Gascoyne shrugged. Clearly the prospect was unpleasant. He poured himself more wine and said, "We owe money, *mon capitaine?*"

"Aye. We haven't paid the chandler for all the provisions

for our last cruise. An' there's what we've taken aboard for this which ain't a generous amount. He'll advance no more."

"That chandler!" Gascoyne said contemptuously. "A fat wineskin! I will talk to him."

"Mr. Muldin's ashore now doin' just that," Wilder said. "We'll know where we stand when he gets back. But there's also our crew to be brought up to scratch. Dast we sail with only enough for two watches?"

"But certainly, monsieur. This little ship sails herself."

"But there's the guns, an' the boarding parties, an' crews to sail our prizes in. No use takin' ships just to sink 'em."

"We can get no men here," Gascoyne told him. "Lucky to keep what we have, with this fleet in, looking to replace sick and dead."

Princess had a motley company: the remnants of the original crew of Irish smugglers, a few Spanish and Portuguese, some Mediterranean corsairs, valued for their skill with knives in the hand to hand of boarding, and a handful of exchanged American prisoners.

"They'd not fill their ships by usin' press gangs, would they?" Wilder asked.

"France is at war, monsieur."

"They've no right to take any but French, an' we've got no Frenchies left aboard."

"Me—I am still French, *mon capitaine.*"

"You'd be no loss," a voice said from the doorway.

"I'll thank ye to keep a civil tongue in your head, Alec Muldin," Captain Wilder said.

Tommy recognized the arrival as one of the prize masters sent away among the first during the Channel cruise—a brief acquaintance terminated without regret. Muldin swayed a little in the doorway, and Tommy caught the reek of whiskey and unaired clothing. One eye was purpling and on the cheek beneath it there was an ugly bruise.

Muldin stepped into the cabin, took a chair, and began to pull off his boots.

"I'll also thank ye to keep your boots on in the cabin," Wilder added.

Muldin paid no attention. "Me feet is near killin' me afther walkin' them hard cobblestones findin' the chandlers." He tossed his boots across the cabin toward the door. "Angel!"

Angel cautiously came halfway in. "Señor?"

"Put them boots in me room, an' in a box 'neath the bunk ye'll find a bottle. Fetch some bread an' cheese too, I'm that famished!"

"Did you talk to the chandler?" Captain Wilder demanded.

"That's what ye sent me for, wasn't it?" Muldin replied in his surly fashion.

"Did ye settle the matter to his satisfaction, then?"

"No, by God, nor he to mine!" Muldin answered, pointing to his damaged eye.

Gascoyne laughed. "You could not handle that fat wineskin?"

"Him an' you too!" Muldin flared. "But not all six of his roustabouts."

"Six or one," Captain Wilder observed, "you got thrown out. Was there aught said about our reckoning?"

"Plenty! He's gonna put a plaster on the ship. He swears he'll libel her against sailing if the account ain't paid." Muldin paused and for the first time seemed to notice Mr. Potter. "Who's this we got here?" he demanded, trying to get his bleary eyes in focus. "Begod if it ain't sonny boy! Does your mother know you're out, sonny?"

"M. Potter is a guest aboard," Gascoyne said. "If you can't be polite, be still."

"Yeah? Well I got something to say to you, Gascoyne, me fine bucko. The chandler sent you a special message. Says the Frogs are gonna search every ship in harbor for reserves an' service dodgers. Says you've dodged so long they'll shoot you for desertion."

"And he would like to have the address of my friend ashore, no? To keep her bed warm in my place."

Muldin made a gesture of hopeless resignation. "That's all this damned Frog thinks of—women."

"And you, only whiskey," Gascoyne retorted.

"Too much of either will get a man in trouble," Captain Wilder observed. "The thing I want to know is, do we sail or don't we?"

"On the next tide, monsieur," Gascoyne urged. "If we do not —maybe never!"

"Sure," Muldin sneered. "You want to get away before they catch you." Too much whiskey had made him uglier than usual, yet he poured himself four fingers from the bottle Angel brought, drank it down, poured again, and cut himself some bread and cheese.

Tommy said, "If my prize money will help, I'll leave it in the venture."

"You would let us have your money," Gascoyne exclaimed, "and not sail with us?"

"Nobody's thinkin' o' takin' him, is they?" Muldin demanded.

"Why not?" Gascoyne inquired softly.

"Because he ain't fit to be trusted with a ship, that's why! Showed that plain enough already—lettin' a fine prize be taken from him!"

"I shouldn't 'a' sent him," Wilder said. "At his age, an' no experience."

"Let us not dig that up," Gascoyne said. "He has already told us he is not sailing."

"Saves me from kickin' his arse overside," Muldin grumbled.

"I'll thankee not to insult him," Wilder warned. "Since he's trusting enough to take shares in the venture, we can sail."

"I will get the ship ready, *mon capitaine,*" Gascoyne said, starting to leave the cabin.

Wilder stopped him. "There's one more thing to settle afore we sail."

"We are attending, *mon capitaine,*" Gascoyne said politely.

"I'll no longer tolerate this wrangling between my lieutenants.

That's to be understood afore I leave this harbor. And I'll remind you, Mr. Muldin, you are second lieutenant not first."

"My money ain't second," Muldin retorted. "We're equal partners in this ship."

"Partners has nothing to do with discipline," Wilder insisted. "An' there'll be discipline in my command. Mr. Gascoyne is first lieutenant, and you'll treat him so."

"You don't have to preach at me like the goddam Pope hisself!" Muldin snarled.

"A man who blasphemes the Pope," Gascoyne warned, "shall have his tongue pierced with a hot iron."

"Who says so?" Muldin demanded.

"The Judgments of Oléron," Gascoyne replied. "You have not heard of them perhaps?"

"I ain't heared o' them," Captain Wilder announced.

"In early times," Gascoyne explained, "before there were King's regulations to govern ships, when captains commanded only by the authority their men gave them, and at their men's pleasure, there was a code to keep discipline. It applied to all—captains and common seamen. The Judgments of Oléron."

"You damned Frogs are still living in the dark ages," Muldin scoffed.

"Now! In your lifetime this code has been used aboard corsairs and smugglers. When there is no law, men make their own."

"We'll have no tongue-piercing code and no hot irons aboard this ship," Captain Wilder told them. "We'll need none, if ye'll but act as gentlemen."

Gascoyne looked at Muldin, sitting in his socked feet, drunk and dirty and bad-smelling, and laughed. "Not the Judgments of Oléron, not *le bon Dieu* himself could make a gentleman of this one!"

"Some day I'm going to kill you, Gascoyne!" Muldin sputtered, choking on his drink.

Gascoyne reached for the galley knife which lay beside the loaf, but Captain Wilder got it first. "None o' that," he warned.

"To cut the bread only, monsieur," Gascoyne protested.

"Sure now?"

"I do not mind his drunken talk," Gascoyne replied and took the knife from the captain's fingers. He cut himself bread and cheese and filled his glass. "Will you not drink some wine, Midshipman Tommy, before you leave us?" He was polite. It was the formality of that politeness that hurt. It sounded as if he were speaking to a stranger.

"I'm not leaving," Tommy told him. "I'm sailing with you."

"Bravo, *mon ami!*" Gascoyne exclaimed. "We will show this drunken lout who can sail a ship." He called upward into the skylight. "On deck!"

"Señor?" Angel's voice came down.

"Look overside and tell me—how does the current march?"

It took but a second for the reply. "It marches slow, señor."

"In what direction?"

"Backward, *señor.*"

Muldin growled, "When Frogs and Dagos get together, who, in God's name, can tell what they're talkin'?"

"It is the end of the flood, *mon capitaine,*" Gascoyne said, "not yet slack water. Midshipman Tommy will have time to take the documents ashore for posting, and pay the chandler, and bring off more provisions. Then, before the ebb has turned, this evening when the breeze blows from the land, we can sail."

Captain Wilder looked at Tommy. "Will you give Dr. Franklin a clean bill o' health on us? I wouldn't want to sail from here leavin' a bad reputation behind."

"I'll write that everything is in order," Tommy assured him.

"Make ready for sea, then, Mr. Gascoyne," the captain ordered.

"Just a minute," Muldin interrupted. "I forgot to mention suthin' that drops a fly in this stew. Got the orders on the wharf just afore I come off to the ship—there's to be nuthin' sail from this harbor 'less she's been searched for Frenchies an' has the port commandant's clearance." He laughed gloatingly. "An' don't that take care of you, me fine French gintleman!"

Gascoyne's echoing laughter was good-humored. "To have a stew," he said, "first you must catch your rabbit."

And Captain Wilder said, "I'll thank ye, Mr. Potter, to help me get these documents ready for mailin'."

CHAPTER THREE

THE TIDE ebbed; the wind blew from the land. It would take a deal of backing and filling in that crowded anchorage to get *Princess* turned around and headed seaward, swinging as she was with her head upstream. But Captain Wilder did not intend to show his hand prematurely: when they were ready to sail, it must be sudden and fast. So, while Mr. Potter had been ashore taking care of last details, they had brought the bitter end of the anchor cable up from the locker and secured it to a quarter bitt, the slack of it draped along the ship's side. And the moment Tommy returned aboard, Captain Wilder ordered:

"Cut the stoppers for'a'd!"

On the forecastle an axe flashed, cutting the cable stoppers. *Princess* was now anchored by the stern, and when she had settled back with the current and taken a strain on the cable, she swung gently around until she was headed straight for the entrance.

"Make sail!" Wilder ordered.

An ax blade cut through the hemp cable. Better to leave an anchor behind than lose time hoisting and so, perhaps, lose the ship.

Princess began to move.

"Guard frigate's flying a signal, sir," Tommy called.

Gascoyne took the long glass from the canvas bag which hung on the binacle. "It is the negative flag," he reported. "It means we must not sail."

"We've got no time to fool with signals!" Captain Wilder

exploded. "What in tarnation makes 'em so slow with that fore-tops'l?"

They heard the roll of drums aboard the guardship, the shrill of pipes. The frigate had cast off her cable. She, too, was making sail. It would be a race for the harbor entrance; in that crowded roadstead she would not dare fire guns for fear of hitting friends.

Under full sail, a touch of the wheel in Reilly's great hands threaded *Princess* in and out between anchored ships, their crews manning the bulwarks to watch her pass. The flag at her peak hung slack, since she ran with the speed of the wind, but occasionally a stronger puff blew it clear, revealing the Stars and Stripes. Then they would hear shouts from the French *matelots*, cheering an ally on.

The guard frigate, no match for *Princess* in agility, soon dropped astern, and by the time they were in the Goulet the chase had been forgotten. Their concern now was the passage of that narrow gullet through which the tide raced to join the sea, and they were glad when they felt the first long Atlantic swell. *Princess* dipped her forefoot into it, daintily at first, then plunging deeper to scoop up green water and fling it aft in shimmering silver spray.

But though they had felt the first swelling heave of the Atlantic, they were not yet in the open sea. Northward, the coastline stretched west to end in a bold escarpment. Beyond, Ushant rose from the sea, a great rock island at the entrance to the English Channel. South of them stretched the Chaussée de Sein, a snarl of rocks and tumbling water, wide near the mainland, narrowing to a point as it thrust seaward, a lance head to impale unwary ships during darkness or in fog. Between these two projections lay the Iroise: open water, yet still a trap; across the seaward side, a corvette was lazily patrolling, her spars and canvas red-gold in the setting sun.

"We'll give that one a wide berth," Captain Wilder announced. "Do we clear the Fillettes, Mr. Gascoyne, if I swing south?"

The Fillettes were submerged at high water, a dangerous pair of sister reefs, but now they were beginning to ruffle the surface as the falling tide swept across them.

"You will clear, *mon capitaine.*"

Wilder steadied *Princess* on a southwesterly heading, holding the lance tip of the Chaussée a point on the larboard bow. The corvette was heading northwest toward Ushant. On these diverging courses, they would draw away from each other rapidly.

"Corvette coming about, sir," Tommy reported, having climbed to the crosstrees to widen his horizon.

It might be nothing more than the reversal of course at the end of a patrol leg. Or it might mean that the corvette was heading back to intercept them. As the ships were heading, after she had come about, they would meet.

"'Bout ship!" Captain Wilder ordered. He swung *Princess* to the heading the corvette had just abandoned. Again they began to draw apart.

"Frigate clearing the Goulet, sir," Tommy sang out from the crosstrees.

It was the guardship. Signals were streaming from her yard-arms. It was clear that she was calling the corvette's attention to *Princess,* for a moment later the patrol again came about to head them off. Blocked from escape to seaward, with a frigate bearing down rapidly from the north, *Princess* was trapped.

"*Mon capitaine,*" Gascoyne said, "we must go through the Raz."

"Never heard of it," Wilder growled.

Gascoyne pointed toward the inshore end of the Chaussée de Sein. "A passage close inshore there."

The captain followed the pointing arm with his glass. "You lost your wits?" he demanded.

Muldin, who had belatedly appeared on deck, rubbing sleep from bleary eyes and reeking of stale whiskey, snatched the long glass from the captain's hand. It took him a little time to focus it, and his hands trembled so that he was obliged to steady it against a stanchion. "Lock him up, Cap," he finally said. "He aims to kill us."

Gascoyne laughed. "You—why not? But *jamais monsieur le capitaine.* Never!"

"This ain't the time fer sech talk," the captain warned.

"Do not alarm yourself, monsieur," Gascoyne soothed him. "I will take you where those warship do not follow."

"Straight to Hell is where he'll take us!" Muldin screamed. "Lock him up, Cap! I'd put him in irons just for thinkin' he could sail through there!"

Gascoyne shrugged. "You will not take even a small risk to avoid prison, messieurs?"

Captain Wilder, before he answered, looked hard at the scars on his wrists. Then he said, "Take the wheel."

Gascoyne steered straight for what appeared to be a riprap of broken rock. The captain fidgeted. He put his glass to his eye, took it down, focused it again, and began talking to himself. "If I could see any kind of opening!" he said.

"One does not, from this angle," Gascoyne assured him. "But there is a channel—it will come soon."

Muldin sat on the deckhouse roof, muttering wildly. Tommy, having come down from aloft, thought it must be Gaelic, since he could not understand a word. But whatever the tongue, Tommy knew it meant no good for Gascoyne. He went and stood beside the Frenchman at the wheel, and prayed, "Please, God, let Gascoyne be right."

"*Voilà!*" Gascoyne exclaimed. A passage was opening in the rocks.

It was not a passage into which a seaman would enjoy taking his ship, rock-girt as it was, with tide-rips swirling in mid-channel. But there was comfort in knowing that Gascoyne had spoken true—there was a channel.

"Now we go through!" Gascoyne yelled above the sound of tumbling water. He glanced across his shoulder toward the two men-of-war still visible in the twilight. "They will not follow," he said and never looked around again.

For a while, there was no more talk. Gascoyne was too occupied, the others dumb. *Princess* stuck her nose into a whirlpool of current that swung her bows off. Rocks loomed ahead, wicked in the dusk. The captain sprang to lend a hand at the wheel. But Gascoyne already had her swinging back. The rocks dropped from sight astern.

"There is no more danger now," Gascoyne said. "For the rest the Raz de Sein is easy."

"Thank God," Captain Wilder exclaimed and mopped his sweating brow.

Muldin disappeared into the cuddy, feeling his way as if afraid to look again and see more rocks.

Gascoyne said, "Midshipman Tommy! Take the wheel!"

Before Tommy had time to protest, he found himself gripping the spokes. He gripped so hard that his knuckles were white against the dark wood.

Laughing at his consternation, Gascoyne said, "I am going to make a coastal pilot of you, *mon ami*."

After his first alarm, Tommy found exhilaration in the danger. Wasn't Gascoyne there with a steadying hand on the wheel when things did not go just right?

"*Non!*" Gascoyne warned when Tommy began to ease away from the coast into what seemed open water on the starboard hand. "We must hold close inshore at this point. There are rocks to seaward."

"I don't see any," Tommy said.

"They are the worst kind, the ones you cannot see; when they stick their heads out, you have some warning."

"How can you remember where all the rocks are?" Tommy asked in wonderment.

"I went out with the fisherman," he replied, "when I was so big." He showed with his hand above the deck how small he had been. "It is why, I think, my family sent me to England to school."

"They thought you might drown?"

"They were sure of it." He pointed ashore to a valley running down to the sea where lights like fireflies flickered in the dusk. "It is my home, where you see those lights."

"Still?" Tommy had always known that Gascoyne was no ordinary Frenchman.

"My people still—*oui*."

"The Gascoynes?"

It amused him. "Papa and Mama Gascoyne? But you are droll, *mon ami!*"

"Well—isn't that your name?"

"I am Gaston de la Caille de Kerguenac," he replied, "*cadet* of that family and black sheep too. As Gascoyne, I do not bring shame to them."

"You could not bring shame," Tommy said. He had never spoken more sincerely.

Reilly came to light the binnacle lamp and, in its soft glow, Tommy saw a shadow on Gascoyne's face he had never seen before.

Night dropped quietly down on Audierne Bay. The sea was smooth. A quarter moon shone opaquely through a veil of stratus cloud. After the smashing of rough water against her bows, the clatter of blocks and the complaining of overworked tackle, the ship was pleasantly still. With canvas shortened, *Princess* cruised cautiously through a Breton fishing fleet, the lights of the small craft bobbing all about them on a long, easy swell.

They sat, in the peace following all that tumult, on the deckhouse roof: Captain Wilder, Gascoyne, and Tommy, talking about what they had best do. Muldin came up from the cuddy and joined them. By the smell of him, he had refound his courage in a bottle.

"Best head west till we're clear o' French waters," he advised. "Then run for Tramore Bay. I can ship ye enough men there to fill our crew."

"I want no more truck with smugglers," Captain Wilder stated bluntly. "We'll try the Western Isles."

"Ye'll ship better men in Ireland than the Dagos ye'll pick up in the Azores or Madeira," Muldin argued.

"But not better than we have right here," Gascoyne said.

"We can revittle in the Western Isles," Wilder persisted. "We still got a little cash money left."

"Men we are speaking of, *mon capitaine*," Gascoyne reminded. He swept his arm around the circle of bobbing lights. "In all the world there are no better seamen than these Breton fisherfolk."

"You mean you'd strip their boats?" Wilder demanded.

"Run press gangs like the bloody English?" Muldin added.

"No, no!" Gascoyne objected. "I will speak with them. We are patriotic, we Bretons. I will convince some of them to sail with us."

"You're a spellbinder, I'll not argue that," Wilder conceded.

"I'd choose smugglers meself," Muldin grumbled. "Don't stink so bad o' fish."

"And you, Midshipman Tommy," Gascoyne said. "You have not spoken."

"If I were one of those fishermen," Tommy answered, "I'd sail with you anywhere."

"Well, then, *mon capitaine*," Gascoyne asked, "shall I go?"

Captain Wilder answered with an order: "Bring her to! Get the jolly-boat over."

Princess came into the wind, and when the boat was overside Booby got in and took the oars, and Gascoyne the tiller. The dim rays of a lanthorn in the stern glinted on dripping oar blades, seeming to move in some mysterious fashion without a rower, for Booby's black arms and torso were invisible in the darkness.

The boat itself disappeared, and then the lanthorn, but they could still hear the beat of oars, fading. A loud hail in the coarse Breton dialect cut the night, and Gascoyne's response. Then the jolly-boat scraped alongside the fishing craft and there was a final rattle of oars as Booby boated them.

CHAPTER FOUR

DEAR Mama and Papa," Tommy wrote from Fort Royal. "We are now at Martinique. Reilly calls it Martinico—most British seamen do. They would like to own it, too. We saw British topsails to leeward as we stood in—Admiral Sir Sam Hood, they say, blockading the harbor of Fort Royal to keep the French fleet out. Seventeen sail of the line we counted. But if M. de Grasse brings the fleet we saw in Brest, seventeen won't be enough to stop him. And the forts and shore batteries here are very powerful.

"We had a good voyage out. Madeira was our only Port of Call, to wood and water and load a cargo of wine and olive oil which we hope to sell here for a good Profit. We also took aboard fresh Vegetables (Potatoes and Onions) and butchered a Bullock and some Sheep. In the Tropics you can't keep meat long without spoiling. Vegetables get the Black Rot unless you sort them frequently to separate good from bad, and keep them well aired. Trouble is, if you don't keep a close watch on the lockers on deck where they're stowed, Men steal them and eat them raw. They say it keeps the scurvy away.

"We took only a few Prizes coming out. A Privateer must look sharp to cut a Prize out of a convoy, and now almost all Trade sails in Convoy. But if there is any chance at all, Captain Wilder takes it. He is a grand Captain to sail with. I like him better all the time.

"Gascoyne is grand too. We sailed short-handed, but he filled the crew from a Breton fishing fleet in Audierne Bay (South of Brest, that is) just by talking to them. He is a Spellbinder, Captain Wilder says. He could be Count de la Caille de Kerguenac if he wanted to. He'd rather be Gascoyne.

"He took me ashore in Fort Royal to meet his Relatives there. An uncle and two cousins. The girls are very pretty.

One is married, although she is quite young. Her sister is about my age—Marie. She is more like a Gypsy than a Breton girl, but then she was born and raised here. It isn't much like Brittany. The men call it Paradise—Palms and Tree Ferns and many kinds of Tropical fruits and flowers. Serpents, too, Reilly says. Of course, they have real Serpents, but I think Reilly meant some other kind! He has a way of telling you something by saying something else.

"Annette is the oldest girl's name. She is sweet and kind and good—like you, Maman. Her mother died of yellow fever. Their name is Kerguenac, the same as Gascoyne's should be. There is always yellow fever here, but sometimes it is worse than others.

"I expect you are wondering why I did not come Home from Brest when finished with Dr. Franklin's business. I would have, except for our Second Lieutenant. He said I wasn't fit to be in charge of a ship as I had proved when I let a rich Prize be taken from me. He was talking about *Vixen*, of course. But how could I help that, under a frigate's guns and my few man all wounded, and the prisoners loose and fighting us? Mr. Muldin (that's the Second Lieutenant's name) said it in front of Captain Wilder and Gascoyne. And when Gascoyne told him I was only visiting aboard and was not sailing this voyage aboard *Princess,* Mr. Muldin said it was good that I wasn't—it saved him the trouble of kicking me overside.

"After he said that, you can see I just had to stay aboard.

"I must close now since we are getting ready to Sail and I must get this to the post station. You have waited too long already for a letter from

"Your loving son,
"Thomas."

He put some crosses at the bottom of the page. "P.S. Papa, please kiss Maman for me. And my sisters too."

When *Princess* had anchored at Fort Royal late in February, and the ship had been made clean and shipshape after several weeks at sea, Gascoyne had insisted that Tommy go ashore with him. "You must meet my cousins, *mon ami*," he urged. "You will see—they are most charming."

M. de Kerguenac, Gascoyne's uncle, and his unmarried daughter, when they are not at the plantation on the windward side, shared a town house with his elder daughter and her husband, M. Boulanger. It was an old house, weather-beaten and in need of paint, Tommy thought when he went with Gascoyne to pay his respects; but it had a kind of dignity and the neighborhood was pleasant and there was a magnificent view across Fort Royal Bay.

The drawing room into which a Negro slave showed them was high-ceilinged, its coolness enhanced by the sparseness of the furnishings and the cool white muslin covers on the upholstered pieces. Closed jalousies shaded the room on the town side, but as Tommy's eyes accommodated to the dim light, he became conscious of a certain genteel shabbiness.

Gascoyne said, as if answering his thoughts, "In Martinique the beauty lies outdoors in the mountains and valleys. Houses are for life's necessities, nothing more."

"It is very cool and pleasant here," Tommy said politely.

"Besides," Gascoyne went on, "I think just now there is a shortage of money."

Then his cousins came in and he bowed in courtly fashion to the older girl and his lips brushed her hand; but he took the younger by the shoulders and studied her. "You have grown beautiful, *ma petite*," he exclaimed. "You were a child when I saw you last." He kissed her affectionately. And then, remembering his companion, "Permit me, Mme. Boulanger, Midshipman Potter, an American officer who sailed with the famous John Paul Jones."

Mme. Boulanger greeted him pleasantly but, to his astonishment, with no comment to indicate she had ever head of Commodore Jones. Nevertheless, in his best imitation of Gascoyne's courtly manner, he bowed low and kissed her hand.

"And Marie," Gascoyne continued, "my little cousin who has grown so beautiful."

Tommy put his heels together and made his very best bow.

"And this young gentleman," Marie asked, "has he always been so handsome?"

Gascoyne laughed. "Since I have known him. He also understands French."

Then they all laughed and the stiffness of a first meeting was broken.

Tommy found himself at once at ease with Mme. Boulanger. She was dressed in a simple tea gown appropriate to the afternoon hour; and although she was not strikingly beautiful, hers was a gradually unfolding charm. It was the beauty of gentleness and gracious manners; and although she was friendly, there was a cool self-containment about her, a feeling of depths unfathomed, perhaps unfathomable.

Marie was all on the surface, Tommy thought, and wore too much of everything: the gold loops in her ears were too large, the slave bracelets on her bare arms too heavy and too many, and her Martinican dress too gaudy. The many-flowered print skirt was full and had a train, with a frill of white lace petticoat showing beneath; the bodice was tight and cut low, and the scarf draped around her shoulders did not entirely conceal this lowness. Yet Tommy could not brush aside her beauty, nor put from his mind thoughts of lithe native women, perfectly balanced beneath their head loads, hips swinging gracefully.

They had been chatting for only a few minutes when M. de Kerguenac came in with M. Boulanger. At the arrival of her husband, Annette Boulanger seemed to draw within herself—a flower closing. She watched expressionless as presentations were made.

M. de Kerguenac was tall and spare of frame, and the white shadows in his black hair added to the distinction of his bearing. It was impossible to miss the family resemblance he and Gascoyne shared. M. Boulanger, on the contrary, was short and corpulent and balding, and he entirely lacked his father-in-law's ease of manner. As to age, their relationship seemed all topsy-turvy. It seemed that M. Boulanger should have been the father, M. de Kerguenac the son-in-law.

When the first exchange of greetings was over, M. de Kerguenac said, "Annette, my dear, will you not order coffee served?" explaining to Midshipman Potter, "Mme. Boulanger is chatelaine in this house for me."

That it was his house, Tommy was glad to know. Glad that M. Boulanger was the alien. Not waiting for the coffee—scarcely waiting for the introductions to be finished—Annette's husband went to a side table and poured a glass of cognac. Having emptied his glass, he refilled it. He did not invite anyone to join him.

Over the coffee, the talk ran to war and fleets and the destruction of island trade. Marie interposed a remark now and then, but Mme. Boulanger did not once speak except as hostess to serve the refreshments.

"What is the name of your ship?" M. Boulanger demanded while pouring his third cognac.

"*Princess,* monsieur," Gascoyne told him. "Privateer."

"A privateer? You came empty across the Atlantic?" Boulanger inquired unpleasantly.

"Not at all, monsieur. We brought a cargo—oil and wine."

Boulanger brightened. "Good. I will dispose of it for you on commission."

M. de Kerguenac explained, "M. Boulanger and I are business partners. I, the planter, make rum and sugar from my cane for him to sell. He also trades in coffee and other island produce."

"When I can transport our goods to market," Boulanger observed bitterly.

"This war has almost ruined us," M. de Kerguenac said. "Planters, exporters, importers—all in the same boat."

"We have no boats!" M. Boulanger observed with an ugly grimace. "There is our trouble! To ship out a cargo is almost impossible; to bring one in, also, unless brought by government convoy."

"It has been long since one of those," M. de Kerguenac lamented.

"Wine and oil are in demand," Boulanger continued. "I can sell your cargo quickly at a good price."

"State the terms of your contract, monsieur," Gascoyne replied, "and your commission. I will suggest it to my captain."

Boulanger turned to his partner. "Since he is your nephew . . ."

"No, no, monsieur!" Gascoyne interrupted. "We would not expect a concession because of that. Your regular commission is what we would expect to pay."

M. de Kerguenac, smiling enigmatically, said, "I do not think M. Boulanger had that in mind."

"What then?"

"One cargo will lead to another," Boulanger said. "I told you— we have no boats. We badly need a fast one to carry our sugar."

Gascoyne laughed. "Island trading? No, messieurs! I have said *Princess* is a privateer. Making war is our business not trading."

"You have also said you brought a cargo of oil and wine," Boulanger reminded.

"That was to help pay the costs of the voyage. We did not expect to catch many ships as a privateer on the way across."

"And you did not?" his uncle inquired.

Gascoyne shrugged and spread empty hands.

"Nor will you catch many here," Boulanger argued quickly. "There are half a dozen American privateers in Fort Royal now. They dare not leave harbor for fear of English frigates cruising outside."

"Our captain does not fear English frigates," Tommy said.

"Besides," Gascoyne added, "not one of them could catch our *Princess*."

"M. Boulanger meant only that risks are great," M. de Kerguenac interposed. "Few trading vessels sail these days unprotected by warships."

"And you wish us to be one of those?" Gascoyne inquired.

"It is not trading in the usual manner," Boulanger commented. "But it pays a great deal better."

"What is it then?" Gascoyne demanded. "Smuggling?"

"What you would call it I do not know," Boulanger confessed with spreading hands. "Trading with the enemy, it might be called."

"Annette," M. de Kerguenac said, "perhaps you would like to take the American gentleman onto the veranda. It will be more pleasant there."

Mme. Boulanger looked questioningly at her husband. He did not answer immediately, his cold shrewd eyes appraising the young American. Then he grunted something and nodded his head, which evidently was taken for assent because the girls got up and moved toward the veranda. Tommy, although he would have preferred the men's conversation, followed.

On the veranda there were cane chairs and a table and at one end a swing-settee. The open side could be shaded by dropping bamboo curtains, but they were up now to give a view of the magnificent harbor.

"Which is your ship," Marie demanded.

It was not difficult to locate the *Princess*. Although there were many cargo vessels lying idle, waiting for a convoy to be despatched under warship escort, and several ships of the line majestically riding at anchor, *Princess*, her scrubbed sides glistening in the sun, her canvas neatly furled and stowed, stood out among them. Here was the slimness of a runner, with the look of a fighter too.

"She is beautiful!" Marie exclaimed. "You must love her."

"Do you like ships so much?" he asked, warmed by her admiration.

"When they are beautiful," she replied. "When they will take one away from these islands."

"Marie is restless," her sister explained. "She would like to travel far away from here."

"You also wish to visit different places, do you not, monsieur?" Marie asked. "Else why would you be here?"

"He is a man," Annette said, "and his country is at war."

"I could dress like a man," Marie persisted. "Will you take me with you, monsieur?"

"Pay no attention to her," Annette cautioned with affectionate tolerance. "My little sister is romantic—she dreams."

"It's all it could be," Tommy said bluntly,"—a dream. We are here to fight in the war."

"You speak French so well," Annette said, anxious to change the subject. "Have you lived all your life in France?"

"I went to school there, madame. My father is on the American minister's staff."

"Do you like France better than America?" Marie asked.

"No." To soften it, he added, "But it is very nice in France."

Annette smiled. "Poor boy! How could you say anything else?"

"Is it wild in America, the way we hear?" Marie inquired "Wild beasts? Indians?"

"We lived in Philadelphia," Tommy replied. "It's not wild there." He was not really interested in their talk; he wanted to hear what Gascoyne and the two in the other room were saying, what plans were being made for *Princess*.

"Do not be impatient, monsieur," Annette said. "They will be through with their business talk soon."

"Have you been in bad storms at sea?" Marie asked.

"Storms and near shipwrecks," he replied.

"Often ships are wrecked, here in these islands," Annette observed. "Last season most of the English fleet—eighteen ships, it was said."

"Two frigates ran ashore near Petite Anse," Marie added. "Where Papa has his plantation."

"They were pulled off later," Annette explained. "But I think they were no longer worth much."

"*Our* fleet had the good sense to leave during the hurricane months," Marie remarked.

"How was it you were nearly shipwrecked, monsieur?" Annette asked.

"I was prize master of a captured English transport," Tommy replied. "When we boarded her in the Channel, Gascoyne was wounded. So Captain Wilder sent me in charge."

"How was she called, that transport?" Marie inquired.

"*Vixen.*"

"It will be a vixen who kills Gascoyne," she remarked.

"Marie!" her sister cautioned.

"She was my first command," Tommy told them with a note of pride."

"I am glad you did not wreck her," Annette said. "But why are you not the captain now?"

Marie laughed. "Clearly he is too young."

"We were captured," Tommy answered, reddening at the girl's disparagement. "An English frigate."

"A frigate is much larger than your ship," Annette observed, looking out at *Princess*. "There was no shame."

"We thought she was French when she came up," Tommy explained.

"How could you tell?" Marie asked.

"Her lines, and she flew a French flag. And her name."

"How was she called?" Marie asked.

"*L'Afrique.*"

"Truly that is a French name," Annette said.

"I'll never forget it," Tommy said. "Instead of being in friendly hands, we found ourselves prisoners. It wasn't long before we were exchanged, though."

"I would like to be in one of your battles," Marie said. "But not storms. Since the big wind I am still frightened. It was—I do not know how many years ago."

"Ten," Annette said. "You were very small."

"The wind blew down everything," Marie said. "For that reason we became poor. And now, when things are getting better again, comes a war to ruin everything."

"You do not know all those things," Annette said. She explained to Tommy. "It is the talk she heard afterward that is in her mind."

"I remember we hid under the bed, the two of us," Marie said.

"Our mother put us there for safety," Annette explained, smiling at the memory. But when she added, "We had our mother with us then," her face was sad.

After that, for a time, they remained silent, looking out at the harbor and the ships. Then Marie said, "You do not take seriously that I would sail with you, monsieur?"

"Of course not."

"*Non!* It was all talk. I was only making fun. But I will leave this island some day. Because I was born here must I stay here until I die?"

"Papa will take you to Paris one day," her sister said consolingly. "When times are better."

"He did not take Mama," Marie flared. "It was the fever took her from this island. He did not take you. He will not take me. But I will not remain here to be married off to some old . . ." She stopped abruptly, shocked by her own words.

Annette said quietly, "I think they have finished their talk inside." Gascoyne was standing in the doorway.

"Come, *mon ami*," he said. "We must make our adieus and return to the ship. We have something to tell our captain."

As they walked to the quay through winding streets, alive with people now that the sun was down and a cool breeze blowing, Gascoyne was silent. But at last a thought escaped him: "What a calamity it would be!"

"If we turn to smuggling sugar?" Tommy demanded, bursting with curiosity.

"Sugar? What are you talking—sugar?"

"Isn't that the calamity?" Tommy demanded. "Smuggling!"

Gascoyne laughed. "To run sugar is nothing. It was of my cousins I was thinking, *mon ami*."

"They are very nice," Tommy said.

"That is it! So nice—Annette. And married to a—a—but, you met him!"

"An old sot."

"Exactly. And what a calamity if it came also to Marie."

"It won't," Tommy replied confidently. "She has her own ideas."

"You got along well with her?" Gascoyne inquired hopefully.

"We talked about a lot of things," Tommy answered.

"You talked—how shall I say?—not like the stale breeze from the bay, but a fresh wind from sea. She sailed with you in her mind to faraway places. Both those girls, I think."

"Martinique is a faraway place to me," Tommy said.

"To them it is a prison. You let sunlight in."

"What I want to know is," Tommy abruptly changed the subject, "are we going to smuggle sugar."

"For that we must see what *monsieur le capitaine* has to say."

"He won't do it," Tommy predicted. "I'll bet anything."

"We would not be breaking French law," Gascoyne explained. "Or American." He laughed at his own thoughts. "It would be droll—*n'est-ce pas?*—helping Englishmen to break English laws."

"Mr. Muldin was a smuggler," Tommy persisted. "I don't want to be like him."

"This is not of M. Muldin's variety," Gascoyne argued. "Where you break your country's laws only to make money."

"Money, yes—but for our ship. If we are to keep active, we must have the money to buy provisions and rum and wine, and sometimes a few coins for the men to stretch their legs ashore. We promise prize money—*oui!* But men cannot live on promises. Ships also die."

"Well—maybe there's no harm in breaking English laws," Tommy conceded.

"View it this way, *mon ami*," Gascoyne pressed his point. "You Americans did not like English taxes—you dumped their tea into Boston harbor. These English in the West Indies like not the English law that says how they can trade. If an English merchant wishes to buy sugar from a French planter to ship home, he may not. Only produce of British islands may be sold in England. Therefore, here, they starve!"

"But with the war on," Tommy argued, "the merchant couldn't get the sugar delivered from a French island, could he?"

"*C'est ça!* For that very reason we are asked to deliver my uncle's sugar."

"Sail straight into British waters?" Tommy demanded.

"Was your Commodore Jones afraid? Not at all! English Channel, Irish Sea, Scottish firths—all were the same to him!"

It put a different light on things. "It would help win the war, wouldn't it?" Tommy said, warming. "Captain Wilder will do anything to win the war."

"*Mon ami,*" said Gascoyne, "anything that helps France, helps win the war. Anything that helps Frenchmen, helps France. *Voilà!*"

CHAPTER FIVE

A MODERATE sea was running, the indigo of its ridges plumed with white. Not a heavy sea, yet *Princess*, down to the gunnels with sugar loaded at Petite Anse, staggered through it under a press of canvas, beating down the white crests that tried to smash their way aboard.

Dominica, its greens and blues grayed by distance, was scarcely more than a shadow. But Martinique, still close, was the green of lush valleys running upward through mountain passes, shading off to lighter greens as they climbed Pelée's volcanic cone, white in its cap of cloud. At the mountain's foot, the shoreline was a froth of pounding surf. Between surf and cloud, cane fields lay green-gold in the sun, with here and there the tall smokestack of a sugar mill rising from a cluster of plantation buildings.

Captain Wilder, agreeable to running sugar until better opportunities could be found, had taken *Princess* around to the Kerguenac plantation on the windward side for loading. Now, clear of the land on the wings of a fresh northeast trade, he was glad to turn the deck over to Midshipman Potter and go below, still shaking from weakness after a bout of fever.

Tommy first saw that everything about the decks was secured for sea. Then, since there were no sails in sight on this expanse of ocean and they were leaving the land, he occupied himself practicing sun sights with his quadrant while, on the roof of the afterhouse, Alec Muldin snored in the sun, dead liquor stewing out of him. Angel sat with his back against the house, plaiting a sennit belt. Booby had the wheel.

"It is for you, Don Tomas," Angel said, putting the finishing touches to the sennit. "Please—you take."

"Better keep it yourself, Angel," Tommy said. "I don't really need a belt."

He was wearing pantaloons of sailcloth, generously belled at the bottoms but scant at the hips to be self-supporting. His cotton singlet was striped with blue, his feet and head were bare, his skin tanned to a golden brown. When he was officer of the watch, there were always men hanging around aft, hoping to be noticed and ready to talk at the slightest invitation. He was as much liked as Muldin was hated.

"To hold the knife, señor, not the pants," Angel persisted. He got to his feet and held the plaited sennit out to Tommy.

"But I don't wear a knife," Tommy told him.

"Better you do," Angel counseled.

"Is there trouble aboard, then?"

"I swear to you, Don Tomas, there will be fighting. These Irish drink too much the whiskey. They play the mean tricks on the Frenchies."

"Do they trouble you, Angel?"

"No! I am Spaniard. And I wear a knife. Always." He patted it fondly, a long-bladed sheath knife on his hip.

"Angel speaks true, Mistah Tommy," Booby called from the wheel. He pulled his own knife from his belt, sheath and all, and tossed it. Tommy caught it but tossed it back. "Better you keep it," Booby urged. "I have one more in my bag."

"Oh, all right," Tommy said to please him and caught the

knife when Booby tossed it back again. He took the sennit belt from Angel, put it on and stuck the sheath through it.

"Mighty handsome belt, Mistah Tommy," Booby said with a broad, white grin. "Mighty handsome officer."

"If trouble," Angel said, "I show you." He drew his own knife and pressed the point gently beneath young Potter's heart. "Up! Between the ribs, señor. No more trouble!"

"Thanks, Angel," Tommy said. "You too, Booby. I'm ready for anything now."

He said it to humor them, having no serious thoughts of trouble. Gascoyne's Breton fishermen were the last people he would expect trouble from. They were excellent seamen, quick to obey orders, never shirking the hardest task aloft no matter how dirty the weather.

But they were a clannish crew, preferring their own company, their own customs, and their own talismans. One of them had brought aboard a pottery image of the Holy Virgin. Its crude colors, although glazed, were dimmed by years at sea, an evidence of long service that enhanced the veneration of the French sailors. They demanded proper care and respect for their Virgin.

Pierre Lebecque, their spokesman, was a craggy giant of a man, with a hawk face that matched his name. He asked, on the first day at sea after leaving Audierne Bay, that his countrymen be allowed a living compartment of their own in which they could keep their *chapelle* and follow their own customs.

Captain Wilder, impressed by the Bretons' appearance and seamanlike manner, genially granted their request. Space was no problem unless the ship became overcrowded with prisoners.

The Bretons had at once hung the statue, in its own little *chapelle*, on a bulkhead, and at the Virgin's feet they had placed a small wreath of artificial flowers. Here they had a shrine before which they could pray for safety against storms, for victory in battle, and a safe return to their homes in Brittany.

But now that Captain Wilder had undertaken to carry cargo, every foot of hold space had become valuable. He had been obliged to rescind his permission and to crowd the seamen together, regardless of race or customs: Irish, French, and bastard mixtures. It promised trouble, and trouble came.

"Don Tomas!" Angel called.

The alarm in Angel's voice brought the quardant down from the young officer's eye. The Breton sailors, both watch-below and watch-on-deck, were coming aft in a body.

Young Potter returned his quadrant to its case, placed the box in a safe place abaft the deckhouse, and stood by for trouble. The Bretons had reached the mainmast, where they halted. With them they had one of the Irish crew, dragged, evidently, against his will and sorely beaten.

Alec Muldin, aroused by Angel's warning, opened a bloodshot eye to see what was wrong. He saw the group at the mast and yelled, "Mr. Potter! Tell them God damned Frenchies they're troublin' a friend o' mine. Tell 'em to leave him go an' git back for'ad where they belong!"

Tommy went to the poop rail, the afterdeck being raised a few feet above the main gangways, and asked, "What do you want?"

"We must speak to *monsieur le capitaine*," the tall man, Pierre Lebecque, answered calmly, yet with purpose.

"Have you a complaint?"

"For *monsieur le capitaine* himself to hear," Lebecque replied.

Muldin, having raised himself to a sitting posture on the roof, called, "Did you tell 'em what I said, Mr. Potter?"

"They wish to speak to Captain Wilder," Tommy answered. "To hell with 'em!"

"It is their right," Tommy retorted defiantly.

Muldin came down off the roof, ugly from interrupted sleep and dying liquor, and fighting mad. But as he started for Tommy, Gascoyne, summoned foresightedly by Angel, came out of the cuddy.

"No!" he called.

Muldin turned on him savagely, and at that moment Captain Wilder came out on deck. "What's all the ruction?" he demanded.

"If these here Frenchies be lookin' fer trouble," Muldin snarled, "by God they'll get it!"

"They asked only to speak with the captain, sir," Tommy reported.

"Let 'em speak an' be quick!" Wilder grumbled. "Breakin' a man out of his bed with all this clatter!" He walked forward to meet them, but he was so shaky that he did not come all the way down from the poop. Instead he sat on the deck with his feet on the ladder treads.

"Speak out!" he ordered.

Pierre Lebecque stepped forward. "It is about our Holy Virgin, *monsieur le capitaine*. She has disappeared."

When Gascoyne had translated, Captain Wilder pointed to the man held by the Bretons and asked, "Is yon the guilty man?"

"It is their belief, *mon capitaine*," Gascoyne replied.

"By God, they'd better prove it!" Muldin growled.

Beads of sweat glistened on Captain Wilder's forehead; each recurrence of his fever left him more the shadow of a man. "Who seen him?" he demanded.

"*Mon capitaine*," Gascoyne explained, "these Irish smugglers hold nothing sacred. They are pagans. They make the Holy Virgin the butt of dirty jokes. They must be punished. One is as good as another for an example."

"I'll hear what the man has to say for himself," Wilder stated.

Gascoyne spoke to Lebecque, and the men holding the accused released him. He stepped into the clear and stood before the captain.

"Name of Hickey," he said.

"And bold as brass," Wilder observed. "Was it you who threw their statue overboard?"

"Suppose you was to have yer sleep on watch-below made nightmare by these Frogs jabberin' afore their idol?"

"I'm askin' the questions," the captain said. "Yes or no—was it you?"

"An' didn't they burn candles while they prayed! Was a man to lie quiet while they set the ship afire an' roast us all to hell?"

Captain Wilder turned angrily on Gascoyne. "I thought I gave orders there was to be no naked lights below decks?"

"True, *mon capitaine*. But religion cannot be changed by giving orders."

"Mebbe not. But I still say there'll be no open lights below decks."

"It is because you are not Catholic that you find danger in a small candle," Gascoyne persisted.

"Small or large, a naked light is a naked light. An' a ship afire burns Catholics and Protestants alike."

"Turn the man loose, Cap'n," Muldin counseled. "I'll take the blame. The men was sore account of losin' sleep, so I told 'em to heave the bloody idol overboard. Tell the bloody idol worshipers to git for'ad where they belong!"

"They do not worship idols, *monsieur*," Gascoyne said. "It is a holy saint they pray to, the Mother of our Lord."

Captain Wilder had come to the end of his patience. "I'm too sick a man to be troubled by sech nonsense," he told them. "I want every damned Irishman cleared out of that compartment into the foc'sle. Put men in with these Frenchmen who kin get along with 'em."

"Now see here," Muldin blustered, "I ain't gonna stand fer no sech treatment."

But Wilder cut him off bluntly: "I ain't, as I know of, asked what you will or won't stand for." And to Gascoyne he said, "As for your people, when we get back to Fort Royal, they can take the matter up with a French court ashore if they're a mind to. There's been no law of the sea broken, throwin' a piece o' clay overside."

"I am glad my men do not understand your English, *mon capitaine*," Gascoyne said unhappily.

"They can understand mine," Muldin flared. "Get for'a'd, ye louts, lest I have ye up for mutiny!"

The Breton sailors did not move. Pierre Lebecque talked earnestly with Gascoyne.

"He says this man must be punished," Gascoyne translated. "If no English law of the sea has been broken, he says you must follow the Judgments of Oléron."

"I must, must I? Does he say just how?"

"He says the hand that threw our Holy Virgin overboard must be cut off and thrown into the sea after her."

"Well, I'm damned!" Wilder exploded and mopped his brow. "What in tarnation be these men—it ain't civilized!"

"If you do not punish him, *mon capitaine*," Gascoyne persisted, "we can expect much trouble."

"Let's have it right now then," Wilder answered. "Call all hands aft."

The men trooped up from below when Reilly passed the word: "All hands lay aft to the mast!" Midshipman Potter went forward to inspect all compartments to make sure the order was obeyed.

"All up and aft, sir," he reported.

"Hoist the colors, Mr. Potter," the captain ordered and waited until the American flag was flying from the peak before he spoke again. Then, having launched into a speech to the assembled crew, he paused every few sentences so that Gascoyne could translate for those who understood only French.

"We've got a good ship here," he told them, "small but fast and mighty useful in this war—this war for American independence. America came about when men crossed the Atlantic to find religious freedom." He pointed upward to the Stars and Stripes streaming clear in the wind. "There ain't gonna be no bigotry under that flag. Every man aboard's got a right to worship as he pleases, except for one thing—there ain't gonna be no open lights burnin' below decks! If you can't pray without a candle, bring your statue topside."

"But, *mon capitaine*," Gascoyne protested when he had finished translating, "they no longer have a statue of the Virgin."

"Where's the ship's carpenter?" Wilder demanded.

Jacobs, the towheaded American, stepped out. "Here, sir."

"Can you make a statue like these Frenchmen had before?"

"Out of wood, sure I can. If they'll show me what they want."

"Colors an' all?"

"I can paint it. We got some colors I can mix."

"Get at it then."

"The statue must have a *chapelle* for protection," Gascoyne reminded.

The captain turned to Tommy. "That's a fine mahogany box ye keep your quadrant in; I stubbed my toe agin it comin' out o' the cuddy. Would ye lend it for a religious purpose?"

"Sir, I'll give it to them," Tommy answered.

"Very good. Now, carpenter, when you've got the statue made and painted, put it in Mr. Potter's quadrant case so they can hang it on the bulkhead, the lid bein' a door which they can open for prayin'. Like a shrine you see in pictures. An' the man who pulls it down will wish to God he hadn't when I get through with him!"

He got heavily to his feet. "Explain that to 'em, Mr. Gascoyne. An' see it's carried out."

Without waiting for an acknowledgment, he dragged himself aft and disappeared below.

CHAPTER SIX

BY THE mark five!"

The leadsman's voice came out of darkness. Except for the hooded binnacle lamp, not a light showed aboard *Princess*.

"Fetch up a sample o' bottom next cast," Captain Wilder ordered.

The leadsman smeared tallow into the cuplike depression in the lead's bottom and whirled the weight round and round in a great vertical arc until the taut line whined. He let go, and they heard a splash forward and the whispering of the line running through the leadsman's fingers as he felt for the slackening that would warn of bottom. Three leather things had passed when the line went slack.

"And a half three!"

He hauled the lead line in, but in the darkness, when he got the lead aboard, he could not see what the tallow had brought up. He ran his tongue across it.

"Coarse sand!"

"Shoals too much on a sudden!" Wilder observed. "Sta'b'd a point," he told the helmsman.

Princess answered her rudder, and the dim binnacle lamp illumined Reilly's face as he leaned forward to watch the swinging compass card. It had become routine for him to take the wheel entering or leaving harbor. Captain Wilder showed great confidence in Reilly.

They had, during twilight, made a landfall on the British island of Antigua, but Captain Wilder had held off running in until covered by darkness. Yet the safety of that cover brought with it certain dangers: he must now grope his way into the land and bring his ship alongside a loading wharf dependent entirely upon soundings, sharp eyes, and the smell of things.

On the larboard hand, a shadow loomed blacker than the night itself. Gradually it became a coastline fringed with white. They must make a similar sighting to starboard to be sure they were heading into Parham Bay.

"Land to starboard, sir!"

It was Midshipman Potter, reporting from the eyes of the ship. They were on the proper course for entering.

Long Island, where the sugar was to be discharged, lay in the very entrance. Deep ships could pass on either side going in to Parham Town at the top of the bay. Although one channel might serve better than the other, depending upon the wind's direction, either was safe. Safe if a ship came squarely into it. In darkness, this was tricky work.

"Cast the lead again," Captain Wilder ordered.

On the larboard hand, what seemed like a setting star appeared. Its yellow rays stabbed the darkness.

"Douse sail," the captain ordered. "Hard asta'b'd!"

Princess had been wearing only topsails and jibs. Now these came in and she ranged ahead on her momentum. The yellow rays drew together in an aureole of light and, closer, a lanthorn in whose glow they saw the stringers of a plank wharf.

"Lay her alongside, Reilly," Captain Wilder ordered. "Gentle her in, lest we knock that rickety wharf down."

Reilly brought her alongside gently.

"Get out just enough lines to hold her, Mr. Potter," the Captain ordered. "We may clear out o' here fast."

The old West Indian hand had brought his ship in so skillfully that officers and men off watch had not been called. "I'll be going ashore now to see the trader," he said. "Get all hands up to discharge cargo."

The wharf was on the inner side of Long Island, sheltered from the prevailing easterlies. This would make stevedoring easier, but it took *Princess* inside a landlocked bay where, after daybreak, she could be seen from the main island. To escape, if an alarm were raised, she would have to navigate one of the channels, beating to windward in all probability to get clear and out to sea.

To add to their uneasiness, English Harbor, the chief British dockyard in the Leeward Islands, lay only five miles away across Antigua's hills. At the dockyard there were always warships revictualing and refitting, and marines; and the regular troops which garrisoned the island were augmented by a home defense force. Every minute spent alongside the wharf after sunrise would be a time of danger.

The crew waited for Captain Wilder's return, impatient to discharge the cargo and sail. Every whip and tackle had been rigged, all hatch covers removed, all dunnage securing the sugar hogsheads cast off by the time they saw the captain returning to the wharf. The trader, a figure in white, walked beside him, and behind the two came a phalanx of dark shadows —the Negro slaves coming down to stevedore the sugar.

The trader drove them to the work, as anxious as those on board to see *Princess* clear and away. Although this illegal practice of incorporating French sugar with British produce was a general thing, planters and island residents being banded in spirit against the mother country, if a ship were reported at his wharf too often, the military might take a hand. A military court would not view the practice kindly.

"They'll have us unloaded afore daylight," Captain Wilder announced as he stepped aboard.

"Splendid, *mon capitaine*," Gascoyne said. "Now you must get some rest."

"I'll not deny I'm tired to the marrow," Wilder replied. He looked exhausted and his hand shook, writing the night orders on the slate which hung beside the binnacle. He talked as he wrote. "We'll need a boat to row guard. There's a couple of brigs-o'-war at English Harbor, trader says. They patrol this part o' British seas off an' on. No tellin' when one may turn up."

"As you order, *mon capitaine*," Gascoyne replied and called to Mr. Potter. "Hoist out the cutter. And choose a good crew for rowing guard."

A patrol off the entrance would be their best safeguard against surprise from seaward. A small boat would sight a man-of-war long before its own discovery, and could give warning in time for *Princess* to get clear of the wharf and run for it, beating out, possibly, through one channel, unseen behind the island, while the man-of-war drove in through the other. Possibly they could get clear without a fight, but if fight they must, under way they would have a chance. Caught moored to a wharf, they would have no chance at all.

"Who keeps the watches tonight?" the captain inquired.

"Me, the first watch," Gascoyne replied. "M. Muldin the middle. M. Potter the morning."

Wilder said, "I'm writing here to fetch me if anything delays unloading, and report anything suspicious." He called, "Mr. Potter!"

"Sir?"

"When you come on watch in the morning, single the lines and make ready to cast off. Rouse me out when all's ready. We'll haul outa here at first crack o' dawn, providin' the sugar's unloaded."

"Aye, aye, sir."

Captain Wilder hung the slate on the binnacle and disappeared below.

The slaves had already started unloading. They laid planks from the wharf to the ship's rail, and *Princess's* men, already having whipped the first hogsheads up from the holds, started rolling them down the planks. On the wharf, the slaves rolled them into a nearby storehouse.

"It will not take too long," Gascoyne observed, pleased at the progress. "We'll soon be back at Petite Anse."

"For another cargo?" Tommy asked.

"Of course. Until we have carried it all. You must go ashore with me next trip."

"I've never been to a plantation," Tommy said.

Gascoyne laughed. "It is not a plantation I will take you to see. It is Marie."

"I thought she lived at Fort Royal?"

"She goes to keep house for her father when he is at Petite Anse. It is lonesome there."

The conversation languished. It was not easy to talk above the noise of blocks and tackles and rolling hogsheads. The hogsheads rolled down the planks controlled by parbuckles, disappeared into darkness, reappeared in the dim light of the dock lanthorns to be rolled away by the slaves, themselves but shadows in the darkness.

After a time Gascoyne said, "My little cousin is attractive, no?"

"She's very nice," Tommy answered.

"*Mon dieu,* but how you found her *ravissante!*" Gascoyne exclaimed sarcastically.

"I've got other things on my mind."

"That Irish *gamine?*"

"Navigation, sailing, how to load and discharge cargo."

"There are other things in life, *mon ami.* You will discover."

"Girls?"

Gascoyne shrugged. "Girls are not the worst thing."

"I think I'll go below and get some sleep," Tommy said.

But he could not sleep. Stripped to the skin, he lay sweating in his berth, hearing the pad-pad of bare feet on the deck above him, the hogsheads rolling, low-spoken orders. The heat was like a fever in his blood; his thoughts turned to Denise. Would he see her again, ever? He could see Marie again if he went ashore with Gascoyne. His heart beat faster. There was no reason why he should not. It was not likely he would ever know Denise better than he did now. They were like two ships speaking in mid-ocean, then sailing different courses. Marie was in Petite Anse, and they were going back.

His thoughts drove any chance of sleep away. He blamed it on the stifling quarters. No one but the sick captain and the half-drunk second officer could sleep in this Turkish bath! He got up, donned a singlet and a pair of nankeens, and went back on deck, carrying his thin straw mattress. A hard bed on the deckhouse roof would be better than suffocation below.

Reilly spoke to him above the racket of the unloading. "Best go ashore, sor, there behind the storehouse. Ye'll get no sleep aboard midst all this clatter."

So, having written on the slate where he could be called to take his morning watch, he went ashore.

Behind the storehouse there were a number of carts standing, and he spread his mattress on the bed of one. The air was sweet and clean. The scent of blossoms swept the ship smells from his nostrils; the night breeze cooled the fever in his blood. The soft singing of the slaves and the pad-pad of their feet on the planking was a soothing lullaby; the constellations in the sky seemed close. Close enough, he thought drowsily, for the masts of a tall ship to touch them.

He awoke suddenly. The stars were fading. The singing voices were still. He heard no pad of feet, no rolling hogsheads.

Oppressed by a sense of danger, he lay still, pulling his mind up from the depths of sleep. It was the quiet, he told himself. They had finished unloading. But if they had, the ship should be getting under way! Yet he heard none of those familiar sounds. But how could he, with a storehouse between him and the ship? His reasoning did not dispel his feeling of alarm. In his haste to find out what was wrong, he ran for the ship, not stopping to bring his mattress.

As he rounded the storehouse onto the wharf he saw that no slaves were working, although some lay sleeping where they had dropped, exhausted by the night's labor. On board *Princess* there was no activity. At only one spot anywhere in his vision was there movement: across the low land of the island's southern point he saw the topsails of a two-masted vessel skimming along the island's rim, hull down behind the land. From the smart, trim appearance of her top-hamper, he took her for a man-of-war brig.

Running, he did not shout a warning, aware that in the morning stillness his voice would carry to the stranger. The distance to her was short, but she still had to round the end of the island and turn toward Parham Town before she would see *Princess* at the wharf. There might still be time.

Aboard, men were sprawled in sleep about the decks. Muldin snored atop the deckhouse. The cutter that should have been rowing guard was tied alongside.

Tommy grabbed Muldin's arm and shook him viciously, and when this did not arouse him, he climbed onto the roof and began kicking him in the ribs. At that moment, Captain Wilder stuck his head out the cuddy scuttle.

"Why wasn't I called when ye finished unloadin'?" he demanded. And then the strangeness of what he saw penetrated his sleep-drugged brain. "What in tarnation be ye up to?"

"He slept on watch," Tommy answered. "He didn't send the boat to row guard. And now there's man-of-war standin' in. We're caught red-handed."

"Come down off there," Captain Wilder ordered. "No use wastin' time on him. Break out all hands!"

The deck was in foul disorder, no attempt having been made on arrival to clear up the running gear ready for sailing. Then, the first thing had been to unload the cargo. Now, as sleepy men roused out, the first thing was to get sheets and halliards clear for running, mooring lines singled, sails, which had been given only a sloppy furl, unloosed. All hands went to work with a will, but before things were shipshape the brig came in sight around the point.

"Hoist English colors," Captain Wilder ordered.

It was common practice for men-of-war and merchant ships alike to fly whatever flag best suited the occasion. They could hope that the brig would pass on to Parham Town, taking them for a legitimate trading vessel.

"Shall we man the guns, *mon capitaine?*" Gascoyne asked.

"First we'll try to fool 'em," Captain Wilder answered. "Keep all the furriners out o' sight below."

"No good fightin' her," Muldin volunteered. "Two guns to our one. Heavier, too!"

The captain whirled on him in fury. "Why wasn't the boat rowing guard?"

"The men was tired," Muldin replied. "I saw no use."

"You read my orders on the slate?"

" 'Twas writ with such a shaky hand I couldn't make 'em out."

The captain looked inquiringly at Gascoyne.

"I gave him full instructions when he took over the mid-watch, *mon capitaine,*" Gascoyne assured him.

"Muldin slept," Wilder said. "But was there no one awake?"

"There was the anchor watch, sir," Tommy reported. "This man—Pierre Duroc."

Duroc was a squat, quarrelsome, ugly-looking man, the worst of the fishing crew. "When M. Muldin slept, why did you not call his relief?" Gascoyne asked him.

"It is not my affair to manage the officers," Duroc retorted.

Captain Wilder held out the slate. "Did he not read the night orders?" he demanded.

When Gascoyne had translated, Duroc shrugged. "I do not read English," he said.

"I'll have more to say about this later," the captain promised. "Just now we've got pressing business." The brig was almost abeam. "Dip the colors!"

Reilly hauled the British flag halfway down and waited for an acknowledgment. But the brig showed no signs of having noticed.

"Begod!" Reilly exclaimed. "She's passin' straight in."

But she had gone only a few ships lengths past before they heard a splash and the sound of cable running through a hawsepipe. As the brig pivoted, swinging on her anchor, they saw that she was rigging out a cutter. Marines were assembling in the gangway, their tunics blood red in the rising sun, their pipe-clayed crossbelts and polished buckles bright in the morning light.

"Shall I not cast loose the guns, *mon capitaine?*" Gascoyne asked for the second time.

"In this fix, guns will only get us sunk," Wilder answered.

The guns were still lashed close to the bulwarks, concealed by canvas covers. And by the time the cutter drew alongside, only a few of the Irish and Americans remained in sight on deck, going about routine ship's work. A casual inspection of *Princess* might well pass her as an armed trading vessel.

The British lieutenant who climbed the side had trouble keeping his legs and his sword from entanglement. But the extremely young midshipman who followed, limited to a dirk by his lack of rank, came up in sprightly fashion. The marines waited in the boat.

The lieutenant, having stepped on deck to face Captain Wilder, said by way of introduction, "Lieutenant Post, H.M.S. *Bulldog*. I must trouble you for some information." He turned to the midshipman, who now stood one pace behind him. "This is Midshipman Lord Garton."

"Cap'n Wilder, gents, at your sarvice," the captain said.

Lord Garton acknowledged the introduction only by a hand placed on the haft of his dirk, a slight inclination of his body, and a belligerent glare. But with or without a display of courtesy, the sight of him brought out cold sweat on Thomas Potter. He remembered Midshipman Lord Garton; his lordship was sure to remember him.

When a prisoner aboard the British frigate *L'Afrique*, which had recaptured the prize that Tommy commanded, this pretentious young nobleman had been a scourge, taunting him, in the helplessness of his captivity, with such epithets as "pirate" and "filthy rebel." Lord Garton was also, it had appeared, obnoxious in the extreme to his own messmates, who gave him a deal of ragging and some physical lumps. His lordship was not one to be either merciful or sporting, and Tommy knew that if he were recognized the jig was up. Yet he feared he could not retreat below decks without attracting attention. He therefore made himself as inconspicuous as possible behind the mainmast, moving about as necessary to keep the huge tree bole between them.

Lieutenant Post was quite affable. "Trading in sugar, I fancy," he said. If not an experienced seaman, as the newness of his uniform and the trouble with his sword indicated, he at least believed in courtesy to his brethren of the sea.

"Aye," Captain Wilder replied, suddenly, to Tommy's astonishment, having become Irish. "Fer Gin'ral Clinton's troops at New York, sor. We was 'bout to start the day's loadin'."

"I'll not detain you longer than necessary," Lieutenant Post assured him. "I come from St. Kitts myself. I know how pressed we are to get our sugar moving."

"Ye be from a plantation fambly thin?" Captain Wilder seemed to be commiserating more than questioning. "I come from Montserrat meself."

"More's the pity, Captain, if your family's in the same fix as mine—like to starve before this war ends." The lieutenant seemed ready to launch into more complaining, but Lord Garton's cough was unmistakably a caution. "I'll have your crew assembled now, if you please," the lieutenant finished.

" 'Tis but a small ship's company we have, sor," Wilder explained. "This war takes most able-bodied men for the fleet. But I'll get them up to see for yourself." He shouted an order: "All hands to muster!"

While they waited, Lieutenant Post said, "The war has smashed our trade to smithereens as well. We have no love for the struggle, we plantation families." But again his guard went up as Lord Garton coughed more pointedly. "Your ship is of British registry, no doubt," he said, with a glance upward at the British colors.

"Aye. Out o' Plymouth," Wilder assured him.

"Plymouth!" Lord Garton exclaimed. "You're a long way from your home port, trading in the West Indies."

"Ach, Your Lordship," Captain Wilder explained, "not Plymouth, England; Plymouth, Montserrat—the island to the sou'-west there."

His lordship looked discomfited at his own display of ignorance. Lieutenant Post hid a smile in a cough behind his hand. "No matter which Plymouth," Post said, "I fancy you are familiar with British navigation laws, Captain."

"Aye. An' a blessin' to British trade they are, glory be!"

"Glory be damned!" Lieutenant Post flared. "Those navigation laws have ruined our island trade."

"You've got no right to talk that way," Lord Garton protested, "because you happen to be a planter's son."

"Because you happen to be an earl's son, my lord," the lieutenant reprimanded, "don't forget naval rank."

Their tug of war, naval rank against nobility's privilege, was in the open. The lieutenant, but recently promoted from the steerage himself, was clearly annoyed by his junior's intrusions and was determined to keep him in his place; the noble midshipman obviously was galled by his senior's curbs. Professionally, neither had had sufficient experience to meet this situation; together they would have been no match for Captain Wilder.

"As I was saying," the lieutenant continued his grievance, "a hundredweight of sugar will fetch a hundred shillings in London. We've got a storehouse full of the stuff and acres of cane ripening. But we can only ship in British vessels, in supervised convoys, and a convoy sails but twice a year, and that not guaranteed till the French fleet is cut down."

"National interest is properly above personal gain," Lord Garton observed with maddening superiority.

"Now see here, snotty!" the lieutenant blazed, honorifics forgotten in his anger, "any more out of you and I'll cob your bare bottom when we are aboard again!"

"I kin see why you don't take kindly to restriction of your trade," Captain Wilder interposed. "'Tis a great pleasure to meet an officer who sees the rights of things an' sphakes so well on it."

"Thank you, Captain," the lieutenant said with a smug glance toward the midshipman.

The crew had been gathering and now waited in something resembling a formation, while others appeared from below, shambling up to join their shipmates. Only Irish and Americans came, and a few Spaniards. Gascoyne was nowhere in sight, having disappeared before the boat arrived. The Bretons had disappeared as well, and remained below.

"'Tis the lot ye see here, sor," Captain Wilder said. "Too few, God knows, but good Britons, most. Good seamen all."

"They look salty enough," the lieutenant agreed, and went and stood before them. "Now see here, men," he began importantly. "His Majesty's Navigation Acts require that all plantation goods be carried in English ships having an English master and a crew two-thirds English. Now then, if any of you are not subjects of the King, step out!"

No one moved.

"Surely," the lieutenant said suspiciously, "some of you are not English." He turned to Captain Wilder. "These dark-skinned chaps?"

"'Tis only they don't understand the King's English," Wilder replied. "Angel! Sphake to the byes."

Angel translated. The Spaniards stepped out.

The lieutenant counted noses at a glance. "Two-thirds good Britons, certainly," he remarked. "And now your officers, if you please."

"Here's me second lieutenant," Wilder answered, indicating Alec Muldin, who, so far, had had the good sense to keep his mouth shut.

"You are a British subject, my man?" the lieutenant inquired.

"I was born British, your honor, an' I've sailed the seas British, an' I hope to die British. Me name's Alec Muldin."

"Splendid indeed." But the lieutenant sniffed suspiciously, catching the smell of stale liquor. "I trust he is not your only reliance," he remarked to Wilder.

"Begod no! There's no better bosun afloat than Reilly here."

Reilly touched his forehead respectfully. "Sarvant, your honor."

"What I'd like to know," Lord Garton interrupted, "is how so many Irishmen come from Montserrat?"

"My lord," the lieutenant said with exaggerated deference, "perhaps you are not aware that Montserrat was settled by Irish stock, and their descendants still have an Irish brogue."

"'Tis the truth an' no lie," Wilder said. "Miny o' the blacks sphake with a touch o' the ould sod."

Lord Garton's eyes held on Booby. "You there, black fella!" he said. "Step out!"

Booby stepped out. "Sarvant, your honor."

"Do you belong on Montserrat?"

"Sure an' I've niver lived nowheres else, your honor, except aboard ship." He might have been Reilly speaking.

"Now ain't it the proof o' what I just said," Wilder demanded and quickly steered the conversation into other channels. "Me first luff is below in his bunk, havin' been up most of the night riggin' ship for loadin' cargo. An' we've got a bright young English lad." He looked around. "Mr. Potter!"

Tommy, behind the mainmast, saw there was no escape. "Here, sir."

"Sthep out, lad, an' pass the time o' day with this foine English gintleman."

Luck, for the moment, seemed with him. Lord Garton had wandered away to have a look at things for himself. But only for a moment. Curious as to what lay beneath the canvas covers, his lordship gave one of them a kick. "Damn!" he bellowed and lifted the canvas to see what he had stubbed his toe on. "Guns!" he shouted. "Big guns!" he called to the surprised lieutenant.

"How big?" Lieutenant Post demanded.

"Can't say exactly, sir. Too big for this small ship, I'd say."

Lieutenant Post said apologetically to Captain Wilder, "There's no time for training our young officers these days—can't tell the caliber of a gun." He joined his junior, lifting the canvas cover to see for himself.

"Hmm! Nine-pounders?" he said.

"Ach, no, sir," Wilder answered. "Naught but popguns. No ship risks sailin' these days without she's armed agin privateers an' pirates."

"Quite right," the lieutenant agreed and returned to the question of officers. "So this is your other mate," he said approvingly, having looked Mr. Potter up and down. "A pity we didn't get him for the Royal Navy."

"Ach, now, sor!" Wilder exclaimed, showing alarm. "Ye'd not be thinkin' o' takin' him from me?"

"No fear," the lieutenant assured him. "We didn't come aboard to press any of your people. And since everything seems quite in order, I suggest you get on with your loading. Come along, snotty!"

Tommy was already backing away toward the cuddy door, but Lord Garton's eyes were on him, growing larger and rounder as recognition came.

"Come along!" the lieutenant ordered again.

Lord Garton's face mirrored his perplexity, his excitement left him without words. The lieutenant was saying good-by to Captain Wilder at the ladder and wishing him bon voyage. Lord Garton plucked at his sleeve.

"What is it now?" Lieutenant Post demanded. "Must you be lifted down to the boat?" He said to Captain Wilder, as one seasoned mariner to another, "It's the curse of the Royal Navy these days—the children they send us to make officers of."

"I think—" Lord Garton began.

"Pray, my lord, do not overstrain yourself," the lieutenant counseled. "And don't overstrain 'The Bulldog's' patience. He'll be waiting in the gangway for our return, and he'll have you at the masthead if I tell him you delayed us."

He pushed Lord Garton through the opening in the rail so that he must either go down the ladder or overboard. His lordship chose the ladder, the lieutenant following so close behind that he trod on the noble fingers, causing them to let go. Midshipman Lord Garton fell backward into the boat, landing on the broad shoulders of a British tar. The sailor grunted under the impact, cursed feelingly, and laid the windless officer in the stern sheets.

Lieutenant Post took the midshipman's usual station at the tiller, gave an order, the boat shoved off.

Aboard *Princess* the tension slackened, as the boat pulled away. But the relief was short-lived. "There's going to be trouble, sir," Tommy told Captain Wilder. "That midshipman knows me."

"His Lordship?"

"We were shipmates aboard *L'Afrique* when I was a prisoner."

"Godamighty!" Captain Wilder mopped his brow.

He remained silent for a moment, thoughtfully watching the departing boat. Then he said quietly, his Irish brogue abandoned, "Pass the word, make sail. No noise, mind! An' cast loose the guns."

In the time it took to pass the word, *Princess* was no longer a sugar trader but a privateer. Men streamed up from below to strip the covers off the guns, cast off the lashings, ready the gun tackles. Some carried powder and ball up from the magazine. Others cast off the mooring lines. Still others stood ready at sheets and halliards.

The cutter, by this time, was halfway to the brig, and Lord Garton, having recovered his wind, could be seen earnestly talking to the lieutenant. The oarsmen ceased rowing, and it appeared the cutter might turn back. But the crew gave way again, putting their backs into the stroke, heading for the *Bulldog*. Lieutenant Post was losing no time in reporting to his captain.

Suspicions had already been aroused, it seemed. The cutter, arriving, was held at the gangway while more marines embarked and a second boat was being lowered.

The brig herself was being warped around, men hauling on

a spring line which led to the anchor cable. In but a few minutes they would bring her broadside battery to bear.

"Headsails!" Captain Wilder ordered. "Lively now!"

The filling headsails pulled *Princess*'s bow away from the wharf.

"Tops'ls!" Wilder ordered. "Fore-to'ga'n't!'

The wind was aloft, the island blanketing it lower down. They must reach up for it.

With canvas drawing, *Princess* cleared from the dock rapidly, turning at the same time away from *Bulldog*. But the cutter was already halfway back, another following. The marines in the leading boat opened fire. The range was long, but musket balls spattered against the deckhouse.

"They're aimin' fer our steering wheel," Captain Wilder yelled. "Get down, Reilly!"

Reilly sat on deck, protected by the taffrail; others on deck took cover. Musket balls were peppering them now. In the cutter, Lieutenant Post, standing in the stern sheets, was shouting at them.

Gascoyne ran to the after gun and sighted carefully; the gun captain blew his match. Gascoyne's upraised arm dropped; the gun belched fire and smoke. The ball struck the approaching boat squarely aft, flinging the bows high as the stern was shattered. For a moment the air was filled with oars, flying muskets, bits of wreckage. Then falling debris splashed where the cutter had been. Oars floated about, thwarts, a water breaker. Amidst this flotsam a few heads bobbed.

Captain Wilder said, "Whether sugar brings a hunnerd shillin's in Lon'on or mildews in the storehouse don't make much difference now. Seemed a nice young feller, too, that lieutenant."

Bulldog had hauled her stern around until her broadside bore on the wharf where *Princess* no longer lay, being already clear and heading for the channel. There was nothing to be done now except give chase. She slipped her cable and made sail, firing, meanwhile, with the single bow gun, the only gun that could be brought to bear.

Princess, her sheets hauled flat aft on the first tack out the channel, had her larboard broadside bearing straight down *Bull-dog*'s center line. It was the raking position ship captains dream of. Her first broadside carried away the brig's fore-topsail yard at the slings, dropping it to the cap. Her second stripped the foremast clean, and the headsails too. The British deck was smothered in a raffle of canvas and fouled rigging. H.M.S. *Bull-dog* had ceased to be a threat.

Obliged to come about twice, beating out the south channel, *Princess* had one last reach to the open sea, with the island ly-ing between her and the crippled brig. She lay down to the task, the sea wind strong in her full-spread canvas. But as she cleared Long Island and came into full view of the entrance to the north channel, another brig was standing in. She had seen *Princess* at the same moment, for her tacks lifted as she came about to intercept.

"Godamighty!" Wilder exclaimed. "She'll have heard the fir-ing. She'll ask no questions."

If he held the present course, he would sail straight into the brig's guns; if he turned away to the southward, he might wreck *Princess* on Antigua's main shore.

"'Bout ship!" he ordered, choosing to risk the latter.

Reilly held her so close to the wind that the leaches trembled; every foot of ground they could gain to windward gave them that much better chance of clearing the point. If they cleared, they would leave the brig with a stern chase, a chase *Princess* could win. And with each passing moment, as Reilly pinched her to the wind, hope rose that she would clear. But the wind sud-denly hauled to the eastward, blowing their hopes away. If they held on longer, they would strike a reef.

"Hard down!" Captain Wilder ordered.

Reilly spun the wheel. *Princess*, like a running horse abruptly reined, answered nimbly. She came into the wind, forereaching while her sails, for a moment, hung slack. Then they filled with a thunderclap and she payed off on the new tack. It all hap-pened so quickly that Gascoyne, intent on the readiness of the guns, was struck head-and-shoulders as the mainboom jibed. It sent him sprawling into the lee waterway and, in that tense moment, as the two ships were rushing at each other, he was left to lie where he had fallen.

Both ships held their courses stubbornly: *Princess* clawing desperately for sea room, the brig determined she could not have it. Steering as they were, they must collide. It was the brig who first gave ground, letting *Princess* pass to windward at musket range. The sides of both ships flamed in a passing gun salute.

For a brief moment the brig disappeared in the smoke of her own broadside and that of *Princess* blowing downwind across her. When she drove out of the murk, she had let fly sheets to spill the wind from her sails lest she pile up on the reef *Princess* had just avoided. They saw her name in large block letters across her square transom: H.M.S. *Growler*. They could not see what damage she had suffered in the exchange of broadsides. On board *Princess* it had been grievous.

Shattered rigging fouled the deck, and wounded too, amongst the tangle of rope and blocks and gun tackle. For some, the suffering was already finished. Near the wheel lay Captain Wilder's riddled body. His eyes stared upward at the sky, as if to hold a last sight of the blue he had been denied in the "Black Hole" at Forton Prison. Reilly, blackened by the gun blasts, still gripped the spokes, altering course to meet the change of canvas, torn as it had been by flying chain-shot. The main shrouds on the engaged side had been dangerously cut; the mast, if not tenderly handled, might go overside.

Hurrying aft from his guns in the waist, Tommy saw Gascoyne sprawled unconscious in the gangway. He ran to him. Gascoyne was still breathing. Then Angel came to help and they made a crude bed of canvas and stretched him on it, and Angel dragged up a gun tub of fresh water and began to bathe Gascoyne's face, sobbing as he mumbled over and over, "Jesus Christ, but I love him!"

Tommy turned away, near tears himself, in time to see Muldin roll Captain Wilder's body over with his boot. "No!" he shouted and ran aft.

"There's nuthin' to be done fer him," Muldin said.

"No decent man would treat a dog that way," Tommy answered and knelt beside the body. He put his head against the captain's chest. There was no heartbeat. He straightened the crumpled legs and smoothed the matted hair from the bloody forehead. Reverently he touched the scars on the bony wrists. Then he closed the staring eyes.

Above him, Muldin was saying to Reilly, "Steady as you go. We'll run north and catch the westerlies. It'll be home boys home for all us Irish."

Tommy had not seen Muldin during the chase or the fighting. But the memory of him snoring on the deckhouse roof when he should have been on watch was something he would never forget. Muldin's failure to carry out Captain Wilder's orders had left them open to surprise. Now Captain Wilder was dead and Muldin was giving orders in his place: orders to quit the work the captain had begun.

Tommy's hand went to the knife in his belt and drew the blade, remembering Angel's counsel: "Up, señor! No more trouble!"

As he looked up to measure Muldin for the thrust, he saw that Reilly was steering with one hand. His left arm hung useless, limp and bloody. Their glances met, and in that brief meeting the old seaman's eyes, deep in their sockets from weariness and pain, told him: "No!"

CHAPTER SEVEN

First the ship.

H.M.S. *Growler*, having kept off the ground, had come about and given chase. If *Princess* was to escape, they must work fast. Quickly they rigged preventer stays to keep the weakened mainmast from going overside. But even with that done they dared not set the mainsail until new shrouds had been rove off—a long and taxing job while the ship was under way. They risked setting the main-topsail, however, and, with the added canvas, *Growler* no longer gained. But she showed no signs of giving up the chase.

Then the wounded.

For the most part, they were cared for by Tommy with Angel's help. They extracted splinters and cleaned and bandaged wounds as best they could. In the beginning of the action, when the marines were firing from the cutter, Reilly had been hit several times by musket balls, yet he had kept the wheel. Then, in the passing broadside, he had received a splinter through his ribs, puncturing, Tommy feared, a lung. When they had patched him up, he was so weak from loss of blood that they put him to bed in an officer's room. Other wounded were turned into their hammocks, after first aid, or made comfortable in makeshift beds on the forecastle deck.

Last the dead.

They sewed them in their hammocks with a round shot at their feet to make sure of their sinking when committed to the deep. Captain Wilder had no hammock, so they sewed him in a strip of new sailcloth, and when the shrouded body had been laid on a grating in the lee gangway, Tommy got an American flag from the locker and covered it. Two Bretons were laid out next to him, their bodies sharing the one French flag the ship possessed. The fourth corpse was Hickey, the man who had thrown overboard the statue of the Holy Virgin. They had no flag for him.

All day they worked repairing battle damage, snatching a midday meal of ship's bread and salt beef, washed down with rum and water or, for the Frenchmen, wine. By late afternoon they had the mast rerigged, but before that Muldin, who had been making frequent trips below, failed to reappear.

"He is in his bunk, Don Tomas," Angel reported. "He is drunk."

So Tommy made the decision to set the mainsail. The mast

took the added stress with only a few groans; quickly they dropped *Growler* astern. But, weary as he was and saddened by their casualties, he had one more task to face. As the sun was swinging low in the western sky, he gave the command: "All hands to bury the dead."

At the wheel, Booby put the helm down to bring the ship up to the wind. They braced the fore-topsail yard aback so that, filling, it worked against the other sails. *Princess* came almost to a stop.

Hickey went first, his few countrymen lifting the body and tossing it clear. Some of the Bretons crossed themselves as the freighted hammock splashed. Other than that, Hickey went unhonored, unregretted.

It was quite different with the Breton dead. Their shipmates knelt near the bodies, their lips moving in prayer, their droning voices an added note to the mournful song of wind in the rigging. Even when Muldin bellowed from the poop, "What's going on there?" they did not halt their prayers, they did not look up.

Muldin had come up from below, his face puffed and blotchy, sodden himself with interrupted sleep, his mood ugly from the dying liquor. His speech was thick, and Tommy caught the foulness of his breath.

"We're burying our dead," he told him.

"Jesus! You think I can't see that! But did ye ast permission?"

"I didn't want to waken you."

Muldin looked up at the fore-topsail, backing against the mast. "Was ye botherin' about wakin' me whin ye laid the topsail back? D'ye think a proper seaman could sleep through that? Or you think I'm stupid drunk maybe?"

Tommy wanted to say that he was drunk and stupid and no proper seaman, but he held his tongue. Muldin swept the horizon with his bloodshot eyes. Astern, the *Growler*'s hull was taking shape above the horizon. In the short time that *Princess* had been hove to, she had gained rapidly.

"Get back on your course," Muldin ordered Booby.

Booby looked questioningly at Mr. Potter.

"We'll bury our dead first," Tommy said.

"Ye'll do no such a thing!" Muldin roared.

"You want us to drop them overboard in the dark of night?" Tommy demanded, his anger boiling up. "Like cowards, sneaking away! These men were killed in fair fight; they're entitled to decent burial in the sun."

"They are, are they!" Muldin yelled, and stormed down from the raised afterdeck, touching only one tread as he came. Passing the mainmast, he seized a belaying pin from the fife rail and ran amongst the kneeling Bretons, flailing right and left. "On yer feet, ye slackers! Did ye not hear my command? Hands by sheets an' braces! We'll have no more o' this nonsense!"

For a moment they were stunned by his onslaught. Then they pounced on him. They knocked him down, they beat him with their fists, they stamped him with feet, bare but hard as teak. They would have beaten his life out had not Pierre Lebecque interfered. He got his people under control, but not until they had belayed Muldin to the main pin rail, his hands lashed behind him, a wooden fid wedged in his mouth to stop his foul cursing.

The Bretons knelt in prayer again and, having finished, lifted the bodies of their dead reverently and dropped them overside. It was now Captain Wilder's turn.

Tommy glanced astern. The brig was getting close; she had begun firing again with her bow chaser. "Wait!" he called, and came down from the poop. He could not let Captain Wilder go without some tending of the side, some word at parting. He walked forward and stood beside the body, not knowing what he was going to say, certain only that something must be said.

"Heavenly Father," he began, "this man has been our father here. He was sick and he suffered, yet he always looked after us, and he never asked his men what he would not do himself. He fought fair and he never plundered prisoners and he buried enemy dead with honor. We can't honor him much when there's a brig chasing us, and trouble aboard besides. So look out for him, God, and give us a little help too. Amen."

At his sign, the men lifted the grating to the rail and tilted the inboard end, and the body of Captain Wilder slid overboard from beneath the flag.

"Brace round the tops'l yard!" Tommy ordered. "Steady on the old course, Booby." There was no time to waste.

Some of the men braced the yard and Booby payed off her head, and the topsail filled with the other sails instead of against them. *Princess* began to gather speed.

Yet the Bretons stood fast where they were.

"Lebecque!" Mr. Potter called, and when their leader stood before him he said, "The men have worked hard—we'll serve out a tot of rum, or a liter of wine if they would rather. And release Mr. Muldin now."

A grumble of dissent arose.

"We are grateful for your wine, monsieur," Lebecque replied. "But your order—why do you give it?" There was no insolence in his tone; his dark brooding face, like rough-hewn granite and as hard, showed no anger. Yet it was plain that he was a man not to be lightly treated.

"With Captain Wilder gone," Tommy answered, "and the first lieutenant disabled, the second takes command."

"He will never command us," Lebecque rejoined. "Never while we live."

"Then I command," Tommy stated boldly.

A murmur of astonishment escaped the men, and laughter.

"No one commands now," Lebecque announced. "We were a French ship with an American master and mostly a foreign crew. Now we are a ship without a captain, without a country. We will elect a captain and plan what we are to do. But first we shall punish this man who blasphemes, this man who, failing his duty, caused us to be attacked."

An old man stepped out from the crowding Bretons, bared his head and ducked it respectfully to Mr. Potter. "With permission, monsieur," he said and, without waiting, began to address his shipmates. He was gnarled and shrunken, and his hands were misshapen from many a hard struggle with stubborn canvas, but he could still hand and reef with the best. The men called him "Gran'père," and it was rumored that he had once sailed as a corsair with the famous Jean Bart, which would have made him over eighty, but he boasted only that in his youth he had gone out in a boat to catch fish for the table of "Le Grand Monarch."

"We Bretons are a seafaring folk," he launched forth. "We heard the roar of the sea in our ears while sucking at our mothers' breasts; we were weaned on tall sea tales; we cut our teeth on the cork floats of nets drying on the sand. We know the Judgments of Oléron. If a man blasphemed the Pope, his tongue was pierced with a hot iron; if a man knifed a shipmate, the hand that stabbed was nailed to the mast and he got no food or drink until he cut that hand off with the knife that had wounded; if a man killed, he was lashed to the body and with it cast into the sea." The old man paused for breath, pointing to Muldin. "That man lashed to the pin rail has done worse than blaspheme the Pope—he has insulted God. And he has killed. Failing in his duty, he has caused the death of several shipmates. He must be judged by the laws of Oléron."

"The hot iron?" someone called.

"Aye. And afterward cast into the sea," Gran'père replied. Ducking his head again politely to Mr. Potter, he rejoined the ranks.

Pierre Duroc stepped out, tough and hard as the name he bore, as squat and ugly as Pierre Lebecque was tall and commanding. "This is old men's talk," he began, "this talk of piercing tongues and cutting off hands and throwing live men into the sea. Let us examine what it is we have. Our fine Gascoyne promised us wealth if we went privateering with him. Have we wealth? We haul sugar and become smugglers, and if the British catch us we hang! I say, if we are to be smugglers, let us return to our own coast where we do not have a great British fleet to keep clear of." He stopped and pointed to Muldin, who only stared blankly, not understanding French. "Let this man lead us, who understands smuggling. Again, if we are to be privateers, let him lead us also. He is not filled with notions of helping to win a war. And, having no conscience, he will do things to make us rich."

"Plunder?" a voice called.

"Plunder? Aye, Whatever is needed he will do." Duroc looked around the ring of faces to see the effect of his words. His own countrymen appeared unmoved by his suggestion, but many of the others spoke out approvingly.

Pierre Lebecque addressed himself to Mr. Potter. "You have heard, monsieur. It is right that you should speak your thoughts."

"It is Mr. Muldin who should speak," Tommy answered. "He has the right to defend himself."

Lebecque stepped to the pin rail and cut the marling that held the fid in Muldin's mouth. He spat the gag out and tried to spit again, but his mouth was dry. "Give a man a drink, for the love o' God," he begged.

"Say what you have to say," Lebecque told him sternly. "Whether you ever drink again depends on it."

"I ain't understood a word of all this jabberin'," Muldin said, "but I got brains enough to know it spelled no good for me. An' they ain't gonna understand me if I explain, which won't do me no good neither."

"Speak," Lebecque urged. "I understand a little the English."

"Not likely," Muldin objected. "You're agin' me."

"Angel, then," Lebecque suggested.

"That little Christer! He'd stick a knife in me an' thank Jesus for the chanct."

"I'll translate," Tommy said.

"You're honest—I'll give yet that," Muldin conceded. "Ye'll repeat it like I say it."

"Go ahead, then," Tommy urged. "These men are getting out of patience."

Muldin scanned the countenances around him: the open, honest, troubled faces of the Breton fisherman; the cruel, avaricious faces of the Western Island riffraff. Men who held to certain standards; others who thought only of booty. "Remind them Frogs," Muldin began, "they was tricked into leavin' their fishin' smacks by Gascoyne's smooth talk. He promised them riches. Instead, they're riskin' their necks haulin' his uncle's sugar. He told them they'd escape service in the fleet; if we go back to Martinique, the French admiral will take over an' they'll end up aboard some frigate."

He paused to give time for translation. His talk deepened the trouble in the Breton faces.

"As for them Spanish an' Portagee," Muldin continued, "tell 'em I'm the bye to sail with if they want plunder. We'll cruise the Spanish Main. They'll have all the rum they can drink, and pockets full o' gold, an' women to live aboard with 'em. Tell 'em that. Just like I say."

When Tommy finished telling them, there were a few cheers and some black looks, for him or Muldin he could not be sure. But there were some vile names called. These were for Muldin.

Tommy continued. "I have repeated what this man said word for word, because I promised him I would. Now I speak for myself. I say you would be fools to follow him. He drinks himself stupid, he is lazy and dirty, he is a liar. But bad as he is, I'll have no part of mutiny or, worse, murder, call it the Judgments of Oléron or whatever you want!"

Lebecque bowed courteously. "*Merci, monsieur.* Now we must consider all these things."

When the men had gone forward to talk privately, Muldin asked, "What did ye tell them, Tommy, lad? What did them Frogs say?"

"I repeated exactly what you said. They're talking it over."

"'Tis a good lad ye are, Tommy, bye. Ye'll not regret standin' by me."

"I didn't stand by you," Tommy replied. "I told them not to listen to you, not to be fools. I should have told them I hate the sight of you."

"Could ye be that cruel, an' me sufferin' to death with thirst? But I'll forgive ye, lad," he wheedled, "if you'll but give me a sup to drink."

Tommy called to Angel, "Fetch Mr. Muldin a pannikin of water."

"Water?" Muldin protested. "For the love o' God, he says give a man water! There's a bottle 'neath me bunk, ye little Dago. Fetch that to me, d'ye hear?"

Angel looked to Mr. Potter for instructions. "He can have a little whiskey," Tommy said.

"We'll be friends yet, Tommy," Muldin said. "You're not a bad lad at all. An' you too, Dutchy, bye," he called to Metzger. "I've watched ye round the ship. There's no better seaman aboard, and' no man gamer. Sail with me an' ye'll be first mate."

"I been in lots o' jails," Metzger replied, "expect I'll be in more afore I'm done. But I ain't swingin' by me neck from no yardarm for piracy."

"An' me just afther sayin' you had guts," Muldin groaned. His eyes fell on Jacobs. "You, there, towhead! What d'ye say? Want to go home rich?"

"I've sailed in three ships now with Midshipman Potter," Jacobs told him. "He's captain enough for me."

Muldin spat. "Him? Captain!" He laughed boisterously.

Then Angel returned, balancing a pannikin brim full and dripping. He held it to Muldin's mouth, while Muldin sucked in great gulps. Suddenly, convulsively, he spat out what he could, choked and gagged on what had gone down.

"He's poisoned me!" he screamed when he had cleared his pipes. "The little Dago bastard's poisoned me!"

"What did you put in it?" Tommy demanded.

"The same as bad men gave our Lord, señor. Vinegar."

Tommy took the pannikin and went to a gun tub standing on deck still with fresh water in it from the battles. He threw the first filling into the waterway to rinse the vinegar out. Then he dipped the pannikin full again and carried it to Muldin and held it to his lips.

Muldin tasted it suspiciously. But when he found that it was fresh, he drank it off slowly. And when he had finished, one hand came out from behind him clutching a belaying pin which he had pulled from its socket in the rail. Somehow, while they had been talking, he had managed to work his wrists free of each other.

He crashed the wooden pin down on Tommy's head.

When Tommy regained his senses, he was in his bunk. The wallowing of the ship in a ground swell told him that she was lying off some island. He tried to get to his feet, but such a wave of dizziness and nausea swept him that he fell back again, flat. He lay quietly, listening for sounds which might tell him what was going on. He slept.

When he awoke, the ship was under way. Close-hauled on a spanking breeze, the short, sharp, jolting pitches told him. He got up and went on deck.

The morning was fine, the wind and spray against his face tonic. From long habit, his eyes swept the horizon. No ships were in sight, only a smudge abaft the larboard beam which could be land. His eyes went upward to the sails: his ears had told him rightly—close-hauled. He glanced into the binnacle without speaking to the Breton sailor who had the wheel. But he learned nothing the sun had not already told him: they were heading north.

Pierre Lebecque was apparently in charge. When he saw Tommy at the forward end of the poop, he passed the word for all hands to lay aft. When they had gathered at the mainmast, Lebecque addressed the young officer: "Your head is clear now, monsieur?"

"Clear enough to hear what you have to say."

"You have carried yourself well, monsieur: you gave us the little *chapelle* for our Holy Virgin, you buried our dead with honor, you have helped us in many ways."

"Never mind that," Tommy interrupted. "What's happened to Mr. Muldin?"

"We put him ashore on Sombrero."

The smudge on the horizon, then, was Sombrero Island. A barren, uninhabited rock.

"You marooned him to die?" Tommy demanded.

"We left provisions and water for two weeks. And whiskey."

"He is not likely to be found in two weeks," Tommy said. "He will die."

"A ship will pass in two weeks, monsieur," Lebecque argued. "We left him a piece of canvas and some oars to make a shelter. During daylight he can use the canvas to signal passing ships."

"If he dies, you are murderers."

"That we left him whiskey is proof we did not wish to kill him. We gave him a chance of life; on board it was certain death."

"Is that all you have to say, Lebecque?" If he handled this with determination, if he displayed the strength and decision Commodore Jones would show under like circumstances, he might regain control.

"No, monsieur," Lebecque replied. "We are ignorant fishermen. We do not read books; we cannot work the machine you carried in the box that is now our Virgin's shrine; we do not understand the figures you mark on the chart to show where the ship is when land is lost from sight. We ask you, monsieur, to be our captain."

His speech filled Tommy with relief more than surprise. Relief that he would not have to fight them to keep command. "On two conditions," he said.

"Speak your conditions, monsieur."

"If I am captain, I will return to Martinique and report all these happenings to the officials there. Otherwise we become outlaws."

"When you are captain, monsieur, you will set the course. That your orders will be obeyed I promise."

The men grouped about, murmuring words of agreement. Encouraging words.

"And I'll only serve until M. Gascoyne is able to command," he told them as his second condition.

"Clearly, monsieur," Lebecque agreed. "It is Gascoyne's right. We pray for his return to health."

"In that case," Tommy said, "I accept. Now we'll swing south again. Hands by sheets and braces!"

"As you order, *mon capitaine*," Lebecque replied and turned to shout a command. The men went to their stations for tacking ship, most of them running. Only Gran'père held back. He approached Tommy and, doffing his hat respectfully, said, "It is well, my son, this thing we did. He was evil in this ship."

The evil was gone. *Princess* was heading back for the French islands. Now they must do something about Gascoyne.

CHAPTER EIGHT

PRINCESS was running south through Anegada Passage. Sombrero, where they had marooned Muldin, lay astern. Guadeloupe, where Tommy planned to set Gascoyne ashore, was still two days away.

The afternoon was fine. Reilly, with a helping hand from Angel, came on deck. "Faith," he said, stretching out on the deckhouse roof, "'tis all I need—a breath o' sea wind in me lungs an' a bit o' sunshine on me face."

Lebecque and several of his countrymen carried Gascoyne up and laid him on a bed of canvas beside Reilly. He, too, sniffed the sea wind; they could see his nostrils working. And when a dash of spray struck his face, his eyelids flickered. Then his eyes, for the first time, opened.

"*Mon dieu!*" he groaned. "But I have great pain!"

"Señor!" Angel sobbed with joy. "Señor!"

"We thought the boom had killed you," Tommy said.

"Has it not?" Gascoyne asked, managing a wry smile. He tried to feel his head but he was too weak to lift his arm. He lay quietly while Angel bathed his face with wet cloths. After a while he opened his eyes again and observed the faces about him. "Where is *monsieur le capitaine?*" he asked.

"Captain Wilder is dead," Tommy told him. "We buried him at sea last evening."

"In battle?"

"Yes, and three others."

Gascoyne lay gathering his thoughts. "I remember," he finally said. "A brig was chasing us." He searched the ring of faces. "M. Muldin also?"

"We set him ashore on Sombrero, monsieur," Lebecque told him.

"Sombrero?" Gascoyne exclaimed. "But there are no people on Sombrero!"

"For that reason we chose it, monsieur," Lebecque replied.

"It can be forgiven," Gascoyne said. He looked at Tommy. "So now you command, *mon ami?*"

"Only until you are well."

"When that will be, God alone can say. You have Reilly to help you?"

"He was wounded too. He is lying there beside you."

"Flat as a flounder, but meself, I don't misdoubt," Reilly said, "and not so wounded as they would have me. Come anither day an' I'll be stumpin' about."

Gascoyne's dull eyes went back to Tommy. "And you Captain Tommy—how go things with you?"

"Do not joke, Gascoyne," Tommy begged.

"Joke? *Mon dieu,* with this pain I joke?"

"You know I'm not your captain."

"You must sail the ship. You must decide what we are to do."

"We are heading for Guadeloupe. It is the closest of French islands."

"You will maroon me too?"

"We'll put you in a hospital," Tommy said. "There surely must be one there."

"You cannot take me to Martinique?"

"It means too long a time at sea."

"You think I will die, eh?"

"You will not die," Tommy told him. "I don't even think of that." He wished that he did not.

"*Bien!* If you say I will not die, I must not. You are to be obeyed, *monsieur le capitaine.*"

"Gascoyne!" Tommy reproached him.

"Well, then, I will make no more jokes if you promise not to leave me on Guadeloupe. It is not fortified, that island. The British may capture it—who can say when? And I would be prisoner."

"Then we must sail as quickly as possible to Fort Royal."

"*Non!* Not Fort Royal! The port commandant, when he found we have no legal captain, might take charge of our ship. What a calamity!"

"Where then shall we go?" Tommy asked.

"I will tell you." But for a time he did not speak.

"I am waiting, Gascoyne," Tommy urged.

"I have lost my voice, I think. I cannot hear myself."

"I hear you," Tommy assured him. "I will do as you say."

"Set a course for Petite Anse, *mon ami.* If I am not better when we arrive, Marie and my uncle will care for me. It is not difficult to enter—that open roadstead."

"I will take you, Gascoyne."

"*Bien.* There I will rest." He closed his eyes.

Again Tommy saw Dominica, a gray shadow in the distance, changing to gray-blue, blue, then green, and beyond it the cone of Pelée, upthrust from Martinique.

They sailed from the Caribbean, north of Martinique, into the Atlantic, and coasted down the windward side, finding a good landmark in the church steeple at the village of Grande Anse. Little Bay—Petite Anse—soon came in sight, and M. de Kerguenac's acres sloping upward from a black sand beach.

Here, across the mountains from Fort Royal, great Atlantic rollers usually surged ashore, pounding the beach until it trembled under a man's foot, turning it creamy white. Ships must take care how close they anchored. But this day the sea was resting; the bay, except for ground swells, was oily smooth. The trade wind blew as usual, but softly, and there was only the laciest ruffle of white trimming the iron-sand beach. Yet, knowing that seas make up suddenly sometimes without warning of strong wind, Tommy anchored *Princess* a cautious distance off. She swung head to seaward and brought up on her cable, riding the ground swell easily. While the men were furling sail, Tommy leveled the long glass on the plantation, anxious to see whether their arrival had been observed.

It was a peaceful scene: the long, brick sugarhouse with its tall stack shooting upward in the morning sun; the cottages of the overseers, the slave quarters; and, set a little apart on a slope above the rest, the planter's house, squat and sturdily built to withstand hurricanes and earthquakes.

In a cove, sheltered from the breakers of the open beach, he saw the big *grommier;* a tree trunk fashioned into a fifty-foot canoe, hauled up out of the water on an inclined launching track.

As he watched, the beat of a drum rolled out across the water. It roused the plantation to life. Men ran down to the cove and cleared away the lashings of the *gommier* for launching.

"They are sending out their boat," Tommy told Gascoyne, who was lying on a pallet on the deckhouse roof. He still could move but little without his head throbbing; sometimes he tried sitting up, but he would soon lie down again, overcome by dizziness.

"I am better today," he announced. "I will remain on board."

Tommy did not believe this. He knew it was because Gascoyne did not want his people to see how sick he really was. But he did not argue.

"They are beginning to load the *gommier*," he told Gascoyne a few minutes later. Mule-drawn carts, filled with hogsheads, were coming down to the cove from the sugarhouse. Field hands trooped along to load the big canoe.

"You must go ashore, *mon ami*, before my uncle comes out and sees the way I am," Gascoyne said. "Say that I am too busy stowing cargo. He must be told, of course, that Captain Wilder is no longer with us."

"We came here to put you ashore," Tommy said, "not to load sugar."

"We have promised them," Gascoyne answered.

M. de Kerguenac had come down to the beach to supervise the launching. Tommy could see his tall figure, clad in white nankeens and a singlet, moving among the slaves. When the canoe was loaded, he held up his broad-brimmed, palm-leaf hat as a signal. Then, watching seaward to make sure that no large waves were rolling in, he swung it down. The drum began to roll. The *gommier* moved down the launching track, pushed by half a hundred slaves.

On his raised bench in the middle of the canoe, the drummer beat a long roll, rolling faster and faster as the canoe gained speed down the launching track, reaching a crescendo as it took the water. Then the beat changed to a steady rhythm, setting the cadence of the stroke.

Once, a moment after being waterborne, it seemed that the heavily laden craft might capsize or be thrown back ashore. Freighted as it was with a dozen hogsheads of sugar plus the weight of eight paddlers, a drummer, and a *commandeur* who, from the stern, steered and gave the commands, there were left only a few inches of freeboard. She lifted sluggishly to a wave that was cresting to break; water poured over the gunnels. The *commandeur* flailed his arm, the drummer increased his beat, the paddlers bent to a faster stroke, driving ahead into deeper water. Now only the humping backs of ocean swells lay between them and *Princess*.

When the first load of sugar had been received aboard, Tommy prepared to go ashore. He would have liked to remain aboard to supervise the entire loading, but Gascoyne was insistent. So he bathed and put on a clean pair of nankeens and a fresh shirt, and combed out and rebraided his queue.

"You must wear a hat, *mon ami*," Gascoyne cautioned. "This sun will cook your brains."

"I have only a tricorne," Tommy told him.

"There is no shade beneath a tricorne," Gascoyne insisted and called, "Angel! When we had English prisoners aboard in the Channel, one forgot his hat. Fetch it from my room." When Angel had gone, Gascoyne added, "I have kept it as a souvenir; now it can earn its passage."

It was a wide-brimmed sailor's straw with a generous double burgee of broad ribbon. Though battered, on Tommy's head it lent a final gallant touch.

When the jolly-boat had been lifted from the stowage in the cutter and dropped into the water, Reilly said, "If me lungs still didn't feel like a blood puddin', sor, I'd pull ye ashore."

"I don't need anyone, thanks," Tommy told him.

"Best take one o' the hands," Reilly urged. " 'Tis surprisin' sometimes what surf can do."

"We need all hands to load sugar," Tommy replied. "It's only a short pull."

Gascoyne said, "Kiss my little cousin for me." The old bantering devilment was in his eyes. "And do not neglect yourself, *mon ami*—she cannot resist you in that rig."

"I won't be going up to the house," Tommy told him.

"But why not? They will make you welcome."

"There isn't time this trip."

"The only time we have is now, *mon ami*," Gascoyne said. "Never forget that. Look at me. Suppose I cannot make the love again?"

The possibility did not strike Tommy as so tragic a thing as Gascoyne's face would indicate. But suppose Gascoyne could never command a ship again! If his dizziness did not leave, and his arm stop shaking!

"I'll come straight back when I've finished our business with M. de Kerguenac," he insisted.

"You think Reilly and me and Pierre Lebecque cannot run the ship while you are gone?"

"Of course I don't think that!" He did not know exactly what he was thinking. His thoughts were all mixed up.

"If you stop to make a little love, I will not tell your Irish *gamine*," Gascoyne bantered. "A kiss is not forever."

It was exasperating. If the talk had been of manifests, and the stowage of hogsheads, or arrangements with M. de Kerguenac for future shipments, he could have waited patiently. But this talk of girls! He went over the side and down into the boat.

As he pulled away from the ship, his eyes took *Princess* in: the tall raking masts, the canvas neatly furled, the web of guys and stays and running rigging. His eyes saw the trim lines of her hull, but his mind was elsewhere. Despite his denials to Gascoyne, despite himself, his thoughts wandered to Denise. "Your Irish *gamine*," Gascoyne persisted in calling her. But was she his? It had been long since their farewell kiss at Portsmouth.

Thinking of that kiss, he forgot Reilly's warning. And, having forgotten, he was surprised by the surf. Suddenly, as a swell crested, he found himself clinging to the boat, swept along in a smother of spune. His wandering mind had not been warned by a steep ridge of blue racing in from seaward.

Dimly, through the spune, he saw the shore. Then men had stopped loading the *gommier* to stare seaward. The crew came running and climbed aboard to get their canoe afloat again. They would rescue him. And think him a bumbling fool.

The crest passed beneath the boat, dropping it into the trough and, for a moment, the turmoil quieted. The boat rode upright, but water was sloshing over the gunnels and he had lost the oars in the first smashing blow. He started tearing at the bottom boards to get something to paddle with. But a second wave, piling up under the counter, lifted the stern so high that the bows dipped under. The boat went cartwheeling end over end.

He grabbed a thwart and hung on, but the power of the sea broke his grip. For a moment, he seemed to fly through the air. Then the sea swallowed him, rolled him, tumbled him in somersaults, battered him. Several times his head struck bottom, and he bounced to the surface for a few gasps of air and froth and sand before going under again.

He was not alarmed at first, striking out bravely for shore. It was losing the boat that worried him, and the ridicule his performance was sure to bring. But as he got closer to the beach, where he could almost stand, the undertow sucked his legs out from beneath him. He seemed to hang there, first struggling in until his feet touched bottom, then sucked out by an undertow against which his flailing arms seemed to have weights on them. He knew that he was fighting for his life.

He fought until a pair of great black hands came out of the spune and grabbed him, and their pull, at the end of a human chain of black men wading into the surf, was greater than the undertow. A giant of a man, bigger even than Booby, picked him up and carried him onto the dry sand and held him up by the heels and shook the water out of him, and then stood him on his feet. His ribboned hat was gone and his sodden clothes clung to him and he had never felt such a fool in all his life.

M. de Kerguenac came running up and began to feel his arms and legs, saying over and over, "Are you hurt, monsieur? We must determine—are you hurt?"

His mouth was gritty with black sand that tasted like iron, and his lungs felt raw. He gagged and brought up salt water and sand, and spit it out. "I'm all right, sir," he assured M. de Kerguenac. "Waterlogged, that's all." Only his pride had been seriously hurt.

"If that is all, monsieur, we are fortunate. It is tricky surf we have here. Our best men sometimes overturn."

It helped put his pride together again. "I shan't get caught that way another time," he said with conviction.

"You must go to the house at once," de Kerguenac urged. "Strangers to these islands catch easily the fever—first wet, then cool wind, last a chill. Marcel will take you." He gave orders in the island patois to one of his men. "Forgive me, monsieur, if I do not leave the beach while the loading continues. They will see to your needs at the house."

The road to the plantation buildings on the hill was only wide enough to accommodate mule carts—a winding slash through jungle growth. Tree ferns and palms and *balisier* lined the roadside so densely that the only vista was the sky. In places, small areas had been hacked from the jungle so that the sugar carts could pass on their way to and from the loading cove. The shouts of the muleteers calling to one another and the screams of jungle birds were the only ties to an outside world. To Tommy it seemed as though he had stepped through a green wall, cutting him off completely from his world of ships.

On the dirt road, their bare feet gave no sound. Rounding a turn, not more than halfway to the planter's house, he suddenly collided with Marie, hurrying toward the cove, followed by an old servant. In that sudden physical meeting, Marie remained for a moment close to him, her hands gripping his shoulders, her eyes, wide with excitement, searching his. "You are alive! You are not dead?" she exclaimed.

He took her hands and held them. She was trembling. "Do you think me a ghost?" he asked.

"*Non!*" she answered. "*Non!*" and sagged against him. "But when that big wave overturned the boat my heart stopped beating."

"You were watching all the time?" What must she think of his seamanship?"

"I have done nothing else since your ship came in sight." She drew away to study him. "You are not hurt—truly?"

"Just a few bruises. The sea let me off pretty easy."

"When I saw it, I ran for the cove. But Zara screamed, 'Come back!' I was not dressed. Nothing! So I must go back and dress myself."

She was wearing a house gown of flowered calico, fitted closely around her throat and buttoned from neck to hem. The hem was drawn up in front and held by a broad scarf around her hips so that it hung just below the knees, giving freedom to her trim legs.

"What a way to receive you at Petite Anse," she said. "Spilling you into the surf!"

"My own clumsiness spilled me; your father's men hauled me out. Except for them I'd still be swallowing sand and water out in that undertow."

Marie covered her face with her hands to conceal her horror at the thought. When she looked at him again, her wild eyes startled him. "That Gascoyne!" she exclaimed. "He knows well this surf is dangerous. Why did he let you come alone?"

"Why shouldn't he?" Tommy flared. "I'm quite capable of pulling myself ashore."

"I observed it," she answered pointedly.

"It was only I didn't see that big wave coming."

"If you had drowned," she exclaimed, "I would have killed him!"

He laughed. "But you are fierce! A man would be safer in that surf."

She laughed too. "Here we stand scolding while you begin to shake. Come, we must strip these wet clothes off." She took his hand and hurried him up the road. He felt the warmth of her concern for him and the frankness of her affection.

At the house, on the broad veranda, he stopped to look out over the Atlantic. The loaded *gommier* was going out again; he caught the sound of the drum, drifting shoreward on the gentle trade. The sea was all sparkling blue, and *Princess* a black swan gracefully riding the ocean swell, and around them the green of jungle and the gold of cane fields.

Marie was tugging at his arm. "Hurry! Dry yourself before

you catch the chill!" She pushed him through a door which opened off the veranda into a small bedroom, simply furnished: a hard narrow bed, an armoire, a small table and chair. As Gascoyne once said, these houses were for living; for beauty, one must go out of doors.

"Zara will hang your clothes to dry," Marie told him and disappeared.

The old *bonne* remained near the window, which, as was custom, had no sash; and when he tried to lower the rattan shade, he found the cord had broken and the roll was tied securely up to keep it from flapping in the wind.

"*Pas nécessie,*" Zara told him with a toothless grin. "*Pas nécessie.*"

Well, if the *bonne* didn't think it necesary, why should he? He began to strip off his soaked garments.

Zara brought a basin of water and a towel. "Wash first in the sweet water," she said. "The feel of salt is not good when you are dry."

When Zara had gone with his clothes, he washed in the fresh water. He had just finished drying himself when Marie called from outside the door, "I have brought dry things for you. Papa's. They will not fit, I think."

"They'll do better than the towel I'm wearing," he told her.

"I will not look," she promised and handed a pair of nankeens and a shirt to him at arm's length through the partly opened door.

As he took the clothes from her, their hands accidentally touched and then, somehow, touched again. "I'll be only a minute," he said.

When he had put on the clothes and opened the door, Marie without hesitation came in. Upon seeing him, she burst into laughter.

"Do I look as bad as all that?" he demanded.

"It is good there is no mirror in this room," she teased still overcome with laughter.

"I'm not as big as your father," he said.

"All the same, you are beautiful," she told him. "But you are tired. After that swim, you must rest."

He looked longingly at the bed; he was tired, he couldn't deny it. Marie pushed him down into the chair and sat on the floor beside him, her legs tucked beneath her.

"Tell me what troubles you?" she demanded.

"Well—didn't I just have a rough time in the surf?" he countered.

"No. It is not that. There are things in your face. You are not the same as when you came to our house in Fort Royal."

"We lost our captain," he explained. "And our ship was nearly captured at Antigua."

"I knew there had been trouble," she said. "Many were killed?"

"Three."

"Gascoyne?"

"No. He is fine. But he has more work to do without the captain."

"You fought so we could sell our sugar?"

"We fought because there is a war."

"You fought to sell our sugar," she contradicted and leaned forward and lightly kissed his cheek. "I am going to repay you." He felt the soft pressure of her breasts against him.

"There's nothing to repay," he said, disturbed.

"Not if I want to?" She looked up at him and her eyes were wells of something he did not undesrtand, something that drove the weariness from him. He got up, taking both her hands, and pulled her to her feet. "Perhaps my clothes are dry?" he said.

"If you are so brave in battle," she teased, "how is it that a girl frightens you?"

"I am not frightened."

"What then? You already have a sweetheart?"

"Not a sweetheart. A girl."

"In America?"

"England."

"Well, then—if you love a girl in England you had better go."

"I did not say I loved her," he protested.

"I know about that girl," she said. "My cousin told me. Is he not coming ashore this time, Gascoyne?"

"He is too busy."

"You do not speak truly. He is wounded, or he would have come."

"He had an accident," Tommy admitted. "But he is getting better. He will soon be well."

"You are speaking true now?"

"Of course. He sent a kiss to you."

"For you to give?"

"How else? 'Give my cousin a kiss for me,'" he said.

"Give it then!"

He gave it, but quickly drew away.

"Do you know what I think?" Marie said. "I think you have not kissed a girl before."

"That was Gascoyne's kiss," he replied. "Your cousin."

"I will give you one now to give to him," she said, and before he knew it she had raised on tiptoe and he felt her arms around his neck and the pressure of her palms against his head, pressing his lips to hers. He felt her body trembling. "*Douxdoux*," she breathed. "You are sweet. And you are not my cousin."

But she did not stay long against him. "All the world can see us here!" she exclaimed and took his hand and led him through a door into an adjoining room. He had a glimpse of *Princess* through the window as they passed—far away, little more than a memory in his wheeling brain.

Marie's bedroom had more comforts, more beauty than the small room they had left. There was a large bed with a satin coverlet, a chaise longue with puffs and pillows, comfortable chairs. A heady perfume lingered in the air. The shades were down.

When she had closed the door, they kissed again. His awkwardness betrayed his innocence. It heightened her desire. She led him to the bed and tried to draw him down beside her. "We will make love, *douxdoux*, if you will promise to love me truly—always."

But he drew her to her feet again.

"You do not love me?" she asked reproachfully.

"No, Marie."

"It is that girl in England!" she accused. "I know!"

"It's a lot of things. Things I can't explain."

"I do not want your explanations!" she flared, her face flaming with humiliation. "I wanted your love. But if your love is for another girl, I hate you. You would not believe how much I hate you!" She flung herself on the bed and, burying her face in a pillow, began to sob.

"Marie," he soothed. "Please." He pressed his lips gently on her cheek.

"Go away!" she cried.

At the door, he heard her voice, weakly: *"Douxdoux."*

"Yes." He waited.

"I do not hate you. Please do not hate me. Some day you will come back?"

"Some day," he replied.

He found his dry clothing ready in the small bedroom. He changed quickly, folded M. de Kerguenac's garments neatly and put them on the chair, and went out onto the veranda. The old *bonne* was sitting cross-legged outside Marie's window. How much, he wondered, had she heard?

"Au 'voir, missie," Zara said and smiled.

"Adieu," he answered and went down the road toward the cove. At least he could face Marie's father with a clear conscience.

The *gommier* was just sliding down the ways with another load when he reached the beach. The drum rolled to a crescendo, steadied to a rhythmic beat. The paddlers bent the paddles with their strength.

As Tommy came down the road, M. de Kerguenac waved to him. "It is the last," he called. "Your ship is loaded. The *com-*

mandeur is carrying the manifest aboard for your captain's signature."

"There is something I must tell you, monsieur," Tommy said.

"Come then, we will sit in the shade and talk until the *gommier* returns."

They sat on a mahogany log under some palms just off the beach, and Tommy told him about Captain Wilder and of the trouble with Muldin and, guardedly, about Gascoyne's accident.

"It is great responsibility for a boy so young," M. de Kerguenac observed gravely, when Tommy had finished.

"You are worried about your sugar, monsieur?"

M. de Kerguenac seemed surprised. "Sugar? What is that— a little sugar. I am worried about you, *mon enfant*. And my nephew. And the others you now command."

"Yes, sir," Tommy said, chastened. "But I have Gascoyne to advise me. It is just that he is dizzy at times." He did not mention the shaking of Gascoyne's arm.

"Gaston is a hard one to kill," his uncle said. "He has been wounded in duels, shipwrecked, shot—*mon dieu*! is there anything that has not happened to him? He will get well."

The *gommier* had returned and the slaves were hauling it up on its cradle. "Will you not come to the house and take *déjeuner*?" de Kerguenac asked.

But Tommy declined. "The sooner we are under way, the sooner we can be back for another load," he said.

"Marie will be disappointed," her father said. "For her it is very lonesome here."

"Next trip, perhaps," Tommy told him.

"When you are in Fort Royal," De Kerguenac replied, "please consider my house your home. You have made a great impression on us all. Besides, you are an ally of France."

"Thank you, monsieur." He began to roll up his bell-bottoms preparatory to launching his boat which had been hauled out of the surf by the men and laid bottom up to drain. The oars had been recovered and lay beside it. His straw hat was on the boat, weighted by a rock, dry but battered to a pulp, its gallant ribbon bedraggled.

"You will not get wet," de Kerguenac told him. "My men will launch your boat."

They righted it and, when he had taken his place on the thwart and was ready with the oars, they ran with it into the sea, black hands and black faces thick along the gunnels, calling to each other and laughing and making great sport of it. When the water was waist deep, they gave the boat a last shove and let it go.

He pulled through several waves until clear in deep water, then he lay on oars for a moment and waved good-by to M. de Kerguenac and his men, still watching from the beach. When they had returned his parting salute, he gave way for the ship.

Coming alongside, he boated the oars; but before climbing the ladder he took a last look ashore. Everything was as it had been that morning on arrival. The *gommier* was secured on its cradle; the mule carts had gone back to the stables; the plantation buildings and the planter's house lay peaceful in the sun.

But though the world outside appeared unchanged, the world of Thomas Potter would never be the same again. He had learned the truth of Gascoyne's words: there were things in life besides ships and guns and men.

CHAPTER NINE

SHORTENED down to storm canvas, *Princess* staggered through a rising sea. The watch huddled in the longboat's shelter or behind the bulwarks, but the helmsman had to face it. Water streamed from Booby's black face. No one braved the deck who did not have to; no one except Reilly. He should have been below but, since he had regained enough strength to get about, not even Mr. Potter could keep him down.

"Wid her belly full o' sugar," the old seaman observed, "she's bound to labor, wouldn't you say, sor?"

Thomas Potter refrained from saying. The sugar worried him. They had made a perfect landfall on Antigua soon after sunrise and they were holding the island in sight, a gray hummock on the western horizon, seen dimly through spray and fine driving rain. If the weather did not worsen before nightfall, he planned to run in, under cover of darkness, discharge the cargo, and be out again by daylight. Remembering their brush with *Bulldog* and *Growler* he was apprehensive; the falling barometer and the rising wind did not ease his tensions. And to make a bad situation worse, a strange sail was bearing down on them. In the war at sea, every ship must be considered an enemy until proved otherwise.

"She's come through bad weather," Tommy observed, the long glass to his eye. "Fore- and mizzen-tops'ls both gone."

"Come through it!" Reilly exclaimed. "Ach, sor, she's brought it wid her."

"Anyway," Tommy decided, "she's not likely to bother us, crippled as she is." He saw that her mizzenmast was jury-rigged.

"Just in case, sor," Reilly said, "I'd best break out the hands an' get the guns ready." He hobbled forward and shouted orders into the forecastle. By the time he returned, it was clear that the stranger was purposely closing *Princess*.

"A Frenchie, by the lines of her," Reilly observed.

"She's hoisting colors," Tommy said. The French royal ensign streamed out from her spanker gaff.

"Reilly!" Tommy exclaimed. "We've seen that ship before?"

"I was thinkin' the same meself, sor."

After studying her for another moment through the glass, Tommy shouted, "It's *her*! It's *L'Afrique*!"

"May the divil take her!" Reilly echoed.

"It's possible she could be French again," Tommy mused. "Hoist French colors till we're sure."

Although she was French by the lines of her hull and by her

flag, they could not be certain. During the long continuance of French-English wars, many ships had changed nationality, some more than once. Tommy had encountered *L'Afrique* the first time in the Bay of Biscay when, as prize master of the captured British transport *Vixen,* he had been fooled by her appearance and her flag. He and his prize crew had cheered her, thinking they were safe under French protection, only to find, a few moments later, that they were British prisoners. Thomas Potter was not to be duped in that fashion again, nor Reilly, nor Metzger, nor any of the others who had been with him on that venture. They would never forget *L'Afrique* in any waters, by any other name, under any flag.

Apparently not impressed by the French ensign that *Princess* now displayed at her peak, the frigate hauled down her own French colors and hoisted British. A spurt of flame licked out from a forecastle gun, a puff of smoke, and a cannon ball splashed ahead of *Princess.*

"Hoist British colors," Tommy ordered. "Hold your course," he told the helmsman.

Despite the fact that again they flew the same national flag, the frigate's gun spoke once more, and with more authority. The ball, landing short, ricocheted over *Princess's* masts.

"We'll heave to," Tommy said, "since she's ordered it. But stand by the guns."

When within hail, the frigate rounded into the wind and backed her main-topsail to kill the way. Her tall sides blanketed *Princess,* lying to awaiting developments. That the frigate intended no good for them was apparent through the open ports, where gun crews could be seen ready at their pieces while gun captains blew their matches to a cherry glow. She forged ahead slowly and there was her name in gold letters across the stern: *L'Afrique.*

An English voice hailed from the poop: "Ahoy there! What ship is that?"

Reilly answered, "*Princess,* your honor. British registry. Tradin' out o' Plymouth—Montserrat."

"Follow me into the lee of Anteega," the voice from the speaking trumpet ordered. "I shall examine your papers and cargo in smoother water."

"Helm astarboard!" Tommy ordered.

L'Afrique was still forging slowly ahead. It would be close, but Tommy judged that *Princess* would pass clear, astern of her. "Guns ready! Hoist American colors!"

The sails filled, driving *Princess* ahead into perfect position to rake the full length of *L'Afrique*'s deck, while only two British stern guns bore on the privateer. "Bring down a mast, lads!" Tommy shouted. And when the frigate's masts came into line, "Fire!"

The broadside brought *L'Afrique*'s weakened mizzen down. *Princess* fired again, adding to the confusion of a falling mast and befouled rigging, then stood away, her own men cheering when only a few scattered shots chased them. They laughed and pounded each other gleefully.

"'Bout ship!" Tommy ordered.

The laughter ceased. Men stared at him in consternation. Even Reilly could not conceal his astonishment. They had got clear without damage; they were out of gun range; the enemy was in no condition to chase. *Princess* was free to sail on about her business, leaving the crippled frigate to struggle with the rising storm. But this chit of an officer was turning back into the fire of British guns. The men stood fast. Not a piece of gear would they touch.

"Hands about ship!" There could be no doubt about this order.

"But, monsieur!" Pierre Lebecque protested.

"You promised to obey my orders as captain," Tommy reminded.

"Of a truth, monsieur. But—"

"Obey then! And be quick!"

Lebecque hesitated for a moment, wiped the spray from his dripping face, turned and gave a sharp order to his men. *Princess* came about.

As she closed the frigate, she ran into some scattering fire. Splashes spouted around her like the blowing of a school of whales. But the danger was soon past. As they crossed *L'Afrique*'s stern, the British guns would not bear, while *Princess* poured in another raking blast. And another. Then she was clear again, standing away.

They could see no flag aboard *L'Afrique*. "She has struck her colors!" Tommy exclaimed in jubilation. The men sent up a cheer. But she had not struck. On the mainmast another flag appeared. She bore away and ran before the storm. *Princess* came about and followed. But there could be no more dueling with the guns; in the smashing seas it would be a useless waste of powder and ball.

"We'll keep close," Tommy said. "When the sea moderates, we'll capture her."

He went below to give Gascoyne a report.

Gascoyne was stretched on the transom settee, wedged in by the back of a chair placed between the table and the transom. "You have got clean away, *mon ami?*" he asked when Tommy entered the cabin. "*Mon dieu*, but I have sweat blood, listening to the cannon!"

"*She* got away," Tommy told him. "We are chasing."

"A frigate?" Gascoyne exclaimed in amazement. "You chase a frigate? Has a boom struck your head too?"

"She's badly crippled in her rigging," Tommy explained, deprecating his action.

"She does not still have guns?" Gascoyne inquired sarcastically.

"Thirty-two 18-pounders," Tommy said. "What a sensation when we bring her in!"

"*Mon ami*," Gascoyne protested, "with our few guns you cannot fight the heavy battery of a frigate."

"We did," Tommy answered.

"And because she is crippled and must run before the gale to keep her masts from rolling out, you think to follow her, and when the storm moderates, capture her?"

"Yes," Tommy said.

Gascoyne sat up. "You cannot carry much canvas running before this wind and sea, loaded down with sugar. Our little ship does not steer well; one need only lie here to feel it. She is sluggish. If these following seas do not broach her, they will break her back and she will founder."

"Then we must jettison the sugar," Tommy announced.

"*Mon dieu!* You bring back my dizziness." Gascoyne lay down again.

For a time they were silent, listening to the swinging rudder as it was moved from side to side to keep the ship from broaching before the great, following seas. A big wave boarded over the taffrail, engulfing the tightly battened skylight, and in the cabin twilight turned to night. They listened to the water gushing through scuppers and freeing ports that were far too small for the great torrent. The skylight turned gray again as the little ship staggered out from beneath her deck-load. The glass washed clear and twilight returned to the cabin. They heard the rudder swing again.

"The helsman's still there," Tommy remarked.

"Poor fellow," said Gascoyne.

They waited in silence through another cycle of boarding seas. Then Tommy said, "You are right, Gascoyne. She will founder if this keeps up—or break her back."

"You must heave to and ride the storm out," Gascoyne counseled. "Storm stays'ls will be sufficient."

"And lose my frigate?"

"You will lose the frigate just the same," Gascoyne argued. "You cannot follow her in darkness."

"The moon rises early tonight—full moon."

Gascoyne sat up again. "*Mon ami,*" he said, "I have been too long below. I must go on deck."

"And countermand my orders? You must not! This frigate we are chasing is *L'Afrique*—the ship that took my first command from me. I have told you of it and of that captain—how he flogged Metzger to make him betray his shipmates, how he

would have hung Reilly as a deserter only a British admiral
intervened; how I might have been hung too, for piracy, except
for some decent English officers on my court-martial. I have
told you all these things before, and you have praised my behavior. Now I have a chance to capture the frigate that captured me, and you tell me I must lose that chance to save your
uncle's sugar!"

"But you are a fierce one, *mon brave!*" Gascoyne said, amused.
"So young, so innocent, and such a fighter!"

"This isn't the time for joking, Gascoyne!" Tommy flared.

"You are in a bad humor, *mon ami*. How long since you have
eaten?"

"I don't know. Last night's supper, I suppose."

"Angel!" Gascoyne called and when the cabin boy appeared,
"we must have some supper."

"Jesus Christ, señor," Angel exclaimed. "We have no soup.
No pot will stay on the galley range."

"Some bread and cheese, then—and wine. *Monsieur le capitaine* has not eaten for many hours."

"You mean Don Tomas?" Angel asked.

"Who else is captain now?" Gascoyne demanded. "You should
take better care of him."

"*Sí*, señor."

"And of me as well. I have not eaten for—let us see—for days,
is it not?"

"You are hungry, señor?" the Spanish boy asked, not believing
he had heard aright.

"Like a wolf," Gascoyne answered, baring his white teeth.

"You hear that, Don Tomas?" Angel shouted. "Our Gascoyne
is hungry! He is getting well!"

"Bring the food," Tommy ordered. And when the boy had
gone he asked of Gascoyne, "You are going on deck? You will
take command again?"

"No, *mon capitaine*. You are going on deck and jettison the
sugar. But first you must strengthen yourself, for it will not be

easy. And me—your talk of capturing frigates has given me good appetite again."

But when he tried to pour the wine, although his arm was no longer shaking, his hand trembled so that Tommy took the bottle from him and filled the glasses.

On deck, when Tommy came up after eating, Jacobs was waiting with bad news. "Two feet of water in the bilges," the carpenter reported. "Gaining. Must be the seams are opening, the way she works in this sea."

"We'll lighten her," Tommy replied. "On deck all hands! Jettison cargo!"

Daylight was still with them: a pallid light beneath massed storm clouds, eerie, threatening worse to come. They removed the battens which held down the tarpaulin over the main cargo hatch, rolled it back, and unshipped the wooden cover. Then they cleared away the dunnage and wedges that held the upper tiers from shifting.

Although Reilly was still unfit to do any heavy work, he was determined to have a part in it. He lashed himself in the shrouds near the open hatch, from where he could control the hoisting operations. A hogshead weighing close to a thousand pounds, swinging at the end of a rope in the void of a violently pitching ship, required guidance. Sometimes, when a succession of big seas struck, it became necessary to stop hoisting. This, from the shrouds where he could see the hogsheads coming up, as well as seas bearing down, was Reilly's job.

When a hogshead was swung out on deck, a gang quickly rolled it to the rail, where a ramp had been constructed; rolled it up the ramp and overboard. These deck gangs, in the opaque light, were shadowy figures scurrying back and forth. But the men in the hold, dropping farther below the main deck as each tier came out, found the lack of light a handicap. Soon they were working by imagination, taking a barrel hitch and hooking on the falls by feel.

Until now, with some added canvas, they had kept *L'Afrique* in sight. But to prevent seas from coming aboard and flooding the open hold, it became necessary to alter course, bringing the combers more on the quarter. *Princess* rode easier that way, but angling away from her quarry, she began to lose ground. And suddenly, night shut down.

The cargo was no more than half discharged, but the men came up from the hold when they no longer had light for working. Lebecque, at Tommy's urging, ordered them to go back. Sufficient tallow dips would be provided, he told them, to light the hold. They still refused.

"They say we have lost the frigate anyway," Lebecque explained. "Why risk their lives?"

"Because we do not see the frigate," Tommy argued, "does not mean we have lost her. The moon will rise soon—we will sight her."

But despite all urging, the men continued to refuse.

"Come," Tommy said at last, impatient with the delay, "I will descend myself. Surely you are not afraid to go where I go."

But whether from fear, or lack of interest, they would not follow him. Only one, old Gran'père, came forward. He wore sealskin boots, the tops lashed just below his knees with leather thongs, for his old shanks and feet could no longer stand immersion in salt water without festering into sores.

"If the young officer goes into the hold, I go too," he told his reluctant shipmates. "If a boy does not fear being crushed by a swinging hogshead, why should an old man?"

But when he started to follow Tommy, who descended the rope ladder carrying a lighted dip in one hand, some of the old man's shipmates held him. "No, no, Gran'père," they scolded. "You are too old. You cannot move fast enough."

"There's oil in my joints still," the old man retorted, "not yet dried up by fear."

In the end, to keep him from it, or shamed by his example, a few followed Tommy below, and then a few more; and finally they had the hogsheads coming out again.

In the eerie light of guttering candles, in the dark cavern

of the hold, heavy with the fumes of raw sugar and human sweat, Hell would not be worse, Tommy thought. Grotesque shadows danced on the bulkheads, and the shadows of swinging hogsheads, falling across the workers, reminded constantly of what would happen if the substance instead of the shadows were to fall.

As they dropped lower, tier by tier, the length of rope increased, the pendulum swings of the hogshead widened, the hazards were greater. But now that the men had started again, they worked at feverish speed to get the job done. Only a shout of *"Gardez-vous!"* would halt the work, when a hogshead got out of control despite the steadying lines they used to keep them captive. "Watch yourself!" And the men would scurry from beneath the hatch opening.

Despite the pitching of the ship and the unruliness of hogsheads, the work was going well when Reilly called down into the hold, "The moon's up, sor."

"Can you see the frigate?" Tommy demanded.

"No sign, sor. Still, a man's eyes can't reach far across these waves 'less he goes to the masthead."

"I'll come on deck," Tommy told him.

He rode a hogshead up, straddling it, clinging to the hook of the tackle block. And when the deck gang saw what they had on the end of their whip, they worked with utmost care to land him gently, right side up, and hands reached to steady him as he slid to the deck, while others unhooked the block and cleared the slings and started rolling the hogshead to the rail.

It was then that a big wave struck, coming out of nowhere to curl high above the rail and crash aboard. The wild, unexpected sea, out of step with the others: a great dark avalanche of water. It filled the deck waist deep between the bulwarks, it overflowed the coaming and poured into the open hatch, it scattered the deck crew as it smashed forward along the gangway, carrying the hogshead on its crest.

The men grabbed at anything for a hand hold: ringbolts, pin rails, each other. But before Tommy could get his hands on anything solid, he was swept forward along with others in a tangled mass of arms and legs. A pair of strong hands grabbed him, hung onto him, checked his forward plunge. The gnarled hands held him while the swirling water rushed past: blinding, choking, bruising. The strength of those hands kept him from going overside.

The little ship fought bravely against the engulfing load. She rose beneath it, water cascading from scuppers and freeing ports, and, in the moonlight, Tommy saw a sight that would remain in his mind forever: old Gran'père was hanging onto him, and someone else to Gran'père, and several others to both of them, all anchored by Pierre Duroc, squat and solid as a rock in pounding surf. He had slipped a rope's end through a ring-bolt in the deck and wound it around his waist, and, with his stocky powerful legs braced, he was anchoring all of them. They owed their lives to him, this little half-drowned cluster, and in that moment Tommy forgave Duroc all his insubordination.

Shedding the water from her deck, *Princess* lifted, her bows higher than her stern, and the hogshead, arrested in its forward rampage by the forecastle bulkhead, started rolling back. A shout of warning from a dozen voices rose above the shriek of wind. Men jumped to hold the barrel and lash it before it gained momentum. They were knocked aside like toys. And once it got rolling along the tilting deck, men's strength could not ensnare it.

Tommy jumped and caught a backstay and swung himself up and clear, just in time. He hung there for a moment. And then he thought of the old man. "Gran'père!" he shouted "Gran'père!"

Men were scattering right and left, climbing, running before the danger as the barrel gained speed on the steepening angle of the deck. It smashed against the afterhouse with a crash that loosened staves. But even above the noise of it, Tommy heard an anguished scream.

He dropped to the deck and ran aft, along with a dozen

others who pounced on the hogshead and held it as if it were a mad beast.

"Take care! Easy! *Prenez garde!*" men called. "Straight up. Lift!"

From beneath the stove-in hogshead, a pair of sealskin boots stuck out.

Oh, God, Tommy prayed, seeing blood mix with spilled sugar as the men lifted the hogshead bodily and threw it overside, *do not let him die.*

But when he knelt beside Gran'père and saw how badly he was crushed, he prayed: *Please, God, take him. Take him quickly.*

Someone brought the *chapelle* from below and, in the flickering light of a lanthorn held close, Gran'père's eyes opened and gazed at the little statue blessing him. He smiled and closed his eyes again.

They wrapped the body in canvas and lashed it on the deckhouse roof where the seas did not reach.

Reilly said, "Do not be grievin', sor. It was his time—Fate had him marked."

"I might have saved him," Tommy said. "I saved myself."

"He was goin' wid you into the hold, only his people held him back," Reilly argued. "They kept him on deck to save him from the danger below, an' on deck he was killed. Would ye blame thim, now?"

It began to rain. Not the fine driving mist of the storm's approach, but hard pelting rain. Overhead, jagged forks ripped the sky, lighting the sea for miles around with blue-white brilliance, cresting the smoky wave tops with silver. Thunder rolled. Farther away, along the horizon, sheet lightning played. As if appeased by the sacrifice of old Gran'père, the storm was moving on.

The wind dropped; the pelting rain flattened the seas; the lightning illuminated the deck enough to speed the work. Soon the hold was emptied, and, when the hatch had been battened down again and all gear secured, every man not immediately needed on deck was sent below to rest.

For the captain, there was no rest. Tommy went into the cuddy and worked up the ship's position on the chart as best he could from rough dead reckoning. After that, he rummaged in the disordered contents of the locker until he found a quill and ink. Day's end required an entry in the ship's log. He wrote:

> "Last part ends with heavy Rain, Thunder and Lightning. Wind abating; Barometer starting up again. In Lat. 15 degrees North, Long. 60 deg. 20 min. West, while jettisoning our cargo Jacques Dubois, of Lambézellec in Brittany, called Gran'père, was badly crushed and died.
>
> "Frigate *L'Afrique* which we are chasing has been lost to sight. Not much help from Moon because of clouds. Will continue Search.
>
> "Thomas Potter, Captain"

He went back on deck. They would search and search and search. They would find her yet.

CHAPTER TEN

IN THE black void of night, off their starboard bow, a red glow appeared. "It might be *L'Afrique*," Tommy speculated. "Afire."

" 'Tis more the look of signal fires," Reilly argued.

"Out at sea?"

" 'Tis a trick they have in these islands—burnin' tar barrels to warn ships o' danger."

"Warning us?"

"I misdoubt they see us yet, sor,"

At times, static charges from the storm rolled up in balls of glowing fire at the ends of yards and on the tips of masts.

"They'll not be seein' St. Elmo's fire on us from where we are.

But *L'Afrique,* now, if she's closer in. They might see St. Elmo's lights on her. Or mebbe see her in a flash."

As they strained their eyes to catch a glimpse of land, a ship, of anything, a fork of lightning ripped out of a black cloud, its tines thrust downward toward the sea, and, like a giant pitchfork, impaled a ship. Blue-white fire ran down masts, shrouds, guys; down every path that would conduct electricity to the water.

"Her sticks is bare as trees in winter," Reilly said.

"It's *L'Afrique,*" said Tommy.

In the brilliance of the strike, in not much more than the blinking of his eyes, he had seen the stump of a mizzenmast.

A red glow appeared when the flash had faded, and the glow suddenly burgeoned into a flaming bush larger, it seemed, than the small hull the lightning had disclosed.

"Blown up!" Tommy said. "Magazine. She's gone."

"An' divil take her," Reilly echoed. But he said it with false relish. Nor was there elation in Tommy's heart, only disappointment at having failed to capture her.

Dawn brought a change of weather. The storm had gone, the wind was back in the northeast quadrant where it belonged; but there was still enough of it to keep a boisterous sea running and make a lee shore hazardous.

Tommy had had a few hours' sleep on the chest in the cuddy, and Angel had brought him some hot tea and warmed beans, since now the galley range could hold a fire. Eating, Tommy made plans. The first thing to be done with the new day was to bury old Gran'père.

It was done in the simplest manner. With the ship brought to for only a few moments, and the hammock-shrouded body on the afterdeck, the waist being awash as *Princess* wallowed in the trough, Pierre Lebecque spoke a few words of parting, and the Bretons mumbled a prayer and crossed themselves. Then a splash, and old Gran'père went down to his last resting place along the hundred-fathom curve.

With it over, Tommy took the long glass and climbed to the main crosstrees to look for any signs of a derelict, any boats, any flotsam. He saw only Martinique: Pelée's lower slopes wreathed in streamers of wind-torn scud, her cone disappearing into thick, impenetrable cloud. At the mountain's foot, sea met land in an unbroken stretch of tumultuous surf where driving combers, smashing against outlying rocks, flung white water into columns higher than a tall ship's masts. The columns, at their tops, spread into lovely fountains and fell back. At their feet lay death.

And then he saw a ship, a tiny thing against that awesome background. She had two masts standing—the mizzen gone—and between the masts were spread a few patches of storm canvas to claw her off the shore. Canvas that Tommy would not have wanted his life to hang on, strained and worn as it must be.

Aboard *Princess*, men gathered on the forecastle head, on the raised afterdeck, in the weather shrouds, watching their enemy make a gallant fight for life. At first they watched with the sympathy of seamen for brothers in distress. "Poor bastards!" they said. "*Pauvre garçons!*" But others covered their sympathy by talk. "The stupid bastards! Gettin' caught on a lee shore!" But in their hearts they knew it could happen to any ship. To them.

As the battered hulk, with its pitifully inadequate canvas, gained ground, sympathy turned to admiration. Foredoomed to disaster, as they had thought her, now there seemed hope. Slowly *L'Afrique* clawed away from shore. If she could clear the Pointe du Diable, she would be safe, for once she got clear of that jutting cape, she would have sea room and to spare. But off that devil's point lay Caravelle Rocks, not far enough off to permit a ship to pass between them and the shore, yet close enough to form a barb on the hook of curving land: a snare for vessels caught too close in.

Princess lay a safe distance off, while *L'Afrique* fought her way out until she had the rocks abeam. A cheer went up from the privateersmen when it seemed the frigate would get clear, but it turned to a groan when her storm staysails blew out of the bolt-ropes in a sudden gust, the worn canvas shredding off downwind. The pressure of wind against her upperworks and hull set her back over the ground she had so haltingly gained.

Tommy, watching through the long glass, yelled, "She's let go an anchor."

"It will never hold," Gascoyne said. "They will drown." He stood in the cuddy door, unshaven, unkempt, looking like death himself.

"We can't just lie here and watch them die," Tommy said.

"Clearly, *mon ami.* You must tow them off."

"Aye. 'Tis the thing," Reilly agreed.

"Go get the sheet cable up, then," Gascoyne ordered. His arm was shaking. "I will lie on the chest in the cuddy, *mon ami.* You can do it without my help. But if you need me, call."

The men turned to without objection when ordered to rouse the cable up from the locker; but when the order came to lay it out in long fleets from forecastle to taffrail, they knew it was to be used for towing and began to grumble. Black looks came Tommy's way. *Princess* was too close against the land for comfort, and drifting closer.

The sea was too rough for lowering a boat to send the tow-rope across, and to get close enough to use heaving lines would be asking for disaster: they must drift the hawser across *L'Afrique's* stem. To be sure that the hemp rope would remain in plain view on the surface, they tied empty casks to it for some distance along the end.

Reilly took the wheel and nursed *Princess* into position for starting the run. Having crossed under *L'Afrique's* stern to get inshore of her, headed seaward, they beat back across her bows, streaming the cable as they came. The buoyed length towed astern, undulating over the waves like a great sea serpent.

" 'Vast!" Reilly suddenly shouted. " 'Tis too much tail, it's swingin' us."

Princess had lost steerage control, and with that gone, she fell off before the wind, the drag of the towrope holding the stern while the bows swung off. In a moment she was heading for the rocks. Men ran to let fly sheets, cast off halyards, kill the headway of the ship. Sails came down on the run.

They hauled in the hawser, fleet after fleet, piling it anywhere in the gangways, anywhere to get it aboard. No one at any time yelled, "Cut!" It took what seemed an age to get the rope in, but they did and, when they had sail set again and Reilly had nursed *Princess* clear of the land, safe from immediate disaster, the men, without orders, began to lay the hawser out, clear for running. Plainly they wanted another try.

This time Tommy knew how much hawser they would tow handily, knew what to expect from current drift, and leeway, and loss of speed from the drag astern. He crossed *L'Afrique's* stem close enough to foul the hawser on it, yet far enough away to let *Princess* pass clear.

On *L'Afrique's* forecastle, men fished with grapnels to get a bight of the hawser aboard. They worked with the efficiency of desperation; no man could afford to bungle now. Having got the end aboard, they secured it to the towing bitts, while others hacked through the anchor cable, cutting the derelict free of the ground. The hawser, now attached to both ships, took a strain as *Princess* forged onward. It straightened out, up out of the water, vibrating like a plucked fiddle string, amidst showering spray. It held. *L'Afrique's* head swung around to follow in the wake of *Princess*, building up a small bow wave as she gathered way. Again a few patches of storm canvas appeared on her stays between the masts, enough to give steerageway and, in some measure, to ease the load.

Having pulled clear of the rocks, the task now was to get her safe at anchor before she foundered. But, as the day wore on, she sank lower and lower until her closed gunports were almost awash. Streams of water gushing from her cambered sides showed that her pumps were working ceaselessly. Her men must be close to exhaustion, yet the dangers of stopping in the rough sea to send assistance across to her seemed greater than pressing on for the southern lee of Martinique.

They pressed on until, as the first dog watch was being set, they rounded Pointe de Salines at the south end of the island. The sea was quiet. After the boisterous waves of the southern run, it seemed as if they had entered a lake.

Yet, from the appearance of *L'Afrique,* smooth water would not be enough. She lay waterlogged, listing badly. They must quickly restore her buoyancy or find a sand beach to strand her on. They kept the towline on her, anchoring *Princess* to hold them both.

Jacobs stood ready with gear for stopping leaks and shores for strengthening weakened bulkheads, and they put all this into the longboat along with their two wash-deck pumps and all the men it would carry.

Reilly went in the cutter, loaded with more men, to be in charge of salvage operations. He was to send *L'Afrique's* captain back.

Gascoyne, now that *Princess* rode quietly in sheltered water, came on deck. He had shaved and bathed and put on clean nankeens and a clean white shirt beneath his light-blue jacket with the silver buttons. His black hair was neatly queued and a gold loop hung from one ear—Gascoyne, dashing as of old. Yet he had not entirely recovered his strength. After a turn or two, observing the activities on deck, he sat on the deckhouse roof to rest.

The cutter was returning from *L'Afrique.* "It is her captain coming to surrender," Tommy informed Gascoyne.

"So you have caught your frigate," Gascoyne said. "*Magnifique!* And your captain too—the one who would have hung Reilly?"

"We'll know in a minute," Tommy answered. But it was a young midshipman who climbed the side. His battered, exhausted condition was testimony of the situation on board.

"My captain's compliments," he said. "He begs to be excused until he gets his ship made safe."

"Captain Beasley?" Tommy asked.

"Captain Lord Ravenscroft," the midshipman replied.

So he was not to have the last word with Beasley after all. "Your captain's request is reasonable," Tommy said, "but as soon as the ship is seaworthy again, I'll expect him aboard to formally surrender."

Gascoyne asked, when the midshipman had got into the cutter and was heading back to his ship, "You are disappointed, *mon ami*, that you did not catch your captain too?"

"I am wondering about his name," Tommy answered. "One of the officers on my court-martial was called Ravenscroft."

"You have a score to settle also with him?"

"A debt," Tommy replied. "I was alone there, a stranger. I was shaking inside, but I wasn't going to let them see it. And this officer—he was a commander—was kind to me."

"It is a name not easy to forget," Gascoyne reflected. "Ravenscroft."

"I'll know him the minute I see him," Tommy said confidently. "After the court-martial he shook hands and said he knew all along I wasn't a pirate, that I had only done what their own officers would do, and that some day he hoped to meet me again. Only not across a green baize cloth. Across green water, and not too much of that.

"And I said, 'About a musket shot?' I wasn't scared any longer —they had acquitted me."

Gascoyne said, "Look yonder there! You may meet him at musket range yet."

L'Afrique was on an even keel now, trimmed properly fore and aft, seaworthy to look at, thanks to Reilly and Jacobs and their men. But that was not all Tommy saw. On her forecastle, men were hacking at the towing hawser to cut it clear, and sail was appearing on her stays and spars. She was getting under way. And, as they watched, a British flag streamed from her peak.

"*Mon dieu!*" Gascoyne exclaimed, "she hoists British colors to take French leave!"

"Cut our hawser at the rail!" Tommy shouted.

Men sprang with axes to cut it clear.

"Hoist jib and staysails!"

"What do you do now?" Gascoyne asked.

"Mount the swivel guns! Boarders away!" came Tommy's answer.

"But she has half our crew aboard," Gascoyne reminded.

"And Reilly," Tommy answered. "We're going to get them back."

The headsails and the swinging rudder cast her toward the moving frigate. Their only chance was to get alongside and board her before she got her guns into action.

"Lay us alongside her forechains, Booby," he told the helmsman. "Swivel guns there!" he called to the men who were mounting the light guns in their brackets along the rail. "Rake her decks when you can, but take care if you see our own men."

Gascoyne called, "Angel! Fetch me a cutlass!"

"Señor?" Angel gasped.

"Be quick!"

"No!" Tommy objected. "You are not well enough!"

"I have always led my boarders," Gascoyne argued stubbornly.

"No," Tommy insisted. "It is time you took command again. I will lead the boarders." He took the cutlass which Angel had brought.

The motley crew of boarders, the riffraff of the Western Isles, long denied the chance to use cold steel, began shouting, as the two ships came together, "À la bordage, mon capitaine! À la bordage!"

They were bare to the waist and their bodies were greased with slush from the galley copper to make them hard to hold in a death grapple. They swung cutlasses, or the short swords like curved bayonets called hangers, and through sennit belts knives were stuck.

The ships fell aboard each other, a sidewise glancing blow, and while men flung out grapnels to hold them, Tommy sprang and caught an open port lid and hauled himself up and through.

All along *L'Afrique*'s side, boarders were streaming up, shouting, "À *la bordage*!" À *la bordage*!"

In the dim light between decks, Tommy saw men, like demons, fighting, and from one desperate melee he heard Pierre Lebecque shout, À *moi, français*! À *moi*!" And Reilly shouted, "Bear a hand, ye spalpeens, least they do us in!"

It was knife and cutlass, handspikes, belaying pins, bare hands. The British sailors, exhausted from storm and fire and labor at the pumps, half starved, deprived of sleep, could not withstand this fresh tide from the privateer. It took only minutes to finish the struggle for command of the great guns; then the tide swept upward through the hatches to the open decks.

Aft, with a few of the afterguard around him, the captain was making a last stand. Charging the poop ladder, a horde of shouting boarders in support, Tommy could not tell whether or not this was the officer who had once befriended him. That day in the cabin, around a green-baized table, he had looked young, handsome, perfectly uniformed. This man, fighting desperately to keep his ship, yet unsupported now, looked more like a scarecrow than the captain of a British man-of-war. His tunic was salt-rimed and cutlass-slashed, he was unshaven, dirty; his burning eyes glared out at Tommy from beneath a bloody bandage.

"I'll trouble you for your sword, sir," Tommy said as the British flag came down.

"This time," the scarecrow muttered, "*your* prisoner," and Tommy knew it was his friend. He took the sword, painfully but with exquisite courtesy extended hilt toward him.

"I dislike confining you," Tommy said. "Will you give me your parole of good behavior?"

Ravenscroft's wry glance took in the conquered deck, his wounded men, the prisoners. He shrugged and said, "What else is there for me to do?"

Tommy gave him back his sword. "I'd like you to keep this," he said, "on your promise not to use it again until you are properly exchanged."

"My word of honor," Ravenscroft replied. His face was pale and wan, he was swaying on his feet, his hand shook when he took the sword.

"Now we must get this wreckage cleared away," Tommy said, "and more canvas spread, if you still have anything in your sail locker, and get this ship into Fort Royal." He called, "Reilly! Pierre Lebecque! Get the work in hand."

Then he turned and caught the falling captain.

CHAPTER ELEVEN

LIEUTENANT GÉNÉRAL des Armées Navales, le Comte de Grasse, Commander-in-Chief of His Most Christian Majesty's naval forces in the West Indies, paced the high poop of his flagship, swinging at anchor in Fort Royal Bay. Fore and aft, he paced, taffrail to quarterdeck.

The Count was becoming concerned with the drain of long service on his health. For more than forty-five years he had served French kings. He had fought in thirty campaigns. In the American War for Independence he had already taken part in eight engagements. His thoughts turned longingly toward home—the Château de Tilly, near Versailles. Among his many friends at court, made comfortable by loving wife and daughters, he could pass his final days in peace. He yearned to feel the rich earth of France underfoot, treading his family acres instead of hard oak decks. His love for home and France was written in his will: no matter in what part of the world or on what sea he might expire, his heart was to be sent home to repose eternally in the chapel of his château.

But, short of death, the Count knew that months must pass, perhaps years, before he would see home and family again. There was much to be done for his King on this side of the Atlantic and, thus far, he had accomplished little.

The thought of the many checkmates given him by Admiral

Sir George Rodney and his able second, Sir Sam Hood, and contemplation of the many campaigns to come turned the good wine of France sour in his stomach.

While he paced, his keen eyes missed nothing. "What is that signal flying on Fort Louis, monsieur?" he inquired of his *major d'escadre.*

M. de Vaugirauld put his spyglass to his eye and observed the flags flying above the battlements. "A ship is arriving, monsieur," he reported. "Two ships."

"*Bien. Merci, monsieur,*" the Count acknowledged and resumed his pacing. His eyes swept the harbor. Where, he wondered, would the port commandant find berths for these arrivals? The fleet already occupied a great part of the anchorage: three ships of 80 guns, a dozen 74's, half a dozen 64-gun ships. Twenty-one sail of the line in all, and numerous frigates besides his flagship, a three-decker rated 110.

But the warships were only part of the concourse at Fort Royal, the French seat of government in the West Indies. The "trade" was assembling to be escorted home to France. Upwards of a hundred merchant vessels of all descriptions were anchored on the fringes of the fleet. And another fifty would be waiting at Cap Français in Sainte-Domingue to join the great convoy as it passed, for, in sailing homeward, ships did not proceed on a direct easterly course. On that route they would battle head winds all the way. Instead, they took advantage of the easterly winds to drive them northwest along the rim of the Antilles, which swung like a great scimitar, the haft close to the Straits of Florida, the blade barring free entrance to the Carribbean and the Gulf of Mexico, the point thrust into the South American continent.

On northwesterly headings they would enter the Gulf Stream, gaining as much as a hundred miles a day even when the wind did not blow. And, somewhere to seaward of Nantucket, where the current stream widened and began to lose its force, and the west winds began to blow, the ships would turn to head, for the first time, toward their destination, riding the strong westerlies across the Atlantic.

"The ships are in sight, monsieur," de Vaugirauld reported. It broke the Count's train of thought and brought his pacing to a halt. Looking seaward, he saw a large ship and a small. The larger had only two of her three masts standing, and she rode low in the water. Her shattered appearance spoke of gun battles as well as storm. Her mizzen being gone, the colors flew from the mainmast, fouled in the jury rigging, so that he could not make them out. By her lines and general appearance she was a French frigate.

The smaller vessel, leading her in, was a topsail schooner having the look of a privateer. A familiar look, the Count thought, and resumed his exercise.

Pacing, he mentally added up his triumphs since arriving in the West Indies with his fleet two months before. Among the first, he numbered bringing the trade convoy safely out from Brest—a hundred cargo vessels of all types, and not a single loss. And he had matched tactical skill with Sir Sam Hood, who had failed to prevent the convoy from entering Fort Royal Bay. Though truthfully, in calm retrospect, he could not call it a great triumph, since he had caught Hood down to leeward, and had outnumbered him besides.

Next, with the Marquis de Bouillé, governor of the French West Indies, commanding the troops, he had attacked St. Lucia, where, in Gros Îlet Bay, the British fleet frequently sheltered. There, riding comfortably at anchor, without strain on either ships or men, it was a constant threat to French ships entering or departing Fort Royal Bay. If Admiral Rodney could be denied this advantageous anchorage, his ships, in order to watch Fort Royal, would have to keep under way, suffering the wear and tear that constant cruising brings.

But at St. Lucia, Sir Sam Hood, although not present himself, had had his revenge. In their first clash he had been outnumbered and outsailed, and he had wisely fallen back on his commander-in-chief, who was cruising in waters farther north,

thus giving Admiral Rodney a single combined fleet with which
to meet the French. But before leaving, Hood had had the
foresight to establish shore batteries in the entrance to Gros
Îlet Bay to look after things during the fleet's absence. He had
left the batteries well manned and supplied, and their fire on
the troops and ships attempting an amphibious attack had
turned the Count's invasion into a retreat.

The next operation had been a victory. With the French
troops still embarked, the Count had attacked and captured
the island of Tobago. But when, following that, he had attempted to do the same thing at Barbados, one of England's
largest and richest possessions and the main supply base of the
British fleet, he found Admiral Rodney's fleet interposed. Yet
the British admiral had refused a general action, being too
crafty to risk his outnumbered ships in waters strewn with
coral reefs washed by strong currents. A damaged fleet, driven
to leeward, might not beat back in time to save the island, but,
kept in being, it accomplished the same result.

This, then, was the accounting: a duel of minds, a threat of
fleets. Thrust and parry and thrust again. In the accounting to
date, there were more minus signs in the Count's addition than
plus. But the final test, M. de Grasse well knew, was still to
come. The war for American independence would be decided
not by armies but by ships. The sea lanes along the American
coast would, in the end, be decisive. If he could gain control
of these water routes, the war would soon be won. Yet he dare
not leave the West Indies until Sir George Rodney's fleet had
been greatly reduced or drawn away.

"Monsieur," de Vaugirauld, at his elbow, said, "there is a
familiar appearance to that frigate which arrives." He handed
his telescope to the Count.

"But certainly," M. de Grasse agreed, after a searching look.
"It is L'Afrique. She was capture from us at Lagos, where we
fought under M. de la Clue." He took the telescope from his
eye. "And now French arms have recaptured her. Magnifique!"

"I regret, Your Excellency," de Vaugirauld said, "it is not the case."

The Count reached for the telescope again. "You mean I cannot recognize a ship I once commanded?"

"Not that, monsieur. I mean she has been captured by American arms, not French."

The Count de Grasse saw the American colors flying from the smaller ship. And aboard the frigate which she was towing, the colors now streamed clear: the American flag above the British.

The Count closed the telescope with a clash and returned it to his *major d'escadre.* Another possible French triumph—small, to be sure, but splendid—must be transferred to the minus column.

"I will talk to the American captain when the ships are anchored," he said. "Please send a boat to bring him aboard."

The Count went below to his cabin, there to immerse himself in discouraging reports: bad condition of ships, lack of provisions and wine, discontent of crews. He shrugged. In forty-five years, it had always been the same. He did not doubt that Sir George, comfortable in Gros Îlet Bay, almost within sight, was faced with the same sort of thing. Yet somehow the fleets managed to keep at sea on distant stations, protecting their sovereign's interests. He unrolled a chart on his big table and began to study sailing routes: currents, winds, storms. The hurricane season was almost on them, here in the West Indies. Whether he took his fleet home to shelter on the coast of France until that dread season had passed, or to the American coast, one thing was certain: they must not remain in these dangerous islands. Yet he must base all decisions on the British fleet, whose presence was always a threat to French possessions. By this threat Admiral Rodney was able to keep a French fleet larger than his own from operations on the American coast. But though a British admiral might pin down a larger French fleet, he could not control hurricanes. The disaster of last season had demonstrated that.

The Count glanced up at a knock and the sound of de Vaugirauld's voice. He was so deeply immersed in his thoughts that, for a second, he could not bring his mind to focus on the two strangers who stood before him, one tall and dark, though unusually pale for a seaman, one young and fair. Both lean and muscular and with the look of danger about them.

"*Mon dieu!*" de Grasse exclaimed. "What have we here—pirates?"

"Of the most elegant sort, Your Excellency," de Vaugirauld replied. "These are officers of the *Princess*."

"*Princess?*" It had a familiar ring, yet he could not recall her.

"The privateer, Your Excellency. She just brought in *L'Afrique*."

The Count de Grasse looked closely at the younger man, again tantalized by a familiarity he could not grasp. The whole affair was one of shadowy memories: the frigate, the small ship towing her, the name, and now, this young officer. And surely there was also a resemblance in the older man to someone he knew.

But though the Count might struggle to remember a lad he had seen but once, and that a great distance from where they now were, Thomas Potter could never forget the Count de Grasse. He thought him the most handsome officer he had ever seen: a man towering well above six feet, powerfully built yet moving with agility and grace, his advanced years evident only in his graying hair, drawn back from wide temples to hang, gathered by a ribbon, on his neck. His eyes beneath heavy brows seemed aware of everything; a patrician nose marked his noble lineage.

When he spoke, his voice held the authority of long command. "We have met before, monsieur?" It ended on a rising note.

"Yes, Your Excellency," Tommy replied. "On the quay at Brest."

"But of course! The young American midshipman. So we meet again. I am pleased." He turned his attention to Gascoyne.

"But you are not American, monsieur." There was no rising inflection now.

"I, Your Excellency, am the same as you—a Frenchman."

"But your ship flies American colors," M. de Grasse said accusingly.

"Our captain had an American commission. But he is gone—killed in action. Midshipman Potter was in command when we captured *L'Afrique*—"

"Only because Gascoyne had been injured," Tommy interrupted. "I only held command until he got well."

"And now," M. de Grasse said, grasping the affair quickly, "between you there is no commission. Your ship has no nationality."

"Since an American captured *L'Afrique*," Gascoyne said, "it seemed only right to fly the American flag."

"And the men who fought to capture her?" the Count inquired.

"French, Irish, American—and the sweepings of many harbors."

"French?" M. de Grasse raised his heavy brows. "French sailors aboard a privateer?"

"We have a dossier on this privateer, monsieur," de Vaugirauld interrupted, a sheaf of papers in his hand. "She sailed from Brest without clearance. The guardship chased but could not come up with her."

"Yes, yes! I remember now," the Count exclaimed. "Nor the Iroise patrol."

"This *Princess* sailed straight through the Raz de Sein," de Vaugirauld added.

"Where," Gascoyne retorted with a laugh, "your warships dared not follow."

"Hmm," M. de Grasse rumbled, stroking his chin.

M. de Vaugirauld continued. "They boarded ships of the fishing fleet in Audierne Bay and took what men they needed."

"We pressed no one," Gascoyne protested. "No Breton came who did not want to."

"They did not come to escape service in my fleet, think you?" M. de Grasse inquired with biting sarcasm.

"How should I know, monsieur?" Gascoyne said with a shrug. "They came—should I inquire into their motives?"

"If they came to escape service, the joke is on them," the Count said and laughed heartily.

"You're not going to take them away from us, are you?" Tommy asked, alarmed.

"We shall see," the Count answered. "Proceed, monsieur," he told de Vaugirauld.

"The ship is now engaged in running sugar for M. de Kerguenac of Fort Royal and Petite Anse. And recently she badly treated H.M.S. *Bulldog*, brig, and escaped from H.M.S. *Growler*, after dealing that ship some injuries. Every ship of the British fleet has been alerted against her."

"*Mon dieu!*" Gascoyne exclaimed. "You must have eyes everywhere."

"And ears," M. de Grasse agreed. "The British, too. When they learn that you have brought in one of their frigates on the end of a towrope, there will be a price on both your heads." He turned to de Vaugirauld. "Have you finished the dossier?"

"There is one thing more," de Vaugirauld answered. "Captain Gascoyne is not Gascoyne at all—he is M. de Kerguenac."

"De la Caille de Kerguenac," Gascoyne corrected.

"In that case, I have known your family many years," M. de Grasse said. "You should be serving in a King's ship, not in a privateer. I am now going to remedy that."

"But Your Excellency!" Gascoyne began.

"Silence," ordered the Count.

"You will remove me from my ship?" Gascoyne demanded, ignoring the order. "You will put me to serve aboard a frigate or ship of the line? I must warn you, monsieur, I am a bad influence. I provoke my messmates to anger—provoke them until they challenge me. Then I run them through. You will gain one officer by putting me aboard, and lost many from dueling."

"Swordsmanship is an invaluable talent in an officer," the Count said, unmoved.

"But surely you do not approve of dueling, Your Excellency?" Gascoyne asked.

"Under some circumstances. But we need not concern ourselves with that. I have not said that I will remove you from your ship. We need such ships and such officers—rascals as you may be, charming as you are. You shall remain in command of *Princess*, M. de Kerguenac. And to save your neck from hanging, should the British capture you, I shall commission you a *capitaine de corvette*."

Tommy, who had stood by silently, except for one outburst, now broke out again. "What's to become of me?"

"As an American and an ally," the Count told him, "you are free to go. As a gallant officer, I beg you to remain. You shall have a commission as *enseigne*." And when Tommy hesitated, the Count continued, "You need not decide at once, monsieur. It is not an easy decision—a change of flags."

"I was thinking of my men," Tommy said. "The ones who have sailed with me—Americans."

"They are welcome to remain," the Count said. He turned to Gascoyne. "Now, monsieur, I have many things to do. You will oblige me by returning to your ship and hoisting French colors at once."

"As you order, Excellency," Gascoyne replied, and bowed, and went toward the door. Tommy, after his best bow, followed.

At the door the Count gave one last command: "You will also hoist French colors aboard *L'Afrique*."

"But, monsieur!" Tommy protested. "We captured *L'Afrique* before you commandeered *Princess* for your fleet."

The Count smiled; warmth in youth was to his liking. "*Bien!* You may keep American colors above British until sundown tonight. But tomorrow morning *L'Afrique* resumes her proper nationality—French."

"As you order, Excellency," Gascoyne acknowledged, and they went out. But they were hardly out of earshot before de Vaugirauld complained wearily, "Another ship to feed, another crew to pay."

"Another pair of eyes," the Count replied. "And a fast ship to carry despatches to General Washington and the Count de Rochambeau. *Princess* will pay her keep, never fear."

His *major d'escadre* brightened. "You have decided, monsieur? You will take the fleet to America?"

"My fleet needs to be in three places at once, monsieur," the Count replied. "To escort the trade home, to go to the American coast and aid Rochambeau, to protect our West Indies while the British fleet remains. Rodney will not remain here through the summer, we can be sure of that. But where will he go?" The Count pointed to the chart. "There are many places, monsieur, many possibilities."

"The American coast, most likely," de Vaugirauld suggested.

"That he will send ships to the American coast to reinforce Admiral Graves, I have no doubt. But how many?" He answered his own question. "Certainly a great many if he thinks I am going there. But will he go himself, or sail for home with his ships most needful of repair? We have reliable reports that the admiral's health is bad—a stricture, or something of the sort. My own health has not been good; no doubt Sir George has heard of that."

"You are thinking of going home, monsieur?" de Vaugirauld quickly asked, unable to conceal his alarm.

"I am thinking of having Sir George think I am going home," M. de Grasse replied, his eyes twinkling. "I shall ask Governor de Bouillé to give me a farewell ball."

"Admiral Rodney will regard it as a wild tale if he hears the rumor," de Vaugirauld argued.

"Exactly. Therefore he must be invited to attend."

De Vaugirauld began to laugh, enchanted with the idea. But his laughter suddenly stopped. "You do not truly think he would honor us?"

"*Non!* But he might send a ship, under guarantees of safe conduct, with officers to attend. He is as anxious to learn what preparations our fleet is making for departure as we are curious about his. He will find there is truly a farewell ball and that our ships are under sailing orders."

"You think he will not suspect your strategy, monsieur?"

M. de Grasse shrugged. "Perhaps. But it can do no harm. And I have reason for writing him now—the prisoners brought in aboard *L'Afrique*. I will offer an immediate exchange. Has not our correspondence on these matters always been most cordial? Did he not bring me some delicacies out from England for my table? At the end of my letter, I shall invite him to the ball. A matter of courtesy, no more, as if I really did not expect him to attend."

De Vaugirauld laughed again. "It can do no harm," he agreed and started to roll up the chart and stow the plotting instruments away.

M. de Grasse halted him. "*Non!* I have still work to do. The American coast is where you think Sir George will go. *Bien!* Where? Boston? New York? Charleston? Or perhaps the Chesapeake Capes? Where?"

When, at last, M. de Vaugirauld left the cabin, his chief was still bent over the chart, plotting sailing routes.

CHAPTER TWELVE

YOUR EXCELLENCY," wrote Admiral Sir George Brydges Rodney, Bart., Commander-in-Chief of his Brittanic Majesty's naval forces on the Leeward Island Station:

"It is with utmost regret that I must decline Your Excellency's kind invitation to a Farewell Ball to be given in Your Excellency's honour by Governor the Marquis de Bouillé. I am distressed to learn that the press of affairs has caused some deterioration in Your Excellency's health, as is also the case with mine; although it is not yet my good fortune to return to England for recuperation as it seems to be Yours to return to France.

"In your kind invitation you were generous enough to include junior Flag Officers, and Captains. Although, for the most part, my Officers are too much occupied to make a journey to attend a social function, by good fortune *Galatea*, frigate, will be passing in the neighbourhood of Fort Royal at that time and I have authorized her Commanding Officer, Captain the Hon. Jones-Loftin, R.N., to enter Fort Royal under a flag of truce to present my compliments to Your Excellency and to Governor de Bouillé, and to represent me at the Grand Ball.

"Believe me, Your Excellency, ever with great respect, Your Excellency's most humble and obedient servant,

"Rodney

"P.S. Captain Jones-Loftin will convey to you my willingness to exchange the prisoners you mention, and he has my authority to make all arrangements."

And so it was that when the Count de Grasse, with Mme. de Bouillé on his arm, led the grand march, the blue, white, and gold of the British Navy mingled with the scarlet, gold, and blue of the French armed forces.

From the crystal chandeliers in the great ballroom of Government House, light from a thousand candles flashed on gold sword hilts and set aglow the decorations of noble and distinguished officers. The candles were flattering to the handsomely gowned ladies, bathing white shoulders and bosoms in soft loveliness while setting ablaze the jewels on many a regally coifed head.

Thomas Potter had never seen such splendor. His own unpretentious uniform, garbed as he still was as an American midshipman, made him feel out of place. But so handsome a youth was not long neglected by the ladies of Fort Royal, hungry for any stimulation, any excitement in this circumscribed island society. And besides, the young American had already a considerable reputation as a—a corsair, *n'est-ce pas?*"

Gascoyne had not waited for introductions; a smile from a beautiful woman was enough. And Tommy soon found that if a smile did not fetch him, a French officer, with punctilious courtesy, soon did. At first it was exhilarating: the beauty of the ladies, the headiness of their perfumes, their bosoms occasionally pressing ardently against him, stirring him, yet at the same time embarrassing him by their closeness. He soon tired of it. He looked around hopefully, thinking that if Lord Ravenscroft were there—his lordship having been turned over to the custody of the governor and given parole—they might find talk more interesting than dancing with these insistent charmers.

Instead of Lord Ravenscroft, he saw Annette. The townspeople of Fort Royal, as well as the aristocracy of government and military circles, had been invited to attend this farewell to M. de Grasse; although Tommy had not expected to see M. and Mme. Boulanger, they were present.

Annette, when Tommy bowed from a distance, gave him a warm smile. M. Boulanger returned only a cold stare, chilling Tommy's first thought of asking her to dance. She was so young and lovely; it seemed a pity she must sit among the dowagers, watching instead of taking part. Yet in the face of her husband's rudeness, Tommy dared not ask her. He had, a few days previously, caused her one humiliating experience. He would not risk another.

Tommy, soon after *Princess* had brought *L'Afrique* into Fort Royal, had gone to see M. Boulanger to explain the loss of the sugar. He had not found M. Boulanger at home, but, Annette had told him, her husband would arrive at any moment. Would he not wait? It had been long since his last visit to their house, and many things had happened—the battle with the English brigs, and with the surf at Petite Anse, and the capture of the British frigate. She was impatient to hear of all this from him.

Her graciousness made him feel at home, and over the teacups he found it easy to tell her of his experiences. The sisters, he thought, were so different. Marie was as free with her charms as she was with her thoughts. But an air of feminine mystery clung about Annette, captivating as an ineffable perfume.

It was pleasant, and an hour sped by. But after he had told

Annette of the storm and the loss of the sugar, she seemed no longer at ease. Her eyes went repeatedly to the door.

"I have stayed too long," Tommy said. "Perhaps I had better not wait for your husband."

"It might be better if I told him about the sugar," she replied. "Why?"

"Trading is very bad now. It is a great loss."

"He will be angry?"

"My husband is hot tempered. He might say things that would hurt you."

"Then I must stay," Tommy said. "I cannot pass my problems on to you."

"Stay then," she replied, "and tell me of the storm—when you pulled *L'Afrique* from Pointe du Diable. I was visiting at Petite Anse that day. We could see you from the house—so tiny in the great waves. Yet you pulled the big ship away. *Mon dieu!* how we prayed for you, Marie and I."

"How could you have known it was *Princess*, madame?" he asked.

"Marie knew. She remembered well from your visits to Petite Anse."

He wondered how much Marie had told her about his afternoon ashore. "But we were far out, madame," he said. "The seas were high."

She smiled. "A woman knows," she said. It was her mystery again. He did not know exactly what she meant, but they were not just empty words, he was sure of that.

"We did only what sailors must do, madame, when a ship is in distress."

"Must you call me 'madame'?" she asked. "It makes me feel so ancient."

"I never think of you as being old," he assured her.

"Are we strangers, then?"

"No. If you will allow me, I shall call you Annette."

"I wish it, Tommy," she replied, a warmth in her manner he had not seen before.

It was at that moment, when formalities were breaking down, that M. Boulanger came in.

"Perhaps I intrude," he said. There was accusation in his tone. "Perhaps you did not expect me to arrive so soon."

"No, no, monsieur!" Annette replied, her face pale. "It was because I expected you at any moment that I suggested your guest should wait."

"My guest?" It was sarcasm thinly veiled.

"I came to see you on business, monsieur," Tommy said.

"In that case," said Boulanger, "Madame may leave the room."

Annette went quickly, without a word. Boulanger ignored his visitor, while he poured cognac for himself.

Ever since Tommy had called with Gascoyne to meet his relatives, he had been aware of the older man's dislike. Nor could he pretend to like M. Boulanger. His boorishness and the discourtesy to his gracious wife were insufferable. But this open hatred!

Having drained and refilled his glass, Boulanger took a chair. "Now then," he said, "your business?"

"I came to report about the sugar," Tommy began.

"You have brought delivery receipts?"

"No, monsieur. We were obliged to dump it in the sea."

"Our sugar!" M. Boulanger choked on his brandy. "But it was not yours to throw away!"

"We were in a storm," Tommy explained. "The ship was laboring heavily. It was either the sugar or our *Princess*—ourselves."

"I have never heard of such a thing!" M. Boulanger raged. "Unless a cargo is badly stowed."

"The casks were properly stowed, monsieur. Believe me."

"I do not believe you," Boulanger replied. "Not one word! I see the whole thing. Bad stowage let the cargo shift. Casks were stove; sugar spilled. There was spoilage by salt water. And to cover your own negligence, you threw it all overboard."

"I do not lie, M. Boulanger," Tommy replied, mustering all the dignity he possessed.

"Everyone lies, when it is of sufficient importance," Boulanger answered.

"I will show you the ship's log. You can see for yourself what the weather was."

"Ship's logs are as big liars as the men who write them," Boulanger countered.

"If you believe that all men lie when it is important," Tommy flared, "I can assure you, your sugar is not that important to me."

"Even if I demand payment for it? We can get no insurance coverage in these waters in wartime."

"I will repay you," Tommy said.

"You are rich, then?" Boulanger sneered. "You can throw money about as freely as you throw sugar?"

"I will pay. Where the money will come from is no concern of yours." At the moment, he did not know himself, his own funds being negligible.

M. Boulanger seemed impressed. "Since you will pay, it puts a different light on the matter. If you had said so at first, I would not have spoken as I did. But a cargo of sugar! Dumped into the sea! *Mon dieu!* But if you will pay . . . come, I have some good cognac here."

"No thank you," Tommy said coldly.

"Come now, *mon ami,*" Boulanger soothed, "do not be offended. I will call Mme. Boulanger and we shall take some refreshment together." He went to the door and called, "Annette! Come at once." Returning, he said, "Your family has large estates in America?"

"My father is a professional man, not a landowner," Tommy replied. "And do not press Madame to return. I must go."

"Well, then," said Boulanger, "if you must go, there remains first the payment. You have a banking connection in Martinique?"

"No. Not in Martinique nor Paris nor anywhere."

"Letters of credit, then? Surely you do not carry specie aboard, considering all the dangers of battle and capture."

For a moment he was at a loss what to answer. Pride had gotten him into difficulty. Then the solution came to him. "*Prin-*

cess will receive a handsome amount of prize money for capturing and bringing in *L'Afrique*. My share will be large, both as part owner and the officer in command when we captured her. I will pay you then."

"*Mon dieu!*" Boulanger flared. "You ask me to wait until then?"

"I do not ask," Tommy said. "You have no choice."

He was glad, when he had got out of the house, that Annette had not come to heel when her master called.

Seeing her now at the ball brought all the embarrassment, all the humiliation of that moment back. Tommy bowed again and went outside quickly, as if by putting distance between them he might put the occurrence from his mind.

The park-like garden was a paradise of tropical shrubs and flowers, traversed by lanes of royal palms, lighted by flambeaux so placed that mirrors on the tree trunks reflected each flare into many, creating a fairyland. Long tables were heaped with the green, gold, and rosy fruits native to the island, enticing salads, and hot dishes of fowl and roasted meats for the truly hungry. Scores of slaves attended the hundreds of guests.

As Tommy walked through the jostling, not too well-mannered crowd a voice called, "Halloa, pirate!" but, for a moment, Tommy could not place the young English naval officer who gripped his arm. Then, up from his memories of twilight in a frigate's 'tween decks, the smell of bilge water and disinfectant, a face came to him.

"Haskins!" he exclaimed.

Tommy had known him as a midshipman during his imprisonment aboard *L'Afrique*. Haskins, now a lieutenant, presented his companion. "Lieutenant Blake of *Galatea*. This is an old friend of mine, Blake. Midshipman—midshipman—damme if I haven't forgotten your name."

"Potter," Tommy told him. "Thomas Potter."

"Thomas Potter—Pirate," Haskins corrected, amused at his appellation.

"A court-martial acquitted me," Tommy reminded, laughing.

"And glad I was," Haskins said. "Though disappointed in a way. First chance I ever had to know a pirate."

"You're quite famous, you know," Lieutenant Blake said. "Haskins has been spinning yarns about you in the wardroom."

"Blake is third lieutenant of *Galatea*," Haskins explained. "I'm fourth."

They sat at a small table and a servant brought a bottle and glasses. Haskins examined the bottle. "Hmm," he said, pleased. "Rum."

"You haven't changed," Tommy said.

"I'd have known you anywhere," Haskins responded.

"I meant your liking for rum," Tommy explained. "Remember the morning of my trial? You brought a bottle to give me courage."

"And drank most of it himself, I'll wager," Lieutenant Blake gibed.

"Young Daspit came along with a bucket of water," Haskins recalled, ignoring the slur about his drinking, "and a black boy to help you wash. Dash wouldn't touch any rum, being on duty, so I drank his share."

"The marine sentry got some of it," Tommy remembered.

"Enough to keep him friendly," Haskins said. "And young Garton—just a sip or two in water to keep him from snitching. The damned little nuisance!" But almost as he spoke, Haskins' tone saddened. "He's gone now—God rest him."

"I was afraid so," Tommy said. "The ball hit squarely in the stern of the cutter."

Haskins looked amazed. "You saw it?" Then the truth dawned. "It was your ship. You're serving in the privateer that mauled *Bulldog* and *Growler!*"

"You heard about it?" Tommy asked.

"It was the talk of the fleet—there'll be no mention in despatches for those two commanders."

"*Princess*," Blake reflected, "privateer. And now she's captured *L'Afrique*. Don't we owe you a sound drubbing if we catch you at sea!"

"First you must catch us," Tommy answered amiably.

Haskins took a good pull at his glass. "That's war for you. Lord Garton almost attended your hanging; you attended his beheading."

"Haskins!" Tommy exclaimed. "Not that!"

"It's what they said—clean off."

They all drank, and for a time they were silent.

The music drifted out to them from the wide windows of the ballroom and they could see the ebb and flow of dancers.

Lieutenant Blake said, "You chaps can sit here and get gloomy sodden, but there's a lot of cheer inside there. I'm for trying some of it." He lurched off toward the ballroom, his legs, steady on a frigate's pitching decks, unsure on solid land.

A servant brought a fresh bottle.

"Do you remember Lord Milholme?" Tommy asked.

"Saluting acquaintance," Haskins replied, becoming more sparing of words as rum gave him difficulty with his tongue.

"Did his arm get all healed?"

"Took it off."

"Not Lord Milholme!" The thought was shattering. "It's hard to think of him with one arm gone. He was the handsomest man I've ever seen."

"Returned my salute with his left, last time I passed him," Haskins said.

"I suppose that ends his career," Tommy reflected.

"That's war," Haskins muttered, sounding more drunk than philosophical. "Arm one time, leg another—lucky to keep breath in your body."

"He won't be coming out to Nevis now, will he?" Tommy said.

"Not likely. Friends of yours?"

"They were kind to me—he and Lady Milholme. Denise and I became good friends too."

"Little spitfire, that redhead."

"You know her?" Tommy asked.

"Went to call one time with Daspit."

"I suppose Daspit sees a lot of her," Tommy asked, fishing.

"He can have her," Haskins said. "Let's get under way."

Tommy was willing. The music had become all discords; the rum had lost its savor. "Where to?" he asked.

"Find some island beauties. But no dancing, mind. Life too short in the Navy; can't afford to waste it." He waggled a finger in Tommy's face. "Beauties—but not for dancing. *Comprenez-vous?*"

Haskins got up unsteadily. Tommy got up too, understanding. Why not? He wasn't likely to see Denise again. And next time it might be his head lopped off by a cannon ball. But before they had quit the table, they found themselves facing two English captains. One of them, to Tommy's joy, was Lord Ravenscroft. They greeted each other warmly.

"This is the American who took my ship," Ravenscroft explained to his companion. "Midshipman Potter . . . Captain the Hon. Jones-Loftin of *Galatea.*"

"Really," Jones-Loftin said, coolly observing Tommy. Then, "Not really! Still," he added, "I understand you were little better than derelict, my lord? No condition to fight even a galley."

It was intended to take him down a peg, Tommy knew, yet he bowed courteously. "It's a pleasure to meet you, sir," he replied. "Perhaps my ship may some day see yours—when you are not derelict, let us hope."

"Come," Ravenscroft said with a laugh, "we are here under a flag of truce. No fighting, no threats of fighting." He sat down. "Come along, sit down. I am ready for refreshment."

So Haskins and Tommy resumed their seats, now in company with two captains.

Jones-Loftin was tall, rather too tall for frigates, and the constant bending to keep from striking his head on the carlings above had given him a permanent stoop. His angular face was weathered and forbidding enough to make a man-of-war's figurehead. When a servant started pouring drinks around, he reached across the table with a long arm and turned Haskin's glass bottom up. "What are *you* celebrating?" he demanded.

"Sir, I'm celebrating the fact I'm not a prisoner," Haskins answered.

"That's cause for celebration," Lord Ravenscroft agreed feelingly.

"And that I didn't have my head blown off like poor little Garton," Haskins added.

"No reason for getting half seas under," Jones-Loftin said.

"Is he one of yours, Jones-Loftin?" Ravenscroft inquired.

"Yes. And he'll spend some time under hatches if he doesn't behave."

"It's a special night," Ravenscroft said. "Let him enjoy it." He turned the young officer's glass right side up again and beckoned a servant.

"I suppose you know you won't be a prisoner much longer, Lord Ravenscroft," Tommy said.

"I've heard something of it. That's why I need company celebrating."

It was plain he would have no help from Jones-Loftin, who was too dry-timbered to celebrate anything.

"We got our sailing orders today," Tommy went on. "We take a large draft of prisoners to Antigua for exchange. I expect we will take you."

"It's in the wind," Lord Ravenscroft replied. "You'll not find many so quick to exchange prisoners as the Count de Grasse."

Jones-Loftin was still studying Tommy. "*Princess . . . Princess . . .*" he was saying to himself, as if to recall something he knew of her.

"With all the actions she's been in," Ravenscroft said helpfully, "you've probably heard of her."

"I've got it!" Jones-Loftin exclaimed. "You marooned a man, didn't you?"

"Yes, sir," Tommy answered. "On Sombrero. He was our second lieutenant.

"And a deserter from the Kings service as well as an outlaw," Jones-Loftin said. "One of our frigates picked him up. An old smuggler with a price on his head. The admiral sent him home to England for trial. Probably been swung from the gibbet on Tyburn Dock by now."

"Odd sort of business," Haskins observed. "Save a man's life so it can be taken away from him later—officially."

Tommy said, "I'm glad he didn't lose his life because of what we did."

As they talked, they became aware of M. de Grasse strolling through the gardens, greeting his guests.

"What's all this about his going home?" Jones-Loftin asked casually. "Not enough victories? Being replaced?"

"It's his health, sir," Tommy answered.

"Looks strong as an ox," Jones-Loftin observed.

It was true. The Count looked a magnificent figure in a blue tailed coat lined with red, the lapels and front heavily roped with gold braid, and the broad moire ribbon of the Ordre Royal de St.-Louis a scarlet slash across his breast. His white wig was neatly curled, but his own graying hair showed beneath it, gathered on his neck with a bow of ribbon. There was no one among the guests nearly so tall, not even Jones-Loftin.

"What's wrong with his health?" *Galatea's* captain inquired.

"They say he has fainting spells," Tommy told them.

"What a pity," Jones-Loftin remarked drily.

There was no time for further conversation. M. de Grasse, having seen the British uniforms, was coming to their table. They all stood and bowed with great respect, Haskins so low that, for a moment, it seemed doubtful that he could regain the perpendicular.

"Gentlemen," the Count greeted them, continuing in his labored English, "I am delighted to see you." He bowed directly to Captain Jones-Loftin. "You and your officers have been made comfortable, monsieur?"

"Were we allies, Your Excellency," Jones-Loftin replied, "we could not have been treated with more consideration."

The Count's eyes twinkled. "It is our enemies we are careful not to make angry." He gave his attention to Lord Ravenscroft.

"And you, monsieur. I do not recall having had the pleasure."

"I am a prisoner of war, Your Excellency. On parole. The former captain of *L'Afrique*."

"Ah, poor fellow!" the Count exclaimed. "How you must feel! I was once a prisoner in England. Only an *enseigne de vaisseau,* clearly not commanding the ship. Yet I was sufficiently disconsolate. But after some months in your beautiful Winchester I had many friends. My heart still warms to them."

"You have shown it tonight, Your Excellency," Ravenscroft replied. "As *Galatea*'s captain has said—we could not have been better treated."

"But we are all human," the Count reflected. "We hunger and thirst alike, have the same fears. And does a Frenchman hold glory in higher esteem than an Englishman? Besides, your Admiral Rodney has always been most courteous to me. I would be obliged, monsieur," he continued, addressing himself directly to Jones-Loftin, "if you would carry a little gift from me to him when you return."

"Command me, sir," Jones-Loftin answered.

"I wish to send some rare wine to Admiral Rodney. If I have two cases delivered aboard your ship before sailing, will you be good enough to see that they reach their destination?"

"If you will be good enough, Your Excellency, to order your fleet not to apprehend my ship."

The Count laughed. "But of course. I shall signal my fleet: 'Admiral Rodney's wine is not to be molested.'" He laughed again. "You are already protected, monsieur. Provided you return straight to St. Lucia. I cannot guarantee your safety if you roam the Caribbean."

He was about to move onward when he noticed Tommy. "And my American ally?" he asked. "Do things go well with you?"

"No longer an ally, Your Excellency," Tommy answered, "one of your officers."

"Splendid!" the Count said. "I am pleased to see that you have already taken up your duties—making my guests, who are strangers, feel at home among us." His bow included the whole group, and he passed on, followed by his retinue which had been waiting unobtrusively in the background.

"Uncommonly decent old chap," Lord Ravenscroft remarked, watching him go.

"These old men-of-war mellow with age," Jones-Loftin observed. "I recollect when I was secretary to Sir Hyde Parker— 'Vinegar' Parker, they called him. Tough old buzzard. After the action against La Motte-Picquet just south of here in the channel between this island and St. Lucia—in seventy-nine it was— Sir Hyde wrote the damnedest letter. Wrote La Motte-Picquet that we were only transient enemies, dependent upon the will of our masters. Said that LaMotte-Picquet's merit as an admiral was stamped on his heart, that he had the greatest admiration for him. I couldn't go that far myself."

"Perhaps," Ravenscroft suggested, "when you have been through what old Sir Hyde had . . ."

"He had the right of it, I'll agree," Jones-Loftin replied. "We're professional men, it's a way of life, a living—like Church or foreign service. We do what London or Paris or Madrid tells us. Enemies today, allies tomorrow."

"Blake is finding a few allies in there," Haskins remarked. Through the ballroom windows they could see Lieutenant Blake dancing.

"Fancy we should go in and do some fraternizing ourselves," Jones-Loftin suggested. "I'm representing Admiral Rodney, you know."

"I'll remain here and fraternize with Tommy Potter," Ravenscroft said. "He's a French officer now."

"You'll fraternize with him here, right enough," Haskins muttered, emboldened by the rum, "but you'll blow him to hell if you meet at sea."

"Of course," Ravenscroft agreed amiably. "Your captain has just said—this is a profession, a way of life. Duty is one thing, friendship another." But before further talk might have steered them into deeper waters, Gascoyne came along with M. and Mme. Boulanger and a beautiful woman to whom they were presented, the Countess Morne-Tilly. Jones-Loftin at once asked the Countess to dance and, a moment later, Lord Ravenscroft followed with Annette.

There still remained four at the table; Gascoyne and M. Boulanger now in place of the two captains. Gascoyne said, "I will drink some wine. This strong spirit is not for me." He pushed the rum bottle away and beckoned a servant.

"Why not strong spirit?" Haskins demanded.

"It gives one ideas. About the ladies, you understand, monsieur. Ideas. But in the end"—he shrugged—"nothing."

Haskins turned his glass bottom up again.

"Cognac," M. Boulanger grunted and glared at Tommy.

They sat silently for a time: Boulanger dourly steeped in his cognac, Gascoyne savoring his wine, Haskins far away in thought. Tommy, through the wide ballroom windows, saw Annette dancing with Lord Ravenscroft. She was radiant, floating gracefully in his lordship's arms. She laughed gaily at, no doubt, some clever sally he had made—a happy, carefree girl.

Gascoyne broke the spell. "Since the English captain has taken my charming partner from me, I must find another."

Boulanger grunted. "These English!" He, too, had been watching the dancers; clearly he found it bitter to see his wife in Lord Ravenscroft's arms.

Haskins sat staring straight ahead, tapping his fingers on the table in the rhythm of the music. Gascoyne finished his wine and stood up. When he had gone, Boulanger drank, wiped his lips, and glared at Tommy.

"Have you received the prize money for *L'Afrique?*" he demanded.

"Not yet, monsieur," Tommy replied. "You'll will hear from me the moment I do."

"I had as well be deaf then," Boulanger grunted.

"You think I would cheat you?"

"No, monsieur. You are too great a fool for that. And I was a greater fool—not putting a lien of attachment against your share at once. In that way I might have had a prior claim. Now the court of admiralty informs me that *L'Afrique* is not good prize, since she is already the property of our King. For that reason, no reward will be paid."

"But we captured her," Tommy protested. "We brought her into port. She belongs to us until the admiralty court makes an adjudication."

"That she was once a French frigate you do not deny?" M. Boulanger inquired acidly.

"Of course not. She still bears her French name."

"And that she was under British colors only because she had previously been captured?"

"What's so strange about that? There are a number of former French ships in British service."

"Exactly. And our King would like to have them back—free of charge."

Tommy was beginning to understand.

"The governor," M. Boulanger continued, "seeing an opportunity to please our fat Louis, has taken possession of the ship from the admiralty court, claiming she is not subject to adjudication. Once the King's, always the King's."

"No prize money at all?" Tommy asked, numb with disappointment.

"Perhaps a small fee for salvage. Nothing more."

"It's a shame to treat us so," Tommy said. "I will talk to the Count de Grasse."

"It will do you no good—he, too, is a servant of the King. And if you think your treatment is shameful, what of mine? You are being denied a profit—something you never possessed; I am out of pocket for the cost of the sugar. One does not grow cane and cut it and boil it and press it without laying out money."

"I am very sorry," Tommy said sincerely.

"It is not your sympathy I want," M. Boulanger snapped. "I find myself denied even the right of libel against the *Princess*. She has become an auxiliary of the fleet, it seems. She too is King's property, not subject to attachment."

"So you have no legal remedy whatever?"

"None."

Tommy began to laugh. He did not know why, exactly. It seemed funny that Boulanger had no redress other than what he himself might do.

M. Boulanger would have struck him had it not been for the dancers returning. Annette was radiant from her dance, alluring on Lord Ravenscrofts arm; and when she laughed at something his lordship said, Tommy realized that he had never heard her laugh before. It was as if a door had been opened into a shadowy room and let in light.

"M. Boulanger," Lord Ravenscroft said, "your lady dances divinely."

"I was not aware of it," Boulanger replied ungraciously. "But then I seldom dance."

"Monsieur deprives himself of great pleasure," Lord Ravenscroft replied, bowing a tribute to Annette. "Madame is also very charming."

"It is a waste of time, this dancing," M. Boulanger muttered in his glass.

Captain Jones-Loftin, having returned to the table in time to hear this interchange, asked, "Will Madame be kind enough to waste a bit of time on me?"

"I do not agree that it is a waste of time to dance," Annette responded with spirit. "I am pleased, monsieur." She placed her hand lightly on the captain's arm.

"*Non!*" M. Boulanger exploded.

"But, monsieur," Annette protested, her hand still on Jones-Loftin's arm, "these gentlemen are the Count's guests."

"You will remain where you belong," Boulanger told her, "with your husband."

"But since you do not dance yourself," Jones-Loftin argued hopefully, "and Madame is so young and lovely. It is unfair—"

"*Non!*" Boulanger interrupted rudely. "Madame, my wife, will not dance again tonight."

Jones-Loftin gently withdrew his arm. "Against a husband's wish," he said, "I canot press my claim."

Annette gave her husband a blazing look of scorn, and for a moment it seemed that she would defy him. But convention was too strong. "If you will not permit me to dance," she said, "I must insist that you take me home."

Haskins broke the shocked silence. Having pulled himself to his feet, he stood unsteadily, gripping the back of his chair. And though his eyes did not seem to see the people at the table, he spoke rationally:

"If you were my sister, madame—and I would be blessed to have one so lovely—I would urge you to dance with Captain Jones-Loftin. He is a gentleman. He knows the courtesy due a lady."

M. Boulanger's florid face flamed with the fires of wrath. "Are you implying, monsieur, that I am not a gentleman?"

Unruffled, Haskins answered, "I could not have been more explicit and remained a gentleman myself."

"Gentleman!" Boulanger sneered. "You are drunk!"

Lord Ravenscroft said, "Drunk, perhaps, but well spoke just the same."

"For which I forgive him all past sins," Jones-Loftin added quietly.

"So!" Boulanger flared. "The English now give us instruction on how to treat our wives. It is a scandal that you, our enemies, are present at this affair. But, since you are, you should have the decency to keep your place."

"It is you who are out of place," Tommy heard himself saying. "These officers are guests of M. de Grasse. They must be treated with courtesy." It brought all of Boulanger's accumulated rage down on him.

"You dare to speak so to me?" Boulanger stormed. "You dare tell me what I must or must not do?"

Annette tried to quiet him. "Monsieur! Calm yourself, I beg you. People are watching. Come, let us go."

"Let them watch," Boulanger screamed. "Let them see a

Frenchwoman, a Frenchman's wife, stand against him with Englishmen. The people will know how to judge. Wives do not behave thus in Martinique."

Tommy said, "They will admire her for her courage, as I do."

"You are an insolent puppy," Boulanger raved. "I will stop your mouth." With the back of his hand, he slapped Tommy across the lips.

And Tommy, with a blow he would regret a thousand times, knocked Annette's husband down.

CHAPTER THIRTEEN

TOUCHÉ!

The blade flicked through, as Lord Ravenscroft dropped his guard the fraction of an inch, and found his breast. But Tommy did not thrust home.

"*Parfaitement!*" Gascoyne exclaimed.

The duelists faced each other again, swords elevated at salute. But Gascoyne halted further practice.

"Rest now, while I bandage your arm," he said.

Earlier, when Tommy was parrying a thrust from Gascoyne, more expert with the dueling sword than Lord Ravenscroft, the blade had ripped the fleshy underpart of his arm.

"Good luck it's not your sword arm," Gascoyne said, as he sponged the caked blood from the wound with water Angel had brought. "In case there should be infection in the morning."

"The lad's ready as he is," Lord Ravenscroft counseled. "Best let well enough alone."

Lord Ravenscroft, as Mr. Potter's second, had made all the arrangements for the duel. He had wanted to accept the challenge himself, claiming that since he had touched off the chain of events by dancing with Mme. Boulanger, thus arousing her husband's jealousy, the fault was his. But, unfortunately, there was no way of getting round the fact that it had been *Enseigne* Potter who had knocked M. Boulanger flat on his back in the governor's gardens.

Gascoyne, although regretting that he had not been on hand to knock M. Boulanger down himself, was delighted that Tommy had seen to the Kerguenac honor. And, since the removal of his cousin's boorish husband from the scene was not to be Gascoyne's pleasure, he thought it fitting that his protégé should be the one to end that unwholesome alliance. Any other outcome was not seriously to be thought of.

Nevertheless, to make sure, Gascoyne had cleared an area in the waist of *Princess* where most of the day he had, with the expertness of one long given to these affairs of honor, put Tommy through a course of training in dueling swords. With Lord Ravenscroft's assistance, he had brought the lad to a keenness that pleased them all.

Gascoyne doused the wound with cognac. At the liquor's fiery sting, Tommy clamped his jaws.

"It will be sore a little in the muscle," Gascoyne said, "but tomorrow we work that out. And you will keep your mind better on your guard. If you think of other things . . ." He made a long thrust, as if holding a blade. "*C'est tout!* You are finished!"

"I know," Tommy said contritely.

That his mind had wandered, he could not deny. All during that session of thrusts and parries, "*en gardes!*" and "*touchés!*" he had been reliving the events of yesterday—the blow given in anger, M. Boulanger stretched on the ground, the challenge.

"Now you must rest," Gascoyne said, after a last inspection of the wound.

But Tommy could not rest. This man was Annette's husband, and he was old. Surely the quarrel could be settled without going at each other with swords. He determined to go ashore and see what amends could be made some other way. And he would say nothing to Gascoyne, sure that if he did, Gascoyne would not let him go. He knew already what Gascoyne would say: "But, *mon ami,* you have been challenged!" It would be as simple as that for Gascoyne. But not for him.

The ship was quiet. Gascoyne was dozing on the cabin transom. On deck, men were loafing at day's end, enjoying a pipe and a yarn. At Tommy's command, several of them put the jolly-boat in the water, and Reilly offered to pull him ashore.

"You're an officer now," Tommy reminded him. "Angel will take me in."

Reilly had been promoted to warrant rank, along with Pierre Lebecque, to fill the vacancies in the officer complement. And Metzger had been appointed bosun.

"Yerra!" Reilly protested. "Whin a man becomes an officer, must he forget how to pull an oar?"

"Don't be pigheaded," Tommy snapped.

"Will ye be listnin' to me now, sor," Reilly insisted. "Whin a man's throubled—which, plain as day, ye are—'tis a friendly counselor he needs. An' who betther than your old friend Reilly?"

"What's that got to do with pulling me ashore?" Tommy demanded.

"Wasn't it me, sor, carried your togs aboard the first ship ye iver joined, and taught ye to swing your hammick so's not to be throubled wid yer kidneys from hangin' in a bight, an' how to lash an' stow, neat an' shipshape?"

"Who said you didn't" Tommy asked. He had learned Reilly's trick of answering one question with another, but he had not learned how to shut Reilly off.

"Thin let's be havin' no more nonsense about who'll pull ye ashore," Reilly said, ending the argument.

When the boat was well clear of *Princess,* Reilly swung broadside to, so they could both look at her, and lay on oars. "Faith, ain't she the beauty!" he observed.

She was freshly painted and her spars newly varnished, and the canvas, new after the storm, all neatly furled in white rolls. The French royal ensign drooped from the staff at her taffrail.

"I wish it were the American flag," Tommy remarked.

"Aye, We've fought some grand battles under the Stars an' Stripes. We will agin, sor, I don't misdoubt."

Tommy, deep in thought, said nothing.

"Whin ye think o' thim grand Donnybrooks," Reilly persisted, "a duel seems a small thing. Yet a man kin be kilt just as dead."

"I wish I didn't have to fight it," Tommy said.

"How come ye got into the mess at all?" Reilly asked. "Fightin' ashore? Ye had a cut lip whin ye come off next mornin'."

"I wasn't fighting, Reilly."

"Some spalpeen hit ye, thin? An' a woman in the offing?"

"No, no! It wasn't that." But Tommy added, "Not exactly."

"Ach, the dear souls," Reilly commented. "Don't they allus be givin' men a rough passage? Was ye defendin' her honor?"

"I suppose you could call it that."

"'Tis naught to be ashamed of," Reilly said.

"The man was old," Tommy replied, "that's why I'm ashamed. And the lady was his wife."

Reilly plied the oars again, in silence for a while. "If ye've been poachin' on a married man's presarves," he said at last, "'tis a bad thing to die for. Yet I don't misdoubt it would be worse on your conscience was ye to kill him."

"I wasn't poaching, Reilly."

"In that case, I'd not duel wit him. He struck you, followin' which ye knocked him on his starn sheets. The score's even. Call the matter off, say I."

"People will think I'm a coward," Tommy said.

"Thinkin' a man's a coward niver made him one," Reilly argued. "I remember a case whin I served in *Barfleur*—not the same thing at all, yet not so different. An officer was challenged who did not want to fight, it bein' a small thing about relievin' late on watch an' no honor involved. But thim young hotheads was always dueling to ease the dullness o' life aboard. They called their messmate a coward."

"He wouldn't meet the challenge?"

"He apologized, bein' in the wrong."

"And they still called him a coward?"

"Until, agin an enemy, he fought repellin' boarders while they cut him to ribbons. The pieces wasn't big enough for the surgeon to sew together."

Reilly pulled in silence after that, while Tommy steered the little boat through the crowded anchorage, a small thing, hardly more than driftwood among those great men-of-war, small as his duel compared to the battles he had been in. He landed the boat gently alongside the quay stairs, and Reilly held it steady with one great hand, both oar hafts in the other.

"Shall I be waitin', sor?" he asked, when Tommy had disembarked.

"No thanks, Reilly," Tommy told him. "I might be ashore for some time. I'll get a waterman to bring me off."

"Mind that story I told ye," Reilly said in final counsel. "If there's no good reason to fight, why be fightin' at all and mebbe get yourself kilt?"

He shoved the boat clear and shipped the oars, and Tommy watched him pull away into the stream. Good, faithful Reilly. He was a friend that could be counted on no matter what happened. Tommy waved to him and turned and ran briskly up the landing stairs. He hurried through the town, unmindful of the oppressive heat, firm in his decision not to fight but to offer an apology. But when, having pulled the Boulanger bell, he was informed by the answering *bonne* that Monsieur was not at home, he felt a welcome sense of reprieve.

"Do you expect Monsieur later?" he inquired.

"No, missie. He is away at St. Pierre."

"Tomorrow then?"

"Perhaps, missie."

"*Merci*," Tommy said. "*Au 'voir*." Tomorrow was another day.

He had turned to go when the *bonne* said, "Madame is at home."

What possessed him, he did not know. When the *bonne* held the door invitingly open, he went in. But, waiting in the drawing room for Annette, he realized the folly of it. It was M. Boulanger he had to face, him and no one else. He decided to leave.

Then Annette came in.

There were violet shadows beneath her eyes and all her radiance at the ball had gone, and when she gave him both her hands they were cold despite the heat. He felt shame to have caused her such distress.

She did not draw her hands away. For a brief moment, no words passed between them, only the intensity of their feelings through their touching hands. She did not suggest that they sit down. Tommy understood; his visit must be short.

"I came to apologize to M. Boulanger," he said, hoping at once to relieve her anxiety.

"For that only?" she asked softly.

"And to tell you how sorry I am to have caused you such embarrassment."

"I am glad you have come. So glad." She withdrew her hands and brushed quickly across her eyes with the back of one. "If you had not come, I was going to see the Count de Grasse."

"To have me kept aboard because I behave so badly when ashore?" he asked, trying to turn it lightly to ease the tension.

"To keep you from being killed."

"I have spared you the trouble of that," Tommy said laughing in his own unease. "There will be no duel."

"Only if you remain on board until you sail," she said.

"But if I apologize? If I tell your husband how much I regret what I did?"

"You do not know my husband. He will insult you for your apology."

"Is he so fond of dueling, then?"

"He has great pride, and having met financial disaster—having to share this house with my father—his pride has become an open sore. He is"—it was difficult for her to go on, but she forced it—"old. Much older than I. It weighs upon his mind. He imagines things." She paused. She could force herself on only by the greatest determination. "I say these things to you because you must not come here again."

"Not even to apologize?"

"No! You must remain on board. Say some duty has come up to interfere. Say anything—nothing. But I beg you, do not meet him."

He was silent for a moment. What would Gascoyne say? And Lord Ravenscroft? What would they think? And Reilly! "You are asking a great deal, Annette," he finally said.

"I know," she agreed. "I am asking much." She was asking more of herself, yet she kept it from her face. But the trembling of her voice betrayed her.

"Annette!" Tommy said. "Is there something else wrong? Something I do not know about?"

"It will not be easy for me if you do not come here again," she confessed. "With you I have had someone young to talk to." She stopped and put a hand over her mouth as if to keep her thoughts from spoken words. "I must not say such things," she said. "It is wicked. But one thing more I must say—do not come again. Monsieur, my husband, is jealous and he is an expert pistol shot."

"Annette," Tommy protested, trying to make light of it, "you are upset. M. Boulanger cannot be jealous of me. I have done nothing."

"You have done nothing?" she asked bitterly. "I will tell you what you have done: you have committed the sin of being young, while he is old; you are handsome, which he is not; your life is adventure, his is a round of contracts, bills of exchange, the price of sugar, tobacco, coffee. You have sails on your horizon, he has only dusty ledgers. He is no fool. He sees himself as he is, and me as I am—and you, *mon ami*. He is jealous of the love he knows you can give, and he cannot."

"If all that is true," Tommy said, "you are right. I should not come here again."

"I am glad that you understand it is good-by," Annette said and gave him both her hands. He kissed them, and when he looked up he saw the deepening shadows beneath eyes misting with sadness; when he took her in his arms and kissed her he tasted the salt of tears.

"Tommy, dear Tommy," she said.

She gave herself fully to his arms, pliant, her lips clinging to his, a kiss not of farewell. Then, as suddenly as they had come together, they drew apart.

Tommy said, "I was very bad. I am sorry. I respect you more than I can say."

"Respect?" The word seemed to startle her. "I thought perhaps . . . perhaps it might be love." She spoke the words softly, as something cherished, the thought itself loved.

"Sometimes a man gets carried away," Tommy said.

"Does he?" And in her trembling lips he thought he saw a smile. "I will forgive you then, if you will promise not to come ashore again, not to fight this duel."

"If that is what you want," he replied, "I promise. I'll do anything for you." It *had* been love, he thought. He loved her very much.

She slipped an arm through his and guided him onto the veranda. It was cool there, a pleasant breeze blew from the water; they could see *Princess*, a black swan plumed with white.

"Even when you do not come ashore," Annette said, "I can see your ship."

"Not much longer," Tommy told her. "We sail in a few days."

"For a long time?" she asked, startled.

"Who knows? But a long cruise, Gascoyne thinks."

"I will pray for you each day," she said, and he thought he had never seen her face so beautiful. "I will pray God to keep you safe. I will also pray him not to bring you back."

Then, suddenly, she was in his arms again, her hair fragrant against his cheek, her head against his breast. "*Mon cher*," she whispered, "others are not so blind as you—my husband knows how I feel."

They moved, unspeaking, to the swing-sette, cool in the shadows of drawn blinds. He kissed her eyes, her hair, her mouth, tasting her love upon her lips. In their ecstasy, kisses seemed not enough. His hands, trembling with an urgency not to be denied, found her bodice. Her hands followed his, covering them, holding them.

"No, my love! Dear love, not that!"

It was a cry of anguish which he could not heed. And though her words forbade, her fingers, fumbling beside his at the opening of her bodice, helped him to go on.

CHAPTER FOURTEEN

IT HAD changed everything. Now there was no other course; he must meet M. Boulanger.

There was no use thinking any more about apologies; you cannot apologize to a man for betraying him with his wife. And with that on your conscience, can you look him in the eye and say you are sorry you knocked him down? Tommy could not, he was sure of that. Nor could he tell Gascoyne that he would not fight the duel; that, to avoid it, he would lurk on board until *Princess* sailed. Clearly there was no escape. No matter if it did mean breaking his promise to Annette, no matter what shame he might feel when facing M. Boulanger, he must meet him. What irony! *On the field of honor.*

That day—the day after his being with Annette—when Gascoyne started him off on another round of dueling exercise, Tommy did not object. Yet, all the time, a solution was fermenting in his mind.

"*C'est ça!*" Gascoyne at last exclaimed. "You are a swordsman now, *mon ami.* I would have no fear for you against the best."

"I've decided to meet him with pistols," Tommy said.

A chain shot tearing through the mainsail would not have caused greater consternation.

"*Mon dieu!*" Gascoyne exclaimed. "But why?" And Lord Ravenscroft said, "I have already informed M. Boulanger's second that the affair is to be with swords."

"You can change it," Tommy insisted. "I am the challenged party; it is my right to choose."

"But, *mon ami*," Gascoyne argued tensely, "with a sword you will surely kill him."

"I don't want to kill him," Tommy replied.

Gascoyne pulled at his hair. "*Mon dieu*, I think you are a little mad! You have a chance to kill this puffed-up toad and you do not want to."

"I'd hate to," Tommy retorted.

"I take it then," Lord Ravenscroft inquired with exquisite irony, "you have no objection to his killing you?"

"Well—" That was a possibility which Tommy had not thought about.

Lord Ravenscroft pressed home his point. "That's what might happen, you know. With pistols, if he gets his shot off first, it could be you."

"No matter," Tommy said with finality. "I'm not going to meet him with swords." It should have closed the door on further argument.

But Gascoyne persisted: "Why did you not tell us this yesterday? We could then have practiced shooting pistols." One way or another he was determined that it should not be his protégé they carried from the field of honor.

"I hadn't decided yesterday," Tommy told him.

"*Mon ami*," Gascoyne argued, with control that gave him pain, "I do not understand. With swords it is in your favor; with pistols he has as good a chance as you."

"Perhaps better," Lord Ravenscroft added. "He may be an expert shot for all we know."

"Pistols," Tommy stubbornly insisted.

Gascoyne, out of patience, shrugged. "We cannot deny a man the right to choose the manner of his death. If he wishes pistols—*bien!*"

"At how many paces would you prefer to die?" Lord Ravenscroft inquired.

They were both disgusted with him, that was plain. "Twelve,"

Tommy said, but one second thought he changed it. "Better make it fifteen."

At that distance even an expert, if his nerves were jumpy, might miss. And M. Boulanger, as Tommy had been told, was an expert shot.

That his decision was foolish, Tommy suspected, and unreasonable, as Gascoyne seemed to think, and headstrong. Yet he saw a certain ironical justice in it. M. Boulanger, when they faced each other at fifteen paces, would think that he was avenging the humiliation of being knocked down in public, when in fact he was being given satisfaction for the betrayal of his honor. And in deciding to meet him with pistols, which would be greatly to the older man's advantage, in some perverse way Tommy seemed to ease his conscience.

But his conscience did not remain at ease. All that long night —the night before the meeting—he was tormented by his thoughts. Sleep came fitfully; finally not at all. The rocking of *Princess* in the easy harbor swell, gentle as the rocking of a cradle, should have lulled him. Instead, he heard every footfall of the anchor watch on his inspection rounds, ticked off the turning of each glass. At last, unable longer to lie in his small stateroom with only his torturing thoughts, he dressed and went into the cabin and lighted a candle, and began a letter to his mother.

"*Chère Maman*," began his letter. "Soon now I am going ashore to fight a duel."

That his mother would not receive this letter for several months, perhaps not at all, and that she could do nothing to help him, made no difference. He poured out his thoughts to her, confided in her, just, as a child, he had many times unburdened himself to her, about small things that seemed important. But this was no small thing, this duel.

When he had finished, he sat staring at the guttering candle, unmindful of the grease which spattered the paper, adding to the stains of tears. Then he tore the letter up and burned it piece by piece in the candle's flame.

In the piling ashes, the candle guttered out. He sat in darkness,

staring upward through the open skylight at the stars. He could
see Orion, the constellation of the hunter. Stars clearly formed
the huntsman's belt, and, with a little imagination, he could see
the sword dangling from it. A sword could have been his weapon.
Had he been a soft-hearted fool?

Angel, coming in to light the gimbal lamp on the bulkhead,
broke his introspection.

"Don Tomas," Angel said, "it is nearly time. You must take
something hot to drink. I will make cocoa."

"Coffee," Tommy told him.

"But, señor," Angel protested, "the nerves. One must hold the
pistol steady. Otherwise . . ." He shrugged expressively.

"Coffee," Tommy repeated sharply. His nerves were already
raw.

Angel went forward, muttering darkly. Tommy took a clean
sheet of paper and began to write.

"Dear Papa and Mama:
    "I am afraid I have not been very good at writing
letters Home, but before we Sail on this Voyage, I want to
tell you what we have been doing. *Princess* has been helping a little to win the war by helping the poor island
Planters get their products—Sugar mostly—to market. But
now I hope we are going to see real action, because *Princess*
has been taken over by the Count de Grasse to be a tender
for his Flagship. And he has commissioned me an *enseigne*.
    "I have met M. de Grasse. He is a wonderful looking man
and a great Fighter, everyone says, strict on his Officers
and Men, but fair. He is a General! Isn't that just like the
French—calling their Admirals, Generals?
    "If I should not get home, ever, I want to say that I
love you both and my Sisters very much. I think of you
always when I pray.
    "In haste, with lots of Love,
            "Your loving Son,
                "Thomas
"P.S. I don't mean to say that I won't get Home. But in
War—who knows?"

He scratched a lot of kisses across the bottom of the page.

He had just time for one other short letter before Angel returned with the coffee. Reilly came into the cabin with him.

"Yerra, 'tis up an' dressed ye are!" Reilly exclaimed. "An' did ye rest well the night, sor?"

"Fine, thanks," Tommy replied, drawing a good hard look from Reilly's shrewd eyes.

"A bit of rest would ha' done ye no harm, sor," Reilly observed.

"I'll be all right when I've drunk this coffee," Tommy assured him.

"'Tis more solid ballast ye'll be needin'" Reilly suggested. "There's time an' to spare—we'll not be shovin' off till anither glass is turned."

"I couldn't eat, Reilly," Tommy replied. "Not a mouthful."

"I've fought no duels meself," Reilly observed, "the practice bein' only for gintlemen, but miny's the time me stummick felt hollow, standin' to at the guns waitin' the first broadside. But after that first divilish thunderclap an' the smoke an' flame an' all, an' flyin' splinters, a man fergets he has a stummick."

"There'll be only one broadside this morning," Tommy said.

"Aye. 'Tis thrue. Yet the principle is the same."

"What principle?" Tommy demanded, drawn into argument despite his uneasiness.

"If Fate ain't called ye up to muster, ye'll be standin' there smilin' whin the smoke has cleared."

"But suppose Fate has?"

"I'll not be supposin' any such thing, sor, by your lave. You an' me will see the day again whin' we stand to the guns, waitin' the first broadside, the Stars an' Stripes above. I make no misdoubt of it whatever."

Reilly could sound very convincing. "Thank you, Reilly," Tommy said.

"I'll just be seein' to lowerin' the boat now, by your lave."

When he had gone, the cabin was lonely, and the hollow feeling that Reilly had banished with his talk, returned. Tommy hurriedly gulped the hot coffee and went on deck.

He stepped from the cuddy into a night still velvet black, but he heard men stirring—the new anchor watch relieving the old—and the squeak of block sheaves and rattle of oars told him they were making ready the jolly-boat. In the waist, where a lanthorn hung from a backstay, he saw Gascoyne's tall figure. He moved forward to join him.

"Ah, you are ready before us," Gascoyne said in greeting. "You slept well, *mon ami?*"

"Yes, thanks."

"Splendid! One needs a steady hand."

But Tommy was aware that Gascoyne had maneuvered him into the lanthorn rays so that he could look at him. Steady hand! He hoped Gascoyne would not see that he was shaking.

"There is a chill in the air this morning," Gascoyne said. Which was absurd, the night having scarcely cooled off, even on the water.

"I'm nervous," Tommy confessed.

"But of course," Gascoyne said amiably. "Your stomach flutters, no?"

Tommy did not answer. His stomach was upside down.

"It is like that before the first duel for everyone," Gascoyne continued. "For some—before every duel. But you—it will pass. When you face him, you will see. It will pass."

"I hope so," Tommy said. He wished that Gascoyne would not be so matter of fact about it. He wished above all that Gascoyne were going with him.

"Listen well to me now, *mon ami*," Gascoyne said, and the amiability had left his voice. "The prisoners for exchange come aboard at daylight. After that we sail as soon as wind and tide serve."

"Without me?" Tommy gasped.

"No, no! But we must clear the harbor." He wet a finger and held it up to test the land breeze, light, capricious. "We must sail before this dies."

Tommy was thinking, *suppose I die?* But he said, "What then?"

"The English milord will meet you at the landing with a carriage. Reilly is going with you also."

"I wish you were," Tommy said. He could not help it.

"You think I have time to go with you to hold your hand," Gascoyne replied gruffly. "*Non!* I have things to do. For one thing, I must get clear of harbor before M. de Grasse becomes annoyed. When he gives an order, it is to be obeyed promptly. But there is another reason; listen well to it. There is a law against dueling. If someone is killed, arrests are made. Only a form perhaps, but arrests. And M. Boulanger is a prominent citizen of this place. It would raise a sufficient storm. Therefore, you must not return through the town. When you have landed with Reilly, the boat will return to the ship. When the prisoners are aboard, I will sail around to Case Navire, God willing, and the wind!" He wet his forefinger and held it up again.

"When the affair is settled, you will drive overland to Case Navire. It is a small fishing village, a little north of the harbor. I will await you there. When I see the carriage, I will send the boat in to bring you off. The English milord comes too."

"Suppose you do not arrive?" Tommy asked.

"Then you must wait until I do." He took Tommy's arm and guided him to the ship's side. "The boat is ready," he said and embraced him. Tommy felt the pressure of his cheek and the scrape of his dangling earring.

"Aim low," Gascoyne said, as a last word of parting. "For his belly. That way you can't miss the heart."

Tommy went down into the boat, his own heart thumping wildly. Above him he heard Angel call softly, "Go with God, señor."

Booby was in the boat with Reilly. The two pairs of oars, with their powerful stroking, pulled the boat clear of *Princess* in great leaps.

"Best take the tiller, sor," Reilly suggested.

Aroused from his brooding thoughts, Tommy shipped the tiller, and, for a time, his mind was occupied with steering the boat through the dark, crowded anchorage. But as they approached the landing, he strained his eyes through the darkness to see whether the carriage was on the quay. If it was not, if Lord Ravenscroft had not come . . . The reek of horse sweat and old harness coming off on the land breeze, the smell of musty cushions and axle grease, dispelled the hope.

"Well, youngster," Ravenscroft greeted him cheerily at the top of the landing stairs, "feeling fit?"

"A bit fluttery," Tommy confessed, "but it will pass—Gascoyne says so."

They got at once into the carriage, Lord Ravenscroft on the seat with Tommy, Reilly on the smaller seat opposite, his back to the coachman, who started off without questions or orders the moment they were in.

"Old hand at duels," Lord Ravenscroft explained. "Knows the ropes."

They skirted the town—still quiet except for barking dogs and a cock-crow—along the water road around to the mountain side.

"I'd better explain the plan," Lord Ravenscroft said. Tommy listened attentively.

"We'll mark two firing points, fifteen paces apart. You'll take your places, one at each, back to back. Then I shall ask, 'Are you ready, gentlemen?' And when you have both replied, I shall say, 'I am about to start counting. When I count "three," you will turn and fire.' Comprenez?"

Could anyone not understand? Tommy was shocked at the casual manner in which Gascoyne and Lord Ravenscroft were arranging for him to kill a man. But if that was the way . . .

"Clear enough," he replied, hoping that his voice would not betray his nervousness. "We'll have our backs toward each other at fifteen paces, you will start counting, and at 'three' we'll turn and fire."

"Aimin' low," Reilly added.

"Exactly," Lord Ravenscroft agreed. He seemed pleased about the whole thing, Tommy thought. "I'll count as steadily as possible," his lordship was saying, "keeping the interval the same so that there will be no advantage to either of you. But once I've said 'three,' turn and let him have it."

"But not so fast you miss," Reilly cautioned.

"Suppose we both miss?" Tommy asked.

"You'll go through it a second time," Lord Ravenscroft told him. "If you both miss then, you can consider honor satisfied. Provided you are both agreeable."

"I'll be agreeable," Tommy said.

"M. Boulanger is bringing his own doctor," Lord Ravenscroft finished. "He will care for either of you—or both."

" 'Tis an omen," Reilly observed.

"A good omen, Reilly?" Tommy queried.

"Not good for him at all," Reilly answered.

After that there seemed nothing to talk about. There was only the clop-clop of the horse's hoofs in the quiet morning air, the creak of axles, and an occasional "cluck-cluck" from the coachman. They passed a graveyard, turned, and drove into a park-like area of tall palms. Tommy wondered what kind of omen Reilly might find in that—a cemetery so convenient. He did not ask.

The coachman pulled to a stop and they all got down. They were the first arrivals, but in the direction whence they had come they heard the whinny of a horse, and soon another carriage appeared. It stopped at a discreet distance from them, and two men got down. One, M. Boulanger's second, carried an oblong case—the pistols. The other carried a small black bag. Tommy could imagine the probes and forceps it contained. M. Boulanger remained seated in the carriage. In the dawn, which had come as suddenly as the lighting of a lamp, he looked very old, his skin like yellow parchment.

Lord Ravenscroft went at once to join the other second, and after a rigidly courteous exchange of greetings, they went together into an open space among the palms and, having made a mark, stepped off fifteen paces. There they made another mark. And to be sure of accuracy, they stepped the distance off again in the reverse direction. Satisfied, M. Boulanger's second opened his case of pistols and, after they had loaded the pair with great attention, Lord Ravenscroft selected one and came toward Tommy.

During all this, the surgeon had maintained a detached manner, correctly neutral. Tommy had begun to feel detached himself; he watched as the other second gave M. Boulanger a steadying hand down from his carriage.

"Come along, youngster," Lord Ravenscroft called, and Reilly said, "The saints presarve ye, lad, an' kape yer hand steady whin ye aim."

Tommy handed him two letters. One, the letter to his father and mother; the other, to Annette. In it he asked her forgiveness for fighting the duel, despite his promise not to. If she could forgive him, he told her, he would never break his word to her again. He would be faithful so long as they both lived.

"You are to post these, Reilly," he ordered, "no matter what happens. No matter what anyone says."

"Aye, aye, sor."

"And, Reilly," he added, as Lord Ravenscroft impatiently touched his arm, "remember, you don't have to kneel to say a prayer."

"Me heart will be kneelin', lad, till it's over an' done."

Then he found himself walking toward a firing point with Lord Ravenscroft, as if walking in a dream. "There's no choice of positions," his lordship was saying. "Clever, the way they laid out this dueling ground. No morning sun in anyone's eyes."

He placed Tommy in position at the firing point, facing a solid wall of palms at the end of the clearing. Tommy wished that some of this formality could be omitted so that they could fire and get it over with.

Lord Ravenscroft talked on: "M. Boulanger is now at the other mark, back toward you. His second and I will be halfway between."

There was silence, and Tommy realized that Lord Ravenscroft had left him and that he was face to face with it, alone.

He waited. He could feel his heart thumping, but it was beating steadily. The fluttering in his stomach had gone.

Lord Ravenscroft was speaking: "Are you ready, gentlemen?"

Tommy checked the priming of his pistol before answering: "Ready." He heard M. Boulanger's reply, and, almost immediately, Lord Ravenscroft again: "I shall now start counting. When I say 'three,' turn and fire." He began to count.

"One."

Tommy glanced up through the palm fronds to the sky. It was a lovely blue.

"Two."

The cadence was unhurried, calm. Tommy took a deep breath.

"Three."

He turned, seeing the flash of M. Boulanger's pistol as his own piece fired, feeling dirt spatter against his legs as a ball richocheted from the ground close to his feet.

M. Boulanger clutched at his heart and fell, his pistol dropping to the ground. Behind him, in long zigzags, a palm frond drifted down.

M. Boulanger lay still, as his second and the surgeon hurried to his side. They turned him over gently, the surgeon, with quick fingers, tearing aside clothing to find the wound. Finally he looked up and said, "I find no bullet hole."

He placed his ear against M. Boulanger's breast, announcing, at last, "It is finished." He methodically closed the eyes staring upward at the blue. "M. Boulanger had not a strong heart," the surgeon said. "Before this, he has had seizures. I will certify to it."

The second urged, "Return to your ship, messieurs, without delay. In case there should be trouble."

"No," Tommy objected. "We will help."

With Reilly assisting, they carried the body to the carriage and arranged it on the seat and covered it with a light carriage robe. The surgeon and the second sat on the small seat opposite, their knees against M. Boulanger's body to keep it from rolling

off. They raised their hats. Adieu. The coachman clucked his
horse into a trot. Tommy thought he had never heard a more
depressing sound than the beat of the horse's hoofs and the
rumble of the carriage wheels as they drove away.

Lord Ravenscroft broke their silence. "Come along," he said.
"I'm on parole, you know. Can't chance getting into a scrape."

But there was still something to be done: the two letters must
be posted before they sailed. Having done that, the coachman
headed along the seaside road for Case Navire.

Long before they reached the fishing village, they saw *Princess*
standing on and off, and the tiny speck between her and the
shore would be the boat coming in to pick them up. A ship
had never looked so beautiful to Tommy; the land had never
seemed so evil.

When he climbed aboard, Gascoyne took him by the shoulders
and held him at arm's length, studying him. "So you killed him,
eh? And without a scratch on you. *Magnifique!*"

"I didn't kill him," Tommy said. "He died."

Gascoyne's jubilation changed: killing in battle, or in a duel,
was one thing; dying quite another. He crossed himself. "May he
rest well."

"It was his heart," Lord Ravenscroft explained. "Had a weakness there, surgeon told us."

"After the duel he told you?" Gascoyne inquired.

"After he was dead."

"*Bien.* Do not feel bad, then, *mon ami.* He was old. He had
lived his life." He embraced Tommy warmly. "How I am glad to
see you back!"

Tommy, still rankling from Gascoyne's cavalier treatment
earlier, said, "You didn't seem sorry to see me go."

"*Mon ami!* Then, for a sou, I would not have let you go."

"You didn't show it," Tommy said.

"Could I let you see that I was quaking and give my fear to
you? *Non!* But next time you will fight with swords. I do not
trust these pistols."

"No more duels for me," Tommy declared.

Gascoyne laughed, and suddenly all the strain of the morning was gone. At his order, the ship heeled to the rudder, and bare feet stamped the deck as topsails were run up and sheeted home. *Princess* lay down to it, heading out to sea, the blue water foaming alongside tipped with the gold of sunlight across Pelée.

"Now we go below and drink some wine to celebrate," Gascoyne said.

Passing through the cuddy, Lord Ravenscroft spoke confidentially into Tommy's ear. "Some day, Mr. Midshipman Potter, me lad, you must tell me how that palm frond got shot down."

MIDDLE PART

July–October, 1781.
Begins hot and humid—hurricane season.
Sailed Leeward Islands under sealed orders.

CHAPTER FIFTEEN

GASCOYNE, at the wheel, his black hair ruffling in the wind, suddenly broke into laughter.

"What is it?" Tommy inquired.

"If we should meet our old friend *Bulldog.*" He glanced upward to the flag of truce flying at the main truck. "How he would growl to see that! On that bone he would choke, *n'est-ce pas?*"

Princess was standing into English Harbor on the Caribbean coast of Antigua, only a few miles across the hills from the Atlantic where she had, in her sugar-running days, nearly been captured by the two English brigs, *Bulldog* and *Growler.* But now the royal ensign of France streamed from her peak, and there was no stealthy approach under cover of darkness. She came openly during daylight, wearing, besides the white flag at her main, a blue flag diagonally striped with yellow at her fore; a prearranged signal for a prisoner cartel.

Gascoyne kept all sail on her, booming through the spacious outer harbor, which served mostly as a hurricane anchorage for the fleet but was now bare of ships. He held on toward two spits of land extending out from either shore to narrow the passage between inner and outer harbors as the wasp-waist of an hourglass separates the two chambers.

"*Mon ami,*" Gascoyne said, as if to reassure Tommy, who was fidgeting from one foot to the other as the land drew closer, "we must show these English that Frenchmen also are good sailors." Only when *Princess* was in the narrow channel did he order, "Shorten sail."

Beyond the channel, where the bay widened again in a land-locked basin, a British ship of the line swung lazily at anchor. She repeated the blue and yellow flag at her fore, as *Princess* boomed through the entrance, shortening canvass as she came. The flag signaled understanding of the arrival's purpose and, at the same time, told the shore batteries in the hills north, east, and west that the stranger was on a friendly mission.

Crossing under the warship's stern, they read her name: *Vengeance.*

"A seventy-four," Tommy reported.

Gascoyne rounded up sharply when they had cleared. "Let go," he ordered and set a topsail backing to kill the headway. There was a splash forward and the cable smoked through the hawsepipe, running out ever faster as the plunging anchor sought bottom, which, in the clear water, seemed but a few fathoms down, but was many.

"Forty-five at the water's edge, sor," Reilly reported from his station on the forecastle.

"Well done, sir," Lord Ravenscroft told Gascoyne, with a seaman's admiration for smart seamanship.

Their arrival caused no visible excitement. Exchange of prisoners, particularly on foreign stations, was common practice. It saved the wasteful employment of fighting men as guards, and spared an unrewarded drain on provisions. Bread and flour were always in short supply. It also mitigated the inhumanity of war, particularly aboard ship where long confinement in damp foul holds made death, at times, seem preferable to the tortures of scurvy and other wasting diseases.

Within the deep bowl of hills where *Princess* lay anchored, scarcely a ripple stirred the smooth water; a mantle of tropic lethargy lay heavy across the naval station. Ashore, the slab roofs of the dockyard buildings, on a bare spit of land jutting into the bay, glared dazzlingly white in the blazing sun. Off the north wall, at the careening anchors, a frigate lay on her side, half of her bottom exposed. In the midday heat, no one was working. Life seemed to have been suspended. Beyond *Vengeance,* deep inside the bay, another ship lay so still at her anchor as to seem painted against the backdrop of hills.

Lord Ravenscroft, who had been observing the surroundings, took the long glass from his eye. "The transport anchored at the top of the bay, there," he told Tommy, handing him the glass, "has the look of your old friend *Vixen.*"

It took but a glance to convince Tommy. "There's no doubt of it," he agreed. The ship had been remasted and her canvas renewed, and the damage to her stern, where *Princess* had poured in a broadside months ago when they had captured *Vixen* in the English Channel, had been repaired and the scars healed by paint. But no amount of paint and trimming could disguise the ship in which he had learned so much, and suffered too.

"Just out from home, I should think," Lord Ravenscroft observed, "from the look of her."

Memories flooded Tommy with stabbing sharpness: his first command, so quickly lost; good moments and bad; victories and finally, defeat. But, sharper than all, the memory of Denise Milholme. After they had become friends, he had thought no other girl could ever interest him. Yet . . . He resolutely put her from his mind. There was little likelihood that she would be aboard after all these months. Besides, there was Annette.

Gascoyne's voice broke his reverie: "Muster all prisoners on deck." Cutters were pulling across from *Vengeance* to get them.

As the first boat drew alongside, a midshipman hailed in a mixture of English and bad French: "*Au bâtiment là! S'il vous plaît.*" He seemed to have run out of words. "I say, aboard there, *mon commandant.*" Some of his men laughed. He gave it up, jumped for the side cleats and scrambled aboard.

"*Bonjour,*" he said.

"Good day," said Tommy.

"You mean to say you're not French?" the midshipman demanded, getting very red.

"Some of us are," Tommy told him, and Gascoyne stepped up and said graciously, "At your service, monsieur."

"I'll thank you to put all our people and their gear into these two cutters," the midshipman told him. "And if you are captain, be pleased to come along as well. Lieutenant Gaither—he's our first, but he's acting captain just now—wishes to have a talk with you."

"With pleasure, monsieur," Gascoyne replied. "But first let me get properly dressed." He indicated his bare feet and pantaloons.

While Gascoyne was below, changing, the prisoners and their possessions were loaded into the cutters. The time had come to bid Lord Ravenscroft good-by.

"Well, pirate," the English captain remarked banteringly, "we've been shipmates how many times?"

"Three," Tommy answered, "if you count *L'Afrique*." It was aboard her that Lord Ravenscroft had sat in trial on him for piracy; had befriended him and, by subtle questioning, had brought out facts resulting in acquittal.

"By all means count *L'Afrique*," Ravenscroft told him. "It began our friendship."

Though enemies, they were friends, of the same race and breed. One, in the eyes of the other, was a rebel against their common sovereign, yet they had fought gallantly as foes and, to their breed, that was enough.

"If you are ever going to tell me about that palm frond . . ." Lord Ravenscroft suggested.

"Nothing to tell," Tommy replied. "I missed, that's all."

"Then you're an amazing bad shot."

"I must have closed my eyes," Tommy offered in explanation.

"I happened to be watching," Lord Ravenscroft said. "Your eyes were open, your aim was high. Fate didn't let you save old Boulanger, but it was a grand try." He wrung Tommy's hand and dropped nimbly down into the cutter. A moment later Gascoyne followed. The midshipman shouted a command, the loaded cutters cast off, the crews got out oars.

With the prisoners out of the ship, all hands turned to scrub-
bing down. They cleansed holds and compartments, opened
wide all scuttles, rigged windsails to fetch in more fresh air.
By the time Gascoyne returned, all was in order, clean and
shipshape.

"It goes well," Gascoyne told them. "As soon as we have our
French prisoners aboard, we sail."

On the quay of the dockyard, they could see a detachment
of prisoners being mustered to be sent aboard in exchange.
But it was not that activity which held the attention of the
crew. They were watching the sails of a brig in the outer harbor,
still hull down across the spit. When she came into full view
in mid-channel, a murmur of alarm arose. The men had not
forgotten H.M.S. *Bulldog*, their old antagonist.

Gascoyne laughed. "We must salute politely as we pass, sailing out."

Pierre Lebecque spoke: "*Mon capitaine*, he does not will that
we sail out."

Bulldog had let go two anchors to hold her across the narrowest part of the channel. She was short and broad of beam;
ugly compared to the sleek *Princess*. He guns were ugly too,
their snouts sticking out from the gunports as if sniffing for a
victim. One broadside from them could reduce the beauty of
Princess to a shambles, and the gun crews were standing ready,
waiting for the order. Alongside, two cutters were being loaded
with armed marines.

"They won't ignore a flag of truce," Tommy remarked, to reassure himself as much as anything.

Gascoyne said, "We did not wear French colors that day
we fought in Parham Bay."

"I don't see what difference that makes," Tommy argued.

"*Mon ami*," Gascoyne replied, "if you had been mauled as
badly as we mauled him, would a change of flags cool your
temper? *Jamais!* But we must be polite and cool his temper for
him."

Then the British boats came alongside.

A commander, followed by a lieutenant, climbed aboard, and after them, marines. Their pipe-clayed crossbelts and polished buckles glinting in the sun, they moved rapidly, as if on drill, dispersing to every salient point: masts, capstan, wheel.

The commander was a short stocky man, oldish for his rank, and there was the lurch of long service in small ships in his bandy-legged stride. He had a round meaty face with heavy jowls, and his eyes were deeply set in fleshy pads, watery in the bright sunlight, the whites bloodshot.

"I command His Majesty's brig *Bulldog*," he announced. "This vessel is now in my hands." It was evident; armed marines stood everywhere.

"You are captain?" the British officer asked Gascoyne.

"*Oui, monsieur.*"

"Captain? So ignorant you do not speak the King's English?"

"I speak English, monsieur," Gascoyne answered calmly, "and it is better so. You must understand clearly what I say. I protest your boarding a ship belonging to His Majesty Louis VI of France, sailing under a flag of true given by your own Admiral Rodney."

"Don't come Admiral Rodney on me," the commander said. "Just let me see your French commission—if you have one."

"But of course, monsieur," Gascoyne answered politely and sent Angel below to fetch it.

"I'll thank you for your name," the commander said while waiting.

"Gascoyne."

"Gascoyne. Nothing more?"

"Only Gascoyne."

"Well, Mr. Gascoyne, my name is Ransom—Master and Commander James Ransom, Royal Navy. I think you will not soon forget my name and rank."

Then Angel came with the commission. He started to hand it to Gascoyne, but Commander Ransom snatched it from his hand. After a quick glance, he said, "Just as I thought. This commission is not a month old. It will not protect you or your vessels for acts prior to that date." He threw the parchment down disdainfully on the deckhouse roof.

Gascoyne picked it up. "What acts, monsieur?" he inquired.

Ransom pointed to his ship. "Do you not recall that brig?"

Gascoyne observed her carefully. "It is possible," he said. "She had only one mast standing when I saw her last—but of course you could put a new one up.

"By God!" Ransom choked. "And from a Frenchman, too! But you will pay for it, mark me! For that and other acts of piracy under the American flag; destroying commerce; smuggling." He paused to get his breath. There was froth in the corners of his mouth.

"Monsieur fatigues himself," Gascoyne said.

Commander Ransom turned and barked an order to his lieutenant: "Rouse up all hands. Search them; search the ship. Seize all weapons—knives, everything."

Gascoyne spoke sharply, as the officer acknowledged the order and was about to move away. "One moment, lieutenant."

"You dare—" Commander Ransom began.

"I warn you not to violate this flag of truce we fly."

Ransom strode to the signal halliards on the main, freed the line from the cleat, and with a vicious jerk started the flag downward on the run.

Lord Ravenscroft had been watching from the quarterdeck of *Vengeance*. "What d'ye suppose is going on over there?" he remarked to Lieutenant Gaither.

"Poor old Ransom, I expect, sir," Lieutenant Gaither replied.

"Parading his seniority?" Ravenscroft asked.

"I'm afraid it's more than that, sir," Gaither told him. "You've heard about his go with an American privateer, I expect."

"Hasn't everyone? I'm surprised he hasn't been laughed off the station for it."

"He has, just about," Gaither said. "I take it he's recognized our visitor as the same ship. And now he'll have his laugh."

"But he can't take a ship that flies a flag of truce," Lord Ravenscroft objected.

"It seems he has, sir," Gaither observed, as the white flag came down.

"And you are not going to stop him?" It was a blunt question; it brought a blunt answer.

"I'll defer to you on that, sir, since you are a post captain. I only look after routine matters while the commodore is away. It puts me under no obligation to combat my seniors."

"If the man's as mad as all that," Ravenscroft mused, "he's not likely to take orders from me—an exchanged prisoner, homeward bound, not in duty status."

"I do think he's gone a bit daft, sir," Gaither reflected. "After all . . ."

The victory of a single American privateer over two of His Majesty's brigs—for her escape could be considered no less than victory—had been difficult to explain. The captains of *Bulldog* and *Growler* had not, in fact, been able to explain it. And although their commodore had not preferred charges against them, wishing, it could be assumed, to keep so glaring a failure on his station quiet, the disgrace still hung, like a black cloud, above their heads. A cloud that only the capture or destruction of the privateer could blow away. And now that she had been caught, no change of nationality, no French commission, no flag of truce was likely to deter Commander Ransom of H.M.S. *Bulldog*.

Lord Ravenscroft glanced in the direction of the tranport anchored deep in the bay. "Who is over there?" he asked.

"She's a letter of marque, sir," Gaither told him. "Merchant captain. But there's a navy captain in passage aboard."

"Does he belong to this station?"

"I suppose you might say so. He's on his way to become naval officer in charge at St. Kitts. They're getting ready to repel boarders over there. Expect old de Grasse to be along any time."

"Hmm," was Lord Ravenscroft's comment as he rubbed his chin thoughtfully. "You didn't mention the captain's name."

"Captain Lord Milholme, sir."

Ravenscroft brightened. "He's not the man to sit quietly by while this sort of thing goes on, if I know Denis. If you'll let me have a boat, I'll just go across and tell him about it. One doesn't violate a flag of truce, you know, regardless of personal scores to pay."

Which was exactly what Lord Milholme told Commander Ransom when, a short time later, he boarded *Princess*.

"What's become of it?" he demanded, glancing aloft.

"I hauled it down, my lord," Ransom explained, "since this pirate was using it to hide his real character."

"Be good enough," Lord Milholme said, "to hoist it up again."

Commander Ransom did not move, nor his lieutenant, nor any of his men. But Tommy, who, with Gascoyne, was standing a little apart from the men belonging to *Princess*, surrounded by armed marines, moved toward the halliards on which the flag of truce was still bent, the flag itself lying on the deck.

"No!" Lord Milholme exclaimed sharply. "I addressed no order in your direction." If he had recognized Tommy, he gave no indication of it. "My order was to Captain Ransom."

The bandy-legged bulldog faced the peer defiantly. But Lord Milhome was such a figure of authority, one tunic sleeve folded back and fastened to hang below the shoulder, a testimony of his own sacrifice for King and country, that only a reckless junior indeed, no matter how much justice he might think lay on his side, would dare disobey.

"Aye, aye, my lord," Ransom answered, and, at a nod, his lieutenant ran the white flag up again.

"Now that we have re-established the *status quo ante*," Lord Milholme said, "let us find some privacy and thresh this thing out."

But though the cabin gave them privacy, through the open skylight a great deal of what went on could be heard on deck.

When the English officers had seated themselves at the cabin table, Lord Milholme stated his position: a flag of truce entering a British harbor must, in honor, be respected. Unless, he added, there were good reasons to suspect trickery. But since *Princess* had brought English prisoners from the French fleet, and lay under the guns of a seventy-four—to say nothing of the shore batteries protecting the harbor—it would take a long stretch of anyone's imagination to suspect trickery. Then he sat back to hear Commander Ransom's explanation.

Ransom told of having, some months before, caught *Princess* smuggling sugar, and of her action when he had tried to apprehend her. Action, he insisted, that clearly put her outside the law, a rebel against the King, a pirate responsible for damage to His Majesty's vessels and for the death of several of His Majesty's loyal defenders. Deaths which, under the circumstances, could only be considered as murder. It was therefore the duty of His Majesty's officers, Ransom argued, to free Caribbean waters of this scourage, no matter where or how.

But Lord Milholme remained unshaken in his position: *Princess* was now under the French flag, her captain held a French commission, she had been permitted to enter English Harbor to deliver prisoners from the Count de Grasse. She must be permitted freely to sail again with French prisoners in exchange. Anything else would be a breach of faith.

In desperation, Ransom questioned Lord Milholme's right to intrude on the actions of the captain of a commissioned man-of-war; an argument that, also, left Lord Milholme unmoved. He was reporting for duty on the Leeward Island Station; whether afloat or ashore was of no consequence. He would assume full responsibility for his acts to Admiral Rodney.

Nothing remained now for Commander Ransom but personal pleading. He became almost hysterical in his frustration, his pleas almost incoherent. "For God's sake, my lord," he begged, "permit me this chance to clean the slate. Let me clear my record."

"You would only foul it more," Lord Milholme told him.

After that, they came on deck quickly, glad to be out of that small hot cabin.

"Captain," Lord Milholme addressed Gascoyne, "there has been a mistake. The ships is yours, but before we clear off, I'd like to speak to your people."

At a order from Commander Ransom, whose earlier arrogrance had given place to hangdog sullenness, marines marshaled the ship's company aft. Lord Milholme addressed them:

"Because Commander Ransom has decided to release your ship, it does not follow that he—or I—approve of your activities. We release you only because the honor of the Royal Navy is more important to us than retribution. You will be permitted to sail, but when you are on the high seas again, clear of His Majesty's island waters, retribution for past misdeeds may overtake you. This is your fair warning."

He waited while Pierre Lebecque translated for those who spoke only French. Then he nodded curtly to Ransom. "Shall we clear off?"

"Sir," Tommy said, while *Bulldog*'s boarding party re-embarked in the boats. "Sir—"

Lord Milholme greeted him amiably. "So our tracks cross again," he said. "Lord Ravenscroft told me you were aboard."

"I hope you are well, sir," Tommy said.

"Splendid." But Tommy wished he had not asked it: he was dreadfully conscious of that empty sleeve.

"And you? I see you still follow your misguided ways."

"Yes, sir." There was no good arguing that one. "Is Lady Milholme well."

"Quite, thanks. She and Denise are spending the afternoon in the dockyard park to escape the heat and stink of shipboard."

"*Mon ami,*" Gascoyne intruded. "Why do you not go ashore and greet them?"

"Splendid idea," his lordship agreed. "Lady Milholme would enjoy an account of your adventures since we saw you in Portsmouth."

They would have much to talk about. What Denise had been

doing in those months. And "Debby," her brother, who was following his father's calling at sea as a midshipman. Denise? So much had happened since Portsmouth . . . "I'm afraid I can't sir," he replied. "We'll be sailing soon."

"Not before dark," Gascoyne said, glancing toward the brig. "The *Bulldog's* mate will be waiting outside. We shall need the cover of darkness to elude that pair."

"I shouldn't wonder," Lord Milholme agreed. "You'll come then, me lad?"

"Thank you, sir," Tommy replied. He did want to see Denise again, beyond anything else.

Commander Ransom had his men in the boats and was ready to leave. Gascoyne tended him to the side. "Forgive me, monsieur le Capitaine Bulldog," Gascoyne said, "that we do not give side honors. We have not yet learned man-of-war style."

"Side honors from a pirate would be an insult," Commander Ransom replied. "As to forgiveness—I will never forgive myself until you swing from a yardarm."

He went heavily down the side into his boat, but, standing on the gunnel, he looked up and shook his fist. "You may get away clear this time," he called up, "but don't ever come into these waters again. If you do, as sure as we have hurricanes in summer, I'll finish you."

He gave an order to his coxswain. The boat shoved off.

CHAPTER SIXTEEN

THE PARK was hardly more than a cluster of dwarf palms and tree ferns around the catchment basin that, along with cisterns which caught the rain from slab roofs, supplied the naval station with fresh water. The volcanic lava foundation of the island provided no wells, nor were there any rivers.

It was cool in the shade of the little park, where a cross

wind blew from the sea; and the two ladies, in soft white dresses, added charm to the scene.

Tommy hoped that it was Lady Milholme's surprise at seeing him, but certainly there was a change in her manner. When they had said good-by at Portsmouth half a year ago, she had kissed him warmly, almost as if he were her son. Now she only gave him her hand. Perhaps it was because he still came as an enemy— or that dreadful empty sleeve.

But Denise seemed ready to take up where they had left off. "Hello, Tommy!" she greeted him gaily. "Did you think I would never get here?" How was he going to tell her that she had come too late?

She was even more beautiful than the memory he had been cherishing. Her red-gold hair no longer hung loosely on her shoulders, as it had the first time he had seen her aboard *Vixen*, but it was dressed in a lovely, grown-young-lady coif. Her eyes had been the green of a stormy sea, that first meeting, and her small breasts had heaved with anger at her being made a prisoner; but there was no storm in the eyes now searching his, and her breasts, molded by the softness of her dress, were a woman's.

"After I heard about your father's arm—" Tommy began but halted abruptly, shocked at his own gaucherie.

"It did nearly beach me," Lord Milholme said, glancing at his empty sleeve. "But I managed to get an appointment."

"It's a shore appointment," Lady Milholme explained.

"I'll have a ship again one day, never fear," her husband said.

"Of course you will, dear," she agreed. "But you may see action enough where we're going."

"Mayn't we all!" Denise exclaimed happily.

"We'll be on St. Kitts," her mother explained to Tommy.

"Old de Grasse may turn up, you know," Denise went on. "And won't that be jolly! I'd love to have a go at those Frenchies!"

"Denise!" her mother cautioned.

"Have a care, me gel," her father added. "This lad's not one of ours, y'know. He's with the Frenchies."

Lady Milholme gracefully turned the conversation into other channels. "Is that splendid fellow still with you, Tommy?"

"Reilly? Yes, ma'am," Tommy answered.

"We owe a great deal to Reilly," Lady Milholme said. "Do give him our best wishes."

Tommy was glad that she remembered. When storm had been driving *Vixen* onto Penmarque Rocks, in the Bay of Biscay, it had been Reilly more than anyone who had saved them from disaster.

"A good breed of men come out of Galway," Lord Milholme said.

"Denis!" Lady Milholme childed with a smile. "That doesn't sound very modest."

"Not me, my dear. We. I was thinking of Debby."

"Is your son getting on well?" Tommy inquired.

"He's still with Captain Jervis in *Foudroyant,* so far as we know," Lord Milholme answered. "Got his baptism of fire in Keppel's fleet when the Admiral turned a trick on D'Orvillers off Ushant. The lad came through without a scratch, we heard eventually."

"But not for a long time," Lady Milholme sighed. "These terrible wars! I might as well not have a son."

Denise said, changing the subject, "Were you really serious when you said we'd meet out here, Tommy? I mean, did you really expect that we would?"

"Sailors can turn up anywhere," he answered.

"This proves it," she said.

"You'll do well to keep your young mind off sailors," her father told her. "Unreliable lot altogether!"

"Not my sailor," Lady Milholme said fondly.

"Take this young chap," Lord Milholme said, half humorously, yet seriously too. "He's joined the French Navy; sailing under the French flag. If he's so tired of America already, you might think he'd come back to us."

Tommy liked these wonderful people so much that he hated to think he would not be coming back to them.

"How did it all happen?" Lady Milholme asked him.

So he told them of his becoming part owner of *Princess*, and how they sailed from Brest without clearance, chased by two warships, and of filling their crew from a Breton fishing fleet; about Pierre Lebecque and the Holy Virgin, and the Laws of Oléron, and how Muldin had been marooned.

"Not so far-fetched, that!" Lord Milholme interrupted. "Those Judgments of Oléron. Not so long ago in our own fleet—in the days of good Queen Bess—our people tied a murderer to his victim and threw both living and dead into the sea; and cut off a man's hand if he raised it against his captain; and, for some offenses, ducked men beneath the keel, or hauled them ashore astern of a boat, and landed them with a loaf and a jug of beer. And a man who habitually slept on watch was lashed on the bowsprit with a knife, which he could use to cut himself loose and fall into the sea, or stay on the bowsprit and starve while tortured by thirst."

Lady Milholme shuddered. "Denis! How horrible!"

"True, just the same, my dear. And we still flog men until, sometimes, they die. And we summarily hang deserters to a yardarm."

Tommy told them of the battle with the two English brigs, and how old Gran'père was caught and crushed by a sugar hogshead; and of how they captured *L'Afrique*, after saving her from the rocks; and, without a legal captain upon returning to Martinique, how the Count de Grasse had taken *Princess* over and given Gascoyne and himself commissions.

"Great God!" was all Lord Milholme found to say when Tommy had finished.

Denise, who had not taken her eyes from Tommy during the story, said, "It's terribly fascinating."

"It's terrible!" Ladly Milholme said. "Why must we always be at war? Killing! Destroying!"

Her question brought no answer; but the sound of a bosun's

call echoing across the basin, and the stamp of feet round a capstan keeping time to chanting voices, reminded them that war still went on.

Lord Milholme said, "*Bulldog*'s getting under way."

They watched her turn in the basin, her fore-topsail backing against the drive of the spanker to twist her round. Her guns were still run out.

"She'll be more than a match for you," Lord Milholme remarked. "And there's likely to be her mate outside."

"Oh, Tommy!" Denise exclaimed.

"They'll not catch us," Tommy said confidently. "You don't know *Princess*—or Gascoyne. No one can outsail them."

They watched silently as sail after sail bloomed and began drawing full; watched until she was hull down across the spit of land. Then Lord Milholme said, "I think I'll walk along and have a chat with the officer in charge of the dockyard."

"Do," Lady Milholme acquiesced, and when he had gone she turned her attention to a book. "I'm reading the letters of Mme. de Sévigné," she told them. "The marquise and your Gascoyne would have known each other had they lived in the same century —she also came from Bretagne."

"Gascoyne sounds simply fascinating," Denise remarked.

"So does Mme. de Sévigné," her mother said, adding, "You two can go walking if you like."

She called after them, "Not too far, dear."

"She's very thoughtful," Denise remarked. "She knows we have lots of things to talk about."

"Yes," Tommy agreed, but he was uncomfortable. Did he call this being faithful to Annette?

They walked toward the sound of caulking hammers until they came in sight of the hove-down frigate. Shipwrights were driving oakum between the strakes of hull planking, while a man with a steaming pot, and another with a long-handled brush, payed the seams with pitch.

"They're behind the times," Tommy observed. "Should be

sheathing her with copper—gives a ship two or three knots more speed."

"How?"

"Barnacles won't cling—or sea grass. Gets rid of all the fouling."

"Don't you ever think of anything besides ships?" Denise asked.

"Well—yes, of course. But ships are interesting."

"You're more interesting to me," she said. "You've changed, Tommy. Changed a lot."

"How?"

"You seem older—a man. That's it, I expect. You're not a boy any longer. It's very becoming. You're really quite handsome, you know, Tommy."

He wanted to tell her how beautiful she was. But in ships lay greater safety. "Don't you want to hear about this new system of coppering? The French are sheathing all of theirs."

"You mean, don't I want to be a spy? Get information from you and pass it on to my father."

"Don't be silly," he said. It seemed quite like old times.

"Was that story you told all true?" Denise asked. "About Gascoyne and Muldin and old Gran'père?"

"Every word."

"You mean you haven't met any girls? Honestly."

"Who said anything about girls?" he demanded.

"That's just it—you didn't. You don't expect me to believe that, do you?"

"I've met Gascoyne's cousins, of course." He was feeling uncomfortable again.

"Are they pretty?" Denise asked.

"Not particularly. Average."

"Why are you getting so red?" Denise asked.

"You haven't changed," he answered hotly. "Nothing but questions! Always questions!"

"Let's go back," she said.

Lord Milholme had returned before them. "It's getting on,"

he announced. "The officer in charge will send us off to our ship any time we are ready. Perhaps we can drop you on the way," he said to Tommy.

"I won't need to trouble you, sir," Tommy told him. "Gascoyne will send the jolly-boat as soon as it gets dark."

While he was speaking, darkness, with tropic suddenness, filled the bowl of hills, mounting upward from land and water, fading the blue of the sky to gray. And then, suddenly, the stars shone down; great sparkling orbs of silver.

Tommy bent over Lady Milholme's hand and kissed it, and she, amused, said, "You really have become French, haven't you?"

Denise put her hands behind her. "No thanks," she said.

Lord Milholme laughed and gave Tommy a hearty clap across the shoulders. "Take care now," he cautioned. "Your Gascoyne looks devil-may-care enough to chance fighting *Bulldog*—both of them, if *Growler's* out there. Don't let him."

"No, sir," Tommy said.

"Shall we walk along to the quay?" Lady Milholme suggested.

"Lead on, Denise, me gel," his lordship said.

In the darkness, Tommy felt her hand seeking his. He took it gingerly. "You really have changed," Denise said. "Is it the war?"

"War isn't any picnic," Tommy replied. "Mutinies and killings and all that."

"I meant because we are enemies," she said.

"Of course not."

"It doesn't make any difference, truly, does it?" she persisted. "I mean, it can't change the way we feel about each other?"

He could answer that truthfully; it wasn't the war that had changed things. But how could he tell her about Annette?

When he did not answer, Denise took her hand away.

Tommy knew he was not being honest, he hated not being truthful; but he searched for her hand and got it back.

She sighed. "At least we're both in the West Indies," she said. "It was terrible, me in England and you, heaven only knew where. But I suppose if you love a sailor, thats what you must expect."

Somehow he must stop her before it went any further. "I don't think we'll be coming back here very soon," he said. "I expect there's a price on our heads by this time—Gascoyne and all of us."

"The war won't last forever," she replied confidently.

They saw the riding lanthorns of *Vengeance,* reflected by the mirror surface of the basin into floating pools of light. Beyond was a dim light that would be *Princess.* They heard the soft splash of oars and saw the phosphorescent blobs as the blades lifted from the water and dipped again.

A boat scraped alongside the masonry landing stairs. "Mist' Tommy?" The jolly-boat had come for him.

"Half a second, Booby," Tommy answered.

"Mind that bottom step," Booby cautioned. "It's all mossy like."

Denise said, "Well . . . Aren't you going to kiss me?"

He wanted to, God knew. Still . . .

"Oh, Tommy!" Denise flared. "How can you be so maddening?"

He kissed her, but she turned her head so that his lips only found her cheek. "That isn't the way we kissed at Portsmouth," he reproached her.

"It was different at Portsmouth, Tommy—we were only children. We've both grown up since then."

In the thick darkness, he felt her presence rather than saw her, and her closeness sent strange thrills through him. He was conscious only of her faint, alluring fragrance, and the wild beating of his heart. He crushed her in his arms and kissed her, and knew that what she had said was true—they had both grown up.

It was but a momentary satisfaction of their hunger; two shadowy figures were emerging from the darkness of the path.

"Denise!" Lady Milholme called. "Are you there?"

"Good-by," Tommy whispered.

"No! Not good-by," Denise answered. "Until we meet. I'll be waiting, darling. If it's forever."

"Denise!" Lady Milholme called again.

He kissed her once more, a farewell touch of lips on lips, passion gone for the moment in the sadness of parting. Then he released her and ran down the stairs to the waiting boat. His heart was singing.

CHAPTER SEVENTEEN

GASCOYNE, enjoying his *petite déjeuner* of white wine, studied the morning position which Tommy, breakfasting more heartily on hot cocoa and ship's biscuit, had worked up by dead reckoning and a quadrant observation of Polaris taken during morning twilight.

Gascoyne said, "Since we are here, and the fleet is not, we must see what new rendezvous we have."

The sealed orders which Gascoyne had opened on the day following departure from English Harbor, had set a rendezvous north of Porto Rico. If there they failed to find the Count de Grasse, they were to open a second envelope.

Gascoyne broke the seal. "Cap Français," he said.

Tommy was glad they were not returning to Martinique. Recent events were all too fresh—the duel . . . Annette. And now Denise back in his life again.

The delay in arriving at the first rendezvous had not been caused by *Bulldog* and *Growler*. Once *Princess* had cleared the outer bay at English Harbor, Gascoyne had swung northward along the coast toward St. Johns, Antigua's largest city, the course he would be least expected to follow. He had kept close inshore, where the mountains cast a band of shadow across the moon's silvery path. They had not even seen the brigs.

But on the following morning they had run afoul of a British frigate; and knowing that the French fleet was at sea, spread

over many miles of ocean, Gascoyne had decided to lead the
enemy northward, away from the fleet's approach, lest the
Britisher make a sighting and scurry off to give the news to
Admiral Rodney.

Managing to keep far enough ahead to escape damage from
the frigate's guns, yet hanging close enough to bait her on with
hope, Gascoyne played the fascinating game through that day
and the next. Then, certain that he had led the frigate far
enough in the wrong direction, during darkness he had reversed
course and headed for the rendezvous. Now, arrived at the area
as the rising sun showed the horizon clear of ships, friend or
foe, they had no choice but to sail on to French Cape.

"The Cape," as sailors called it, was not a cape at all, but a
city of low, tile-roofed houses baking in an oven of high encircling mountains; a harbor, landlocked and well guarded by
forts, sheltered from Atlantic storms by a bulge in the northern
coastline of Sainte-Domingue.

The anchorage was reached through a narrow winding channel which could be navigated with safety only at certain stages
of the tide, and then only if the wind blew fair, for there was
no room for tacking. When *Princess* stood in, it was crowded
with ships.

Waiting for Gascoyne to return from the *Ville de Paris,* where
he had gone at once, upon anchoring, to report arrival, Tommy
counted nearly two hundred merchant vessels, besides the flagship and all her fighting brood. Tired of counting, and of waiting, he gave up and went below, convinced that he had seen
the largest fleet of ships ever assembled.

Meanwhile, Gascoyne had been kept waiting in the passage-
way outside the flagship's great cabin, cooling his heels while
many officers of rank passed in and out from conferences with
the commander-in-chief.

"I have reported your excursions to His Excellency," the *major
d'escadre* informed him. "He found it so interesting he desires
to see you. You must be patient; His Excellency has many difficult decisions to make."

It was an understatement. The Count de Grasse was facing decisions that would have crushed most fleet commanders. Decisions that might bring the American war to a victorious close, or abandon it to a wasting end.

His was the responsibility of getting the "trade" convoy safely home to France. If he were to sail it without adequate man-of-war escort—and "adequate," with a British fleet about, meant a great part of his force—he would risk its being captured or destroyed. If he held the convoy in safety at Sainte-Domingue, while he took his fleet to the American coast, disappointed merchants would complain bitterly. Their friends at court would demand his head. And although the Count understood the urgency of bringing support to Washington and Rochambeau, he was too competent a strategist to divide his fleet: he must arrive on the American coast in sufficient strength to outnumber a combined British force, or he had better not go at all.

Not go? And lose the war!

The urgency was impressed upon him by communications brought from Boston by the frigate *Concorde*, awaiting him at The Cape when he arrived. The most urgent came from the Count de Rochambeau, commanding the French armies in America. If the French fleet did not soon arrive to establish control of coastal sea lanes, Rochambeau had written, the war must, before long, come to an inglorious end. It was essential, first, that British troops be denied reinforcement from England, as well as arms and munitions and all manner of supplies; and that concentrations of force at one strategic point or another by water transport be prevented. Second, His Excellency, the Count de Grasse, must not only bring his fleet, he must also bring troops from the West Indies. Four or five thousand at the very least.

Troops from the West Indies? He had no troops under his command!

There was also an urgent plea from the quartermaster general of the French armies in America, to bring him funds. It had become impossible, the quartermaster general wrote, to convert French bills of exchange into cash without paying an intolerable premium—their war chest would shrink as much as 30 per cent. And even if they could accept so great a loss, ruinous to even think of, there were not sufficient funds available in the American Colonies, at whatever rate of exchange, to supply French needs. His Excellency, the Count de Grasse, must therefore bring with him, at the very least, 1,200,000 livres.

A million and a quarter livres! Mon dieu! Where was such a sum to be found in Sainte-Domingue?

In addition to these requests, so urgently expressed as to be in the nature of demands, he was given instructions about his plan of operations. The French minister to the Colonies, the Chevalier de la Luzerne, wrote that General Washington urged the Count de Grasse to bring his fleet to the American coast immediately, and that he appear off New York, there to destroy the British blockading squadron while, on land, the allied armies attacked General Clinton's positions.

General Washington had been thoughtful enough, the Chevalier wrote, to recruit a number of pilots familiar with the approaches to Sandy Hook and the bar across the entrance to New York Harbor, and had sent them forward aboard *Concorde*. Thus, it was to be trusted, the Count de Grasse would be relieved of any hesitancy he might feel about attacking in unfamiliar waters.

This plan, monsieur le ministre, I do not intend to follow.

The Count could answer in this cavalier fashion, knowing that he had full authority to decide when he would come, where he would strike, or even whether he would come to America at all, depending upon the situation in the West Indies and Admiral Rodney's fleet. He had been furnished with a copy of a letter written by the Marquis de Castries, French minister of marine, to Rochambeau.

"M. de Grasse," the letter said in part, "who commands in America, will advise you of the time he will visit your waters. He commands twenty vessels; he will gather another ten in the West Indies; you will have eight, commanded by M. de Barras, to give him. Then, master of his movements to unite or separate his forces, I hope that in due time he will be master of the coast of America, and join with you if you wish to form any plan in the north."

Clearly the responsibility was his alone.

Washington and Rochambeau must have assistance quickly.

"Show M. de Kerguenac in," he told his orderly.

The Count gave his visitor the courtesy of rising, and Gascoyne saw how he had aged in but a few months. The rugged old sailor's great frame seemed to sag beneath the weight of his responsibilities. He remained standing: a man to whom minutes were precious.

"I have your report on the British frigate, monsieur," he began at once, "and how you led her astray. I wished to thank you in person, and to make sure that you saw no other enemy ships."

"We saw no others, Your Excellency," Gascoyne replied.

"Nevertheless," the Count argued, "if Admiral Rodney is scouting Anegada Passage, he will also be watching Mona and the Windward Passage as well. I fear he has spread a net to catch any convoy homeward bound."

"Without doubt, monsieur," Gascoyne agreed.

"Without doubt," the old seaman mused. "But he will catch none, monsieur, for I intend to keep the convoy safe here at The Cape until I can give it proper escort. Let the merchants have my head if they can get it."

"I have no fear for you, monsieur," Gascoyne said.

The Count stood thoughtfully for a minute. Then he said, "I like well the way you serve me, monsieur. When you have transferred the exchanged prisoners, according to M. de Vaugirauld's instructions, prepare your ship for sea. You will undertake another mission."

Only then, when Gascoyne was departing, did the Count show the warmth of his great heart.

"Your uncle was well, when I last saw him at Fort Royal—his charming daughters too." The Count looked grave. "But there is much yellow fever now."

"They have had much experience with it," Gascoyne said. "They understand the care to take."

"And your American midshipman?" the Count inquired. "He carries himself well."

"Without him my ship would seem empty," Gascoyne replied.

"*Au 'voir*, then," the Count said in dismissal. "May God sail with you."

Princess rode the Gulf Stream northward. Her men, driven up from below decks, cursed the soggy heat. But Gascoyne thanked *le bon Dieu* for the current's strength. Even without canvas set, even if there had been no wind, *Princess* would still be making good three knots over the ground in the general direction of their landfall. Speed and ever more speed he strove for; great events might hang on their arrival. His thanks went up not only for the current, but also for the fresh wind from east-northeast.

But the men, seeing nothing but the deep indigo of the stream and the hot vapors rising from it, and drifting islands of seaweed, cursed the folly that had ever set their feet upon a ship's sweltering decks.

They had been worn to shadows, on short rations as they were, hauling on sheets and halyards, and trimming yards, while the great fleet of M. de Grasse turned and twisted in the baffling winds of the old Bahama Channel, drifting sometimes in calms, anchoring more than once to avoid stranding on coral reefs. Finally the armada had spewed out into the Strait of Florida, and *Princess* had parted company to scud ahead on duty assigned. Three days had passed since they had last seen their fleet—twenty-eight sail of the line plus frigates and auxiliaries—tacking northward in cruising formation of three columns.

Now *Princess* shared the wide expanse of ocean with only one other: a fat merchantman down to the gunnels with cargo, slow, promising easy capture. When she had been clearly made out, the boarders—the riffraff of the Western Isles, and the Mediterranean corsairs—got out their cutlasses and began sharpening their knives. Some got slush from the galley copper to grease their naked bodies.

"Bueno!" they said. *"À la bonne chance!* Tonight we eat well and drink wine again!"

But when Gascoyne gave no sign of changing course, their jubilation turned to grumbling. They glanced aft frequently, listening for Gascoyne's order. And when no order came, no shifting of the helm, the fiercest of them set up a shout:

"À la bordage, mon capitaine!" "Will you not take this prize?" "See how her belly is fat; this fine goose will feed us well!"

Yet Gascoyne, knowing how poor their rations were, how bad the water, and no wine, held his course. At last, however, when the grumbling had turned to bitter jibes and muttered threats, he called, "Pierre Lebecque! Lay aft all hands!" And when the men had gathered in the gangways, with Tommy and Reilly and Pierre Lebecque beside him on the raised afterdeck, Gascoyne spoke, as a father disappointed in his children:

"Mes enfants," he began, "we are sent by our commander-in-chief to see and not be seen, to run, not fight. We are sent to be his eyes, his ears. Why? Because His Excellency knows well how our *Princess* is fast, how her men are brave. You have shown it already many times. Yet now you would fail him by delay. Now for food and wine and prize money you would bring disgrace upon our ship. You want money, eh!" His voice hardened; honey no longer dripped from his words. "Let me tell you, then, what our great chief has done. When he could not raise the money required in America to support the French armies there, he offered his plantation on Sainte-Domingue and his estates in France as pledge. A million and a quarter livres—think of that! His ruination if the war is lost. Even so, the money could not be raised. But a Spanish ally helped him in his need, raising the money in Havana—some of it from ladies' jewels, one hears. We can believe it. Did we not go to Havana to tend the frigate that was carrying the gold to M. de Grasse?"

"Basta!" some of the men called. "Enough talk!" "They have gold, why not us?" *"À la bordage, mon capitaine!"* Some of them climbed onto the bulwarks to see how close now their intended victim was.

"Enough?" Gascoyne said scornfully. "No, it is not enough for your swinish ears. But I will tell you more—I will show you just how crass you are."

His scorn for them recaptured their attention.

"Besides the money, His Excellency was asked to bring troops to America. Troops to reinforce our own Lafayette. Do you understand? This marquis has left his comfortable life in France—his food, his wine—for the hardships of war with General Washington. And since he is hard pressed, troops are needed to save those already there. Troops are not easy to find. True, there were French soldiers on Sainte-Domingue—three thousand infantry, artillery, dragoons. But they had been promised to the Spanish admiral, Don Josef Solano, for attack on Florida. Yet, when M. de Grasse explained the need, this Spaniard released his troops for service in America at this moment of great emergency. Now our chief can sail. He has the gold, he has the troops. But he has not got them to America, you understand. He requires information. Where is the British fleet? Waiting off the Virginia Capes? Anchored in the Chesapeake? How many ships? How strong? These things he must know if he is to succeed. And who has he sent to get this information for him? Our *Princess*, with her speed."

As he talked, a hush fell across the deck. Eyes that a moment before had blazed with anger, now grew warm with respect and admiration.

"Are we to do less for our own chief than did those Spaniards?" Gascoyne finished. "Are we to fail him for the sake of plunder, to fill our bellies, to guzzle wine?"

"*Non, mon capitaine!*" they shouted. "*Jamais!*" They threw down their cutlasses, sheathed their knives, began cleaning the greasy slush from their bodies.

"*Bien, mes enfants*," Gascoyne said, honey in his voice again. "You have behaved in a worthy manner. Me, I have a small quantity of wine for my own use. Not much is left, but what I have, I will share."

"*Non, mon capitaine!*" they shouted. "We will have wine

again when our fleet wins the war!" "Those soldiers ashore! Those lazy pigs! They must have seamen to win for them!" "To lead us, *mon capitaine,* you must keep your strength. We will not drink your wine!"

So *Princess* held her course. The fat cargo vessel sailed unhindered on her way.

Three days later they made their landfall on Cape Henry, and opened the entrance to Chesapeake Bay. And since, off the capes, they had found no British squadron cruising, nor sails on the horizon that might be scouting frigates, Gascoyne cautiously sailed *Princess* through the channel between Cape Henry and Cape Charles.

The great bay was empty.

They coasted along the eastern shore, passing lush meadows, a hamlet here and there and, occasionally, a stately manor house set back from the water's edge across broad lawns, with slave quarters and smokehouses beyond. On an offshore puff of wind they caught the smell of hickory smoke, of hams and bacons curing.

" 'Tis a grand place to have a farm," Reilly observed wistfully. "Pigs an' chickens an' all."

"It's a wonderful country," Tommy agreed.

"Virginny too," Reilly said. "Once, in a ship carryin' brick, I went up the Rappyhannock, acrost on the other shore. Red brick it was, fer a grand mansion house near Fredericksburg."

"I meant all America is wonderful," Tommy said.

"Aye. Is ut good farm land where you was born, sor?"

"Pennsylvania? The best, I think. But I was only eight when we went to Paris."

"When the war's done," Reilly said, " 'twould be a grand thing to have a farm."

"Do you think we'll win, Reilly?"

" 'Tis in the fleet's hands, sor; whichever gets here first—the white flag with the gold flowers, or the bloody red—will turn the trick."

They cruised north until they could see the anchorage off Baltimore; as yet they had not seen a single British man-of-war. They ran south again, exploring bays and river mouths, cruising during daylight, anchoring at night. The Patuxent was bare, and the Potomac.

At the mouth of the Rappahannock, Reilly said, " 'Tis where we brought the red brick, sor. Grand farm land it is." There was a lugger loading hogsheads at a plank wharf.

"Tobacco," Tommy said.

They could smell the rich fragrance of the leaves, curing in a nearby shed.

"A barnyard smells sweeter to me nostrils," Reilly remarked.

"We might have a farm one day," said Tommy.

It was a pleasing thought. Caught up in these great events, Martinique—Annette—seemed far away; Antigua and Denise. But now, for a brief moment, talking of farms, he thought of them. He could not see Denise in the peaceful, well-ordered life of a plantation.

Reilly said, "I'll just take a cast of the lead, sor. Against there bein' any shoals."

They cruised on down to the York River, and it was there they saw the first sign of British activity: a frigate and several sloops-of-war, anchored with a number of transports. But so few ships could not presage any great movement of troops. And when they found no British men-of-war in the James River, which they investigated as far as Chickahominy Creek, beyond which no deep ships could safely navigate, it was clear that no strong British force had come.

"*Mon dieu*, if M. de Grasse will only arrive!" Gascoyne said. "He can sail in without firing a gun."

"It won't be long," Tommy remarked.

"Ten days, *mon ami*. Now we must watch to carry him a warning if a British fleet comes first."

For the watchful waiting, they found a smooth anchorage in Lynnhaven Roads, under the shelter of Cape Henry. Here, free of curious eyes ashore, since there was no town or habitation nearby, they could watch the approaches to Yorktown and the upper bay, as well as the James River. And, in the event a British fleet did come, they could slip out quickly, with small chance of being caught inside.

The anchorage had other advantages: a wide sand beach where the men could bathe; where, from time to time, they hauled a seine to keep the mess supplied with fish. Nearby they found a stream of clear sweet water where butts and casks could be refilled, and from the wooded shore they replenished their stock of galley firewood.

But life was not all ship-keeping and relaxation; they must be constantly alert for enemy sails on the horizon. This was the weakness of their anchorage: the wooded knob of hill that formed Cape Henry obscured a great arc of the Atlantic. Since they could not see across the hill, they climbed it and hacked out a clearing in the scrub thicket and bramble patches at the highest point, and put up a canvas shelter.

While the men were clearing the ground, Tommy, having brought the long glass ashore, with Reilly to spread and hold the chart for him, surveyed the panorama. The flood tide was ripping across the Horseshoe Shoal, which lay between them and Point Comfort. Beyond, on a finger of land between the James and York rivers, was Yorktown where Cornwallis stood entrenched. Near the mouth of the York, Tommy saw some specks that might be ships.

"Must be the frigate and transports we saw when we passed there the other day," he told Reilly.

"More o' thim now, sor?" Reilly asked.

"I don't think so," Tommy replied.

" 'Tis restin' his lordship must be, thin," Reilly observed. "Thim few ships is not enough to move him out, nor yet likely to 'uve brung much to him."

"He'd need a whole fleet," Tommy said.

"Aye. Whichever gets here first—the red flag or the white—will be the difference."

South of them, the James wound down from smoke-blue ridges

and James Town slept in the sun; and not far away was Williamsburg, capital of Virginia, where Lafayette's army was bivouacked.
In that direction, also, all was peaceful. This great bowl of bay
and hills and streams was the amphitheater of war; yet nothing
moved. Only the tides ebbed and flowed unceasingly across the
Horseshoe, and each changing tide brought hope, as the army
commanders watched for the arrival of a fleet: Cornwallis looking for his own to take him off—to extricate him by sea from the
untenable position Lafayette had maneuvered him into—or to
bring him enough troops so that he could break out overland.
Lafayette, watching for a sight of the fleurs-de-lis of his homeland, bringing him reinforcements after which he would complete the encirclement of Cornwallis and, by attrition, bring his
old antagonist to surrender.

Between the hill on which they stood, and Cape Charles ten
miles northward, there was a broad shoal. "Here it is, right
here," Tommy exclaimed, putting his finger on the chart. "The
Middle Ground."

At half-tide it was a dark purpling shadow, turning to sea
green when the flood tide swept in from the Atlantic, muddying
to yellow when the ebb carried the silt of half a dozen Maryland
and Virginia rivers out to sea.

"'Tis strange, the contrariness o' nature," Reilly observed. "A
fine broad bay where all the ships o' the world can navigate, an'
a fine wide channel for thim to pass in an' out, an' in the middle
of it she sticks a lump o' ground to turn a shipmaster's hair
white, beatin' in or out on any but the fairest wind."

"It's not getting out that worries me," Tommy said, "but will
our fleet get in."

Reilly added a benediction: "Aye—afore old Rodney does."

They left a lookout posted on the hilltop, the watch changing
when the anchor watch changed aboard, and an officer inspected
frequently to make sure the men on duty kept alert. The lookouts
could signal *Princess,* lying in full view of them below, and
they had American, French, and British flags to signal the nationality of approaching vessels.

Days passed, however, without a flag's being used. Then, aboard *Princess* one morning, they saw the British flag flying on the hilltop. Gascoyne at once began getting ready to sail: they must not take the least chance of finding themselves blocked in. But he sent Tommy and Reilly ashore to get more information.

In the hot dog days of August, it was a grueling climb, and they were panting when they reached the top and saw two British frigates standing in. The eyes, it could be assumed, of an approaching fleet.

The frigates cautiously wearing only topsails, passed through the capes; but as the bay opened up before them, clear of ships, they set more sail and proceeded boldly, one up the bay toward York, the other into the James.

Princess was riding at shortstay, ready to cut and run if the frigate approached, but the British evidently took her for a local trading vessel, since they did not investigate. And when the lookout signaled that these were the only two ships in sight, routine aboard *Princess* soon returned to normal.

On the day following—the tenth since their own arrival in Chesapeake Bay—neither frigate having reappeared, Tommy was toiling up the hill with the long glass, hoping to locate them somewhere in these broad waters, when he heard a rustling in the underbrush. Startled, he stood absolutely still, thinking it might be an animal, although they had seen no wild game about; or, by chance, an Indian. Immobile, listening, he was suddenly seized from behind, his warning outcry stifled by a hand clapped over his mouth. In but a few seconds he found himself gagged, his arms pinioned behind him, and two men in the uniform of French dragoons were pulling him through the scrub and brambles. Since they were French, Tommy was more annoyed than alarmed, being unable to make his own identity known because of the gag. But he knew that eventually he would have his chance to explain—and demand an explanation.

Emerging from a thicket onto the bank of the stream from which, where it poured into the bay, *Princess* had been watered, he saw a squad of dragoons making camp, their picketed horses swishing their tails under a cloud of gnats, pawing almost in frenzy. A noncommissioned officer, stripped of tunic and long boots and heavy kepi, was lying on his belly, drinking from the stream. He looked up, when his men dragged Tommy before him, rolled over again to submerge his face and guzzle, then sat up.

"This hellish heat!" he grumbled.

He spoke in French, but with such a strange accent that Tommy could hardly understand him. He was young, with blond curly hair, and his thin sensitive skin was peeling from exposure.

"These damned flies!" he cursed, using a hand for a fan, meanwhile listening to his men report that they had found this English officer skulking in the bushes.

"Why do you spy on us?" the sergeant demanded in English more heavily accented than his French.

Tommy rolled his eyes and made queer grunting noises around the gag until, realizing that he could not answer because of it, the sergeant ordered the gag removed.

"Come now, speak up," he commanded. "It's too damned hot for trouble."

Tommy replied in French. "I am not spying, monsieur. I am watching for a fleet—English or French."

"You are not English?"

"American. But from a French ship. We were sent to scout ahead by the Count de Grasse."

"Truly? He is coming then?"

"He should be here any day," Tommy assured him.

The sergeant said to his men. "You are fools. He is not English."

"Do you think we do not understand our own tongue?" one of them demanded.

"You do not understand common sense," the sergeant replied without rancor. He seemed a very pleasant young man. "So you are American?" he said. "You fight on our side."

"Your pardon, monsieur," Tommy answered, "but I think it is you who fight on ours."

"Either way," the sergeant replied, laughing, "we must both fight these damned flies!" He laughed again. "We thought we had caught a spy, and we find a brother-in-arms."

"May I ask, monsieur," Tommy inquired politely, "what you are doing here?"

"We crossed from the Williamsburg side yesterday, at Burwell's Ferry—it is from Lafayette's army we come. Our major is an aide-de-camp to the Marquis. We are to watch for the fleet of M. de Grasse, and when it arrives our major will go aboard at once and urge the Count not to lose a moment coming to M. de Lafayette's assistance."

"Are things as bad as that?" Tommy asked.

"Figure for yourself," the sergeant suggested. "Lafayette has two thousand men—untrained Americans, for the most. Cornwallis has seven thousand, all seasoned troops. The old redcoat laughs at our general—calls him 'the boy'. True, the Marquis is young, but it is not lack of years that will beat him; it is lack of troops. If Cornwallis starts for South Carolina, where there is another British army to join and strengthen him, do you think our two thousand men can stop him? Not at all! It is quite impossible, monsieur. You can see that for yourself, although you are a sailor."

"M. de Grasse is bringing reinforcements," Tommy assured him.

"It will be a happy day when he arrives," the sergeant said.

Tommy feared, for a moment, that the good news had been too much for the young sergeant; his eyes were popping from his head, the smile had fled his boyish face, he got to his feet and stood as rigid as a tree.

"You are a fool," a voice behind Tommy said, "and besides you talk too much." Tommy turned to face a French major who indicted him with a pointing finger. "You have been giving information to this spy."

"Do not argue," the major ordered. "You Swedes are all pig-headed. I tell you, this is a spy. There is a British frigate in the cove below here; her men are filling water casks and cutting wood. And this one comes ashore to spy on us, and you tell him everything!"

"Monsieur," Tommy interrupted, knowing now where one of the frigates was, "I am not from the English ship; I am an American. I am not a spy, but an ally."

"My commandant," the sergeant said, "he is not a spy—he told me so at once."

The major nearly choked. "*He* told you so! Why must they send a Swede with a thick square head to help me on this journey!" But he took a calmer look at his prisoner. "You have some identification, perhaps?"

"If you will come to our lookout post where we watch every day for the French fleet, you will find some of your countrymen. They will identify me."

"Come along then," the major ordered. "Prove to me that you are not English. I should not like to shoot you as a spy."

"No, sir," Tommy agreed. "I would not like you to."

He led the major, with the sergeant and two dragoons following them, toward the hilltop. As they approached the lookout post they heard shouting and, reaching the crest, they saw that the lookouts on watch were greatly excited.

"*Monsieur!*" they shouted when they saw Tommy. "Look! Look! A fleet arrives!"

To the southeastward, sails lay along the horizon like puffs of gray cloud. A few hulls had already climbed over the world's rim, but at so great a distance they could not be clearly distinguished.

"Think you it is M. de Grasse?" the major asked, himself showing great excitement.

"It is the quarter from which his fleet should come," Tommy replied.

And then, removing any possible doubt, he saw the tall three-decker, *Ville de Paris.* "It is M. de Grasse who comes!" he shouted.

The Breton sailors threw their caps into the air, hugged one another, danced around in sheer joy. "It comes! It comes!" they shouted. "Our fleet has arrived!" One seized French colors and waved the flag madly, while another began signaling to *Princess.*

The young sergeant grabbed one of his dragoons and danced. The major looked at Tommy; Tommy looked at him. Then, as if moved by the same impulse, they seized each other and joined the dance.

After the first excitement, when things had resumed a semblance of calm and they were recovering breath, the major said, "I am glad I did not shoot you, *mon cher.* You dance divinely. And now if you will see that I am taken aboard the French flagship when M. de Grasse anchors, I shall be doubly glad."

CHAPTER EIGHTEEN

HIS EXCELLENCY, the Count de Grasse, for the first time in months slept well. His fleet, riding safely at anchor in Lynnhaven Roads, had stoppered Lord Cornwallis inside Chesapeake Bay as tight as a cork in a bottle of wine. Furthermore, while the fleet remained there, no reinforcement could reach the British army from sea. No relief. No rescue.

Since the fleet had anchored, four days earlier, on the last day of August 1781, M. de Grasse had accomplished much. He had received from Lafayette's aide-de-camp news of the French-American general's dire need, and had at once begun landing troops brought from the West Indies to reinforce him.

An officer from General Washington's staff had arrived to request water transport for the armies moving south into Virginia. In response, he had ordered his lightest draft vessels stripped of all unnecessary men and equipment to provide transport, at the head of the bay, where the Elk River empties. These ships would carry the troops down to the York Peninsula to maneuver in concert with the Marquis de Lafayette against Cornwallis.

The Count had also learned from General Washington's emissary that M. de Barras, commanding eight French sail of the line, had departed Newport for Chesapeake Bay, bringing aboard his ships the heavy artillery of the marching armies. And, from the captain of the captured British frigate *Loyalist,* he learned that although ill health had obliged Admiral Sir George Rodney to return to England, Sir Sam Hood had come to the American coast to reinforce Admiral Graves.

But on the fifth September morning, while the Count took his forenoon exercise, pacing the high afterdeck of his flagship, his *major d'escadre* rudely interrupted his self-congratulations.

"Monsieur," de Vaugirauld reported, "they are signaling from the station on the hill."

It was true. A British flag was being waved.

"Ships? Of course," the Count observed. "But British? No. Surely it is M. de Barras with his eight sail coming to join me."

But soon one of his own offshore patrol frigates drove through the Capes to report the approach of a large British fleet: nineteen of the line and frigates.

"So, it is not M. de Barras after all," the Count mused.

"If he comes now," de Vaugirauld observed, "he will be destroyed. Eight cannot fight nineteen, monsieur."

"God forbid!" the Count exclaimed. "But we must lend a hand. Make signal to our fleet—up anchor; form battle line."

It was a daring thing to do, a gallant thing. In its tactically sound anchorage, his fleet could stand any assault through the constricted entrance. But if he sailed, he took great risks, even though superior in numbers, for his ships must pass seaward through the narrow channel, one at a time in single column, then form battle line outside before the enemy could strike with his full force. Should the French loss in action be great, the British might slip in, pre-empt the anchorage, and so bring his whole campaign, his whole well-laid plan to naught. Against this stood the situation of M. de Barras and his eight, sailing into certain destruction.

"We must take care at the Middle Ground, monsieur," the Count warned his *major d'escadre*, "lest a ship or two be stranded. I need all my ships afloat, you understand."

"We can anchor a ship there to mark the limits of the shoal," de Vaugirauld suggested.

"But not a large ship," the Count replied. "I shall need all my large ships in the fighting."

"*Princess*, monsieur?"

"Gascoyne? Splendid!"

The Count's spirits soared with the flying signals; his eyes, watching the anchors come dripping from the water and the canvas fill, burned with the eagerness that had bolstered him in many a fight. Impatience to be out and into battle put new spring into his long stride. He beamed with pleasure, seeing *Princess* in station as a guiding beacon at the Middle Ground.

She was a safety mark, telling the deep-draft ships how far north they could hold without touching the ground. From her deck, the sortie was a sight Thomas Potter would never forget. Sometimes a man-of-war, battle flags streaming from every masthead, sails bone-gray from long weathering, drum-taut in the fresh northeast wind, came so close as to tower above the small clipper. The bluff bows, smashing down on ocean combers, piling through the entrance, were veiled in spray. The spume blew back across *Princess*' deck, the big ships came so close, rolling and pitching her in the waves of their passing.

"*Mon dieu!*" Gascoyne exclaimed, wiping salt spray from his face.

"Must they come so close?" Tommy asked.

Their own yawing in the current gave the answer: at ebb tide, there was a strong southerly set across the entrance.

"The slow sailers will have trouble, *mon ami*," Gascoyne said. "You will see. Before they are clear, we shall be rescuing people from Cape Henry, where they will run ashore."

The leaders had no trouble. *Auguste* came first, wearing the flag of M. de Bougainville, *chef d'escadre* of the van division.

"Antoine de Bougainville," Gascoyne remarked. *'C'est magnifique!* He has sailed round the world, islands have been named for him, and flowers, and now he leads into battle."

The Count de Grasse, in his three-decked flagship, led the center. M. de Monteil, in *Languedoc*, brought up the rear. But in spite of every precaution, although Princess clearly marked a safe course, some of the slower sailers, making excessive leeway, were set dangerously close to Cape Henry and were forced to tack ship to claw off. This threw the formation astern into confusion, opening a wide gap between van and center, as well as presenting a ragged formation to the enemy.

"See how he comes downwind to attack," Gascoyne observed, intently watching the British fleet. The British admiral had the weather gage; his ships bore down in tight battle formation, at a cable length from each other on bow and quarter bearings, so that no ship could blanket the guns of any other.

"He throws his whole strength at Bougainville's divison," Gascoyne said. "He will smother him before the center can get up," But suddenly Gascoyne shouted jubilantly, "He throws his chance away!"

At the last moment, perhaps wary of shoal water, perhaps fearful of giving up his weather gage, the British admiral wore his fleet round and came up parallel to the French column, heading seaward.

"God be thanked," Gascoyne breathed.

The British had thrown away their golden opportunity.

The French center closed on the van, the formation tightened, and now, when the British closed the range to force a decision, they met a devastating fire.

This first clash was all that *Princess* saw. The two fleets hauled steadily eastward, lost in the mists of distance and the fog of battle. Black clouds of smoke hung above them, the great guns sent thunder rolling shoreward and, as night fell, the flashes of their broadsides stabbed the sky with lightning. But darkness

soon put an end to the fighting; only the stars knew how the
fleets had fared at sea.

Chesapeake Bay again was empty; the great amphitheater of
war lay as quiet as when Tommy had first seen it. Lafayette
still waited near Williamsburg. At Yorktown, Cornwallis still
manned his trenches. But now, at Elkton, far up the bay, ships
waited to bring the armies of Washington and Rochambeau
south by water to Lafayette's assistance. And off Cape Henry,
beyond the land's horizon, two great fleets were fighting to
decide the fate of all.

The waiting at Elkton, where *Princess* had gone as soon as
the fleet had got safely to sea, seemed endless. It had been
General Washington's plan to move his armies by water down
the Delaware to Wilmington, leaving only a short march cross-
country to the head of the Elk River before embarking in the
French ships De Grasse had sent for the final leg down Chesapeake Bay. But lack of water transport on the Delaware had
obliged a forced march all the way.

Meanwhile, the crews of the French ships waited, hopefully
at first, then uneasily, and, as time dragged on, with sinking
hearts. Perhaps there had been a disaster; perhaps a British army
had waylaid the marchers.

But their spirits lifted when, at the end of a week, news came
that M. de Grasse had returned, victorious, to his anchorage
inside the capes. M. de Barras, as well, had got in safely.

The packet that brought news of M. de Barras, brought mail
from France, and Tommy received a letter from his father, written before, at home, they had received Tommy's missive from
the West Indies.

"My dear son," the letter read:

"The only news that we have had from you since you
posted a letter at Brest, telling us that you had decided to
make another cruise in the privateer *Princess*, was information which Dr. Franklin received in the form of complaint
from M. de Vergennes. In his complaint, the French Minister stated that *Princess* had cleared from Brest against or-

ders, that she had refused to halt when so commanded, and that, to cap the climax, she had impressed a French crew from a fishing fleet in Audierne Bay.

"Now, my dear Son, I know that you are not the Captain, and therefore could not be responsible for these piratical acts; yet it pains your Mother and me greatly to think of you in such bad Company. We pray that upon your arrival in the West Indies, where, Dr. Franklin tells me, your Ship is bound, you will lose no time in quitting such a Ship and such bad Company, and return to your hearth and home.

"I am enclosing a letter from Dr. Franklin, addressed to the Count de Grasse, begging His Excellency's favor to see that you get passage home in a returning transport or other suitable craft. Do not delay in presenting this letter to His Excellency, I beg you.

"For the rest, your Mother and the Children are well, but our minds are full at the moment of the dangers you are in, and our hearts are heavy with fear. So, dear Son, please return to us."

The word "children" in this last paragraph was badly smudged, and closer inspection convinced Tommy that the word "other" had first been written and then erased. *Other children! Quit this bad company and come home!*

He was so angry that he felt no sadness at his father's plea, and he regarded Dr. Franklin's letter with distaste, as if it were a hateful thing. That his father could believe he would abandon the great events that engaged him to run home for safety, reddened his cheeks. But calmer thoughts followed this first flush of resentment.

Perhaps he should take his father's counsel and present Dr. Franklin's letter. M. de Grasse would surely give him transportation home. Home! To himself, though he would never admit it to his parents, he could not deny that this was a hardlying trade he had chosen to follow. The sea was cruel. He thought of the good food at home, the soft down beds, the warmth and love of family gatherings around a blazing hearth. Perhaps if the opportunity came . . . He had just opened his sea chest to put the letter away for future use when he heard Angel shouting wildly, "Don Tomas! Señor! They come! The soldiers come!" Throwing the letter in, he slammed the lid and rushed on deck.

All that day troops streamed into Elkton to embark upon the transports; all the next day, and the next. French grenadiers and dismounted hussars, four thousand of them when all the columns arrived, well equipped, swinging along proudly beneath the flag of France, their traditions marching with them in waving regimental banners, battle-scarred in many lands. The sight of them made Tommy feel proud.

But his eyes misted when the Americans arrived, half the number, ill clad, gaunt with hunger, shod, many of them, only with rags to protect their bleeding feet. Troops from Providence, Stony Point, Kingsbridge, and White Plains, marching into Virginia, making their own traditions in each new fight. When they pitched camp at Elkton, it was the thirty-fourth bivouac of the march.

Through New Jersey they had marched, American and French, into Pennsylvania and on to Delaware, the weary men putting at least fifteen miles behind them each day before, at night, their bivouac fires challenged the fireflies. Hot days and rainy days; rocky roads and sandy stretches; stubble fields. They ate short rations, and slept, when it rained, under spreading trees or sheds or haymows. In good weather they had stars for a roof.

But always they pressed forward, their leaders knowing that the Count de Grasse must return to the West Indies before October was gone. September had already come.

For many the journey was not ended, even at Elkton. The small ships waiting in the Elk River could lift only four thousand; the other two thousand must be marched around the head of the bay to Baltimore and, finding no ships there, go on to Annapolis, where larger ships, sent by de Grasse, had sufficient depth of water to come in.

Soon Chesapeake Bay bloomed with sails: large ships, small ships, craft of every kind, each packed to the rails with soldiers. In and out, around shoals and bay islands, they beat their way, now with wind and current working together to speed them on, again with wind bucking tide and progress slow. At times, when the wind blew foul, they must anchor or lose ground.

But each day brought transports into the James River, and the troops, landed near Williamsburg, marched to support the army of Lafayette, already reinforced by the troops and artillery from the West Indies. At last the bay was clear of transporting ships; the troops were all ashore. The trap was ready to be sprung. They could march now toward Yorktown, sixteen thousand strong.

Each time Tommy opened his sea chest, Dr. Franklin's letter stared at him accusingly, until, unable to bear the thought of causing unhappiness at home, he tucked the letter under everything, at the bottom of the chest. But he would write; he would explain things. When they knew that he was not a pirate but a commissioned naval officer serving the Count de Grasse, they would feel better about it.

"Dear Mama and Papa," he began: "The most wonderful thing has happened!

"A few days ago *Princess* was sent to James Town with Despatches for General Lafayette, and we brought back a pouch of letters from Williamsburg to be delivered to the Flagship. Booby—I've told you about him—rowed me across to the *Ville de Paris* with the mail pouch, and, as we approached, there came in ahead of us a large boat from the captured British ship *Queen Charlotte*. The French crew were all in their best uniforms, and, in the stern sheets, was a company of American and French officers. As this boat came alongside the Flagship, the crew tossed oars and there was a great blowing of Trumpets on board and the roll of Drums, and I could see that the jolly-boat of the privateer *Princess* had no business in such grand company. Still, there was the Mail to be delivered.

"So I ordered Booby to pull around to the Larboard side, and when I went up the ladder no one noticed me, all hands being faced to Starboard at salute while saluting guns were fired. As I stepped aboard on the Larboard side of the Quarterdeck, a tall, handsome officer in a General's uniform stepped aboard to Starboard and raised his hat, holding it high while the guns crashed out. Thirteen guns were fired in succession, which I don't think was very good. I mean, the officer was General Washington. He should be treated like a King. They should have fired a hundred guns for him.

"The moment the last gun was fired, the Count de Grasse rushed across the deck and embraced the General and kissed him on both cheeks, and then he kissed Rocham-beau, and after that, Lafayette. He looked young and shy —not like a fire-eater. The Marquis de L., I mean. There were some other American officers too, but they did not get kissed. I think they were just as well pleased, because they looked embarrassed when M. de Grasse kissed our General.

"*Major d'escadre* De Vaugirauld called for the ship's company to cheer General Washington, which they did with a will, and cheered the Count de Rochambeau as well, and Lafayette; and all the anchored ships dressed their rigging with every Flag they possessed. Then the Senior Officers went into the Admiral's cabin to drink toasts, and I delivered the Mail to the Officer-of-the-Deck and got a receipt for it, and went down to my boat and so back to *Princess*.

"She seemed awfully small after being aboard the great *Ville de Paris*, but even if she is too small to get into the real action, we do have a part in what is going on. It was a wonderful Experience.

"I received Papa's letter enclosing a missive from Dr. Franklin to get passage for me Home. I haven't presented it *yet*. When he knows that I am not a pirate, but a French naval officer with His Excellency, the Count de Grasse, I don't think he would want me to give up and come Home. Would you, Papa?

"I must close now, since we have just received orders to get under way. I love you both dearly—my Sisters too—and when the War is over, I'll come straight home.

"Your loving son,
            "Thomas

"P.S. Did you get my letter which told you I am now an *Enseigne? Princess* is a man-of-war, and Gascoyne is *Capitaine de Corvette.*"

While the combined armies marched on Yorktown, M. de Grasse deployed his ships to block every avenue by which Cornwallis might escape. He sent one squadron to the mouth of the York River to blockade the ships inside, and, as well, to land troops on the Gloucester shore, across from Yorktown, to hem in the British cavalry encamped there under Colonel Tarleton, whose reputation as an intrepid and unpredictable antagonist had spread afar.

To this blockading squadron, *Princess* was now attached. Her light draft and speed and handiness fitted her for lifting small detachments to points where the tactical situation might demand quick reinforcement.

For a time, on the water, all was quiet. But the sound of musket fire, rolling out from the land, told the seamen that the soldiers were closing the trap on the British redoubts. For the ships it was a waiting game. Yet if Cornwallis should attempt to extricate his army by water, leaving only a holding force in his Yorktown position, the burden would shift to the fleet.

Princess, anchored inshore of the blockading squadron, kept lookouts aloft to watch the river, and a sea watch on deck to handle sails quickly. Soon after midnight of their arrival, the man at the main crosstrees shouted, "Deck there! Ships be under way on the river!"

Lights were moving on the water. Not the normal riding or running lights displayed by ships but large globes of orange-red, as if the ships themselves were huge lanthorns.

The foremast lookout hailed, "*Mon capitaine!* Five come out!"

The glare of their inner fires betrayed them. Incendiaries!

Sails full-set, they rode the river current seaward, blazing fore and aft, steering straight into the French squadron. The blockade must either break or burn. But no matter which, in the confusion and panic the way would be open for transports to escape.

At the first cry of alarm, Gascoyne ordered the anchor up and got *Princess* under sail. But there was little they could do. All around, French warships were getting under way. Some broke their anchors from the ground and drifted, hoping to drift clear. Others, not even taking time to slip their cables, cut and ran. Two ran aground.

The fire ships had come close enough by this time to light the scene brightly, revealing the panic aboard the men-of-war. French sailors, roused from slumber, ran crazily about the decks. It was order, counterorder, disorder. When one ship commenced firing her great guns, others followed her example. They fired at the incendiaries, at each other, at anything that moved. When they began firing at *Princess,* there was no other course than to clear the area.

From her rigging, Tommy watched as the fire ships drifted through the French squadron, their own sails, by this time, ignited by the tongues of flame licking up from the holds. Yet they drove onward with the current, steered by tillers spiked amidships, for no living thing could exist aboard. At some time on their course seaward, they had been abandoned by their crews.

Heavy rain squalls came on. But a deluge could not have extinguished the infernos of holds crammed with fagots soaked in pitch. Miraculously, though, no French ship was run afoul, nor were any set afire by flying embers. And, though the blockading squadron had been thrown into confusion, no transports attempted to make a sortie. Though alarming, the attack had proved a failure. In the end, the fire ships drifted onto mud banks, there to burn themselves out, lighting up the bay for miles around.

All that day, and for days therafter, the roar of cannon and musketry rolled continuously across the water. Its crescendos marked the French-American advances, as echelon followed echelon, seizing the outlying British salients, destroying or pre-empting them as the lines drew tight around the British redoubts.

"Faith," Reilly observed, "an' haven't they go his lordship in a puddin' bag!"

It was more like a horseshoe. The allied armies were de-ployed in open trenches which formed a U about the British position. After each successful advance they dug new trenches, squeezing the British into an ever-shrinking area of resistance. Although at times a successful British counterattack might expand the perimeter temporarily, as red-coated troops seized allied trenches, implacably the squeezing process continued.

But as the ends of the U moved closer and closer to the river, they became vulnerable to gunfire from British ships at anchor. Now the objective of the fire ship raid became apparent: by damaging French warships, or at least by impressing French commanders with the hazards of remaining so close to Yorktown, Cornwallis had hoped that M. de Grasse might withdraw this squadron.

But when the two English warships in the river began en-filading the allied trenches, the French squadron, having re-formed after the raid, moved in even closer to lay a thick blanket of cannon fire across the British ships.

French guns hurled red-hot shot which set several transports afire and hulled the 50-gun ship *Charon* so that she settled on a mud bank, her upperworks burning to the water's edge. *Guade-loupe*, frigate, and several sloops of war were obliged to retreat further into the river to get out of range. And so the enfilading of the allied trenches ceased.

Aboard the French ships, waiting again became the order of the day. Wait, watch, and stand ready, while ashore the allied armies closed the U relentlessly. On the night of October 15, this dull routine was broken. A call for help came from the Gloucester shore: Cornwallis was crossing from Yorktown with his army to join forces with Colonel Tarleton. If the crossing in force should succeed, the combined troops might drive through the limited allied resistance at that point and break out into open country.

The call for help brought immediate response: land the marines.

While reinforcements were being landed, the *chef d'escadre* ordered *Princess* to proceed inside the river and observe the extent and scale of the movement. The weather had turned boisterous: no moon, no stars, and driving rain squalls. Although this cloaked the movements of *Princess,* it also covered the British. But "observe" was the order. So Tommy crawled out on the bowsprit and lay there, beneath the headsails, watching for boats. Through the driving rain he caught occasional glimpses, but he was puzzled. They were moving from Gloucester to Yorktown, the reverse of what had been reported. Then as one came close, he saw that it carried only a boat crew.

"Empty!" he shouted to Gascoyne. "They're crossing back to Yorktown empty!"

It was evident that part of the British army at least had got safely across to Gloucester. Yet Gascoyne was not satisfied; he must know more before returning with a report to the *chef d'escadre.* He tacked slowly back and forth, from one river bank to the other, nosing steadily closer to the British position.

As the night wore on, the storm increased. The gusts came so hard that Tommy lashed himself to the sprit, lest he be blown overboard. The constant soaking, and the wind, chilled him until he could hear his teeth rattling. Yet he stayed.

"Boats!" he shouted. "Boats all around us! Loaded with troops."

Princess could have blasted some of them with her guns, but there was no need. The storm spelled their destruction. Oarsmen were pulling desperately; soldiers bailed to save their lives. A boat swamped a short distance ahead, and Tommy saw the heads of men bobbing in the water, heard their faint cries, saw their arms reaching up to catch a rope, anything for succor.

But though he reached down, he could not help them. It mattered little. They were so many; he only one.

All around *Princess* boats were struggling to keep afloat. Those that did, turned back toward Yorktown, in full retreat before the storm.

With the coming of daylight, the wind dropped, the roughened river became smooth again. Gascoyne brought *Princess* within hail of the squadron flagship to report that the attempted crossing had ended in failure. From the flagship, the *chef d'escadre* could see for himself boats streaming back from the Gloucester shore loaded with soldiers. Now that his desperate attempt to break out had failed, Cornwallis was regathering his troops to fight to the end, where he stood—at Yorktown.

On that day, the 16th, gunfire again rolled from the land, as the British launched a vicious counterattack. But having been long without replenishment of ammunition, the assault could not be sustained. The blare of bugles soon halted the charging men; the trenches which had been their objective remained in allied hands.

On the morning of October 17, a stillness lay across the land. As the day wore on, a white flag appeared above a British parapet. *Princess* was sent off to carry the news.

With all sail set, she stood clear of the blockading squadron on duty assigned, and Tommy wrote in the ship's log:

"Under way for Hampton Roads, carrying Despatches to M. de Grasse. This day, at ten and a quarter o'clock, a white flag was raised above a British redoubt and a Drummer Boy came up in full view and beat the Long Roll, understood as a request to Cease Firing. General the Lord Cornwallis and his entire army must now surrender.

"Clear and cooler. Light airs from NE.

        "Thomas Potter, Ensign"

LAST PART

January–February, 1782.
Begins with squalls and heavy rain.
Action at St. Kitts.

CHAPTER NINETEEN

THE FALL of Yorktown, with the loss of seven thousand troops and their equipage, doomed the British land campaign. But there still remained the war at sea. Admiral Hood, now that October had run out and the hurricane season with it, would take his ships back to the West Indies. It was high time, the Count de Grasse decided, to return himself, lest His Most Christian Majesty's position in the Caribbean be overturned. On the other hand, if the French fleet got back before Admiral Rodney arrived from England with refitted ships, French holdings in the Caribbean might be increased.

With the business in the Chesapeake cleared up, except for salvage operations which did not require the presence of his fleet, M. de Grasse turned his attention to getting the trade convoy, waiting for warship escort at Cap Français, safely home. To alert the merchant ships for sailing, he sent *Princess* on head.

The Cape, when *Princess* tacked in through the winding channel, looked no different from when Tommy had seen it last: the same low, tile-roofed houses, the same encircling hills, the same shimmering heat and smells. Yet, to Tommy, things were different. Then, they had been leaving the West Indies behind; now, they were coming back. Fort Royal would be next. He was not looking forward to Fort Royal. He did not know exactly why, yet it was a feeling about Annette. He did not want to face her. But perhaps he would not have to. Most likely she would not want to see him.

"What will you do when the war is over?" he inquired of Gascoyne, who was across the table from him, lounging on the transom. The checked cloth was spread, as it always was in harbor, with glasses and a decanter set out, and, since the ship hardly rocked at all in that smooth landlocked anchorage, the airports in the side were open as well as the skylight above the table. There was a certain coziness about the little cabin. Storms could be forgotten; the discomforts they underwent at sea.

"What will you do?" Tommy asked again of Gascoyne, who seemed to have lost himself in the bouquet of the wine.

"Me, I am a sailor," Gascoyne answered. "You too, eh?"

"I'll go home as soon as it's over," Tommy said. "Paris."

Gascoyne refilled his glass. "When the war is over," he said, one hand caressing the beading which ran around the transom, "I shall ask M. de Grasse to give us back our little ship."

"Do you think he will?" Tommy asked.

"Did he not promise?"

"No. He only said, 'Who can tell?' "

"It is the same thing. We have served him well. Besides, when there is no longer war, what will he need of our little *Princess*? You will see. She will belong to us again—you and me."

"But what then?" Tommy asked.

"Listen. We shall form a trading company. My uncle too. He will manage things ashore. We—you and I—will sail through the islands trading—French, English, Dutch islands—when the peace has come. Spanish islands too. When we have made much money, we can buy another ship. Captain Tommy you will be. Better than a dull life in France, eh, *mon ami*?"

"But my family lives in France."

"Forever?"

"Well—" He had not thought of that. "When the war is over, I suppose my father will move back to Philadelphia."

"*Très bien!* When we have our second ship, you will sail to Philadelphia. Those strange ones—how do you call them?—

Quakers?—do they not put sugar in their coffee, and drink rum?"

Tommy laughed. "Not Quakers—not rum and coffee. But there are lots of other people in Philadelphia."

"*Bien*. You will sail to Philadelphia—coffee, sugar, rum. You will make your father proud, seeing your ship at a wharf, or lying in the stream. 'My son's ship,' he will say, pointing her out to friends. 'My son, Captain Thomas Potter.'"

"I see now how you got the Breton sailors to sail with you." Tommy laughed.

Gascoyne laughed too. "It sounds good, eh? We will become rich. My poor uncle too."

"Are they very poor, Gascoyne?" Tommy asked.

"How do you call it? Church mice! But it will change after the war. There is no trade now, you saw that for yourself. Little comes out from France to sell, and the produce which should be selling in France lies here in these ships."

"They will be going soon," Tommy said.

"But it will be a long time before the money comes back. And to make things worse, yellow fever is very bad this year. I heard on shore that many are dying. Those who can, have quit the hot cities and gone to the windward side."

"Annette?" Tommy asked.

Gascoyne shrugged. "I do not know. Perhaps she stays at Petite Anse with Marie."

Reilly's voice down the skylight halted their conversation. "Three sail o' ships standin' in, sor. Frenchies."

From the deck they could make them out: *Victoire* leading, *Valliant* and *Triton* in her wake. Now, at last, the convoy would go home.

Valliant and *Triton* remained outside to form the ships up; *Victoire* stood in. Some of the merchant ships were already heaving in their anchors, anxious to be off.

But on the next day, ships were still clearing, every hour that wind and tide served. It would be yet another day before all were out. Meanwhile, Gascoyne received new orders from

Victoire's captain: *Princess* would return to Chesapeake Bay to assist in salvage operations and form a link for despatches with M. de Grasse, who, with the remainder of his fleet, was en route to Martinique.

The sight of the ships forming up to go home, the thought of long months at sea before he saw home again himself, was too much for Tommy. He decided to present Dr. Franklin's letter to the captain of *Victoire*. He would request passage for himself and Reilly. And he would not tell Gascoyne about it until it had been arranged, lest he be persuaded to change his mind. Gascoyne was dozing on the transom. Tommy got the letter from his chest and went on deck.

A lot of the Bretons were in the waist, watching the convoy sail, and, seeing him, they crowded around. Since the unpleasant affair of Muldin, and the taking of *L'Afrique*, Tommy had had their admiration and, more, their friendship and trust.

"The convoy is sailing," one of them said, "yet we have no order to lift our anchor."

Another spoke: "One hears we are not returning to France, but to America, monsieur. Is it true?"

"You'll have to ask the captain about that," Tommy told them.

Behind him, Gascoyne spoke, his bare feet noiseless coming from the cuddy. "It is true," he said.

"We will not go!" Pierre Duroc declared, and a clamor, supporting him, rose from his shipmates:

"The war is over; we will go home."

"We ask for nothing except our right."

"We are fishermen, not *matelots*."

"*Mes enfants*," Gascoyne said quietly, "listen well." At the magic of his voice they fell silent, even Pierre Duroc.

"You have said it—you are fishermen. When you have hauled a few trawls—scarcely enough to cover the bottom of your hold with fish—do you turn your boat around and sail for home? *Non!* Nor do we go home until our work is done."

Duroc spoke again. "The British have surrendered. Did we not see it with our own eyes?"

"One swallow does not make a summer," Gascoyne continued, "nor one battle win a war. When our King needs us no longer he will tell us so."

Duroc hawked disrespectfully and spat across the rail. The wind blew drops of spittle onto Gascoyne. He wiped his face with his hand and said, "You did not learn your seamanship at Audierne?"

"Lambézellec," Duroc replied.

"I knew such a lubber could not belong to Audierne," Gascoyne said with a disdain that brought guffaws from Duroc's shipmates, and they made jokes at his expense.

But it eased their discontent only for a moment.

"We have been too long at sea," one of them said. "Too long from home." And another supported him: "It is time we slept in beds ashore again. Had some decent food, and wine that has not turned sour from seasickness."

"I am Breton too," Gascoyne reminded them. "Do not forget that. Such child's talk does not become our fisherfolk. Nor will Our Lady look with favor on us if we cannot stand hardship." He elbowed his way through the crowding men and started down the ladder into their living compartment. "Come," he urged from the ladder, head and shoulders above the deck, "say a prayer with me to the Blessed Virgin. She will bring peace to our hearts."

"Gascoyne is right," someone said, and they followed him, man after man, down the ladder. Only Pierre Duroc hung back, but he listened at the hatch.

Tommy listened too, hearing the voices of men kneeling before the *chapelle* to pray. They prayed *le bon Dieu* to quickly bring them peace so that they could return to their fishing grounds, to their wives, their families; they asked the Holy Virgin to give them patience, to ease the loneliness, the homesickness in their hearts. They begged for safety in their lives so that they could see the shores of Brittany once more before death came for them.

They were still praying when Gascoyne came quietly up the ladder and out on deck. "Do not be troubled, *mon ami,*" he said, seeing Tommy's troubled face. "They will sail with us— with you and me." His eyes fell on Pierre Duroc. "But not this one. He will not." He moved threateningly toward the tough, squat Breton. "Pack your gear, Pierre Duroc. Get off this ship."

It caught Duroc aback. "But where shall I go, monsieur?"

"To the devil, for all I care. When I have set you ashore, you are no longer one of mine."

"But I have no place to go ashore," Duroc protested.

"Just the same, if I find you still aboard in half an hour, you will prefer to go to hell." He turned his back on the trouble-maker and went below.

"Monsieur," Duroc said to Tommy, "I do not wish to be sent out of the ship in disgrace. Speak to him for me."

"For your behavior to him, you deserve what he has ordered," Tommy replied, "but because you once saved my life, I will speak to him."

But before following Gascoyne below, Tommy took Dr. Franklin's letter from inside his shirt and tore it into strips, and strips again, and threw the pieces overside.

It had been early June when *Princess* sailed from Fort Royal for English Harbor with the cartel of prisoners to be exchanged. It was early January now. Their assignment on the American coast completed, they were returning to Martinique. The old ones of the crew—the Irish smugglers—had deserted in Chesapeake Bay the first opportunity they had. The Americans had not. They had been too long with Midshipman Tommy to make a change. The Bretons had not deserted either: *Princess* was their best chance of getting home. They put their faith in Gascoyne. Had he not said it? He was Breton too.

Running out of a heavy rain squall, there was Martinique— the cone of Pelée thrusting skyward through a layer of thick gray cloud. Rain engulfed them again, and, when it cleared, they saw many ships. A shout went up from deck: "Our fleet! Our fleet!"

Pierre Duroc was shouting with the rest, for Gascoyne had listened to Tommy's plea and let him remain on board.

"Even a lubber can recognize *Ville de Paris*," Gascoyne remarked, with a glance at Duroc which made the troublemaker hawk and spit, but this time with care, downwind.

"We will join the flag for orders," Gascoyne said. "Come about."

The fleet was close-hauled, standing eastward, its battle columns guarding a conglomeration of transports. It would not take *Princess* any great time to overhaul them, but darkness fell while she was still on the fringes.

At dawn, fetching morning cocoa, Angel roused them with shouts of: "*Nieve! Nieve!*" Almost ahead, they saw what seemed to be a snow-capped mountain. "Look, Don Tomas!" Angel yelled. "It appears like the Sierra Nevada."

"It isn't snow," Tommy told him. "It's cloud."

It was Nevis, its high cone always seeming snow-clad. There, or at St. Christopher, soon visible to the northward, M. de Grasse was launching an invasion. That it was to be "St. Kitts" first, became clear when he anchored his fleet, transports closest inshore, off Basseterre, the capital city.

The ships strung out close to land along the sheltered roadstead, and at once the transports began debarking troops. *Princess*, because of her shallow draft, was sent close in to cover the landing of cannon from an artillery transport.

The British, caught off guard, offered little resistance. Troops and artillery streamed out of Basseterre, heading for Brimstone Hill, a fortified eminence northwest of the capital behind the coastal town of Sandy Point. They took but small interest in the transport nosing up to the land, covered by *Princess*. But, when the transport ran upon rocks and bilged herself, settling on the bottom with only her upper deck clear, the British quickly diverted some cannon and mortars which they were hauling to the top of Brimstone Hill, to attack this helpless target.

But the fire from *Princess* hampered the unlimbering of their pieces. First discouraged by the heavy fire from so small a ship, then dismayed when they saw the smooth water between transports and shore crawling with boats loaded with soldiers, they gave it up. If they were to fight another day, they must take shelter behind their prepared fortifications. In their haste, they abandoned cannon and mortars. The capture of these pieces in some degree compensated the French for the cannon lost in the foundered transport.

By nightfall, six thousand French troops had been landed. The British regulars, and militia, were encircled on their hilltop. The fleur-de-lis flew above Government House in Basseterre, where the Marquis de Bouillé established his headquarters.

The flag caused no great consternation in the capital: invasion had been the island's history. Some two hundred years before, French and English had invaded together to take the island from the Caribs. Then came the Spanish to take it from the French and English, who had settled side by side to cultivate the land. The Spaniards, adventurers rather than colonizers, after sacking the island and deporting all the European planters they could get their hands on, departed. Then, Frenchmen who had hidden in the hills came down and worked their land again. But soon British arrived in larger numbers and took possession. So it had been through the decades: one flag, then another.

Now the French were back again. De Grasse controlled the sea approaches; the Marquis de Bouillé held Basseterre and the surounding land. But the British held Brimstone Hill. And, as long as they held it, the French did not truly possess the island.

A week of siege passed, and still the British held. M. de Grasse had not expected much more time than this before help came to the beleaguered garrison by sea; therefore he was not surprised when, in the last week of January, outlying frigates brought him news of a large British fleet. It was rounding Montserrat from the south and heading northward toward his anchorage.

From the lofty poop of *Ville de Paris*, M. de Grasse counted twenty-two of the line. This would be Admiral Hood: if Sir George Rodney had got back from England there would be more. In his own fleet, de Grasse had twenty-six, a superiority he would not again have, once Rodney arrived, until fresh support came out from France. It seemed a golden moment to increase his numerical superiority by weakening Hood. Besides, on arrival, M. de Grasse had not anchored his fleet in a formation suited to battle, his concern then being the rapid debarkation of troops. It seemed wise, therefore, to meet Hood's approach under way, hoping by skilled maneuvering and superior numbers to deal out a crushing defeat. He sent transports and auxiliaries under the lee of Nevis to await the outcome.

With his battleships in tight cruising formation, he stood south during the night, batteries manned and alert. At dawn, they found the British fleet several miles to windward, bearing down, it appeared, to engage. De Grasse therefore brought his fleet about to meet the challenge, forming in line of battle on bow and quarter bearing, angling across the British line to prevent movement northward into the area of land operations off St. Kitts. But his leading division failed to understand, or, understanding, did not obey, bearing away from the enemy instead of closing to attack.

Quick to seize his opportunity, Admiral Hood made all sail for the anchorage so recently secure in French hands, and, although by the narrowest of margins, reached it without having his rearmost ships cut off, despite all French efforts to intercept him.

It was a stunning reversal: the British now held the anchorage, the French must drive them out. The odds still remained twenty-two against twenty-six, but Hood's plan of mooring more than equalized his lack of numbers. He anchored his van and center on a line running east and west, almost perpendicular to the shoreline, the eastern ship lying close in, to prevent any passing between it and the land. His rear division stood on northward to anchor just inside the hundred-fathom curve, where the holding ground was good, the line slanting shoreward. The two sections of the fleet now lay, like a partly opened hinge, at an angle to one another, the guns of one section protecting the flank of the other. And to be sure that the guns could always be brought to bear against attack, spring lines were run from the sterns to the anchor cables, so that the ships could be hauled this way or that into the best position for gunfire, and held there.

Here was a floating glacis of compactly anchored ships, bowsprits overhanging taffrails, great guns covering every angle of approach, the open side protected by the island. Ships and men could wait confidently for the French assault.

M. de Grasse launched attack after attack, day after day; but aside from necessitating the exchange of ships in the British formation, bringing undamaged vessels from the less exposed positions to relieve those in the vulnerable salient which had been heavily damaged, nothing was accomplished. The French army's lifeline to its fleet remained severed.

A second week passed, and a third. The French ships, after months of cruising and the drain of the battle off Cape Henry, were grievously in need of refit. Stores, ammunition, and provisions were nearing exhaustion; there was no wine for the overworked crews of these undermanned vessels; the sick rate had soared appallingly.

Spirits were lifted, however, in the first week of February, when two fine sail of the line were sighted, arriving from France. But their *chef d'escadre*, the Marquis de Vaudreil, brought crushing news: they were the only two of a large squadron to escape after defeat in battle with Admiral Kempenfelt off Ushant. The supply convoy which this squadron had been escorting to the West Indies had been scattered to the four winds. And, to further darken the outlook, it was reported that Admiral Rodney had sailed from Spithead with a large force to resume command on the Leeward Island Station and strengthen the British position in the West Indies.

So there it was: no further reinforcement could be excepted, no stores, no provisions, no replacement of dead, wounded, and ill. And, perhaps, the sails of Sir George Rodney's squadron were just below the horizon. Yet M. de Grasse was not ready to abandon St. Kitts. He would hold on for another week, give the Marquis de Bouillé time to put on a last ounce of pressure to force capitulation of Brimstone Hill. But if, after a week, the British had not surrendered, M. de Grasse would be obliged to withdraw his fleet to the fortified base at Fort Royal. To remain at St. Kitts, weakened, his ships constantly cruising, would be courting complete disaster.

Having made his decision, he faced the problem of getting his ultimatum to M. de Bouillé, since Hood's fleet had cut off all communication with the shore.

"Where is our Gascoyne?" the Count demanded of his *major d'escadre*. "He is so clever at maneuvering in and out of ships, and navigating in shoal waters. I can use that skill now."

"*Princess* is sheltering in the lee of Nevis, monsieur," de Vaugirauld reported.

"Signal for her to come up at once," the Count ordered.

Princess, footing stealthily through the velvet darkness, hugged the land north of Sandy Point. The knowledge gained while covering the foundered artillery transport greatly profited Gascoyne, running in now to execute the Count's mission. The hulk lay resting upright on the bottom, firmly anchored by the weight of cannon inside, the masts rising straight up from the main deck, which was awash at high water. Before sunset, Gascoyne had taken bearings, lining the masts up with a church spire on the outskirts of Basseterre. The masts would be a leading mark, illuminated by the gun flashes from Brimstone Hill; and the top hamper would provide some cover if he could keep the hulk between *Princess* and the flashes of the guns, never ceasing while the siege continued.

There was not a single light on board; even the binnacle lamp had not been lighted. The helmsman steered by the stars and the guns and an occasional glimpse of the hulk's masts in the flashes.

Tommy stood beside Gascoyne near the wheel. "This is dangerous, this thing you are to do for M. de Grasse." Gascoyne said. "I do not know how I should tell you about Annette—your mind must be untroubled while you swim ashore and land inside the fighting lines."

A numbness gripped Tommy. "Annette?" he managed to say. "Is something wrong?"

"The fever has taken off Annette," Gascoyne said.

It seemed for a moment as if *Princess* had touched the ground, but the shaking was inside him, and not the ship trembling. Dear Annette! She had given him her love and he had taken it. Yet he had failed her, breaking his promise about the duel, and, after taking her love, dreading to see her again. Now he never would!

Gascoyne moved away, making a pretense of testing the drawing of the canvas with his own hands on the wheel. When he returned he said, "M. de Grasse gave me the news when I went aboard the flagship to get our orders. My uncle also was very ill. He is better, M. de Grasse assured me."

Gascoyne's matter-of-fact telling steadied Tommy. His mind must be untroubled for this mission; he must keep himself controlled. "And Marie?" he asked, trying to keep emotion from his voice.

"The fever did not touch Marie," Gascoyne replied. "She goes now to live in France with her father. He can no longer stay on Martinique—to lose wife and then daughter is too much."

So Marie would have her wish, Tommy thought. Perhaps, after everything, Annette had had hers too. Oh, Annette!

Gascoyne was speaking: "It was St. Kitts where your Lord Milholme was going, *n'est-ce pas?*"

"Yes," Tommy replied.

"Perhaps he has been taken prisoner. What good luck if you should meet him ashore."

Knowing that Gascoyne's talk was to keep his mind from other things, Tommy did not answer. Was it the dangers ahead that Gascoyne did not want him to think about? Or Annette? The danger might keep him from thinking of Annette. He welcomed it.

In a burst of gun activity on Brimstone, they saw the masts of the hulk, not far away. "Steady," Gascoyne cautioned the helmsman, and began stripping the canvas off *Princess* until, when the last sail was doused, she carried only enough steerageway to glide noiselessly alongside the wreck.

"*Mon ami?*" Gascoyne said softly.

"Ready," Tommy answered, stripping off shirt and trousers to stand naked, a white shadow in the night. Gascoyne walked to the rail with him.

"You have it clearly?" Gascoyne asked. "We remain here until an hour before dawn. If you are not back then, we must leave. But we will return tomorrow night."

Reilly fastened a bundle of clothing between Tommy's shoulder blades, held in place by sennit bands under his armpits: shoes to keep his feet from being cut when he traversed the limestone rocks ashore, nankeens and cotton singlet so that he could present himself decently before the Marquis de Bouillé when delivering the ultimatum from the Count de Grasse.

"They'll kape dry, sor," Reilly told him. " 'Tis waterproof, that bit of oiled cloth I've wrapped thim in."

Gascoyne said, "You will be inside French lines where you land. But take care, lest French patrols shoot you. Do not forget the Count's password."

"Best kape it on the tip o' yer tongue ivry minute, sor," Reilly cautioned.

"I will, don't worry," Tommy said and started down the side cleats.

"*Au 'voir,*" Gascoyne called softly.

Angel reached down and touched his hand, just before he

let go to take the water. "Go with God, señor," he whispered.

Tommy let go of the ship and swam away, slowly, splashing the least possible.

CHAPTER TWENTY

TIME was running out; the sand stood low in the first glass of the morning watch. Near the rail a group of shadows huddled, becoming men when the flashes of French cannon encircling Brimstone Hill, and the return fire of the British batteries, cast a red glow on their faces.

Booby, in his brooding voice said, "Ain' gona be much left o' Sandy Point town, all that shootin'."

"You know Sandy Point?" Metzger asked.

"Been theah. Knows Basseterre best. Been theah many times."

"Christ! You think he's gone all the way to Basseterre?" Jacobs asked.

"Doan' know. All I knows is one of us shoulda gone along of him?"

"Didn't we ast him more than once to leave one of us to go wit him?" Metzger fumed.

"They coulda sent him in a boat," Booby persisted.

"They'd 'a' seen a boat from the hill afore it was halfways in," Jacobs argued. "If the lobster-backs didn't start shootin', the Frenchies would."

"Ain't no comfort, losin' a friend," Booby brooded.

"Don't shed no tears yet," Metzger counseled. "He ain't been gone that long."

"Just all the mid-watch and half the first, that's all," Jacobs observed gloomily.

"An' a glass already in this," Booby added and went to turn the sand glass standing on a shelf in the binnacle.

Reilly elbowed his way through them and stood listening at the rail. "Hist!" he cautioned.

In the distance, toward shore, they could hear soft splashing. Soon it became unmistakable: the even beat of a swimmer's stroke.

"It's him all right," Jacobs said.

"Praise be to God," Reilly exclaimed. "Fetch the captain."

But Gascoyne was already there. "Spread out along the rail, fore and aft," he ordered. "How he will be tired!"

In but a few moments they saw him: at first a phosphorescent whirlpool in the water; then he rippling flashes of his arms as he paced himself, for Tommy was very tired and if he did not concentrate on his stroke, he found himself making a great deal of disturbance without gaining much distance.

He saw the tall masts of the foundered transport, and a dark shape lower down that would be *Princess*. A few more strokes would do it. But it took more than a few before he made it alongside and felt two great hands slip beneath his arms, and then a powerful arm slipped around him, and heard Reilly saying, "The saints be praised—wid the gunfire an' sharks an' all."

Reilly raised him up to hands reaching down from the deck to lift him aboard, and Gascoyne was embracing him, wet as he was, as he stood dripping on the deck, getting back his breath.

"You lost your clothes, *mon ami*?" Gascoyne asked. "You did not stand naked before M. de Bouillé?"

"I didn't want any extra weight homeward bound," Tommy replied. "Some French soldier will make good use of them."

"Tell me what passed," Gascoyne said.

Angel came with a towel and began drying Tommy. "You must not catch the chill, señor," he scolded, rubbing vigorously.

"Easy!" Tommy cautioned. "I don't want to be skinned alive twice in one night."

"The Marquis was angry?" Gascoyne asked.

"When I first gave him the Count's ultimatum," Tommy replied.

"But naturally," Gascoyne said. "What will become of him and his troops if our fleet sails away?"

"He understood things better when I explained about the shortage of food, and magazines nearly empty, and no store-ships coming. He would take Brimstone Hill before the week was up, he said. The British must have fired away most of their ammunition, and they have had no fresh supplies of food, and drinking water must be getting low. One week more, the Marquis thinks—ten days at most."

"Our troops are of good temper?" Gascoyne asked.

"What I saw of them."

"And the town? Things go well there?"

"If you mean Sandy Point, there's not much of it standing."

"Basseterre?"

"The Marquis was at his field headquarters, so I did not have to go into town. There is much yellow fever in Basseterre, the Marquis said."

"There is always yellow fever," Gascoyne said.

"It is very bad, with so many soldiers," Tommy persisted. "And getting worse."

"Us—we have the clean sea air," Gascoyne observed casually. "Now we sail. And you must get some sleep."

Angel had finished drying him and had brought some clothes which Tommy was putting on. "No sleep yet for me," he said.

Gascoyne took his shoulders and pulled him close to see his face. "What troubles you?" he demanded. "Your friends are in Basseterre? The Irish girl."

"I think so. The British soldiers took no families with them on Brimstone Hill."

"It is too far, if you are thinking we should help them, *mon ami*," Gascoyne said. "The night is nearly gone."

"Only ten miles," Tommy argued.

"With the ship—two hours. Overland—who can say? Nor how long to find them in the town."

"You will sail away and leave them?" Tommy asked heatedly. "To die, perhaps. Like poor Annette."

"We cannot fetch them out tonight," Gascoyne insisted. "Now, even, we may be under British guns at dawn."

"Tomorrow night?" Tommy urged. "The moon is down again tomorrow night. You were coming back for me. Come back for them."

"*Bien.* If you want to come back, we come."

"I will stay here to find them," Tommy said. "When you return tomorrow night, I will have them waiting here."

Duroc broke in, speaking with exaggerated courtesy, yet with trouble in his voice. "*Mon capitaine,* you would not risk our lives for ladies?"

"When I will not risk my life for a lady," Gascoyne replied, "it will not be worth keeping." He addressed the others. "How say you from Audierne? Shall we help Midshipman Tommy save his sweetheart?"

Tommy was glad that it was dark; yet he warmed to their response:

"But of course, monsieur!" "How could we not?" "But not alone, *mon capitaine;* some of us must go."

"Clearly," Gascoyne agreed. "He will need companions."

"By your lave, sor," Reilly said, "I'll go with the lad." And Booby said, "Me, too, sah. I knows the ropes in Basseterre."

"Good,' Gascoyne said. "And you will need a boat. Ladies must not be asked to swim."

"Best lave the longboat, sor," Reilly suggested, "in case there be several who wants to come."

"You think we run a boat service to Nevis for stranded English ladies?" Gascoyne demanded.

"Is that where you will take them?" Tommy asked.

"English to English," Gascoyne replied. "Hurry—the dawn comes."

The men, crowding around to hear the talk, began to volunteer.

"Four, to keep the boat, will be enough," Gascoyne told them.

The longboat was lowered quietly into the water, and Gascoyne gathered the party around him to give final instructions. "The four who keep the boat will secure it between the wreck's masts where it will not be noticed during daylight. Two will go with Midshipman Tommy."

"Reilly and Booby," Tommy interrupted.

"*Bien*. When you have the ladies, bring them back to this beach and show a dim light after dark tomorrow night. You, in the boat, when you see that light will go in to bring them off."

Murmuring their understanding, the men who were remaining with the boat dropped down into it.

"Tomorrow night, when it is dark," Gascoyne told Tommy, "you will bring the ladies to the wreck. Safer to wait out here than ashore. Besides, when I come, perhaps we have no time."

"And if you don't come?" Tommy asked.

"I will come."

They walked together to the rail. "Until tomorrow night then, "Gascoyne said.

"In this same place," Tommy answered and dropped quietly down into the boat.

Above him he heard the soft rustling of canvas as jib and staysail were carefully hoisted, and the lapping of water along her hull as she began to move. With a ruffle of white lace at her waterline, *Princess* slipped ghost-like through the darkness and disappeared, leaving the boat rocking in the swell of her departure.

The men began to secure it between the wreck's masts. Tommy said, "Ready, Booby? Reilly?"

"Best rest a bit, sor, afore ye start another swim," Reilly suggested.

"No time," Tommy answered. "We must get ashore before daylight."

The day was breaking when the three swimmers dragged themselves from the sea on a rocky stretch of coast, set by the current some distance from their planned landing beach, yet far enough from Sandy Point to escape observation.

"Yerra!" Reilly gasped. "Ye niver warned us the undertow was strong as the divil hisself."

"It wasn't when I swam in the first time," Tommy managed

to reply. He was retching violently, but only salt foam came up from a stomach long without food.

Booby said, "Nevah kin tell 'bout them currents. Times comes a tidal wave, throws big ships right up on land. Othah times sucks the water right outa harbors."

"Faith, an' didn't it nearly suck us back to Ameriky?" Reilly grumbled.

They spread their clothes on the rocks to dry. "We'll rest a few minutes," Tommy said, and they stretched out on some flat rocks. But not for long. In the wind and the heat of the rising sun, their clothing was soon dry. They dressed and started off.

The footing along the old, crevassed lava streams on the lower slopes of Mount Misery was dangerous, and a noisome smell of brimstone, coming from fissures in the volcanic crust, hung over the land. In a short time, between the bad footing and fighting through rank underbrush, their clothes were wet again, sticking to their skins.

"These rocks is murther to a sailor's feet," Reilly complained. "The man who named this Mount Misery must ha' walked through here."

"Doan' like this devil stink neither," Booby added. "Hell ain't far under heah, I specs."

"We'd best cut across and go in on the coast road," Tommy decided.

"Aye," Reilly agreed. "Betther take the chance o' bein' picked up by patrols than murther our feet trampin' cross-country."

When they had got the road in sight, they were on a hillside overlooking the Caribbean. Northward, across the sparkling blue, they saw no patch of white that might be the sails of *Princess*.

"Praise be the saints an' all," Reilly said jubilantly, "the little ship's got clane away."

They sat down to rest themselves amongst the sage and fragrant myrrh covering this seaside slope. Below them the British fleet lay so close that the shrill of bosun's pipes and shouted orders, starting the day's routine, drifted up to them. Southward, hull down, the sails of the French fleet dotted the horizon, reaching toward Basseterre.

"M. de Grasse is going to try again," Tommy remarked.

"Aye," Reilly agreed. "Still an' all, I misdoubt he'll iver break that wall o' ships."

"Best be movin' along," Booby said. "Mighty far yet to town—road climbs up an' down."

On the coast road to Basseterre they met no patrols, and, when a convoy of provision carts from the French camp passed them, going into market, Tommy's fluent French got them a ride.

Basseterre seemed peaceful enough that morning when the provision carts drove in. But the steady ripple of gunfire from the direction of Brimstone Hill was a reminder that the fate of the island remained undecided. The market place seemed little concerned with the fighting; here, as on most of the other islands, the residents took no sides, wanting only an end to the war, so that they could lead their peaceful lives.

The provision carts made slow progess through the crowds that milled in the central square: sweating humanity shading from light brown to ebony, their chatter like the rush of confused water, for they spoke in many tongues and in a patois mixture of all. Countrymen sat beside piles of vegetables and tropical fruits: green, yellow, orange, red. Booby, the cart abandoned, searched their faces to find an old friend. But nowhere did he see a familiar face.

The sun, by this time, was nearly overhead, and they had not had anything to eat. So they halted their quest long enough to refresh themselves with bananas and mangoes and small fragrant Spanish oranges.

"How long since you've been here, Booby?" Tommy inquired.

"Dunno, 'zactly, Mist' Tommy. Six year. Eight, it could be."

"Fer the love o' God!" Reilly exploded. "Ye'll not be thinkin' to see the same faces sellin' produce?"

"Six, eight years ain't nuthin'," Booby answered. "By 'n' by I'll see someone for sure."

They started again, working the fish market where boats, half full of water to keep their cargoes of silvery fish alive, had been hauled up on the land. It was here, at last, that Booby found someone he knew.

The man's welcome to Booby was friendly enough, but he looked suspiciously at Tommy and Reilly. With the island still a battle ground, today's victors might be tomorrow's vanquished. It was safest not to take sides.

Booby explained, "My officer looks heah for friends. We are from a French ship."

"The French have arrived but lately," the man replied. "I have not yet made acquaintances."

"I am looking for an English lady," Tommy said. "Tall, very beautiful. Proud."

"A milord's wife," Booby added.

"A milord's wife would not come to this market," the fish-monger said.

"She might with her servant," Tommy argued. "To select a fish for dinner."

"A fine *balaou* for the milord," Booby said. "Or a *couronné*."

"It might be that her daughter would come with the servant," Tommy said. "She is very beautiful, like her mother."

"A redhead, she is," Reilly added.

"It is strange," the man said. "You come from a French ship seeking English friends." He pointed in the direction of the gunfire. "Every day they try to kill each other—English and French."

"I mean them no harm," Tommy insisted. "They helped me when I was a prisoner in England; now I would like to help them."

"I have seen no one like that," the man said, "but I will inquire of these others."

His questioning only brought suspicious glances from the other fishmongers, and some muttered threats.

"We're wasting time here," Tommy said. "Try to find someone else, Booby."

But as they walked away, a man followed, and when they
were clear of the others he spoke to them. "I have seen your
English ladies," he said, "a tall proud lady and sometimes a
young girl."

"An English officer's wife?" Tommy asked.

"Sir, I have never seen an English officer in the market buying
fish," the man replied.

"Do you know the lady's name?" Tommy persisted.

"The white servant who comes with her calls her always
'milady.' The young girl is called by a strange name."

"Denise?" Tommy asked hopefully.

"It is possible," the man replied. "A strange name, it seemed."

"Will you take us to where they live?" Tommy asked.

"My son will. He has carried fish there." He whistled between
his teeth, and a spindle-shanked boy with a potbelly dragged
himself from the shade of a boat where he had been guarding
its cargo of fish. He did not look very bright.

"You remember the ladies, my son?" his father asked.

"Which ladies, Papa?"

"The English 'milady' with the daughter of the red hair."

"I remember, Papa."

"This gentleman wishes to find them. You will take him to
their house."

"Will he pay me?" the boy demanded.

"He will pay *me*," the father replied, giving his son a good-
natured cuff.

"Does the boy truly know?" Tommy asked, before paying
anything.

"We do not cheat," the man said haughtily. "If I took your
money and did not know, it would be a Judas trick." And after
that he refused the offered payment.

"Ach, sor," Reilly counseled, "the fair thing is give the money
to the lad—whin he gets us there."

"It is fair," the father agreed. The boy started off at once.

They had trouble keeping up with him as he squirmed through the jostling crowd; but soon they were clear of the market and the boy led them through narrow, winding streets lined with shops and business houses, most of them shuttered because of the war. They came at last to a residential quarter. The streets here were wide and clean, and lined with neat homes of gray stone, with wooden upper stories.

" 'Tis more like ut," Reilly said. "Dacent people live in these houses."

But, as their hopes rose, the boy appeared to be discouraged. He shot nervous, darting glances at the houses. Several times he seemed to be on the point of stopping, only to start again, his jog trot more rapid.

"Faith now," Reilly remarked, out of patience, "we've cruised this strate more than once, wouldn't you say, sor?"
that he had been gulled.

"It looks familiar," Tommy conceded, although hating to admit

"Avast, ye young spalpeen!" Reilly shouted.

The boy stopped in his tracks and waited, his face twisting with fear. When they came up to him, Booby caught him by the scruff of the neck and shook him, and Reilly said, "Sphake true, lad, have ye lost your bearings?"

The boy only whimpered in his fright.

"I will beat your Judas arse till you speak us true," Booby threatened.

" 'Tis where his brains is," Reilly said, "but 'twill not help to beat them out."

"Let him go," Tommy ordered. "He doesn't know."

The boy ran off, not stopping to take the coin which Tommy offered.

"We'll have to try door to door," Tommy said.

So they went from house to house, Reilly on one side, Tommy on the other, while Booby patrolled the street, his eye on passers-by. Frequently doors were slammed in their faces before they had their question out. Sometimes their inquiry would arouse enough curiosity to permit a few more questions. But, after many houses, they were still no nearer success.

Then, at last, came a door where the quadroon servant's nervousness aroused Tommy's suspicion.

"Tell me," he demanded, "do English people live here? I am a French officer. If you lie to me I will have you punished."

"There are no English in this house," the girl answered, trembling with fright. "No sick."

"Let me in," Tommy ordered, "or I will call the soldiers." But he prayed that soldiers would not come along to interfere.

His threat threw the maid into a panic. She tried to close the door, but Tommy got one foot inside, while the maid cried out, "Come quickly, someone! Robbers! Thieves! Help!"

Someone came, and Tommy heard a heavy piece of furniture being dragged up and set against the door; but with his foot inside, it could not be entirely closed. Yet, with all his weight, he could not force it open.

A woman's voice called from the depths of the house, "In the name of God, what's all the Donnybrook?" There was something familiar about her Irish brogue. Someone he had heard before.

Another woman answered, "There's a thief tryin' to break in, mum."

He had heard that voice before, as well.

The first voice shouted, "He'd better break right out, before I come down and break his skull." And Tommy knew.

"Mrs. Major O'Cassidy," he called. "It's Midshipman Potter. I was prize master aboard *Vixen* when you were a passenger. After we captured the ship in the Channel."

"Hawkins!" the voice called. "What's become of your eyes? Just squint through the crack, now, and see is he lying or not."

Mrs. Hawkins! The sergeant's wife who acted as servant to the officers' wives aboard *Vixen*. She was peering at him through the crack of the door. "Lawks, mum," she reported, " 'tis no lie at all. It's the 'andsome young lad who done hisself so 'andsomely aboard."

"Unbar the door then, for the love o' God!" Mrs. O'Cassidy shouted.

There was a scraping inside as the heavy object was removed to permit the door to swing open, and Tommy stood facing Mrs. Hawkins, sharp-tongued and straggly-haired. Her hair was grayer than when he had last seen her, and straggling more than ever; but in the certainty that the Milholmes could not be far away, he nearly kissed her. He did kiss Mrs. O'Cassidy when she appeared a moment later, lean and leathery and horse-faced, still the hardened campaigner.

"I'll thankee to explain your advances," she said, but she looked pleased.

"I'm looking for Lady Milholme," Tommy told her.

"Ye've come too late."

"The fever?"

"Aye!"

Her horse-face swam before him and his knees were buckling; but he felt her hand beneath his arm and heard her shouting for Hawkins. "Fetch the brandy," Mrs. O'Cassidy ordered, "before the midshipman faints altogether."

Then, half propelled, half floating on the strength of her arm, he found himself in a small parlor off the entry hall. She sat him down on a sofa.

Her sharp eyes noted the deep circles beneath his, and the skin drawn taut across his cheekbones. She shrewdly guessed the reason. "When a man's been up the night, an' no breakfast, 'tis no shame at all. Leave your head hang down till the blood runs back."

She held him bent over, his head almost touching his feet, until Hawkins came flying in with a decanter of brandy. The bending had brought color to his cheeks again, but Hawkins poured the strong liquor for him just the same.

"Not bung full," Mrs. O'Cassidy cautioned. "'Tis to make him feel better, not to get him drunk. And a drop o' water lest he strangle on it."

She held a glass for herself while Hawkins poured until there was little space for dilution. "With all this yellow jack about, I always add a drop o' spirit to purify the water," Mrs. O'Cassidy said. She tilted her glass in Tommy's direction and drank.

Tommy drank his down in one gulp, while Mrs. O'Cassidy studied him over the rim of her glass. The brandy gave him courage to ask, "When was it?"

"What?" Mrs. O'Cassidy demanded.

"Lady Milholme."

"If ye mean what I think ye do," Mrs. O'Cassidy told him, "it ain't happened yet. I only meant you came too late to see her, bein' down, as she is, with fever. There's a medico upstairs with her now. We'll know soon how bad it is."

She took a good pull at her glass, wiped her lips with the back of her hand, and called, "Hawkins!" And, when Hawkins appeared, "Tell Maria to set a place at table for Midshipman Potter. The poor lad's had no breakfast."

"I'm not alone, ma'am," Tommy said. "I've got two men with me."

"And are they banging on doors too?" Mrs. O'Cassidy asked.

"Reilly is. Booby's patrolling the street."

"Go fetch 'em, Hawkins," Mrs. O'Cassidy instructed. "Two hard-lookin' characters who smell of ships. Bring 'em into the kitchen and feed 'em the best breakfast you can manage."

"That I'll do, mum. They be outside now, watchin' the house— I remember thim from the *Vixen*."

When Hawkins had gone, Mrs. O'Cassidy took another good pull at her glass. "We should be hearing from upstairs any second now."

"Where's Denise?" Tommy asked.

"Upstairs with her ma, where she should be. His lordship's on Brimstone Hill, tryin' his hand at soljering."

"Your husband too, ma'am?"

"Where else would the dear major be! He's first battalion, Royal Scots, and if I know me lovely man, he's responsible for the one hospital in this town being full to overruning with wounded Frenchies. It's because o' that we can't get her lady-ship cared for proper; and won't the O'Cassidy hear from me!"

"We must get Lady Milholme away from here," Tommy said.

"Away to where, for the love of God?" she demanded.

"Nevis is closest. It's English. There must be a hospital."

"Has it gone to your head now, that drop of brandy?" Mrs. O'Cassidy asked. "D'ye think the Frenchies are letting boats come and go freely? They're searching houses too, and when they find anyone down with fever, they cart 'em off to the pest-house instanter."

"Listen,' Tommy urged. "The ship that brought us in will be back off Sandy Point tonight. We must get Lady Milholme there."

"Hmm." Mrs. O'Cassidy twisted her glass thoughtfully. "I'm not sayin' it ain't a grand idea," she finally said, "but could she stand the journey? There's the rub."

"The doctor will tell us."

"We don't dare trust him to ask. He's an old Spaniard Denise dragged in off the street—the only English medic being up on Brimstone with the militia, carin' for wounded."

Before Tommy could argue further, they heard quick foot-steps in the hall and, in the doorway, Denise appeared. The sight of her brought Tommy up from the sofa; the sight of him seemed to frighten her.

"Tommy!" she exclaimed.

"Denise!" He moved toward her, but she backed away as if afraid. "Denise!" he said again.

"You are real?" she asked. "You're really Tommy?"

"Big as life an twice as handsome," Mrs. O'Cassidy said. "Come in, child, and tell us about your mother."

"I've come to take you both away," Tommy explained.

"Oh, Tommy!" Denise cried and came to him with a rush

that filled his arms with her for a moment. "Oh, Tommy, I'm so awfully, terribly glad to see you!"

"There now, me dears," Mrs. O'Cassidy said and wiped her eyes.

"Heaven must have sent you, Tommy," Denise said. "We're in such a frightful mess."

"What did he medico say?" Mrs. O'Cassidy demanded.

The doctor came in just then: a small, dried-up old gentleman with a white mustache and a pointed beard and the manners of a grandee. His sharp eyes held compassion in their quick glance, as the young people drew apart.

"It is not yellow fever, señora," the old doctor replied.

"You couldn't be wrong, now?"

"Señora, I have lived on this island many years. I have seen malaria, yellow fever, and plagues brought in on ships by rats. The symptoms in this case are not the same. I find no vomiting of blood, no bleeding gums, no jaundiced skin."

"What would you call her sickness then?"

He shrugged. "I do not know. There are no pustules that come with the smallpox, but the skin is mottled—a spotted fever of some sort. But not yellow fever, I am certain."

Denise sat down quickly in the nearest chair. Her lips moved in prayer. Hawkins, who had followed the doctor in, began to weep.

"And what's the tears for now?" Mrs. O'Cassidy demanded.

"If she's got fever and spots they'll be cartin' her ladyship off to the pesthouse, ain't that reason enough?" Hawkins dried her eyes and appealed to Tommy. "Don't let 'em sir; you can't imagine what it's like. The Frenchies face cannon brave enough, but fever gives 'em a fright. They cart people off to that charnel house every day. They die like flies."

"Your servant speaks true, señora," the doctor said. "When the French hear of this sickness they will come for her."

"And ain't they searchin' every house, mum!" Hawkins exclaimed, again in tears. "Maria says they're goin' through the town."

"True, they are searching," the doctor agreed. "But if they were not . . . I still must report this case to the authorities."

"But wasn't you just after telling us it's not the yellow curse at all?" Mrs. O'Cassidy demanded.

"Any fever must be reported, señora. Fever—it frightens them."

"Oh, please, please," Denise begged. "Can't you pretend you've never been here?"

"I am obliged to report, my child," he answered compassionately. "I would be disbarred from practice if it became known. Perhaps put in prison."

"None of us would give you away," Denise assured him.

Then Tommy interceded. "If I got the patient off the island, you would have no obligation then."

"You have the means?" the doctor inquired. "A ship?"

" 'Tis me distress and all," Mrs. O'Cassidy apologized, "that's kept me from mentioning it sooner: this is Mr. Midshipman Potter, who's come with his ship to take the ladies off."

The doctor bowed courteously, studying him. Denise begged, "Please, please let him. You can see he's the kind of man who will do what he says."

The old doctor bent gallantly over her hand. "I would be of stone," he said, "could I withstand such pleading." He turned to Tommy. "I will say nothing until tomorrow. If the lady has been moved by then, I will say nothing at all. I rely on you, señor."

He bowed to Mrs. O'Cassidy. "Give me a moment, Doctor," she said, "till I fetch your fee."

"There will be no fee," he replied, "except your promise not to move the patient until after dark. Someone would surely see and tell. It would mean much trouble for me."

"You've got the heart to match your noble looks, señor," Mrs. O'Cassidy told him. "Ye can sleep without fear, and your conscience clean."

His bow in the doorway took them all in. "Go with God, my friends."

After they had eaten, Reilly had gone into the town with Booby to find a reliable carter for the drive to Sandy Point. Denise had immediately gone upstairs again to sit with her mother; Mrs. O'Cassidy had insisted that Tommy get some sleep, "against the coming night."

It seemed to Tommy that night would never come.

The enormity of the task he had undertaken, the improbability of transporting a sick woman that far without investigation by patrols, which would surely send her to the pesthouse, and the difficulties of getting her aboard and properly cared for if they ever reached Sandy Point, tormented him.

Off the harbor, great guns roared: M. de Grasse was again battering at the British wooden wall.

But at last Tommy slept.

He awoke with Reilly's hand on his shoulder. Night was dimming the windows. "'Tis close on dark, sor," Reilly reported. "There's a cart standin' behind the house, an' a driver who knows the coast road. As soon as ye've had a bite, we'd best get under way."

"I'm not hungry, Reilly," Tommy told him. "We'll start straight off."

"Have a good wash first, sor," Reilly counseled. "The lovely feel of cool water will put new life in ye."

There was a washstand in the room and a jug of water, so Tommy washed himself quickly and got into his singlet again. It made him feel so much better that he stopped long enough in the kitchen to eat some of the cold fowl that Hawkins was packing in a hamper, and some manioc bread, washed down with a glass of claret.

When he went out, he found that Reilly and Booby had already loaded the cart; so the task now was to get Lady Milholme in. They lifted the mattress from her bed without disturbing the heavy stupor of her sleep, and carried her downstairs carefully, placing the mattress gently on the bottom of the cart without her realizing that she was no longer in her bedchamber.

They tossed some cushions in for the others to sit on and,

having helped Denise in beside her mother, Tommy made a final check to make sure that all their belongings had been loaded. He found nothing of Mrs. O'Cassidy's, and when he went inside to urge her to hurry, she only smiled.

"I'll be needing no traps where I'm not going," she told him.

"But you must go," he urged.

"You'd not be thinkin' I'd run off and leave the dear major?"

"You don't think I'll go away and leave you here," Tommy countered.

"And why not, now?"

"There's yellow fever, for one thing."

"And haven't I seen it, and the cholera, and the bloody sweats, in one part of the world or another, and never run?"

"But the soldiers," Tommy persisted. "They may get out of hand after they take Brimstone Hill."

"The only brimstone them Frenchies will take is what they get in hell, where me dear major is sendin' them as fast as possible. Besides, what soldier is blind enough to make amours to me?"

"But you can't abandon Lady Milholme," Tommy urged as a last argument.

"Get along with your nonsense! Hawkins can do for her better than me; and her own daughter along as well. Besides, who would tell his lordship and Sergeant Hawkins what's become of their wives, if they was to come home after layin' the Frenchies out and find them missing. And the O'Cassidy."

He saw now why the major loved her, horse-face and leathery skin and angles where curves should be. He wanted to tell her he thought she was grand. But all he could say was, "I hope Major O'Cassidy gets home safely."

" 'Tis a generous thought, and him your enemy," she replied. "Get along now—go with God like the good doctor told ye." But, for a minute, her sinewy arm closed around his shoulders until he thought the bones would crack.

Tommy rode on the seat beside the carter, where his fluent French would be useful if they met patrols. Reilly and Booby rode inside with the women. As the driver clucked to his horse and the cart pulled out, Mrs. O'Cassidy waved from the veranda, a lonely figure, little more than a shadow in the light from the window. The mistiness that welled up in his eyes turned the house and the lonely figure into a golden blur of lamplight, so that Tommy could no longer see her. But he waved, and waved again as the cart swung into the street.

CHAPTER TWENTY-ONE

THE LONGBOAT rocked gently in an easy ground swell. Lady Milholme stirred restlessly on her mattress, on the floor boards in the stern sheets. Hawkins dipped a cloth overside and dampened the fevered woman's forehead, wet it again and laid it, cool and dripping, on Lady Milholme's face. Denise, her head pillowed on Tommy's shoulder, slept.

The mid-watch was nearly at an end. *Princess* had not come.

The trip from Basseterre had been uneventful. Twice they had been stopped by patrols, but Tommy's french, and the password given him for his visit to M. de Bouillé's headquarters, had got them through without inspection. And, since the carter knew a cut-off to the beach, they had not actually passed through French picket lines. The strand where he had brought them seemed rather far for signaling to the boat, but not long after they had shown a lanthorn the boat came in. And with so many to help, it had not been difficult to move Lady Milholme without disturbing her.

But now, after everything had gone so perfectly, *Princess* had not come.

The men talked in whispers, tense, uneasy. "Why ain't them sodjers on the hill shootin' tonight?" Metzger demanded.

"Whyfor dey be shootin'?" Booby asked. "Suppose they cain't see nuthin'?"

"To light up the wreck's masts, you dumb bastard," Metzger said.

"Whyfor?"

"So Gascoyne can find his way back. Why else?"

One of the Bretons spoke up. "Ver' fine sailor, Gascoyne. Of the best. He will come."

"He'd better hurry," Metzger grumbled. There remained, at the most, two hours of darkness.

Reilly came and sat beside Tommy. "What do you think, Reilly?" Tommy asked.

"Faith, an' what do I not! He might 'uve put the little ship ashore, holdin' close to the land to keep as far as can be from the British. Or they might 'uve caught him yesterday morning when he was getting out."

"Or tonight, trying to get back," Tommy added.

"Just so, sor."

They sat in thoughtful silence for a few moments before Tommy said, "At daylight, if he hasn't come, we'll have to take Lady Milholme out to the British flagship."

"Or ashore to French headquarters, sor," Reilly said.

"We can't do that," Tommy argued. "They'll send her to the pesthouse."

"An' us to prison, if we go out to Admiral Hood," Reilly said.

"You don't have to go, Reilly," Tommy told him.

"Ach, now, sor. We'll leave the Frenchies swim ashore, an' Metzger an' Booby an' me can pull the boat out."

"Ship acomin', Mist' Tommy!" Booby's black skin concealed him in the darkness, but from his voice he was standing on the wreck's submerged deck.

"Do you see her?" Tommy asked.

"Hears her," Booby answered. "Feels her too."

No one else did. Nor could they see anything approaching.

"He's got a nightmare," Metzger growled.

"I feels her through de water," Booby insisted. "Close."

In but a few moments they saw the curl of a phosphorescent

bow wave and a smoky-white streak along a waterline. A ship was passing to seaward of them toward Basseterre.

"Best show a light, sor, afore she passes us," Reilly suggested.

"Supposed it ain't our ship," Metzger objected. "Maybe *Bull-dog*, sniffin' round. Or *Growler*."

"Stow the talk," Tommy ordered. "Show a light."

They had kept the lanthorn lighted, hooded with a piece of canvas. Reilly pulled the screen from it and showed the light above the gunnel. He lowered it, showed it again, and once again. Then he rehooded it. The bow wave had begun swinging toward them.

They heard the rustle of lowering canvas, and the streak of phosphorescence faded. They sat tensely waiting, wondering: friend or foe?

Then, out of the darkness, came Gascoyne's voice: "*Mon ami!* Are you ready?"

"Ready," Tommy answered.

"Come alongside then. Be quick."

Many hands reached down to receive the lifted mattress. "Careful," Tommy cautioned. "The lady is very sick."

Denise went next, and Hawkins, and after them the scrambling men, as falls were hooked on and the boat hoisted, with *Princess* already moving through the water, sail set again.

"I was afraid something had happened," Tommy said.

Gascoyne did not reply for a moment, intent on the ship and sails. "We must hold close to the land," he finally said. "There's a patrol between shore and the British fleet."

"That's what delayed you?" Tommy asked.

"Three times I tried to slip past, but each time there was a brig blocking us."

"But they couldn't have seen you," Tommy argued. "You showed no lights."

"He can smell," Gascoyne answered. "It is that damned *Bull-dog!*"

"Do you think he actually saw you?"

"Tonight, no. But yesterday morning—I think so. Dawn caught

SEA ROAD TO YORKTOWN   261

us before we had turned the island. I recognized him. Would
he not recognize us?"

"He will never forget us," Tommy said.

They held close, smelling the sulphur off the land, and before
dawn unmasked them, they were off the northern end of the
island. Eastward the sky brightened suddenly: first lemon, then
orange, then bright gold. The morning light caught the bold
white cliff at the south end of St. Eustatius, five miles to the
north. The channel between the two islands was clear of ships.
But astern, a long way back near Sandy Point, they saw the sails
of a brig.

"Can he see us, do you think?" Tommy asked.

"In this light?" Gascoyne replied. "But of course. He will
never catch us, though. We are too far to wind'ard."

No ship could give *Princess* that much head start and catch
her on a beat to windward. Tension eased. The cook lighted
his galley fire. An appetizing smell of breakfast drifted through
the ship.

In the cuddy, Lady Milholme was asleep in a swinging cot,
with Denise beside her on a bed made up on the quartermaster's
chest. Hawkins had been given one of the tiny rooms below.

A few hours' run down the Atlantic side of St. Kitts, which
now lay between them and *Bulldog*, and they would be at Nevis.
They had reached Black Rocks, a massive length of old lava flow
creamed by Atlantic breakers, halfway down the island, when
someone yelled, "Look aft there!"

Moments earlier they had passed through a rain squall, and
now, astern, driving out of it they saw a brig. The sight brought
men huddling, pointing, arguing. Some crossed themselves.
Superstition lay heavily across the deck; did the *Bulldog* have
supernatural power to hound them wherever they went?

"Is ut blind ye are," Reilly scolded, "as well as stupid? 'Tis
not *Bulldog* at all. Yon's got a tall mainm'st; *Bulldog's* is short,
since we shot it down that time at Parham Bay."

They might not have understood his English, but they felt his
confidence.

"The dogs hunt in pairs," Gascoyne said. "But *Bulldog* or *Growler, mes enfants,* we have a brig to fight."

Before the wind, as they were running, the square-sailed brig had the advantage of them.

"She must have been lying in Deep Bay," Tommy conjectured.

She could not otherwise have appeared so close to them, even though visibility had been low in the rain squalls. They had not seen her, passing the entrance to the bay, but she had seen them. And now she was in full chase. Stunsails blossomed at the end of every yard, filling out a towering rectangle of canvas that dwarfed the small hull carrying it.

"This is bad, *mon ami,*" Gascoyne said. "Get all hands up."

They hauled the main boom across to sail "wing and wing," but still the brig gained.

They got a spare jib up from the sail locker and rigged it on a sprit on the foremast to balloon out opposite the other head-sails.

Now they held their own; but that was not good enough. A sail blowing out of its gaskets, a parted halyard, a yard sprung by strain, and the brig would be at gun range in no time. They manned the wash-deck pumps and wet down the sails, so that no breath of wind could escape through the porous canvas. They began to gain a little.

Charleston, the capital of Nevis, lay two-thirds of the way down the western shore. To reach it, they must swing southwest through the Narrows, a passage between Nevis and St. Kitts. There were coastal towns closer, but only at Charleston were they likely to find a hospital. And if they should find none, surely Government House would give sanctuary to an English peer's wife.

Gascoyne did not turn into the Narrows immediately upon passing Scotch Bonnet at the southern end of St. Kitts. He held on until nearly in mid-channel, in this way keeping the full strength of the wind. The brig made the mistake of trying to cut across and, soon blanketed by the island, lost her wind and valuable time with it, getting out into mid-channel where her sails would draw full again.

Meanwhile, *Princess* was booming along with a margin of safety to clear the corner of Nevis. They would set Lady Milholme ashore at Charleston and be out, running for the cover of their own fleet's guns before the brig got there.

"There's anither brig standin' clear o' Nag's Head, sor," Reilly reported.

This brig was coming around from the western side of St. Kitts. It was *Bulldog*, there could be no doubt, since her mainmast was shorter than it should be. Commander Ransom's strategy was apparent; knowing that *Growler* was patrolling the Atlantic side, he had not bothered to chase *Princess*, seeing her go north about St. Kitts. Instead, he had run south as fast as possible to cut through the Narrows and intercept her there.

Princess was trapped in a channel only three miles wide, and a more powerful enemy was blocking each end.

Gascoyne looked at Tommy. "We cannot fight with the ladies aboard," he said. "If we set them adrift in the longboat they would be picked up."

"I think it would kill Lady Milholme."

"Then we must surrender," Gascoyne said. "She would never live through a battle."

"We could try Newcastle," Tommy suggested.

"It is very small. There would be no hospital."

"At least we could get her ashore, into the hands of English people. And then run for it ourselves."

"And fight a little too, eh?" Gascoyne answered and gave an order.

Newcastle, as they ran down to it, grew out of the foreshore: a cluster of houses, the smokestack of a sugar mill and the compound buildings; and beyond, the green and gold of cane fields on the lower slopes of Mt. Nevis.

"No shore batteries," Tommy reported, studying the shoreline through the long glass. "No ships at anchor."

Here vessels must load in an open roadstead: a shallow crescent of bay between two projecting points of land. Yet it was well sheltered from ocean rollers and northerly storms by neighboring St. Kitts, just across the Narrows.

"Man the longboat, Reilly," Gascoyne ordered. To Tommy he said, "Come." They went into the cuddy together.

"Are we nearly there, Tommy?" Denise inquired as they entered. Earlier, he had told her of the plan to land at Charleston.

"It has to be Newcastle," he replied. "There are two brigs chasing us."

His voice aroused Lady Milholme. "Is that you, Tommy?" It was the first time she had seemed aware of him."

"Yes, ma'am."

"Do not risk your ship for me," she said. "Newcastle will do—anywhere. But don't let Commander Ransom catch you."

"Permit me, madame," Gascoyne said. "There is not much time." His fingers searched for her pulse and, satisfied with what his fingers told him, he bent and gathered Lady Milholme in his arms and carried her from the cuddy.

They placed the mattress in the longboat and laid her on it, and Denise and Hawkins got in beside her, and the crew got in and readied their oars. When *Princess* rounded to off the wharf, they lowered the boat and cast it off the moment it took the water.

"Do not go into the town, lest they take you prisoner," Gascoyne called as the boat pulled away, with Tommy at the tiller and Reilly setting a stroke that bent the ash blades. "Only on the wharf."

Townsfolk were gathering at waterside: a mixture of white, black, and brown, drawn by the sight of three strange sails bearing down on their quiet harbor. On the village green, troops were assembling. Some wore uniforms, some only military headgear or tunic. Some were distinguished as soldiers only by the muskets which they awkwardly shouldered. A few were hitching mules to several pieces of field artillery.

When the men carried the mattress with Lady Milholme up

the green-slimed landing stairs, the crowd watched with idle curiosity, exchanging comment among themselves, but no one made an objection. A detachment of the militia was marching toward the wharf, the noncommissioned officer in charge "hup-hupping" in a futile effort to keep them in step. Late arrivals came running after the men in ranks, muskets at trail or tucked under their arms like fowling pieces. Clearly an alarm had been sounded in the town, and the workers of the sugar *atelier* were turning out to repel invasion.

Tommy faced the villagers. "Is there a hospital here?" he asked.

Someone laughed. "Here?" And a man said, "Nearest is Charleston. Close on eight mile. Bad road."

Hawkins bristled. "Her ladyship ain't movin' eight miles. If there ain't a hospital in this town, some kind soul has got to take her in."

"There's a nurse, here," the man said. "Nurse an' midwife. Knows a lot about sickness, Nurse Simpson do."

Tommy said, "You must find her, Denise." He faced the crowd again. "I'll thank someone to take this young lady to Nurse Simpson."

"Happen I can," a man offered. "I be goin' that way."

Denise hesitated. Reilly had brought a piece of canvas from the boat, and Booby had collared several black boys and posted them like awning stanchions, holding the canvas to give Lady Milholme a patch of shade. Hawkins waved the flies from the sick woman's face with a palm leaf.

"Dare I leave her, Tommy?" Denise asked.

"I'll be here with Hawkins," Tommy assured her.

"Come along, miss," urged the man who had offered to take her.

So they hurried away together, passing a detachment of militia coming onto the wharf as they left it.

Hawkins said, "Lawks, sir, ain't you done enough? I'll see to her ladyship; you'd best clear out afore those soldiers get here."

"Whyfor dey call de army out?" Booby brooded. "Scared o' harmless folks like us?"

"Brimstone Hill has surrendered," a man replied. "Old de Grasse will be after this island next. That's who we thought it was when we seen your ships comin' in."

The brigs were very close. "They'll not fire on *Princess*," Tommy said, "lest they damage the town."

"Just the same, sor," Reilly urged, "we'd best get back aboard afore these play soldiers make us trouble."

"Get the men in the boat," Tommy agreed. "I'll be along in a minute." He spoke to Hawkins. "Take good care of her—of both of them."

"Don't bother your head about us now, sir," Hawkins replied. "We're with our own people. Look out for yourself."

From the top of the stairs Reilly was calling, "Come along, sor, for the love of God!"

Tommy knelt beside the mattress and kissed Lady Milholme's forehead. "Debby?" she murmured.

"Everything will be all right now," he told her. "You'll soon be well."

"Debby? Is it really you?"

If it would comfort her to think he was her son . . . "Yes, dear."

"Thank God you're home." She sighed. "These frightful, frightful wars."

The soldiers were close now. Tommy kissed her again and ran for the stairs.

When the boat was clear, he ordered the crew to lay on oars, waiting to see what the militia would do. The formation broke ranks. Several men, having bent over the mattress, drew away. One of them began shouting at the boat.

"Sergeant Busby here," he yelled. "You can't put sick ashore without a medical certificate—against this harbor's rules o' quarantine."

"Never mind the rules," Tommy shouted back. "Just take care of her, that's all."

"Suppose she's got the plague?"

"She's only got a fever," Tommy assured him.

"What kind of fever—yellow?"

"Just fever. Nothing contagious."

The sergeant conferred with his men. Then he ordered, "You come back here and take her away, else she stays right here in the heat an' flies. There's not a man will touch that mattress."

"We'll have to go back, Reilly," Tommy said. Reilly already had the boat swinging.

Tommy did not know just what he was going to do; he knew only that he could not leave a sick woman in such unfriendly hands.

"Lie off, Reilly," he ordered. "Better I swim for it than have them take the boat."

"Remimber this, sor," Reilly counseled. "'Tis no time for fightin', at all. If they won't listen to reason, bring her ladyship back on board."

They could do that, of course. But Denise? Leave her!

The brigs, having driven their quarry into a cul-de-sac, were proceeding with caution. *Growler* had hove to off the eastern point, *Bulldog* off the western. No matter how *Princess* might double back, toward the Atlantic or the Caribbean, one of them would be lying athwart her course.

Tommy ran quickly up the landing stairs, facing, at the top, a ring of threatening faces. The field pieces were rumbling along the shore road, drivers lashing the mules into a gallop. Opposite *Princess*, they wheeled and began to unlimber. It was a big day for the militia.

"Now see here," Tommy began firmly, "you can't really mean you'd leave this lady to die in the sun. She is Lady Milholme, the wife of Captain Lord Milholme, a countryman of yours."

"Catch yellow fever as easy from a lord's lady as from a scullery wench," the sergeant replied.

Hawkins stopped fanning Lady Milholme and stood up. "First time I was ever ashamed of bein' English," she fumed. "While our men was fightin' atop Brimstone Hill, our enemies come along an' risk their lives savin' us, only to have our own people turn us away."

"Enemies?" Sergeant Busby demanded. "Bean't you English?"

"I'm an American," Tommy answered boldly, "from a French ship."

"Seize him, lads!" the sergeant ordered importantly.

His men were not all of the same mind. "If they was kind enough to bring her ladyship here, like this woman just said—" one of them began.

But the sergeant cut him off: "If you won't take my orders, you'll take the major's."

The major came bustling up: a country squire in uniform. His florid face was streaming in the heat, and he was puffing from pompousness and overeating.

"What's all the row here?" he demanded.

"Sergeant says to seize this here good samaritan," one of the men replied.

"Nonsense," the major said. "Allow me," he said to Tommy. "I am Major Smith-Boulton, magistrate here, plantation owner and all that. I talked to the young lady in the village. She'll be along straight off with Nurse Simpson."

Tommy could see Denise and a woman coming from town

"Can't see why a man who dumps a cargo o' yellow fever on our wharf should be kindly treated," Sergeant Busby grumbled.

"I've told you her ladyship hasn't yellow fever," Tommy insisted.

"I seen him kiss her," one of the onlookers volunteered. "Not likely he'd do that if she had yellow."

"Kissed her twicet," a woman added. She bent over Lady Milholme to observe her, a friendly gesture, showing that she did not fear contagion. "Seems like we could do something for her, poor soul."

"We shall," the major announced. "She's to be taken up to Boulton Manor at once."

Denise arrived then and came straight to Tommy, while Nurse Simpson gave her attention to Lady Milholme. "Oh, Tommy," Denise reproached him, "why didn't you leave before the soldiers came?"

"He did, mum," Hawkins told her. "Left an' come back, of his own free will."

"Just like you, Tommy!" Denise exclaimed.

"Could I leave your mother here on the wharf?" Tommy asked. "The sergeant said no one would so much as touch her mattress."

"They'll touch it right enough," Smith-Boulton said. "Here, some of you, lift that mattress up."

Some hung back, more fearful of contagion than of the major's wrath; but enough stepped forward.

"Gently now," the major ordered. "Take her straight up to Boulton Manor. Nurse Simpson will see to her." He turned to Tommy. "Your charges will stop with us, sir, until her ladyship is better. As for you, I suggest you clear out as fast as you can."

"Just a moment there," Sergeant Busby objected. "All well an' good—'ee didn't bring yellow fever. An' no one says the major can't turn his home inter a hospital, if he's a mind to. But no matter what favors this man's done the ladies, he's still an enemy o' the King."

"My good fellow," Smith-Boulton observed condescendingly, "I think those two men-of-war lying outside can take care of the King's enemies without our help."

"But he might be killed!" Denise protested. "That terrible Captain Ransom might hang them all as rebels."

"Just so," Smith-Boulton agreed. "So I suggest, sir, that you surrender to me. Your boat crew as well. We'll treat you decently here, I'll see to that. Prisoners of war. Parole if you like. Better than being sunk, or God knows what, as her young ladyship has just said."

"Thank you, sir," Tommy answered. "But if you'll permit me, I prefer a fighting chance."

The men were carrying Lady Milholme shoreward along the wharf, three on each side, the black boys proudly holding the canvas above her—a canopy shading a potentate. Nurse Simpson walked beside the mattress, her fingers on Lady Milholme's pulse. Hawkins waved her palm leaf to keep the flies away.

A cannon shot reverberated across the harbor. A cloud of smoke belched from *Bulldog*'s side, and an answering cloud of dust flew up from a field beyond the town where the ball, having hit short of *Princess* and ricocheted, buried itself.

"The blasted fool!" Smith-Boulton stormed. "Has he no better sense than fire into town! Best get your ship out of here, young man, before he knocks a building down."

"Aye, aye, sir," Tommy answered, and sprinted for the stairs.

At the top, he turned for a last wave. Denise touched her fingers to her lips. He ran down to the waiting boat.

Princess was sweeping shoreward in a wide turning circle to meet the boat; and with falls quickly hooked on, men on deck ran it up with the crew still in it, while others were crowding on sail.

Gascoyne gave Tommy a brief glance. "Trouble ashore, *mon ami?*" But his eyes went quickly back to the brigs and the sails, and his thoughts to how best they could escape.

"They're in good hands," Tommy told him. "There's a decent major there, magistrate of the town and leading citizen. He's taken them in."

"Splendid!" Gascoyne said. "We'll head for *Bulldog*—if he wants revenge, we shall give it to him."

"The major wanted me to surrender to him," Tommy continued. "He said we'd do better with him than getting sunk."

Gascoyne laughed.

"They say Brimstone Hill has surrendered," Tommy told him.

"*Magnifique!*" Gascoyne said.

Bulldog, as *Princess* approached, tried a ranging shot. Short. *Growler* held her position off the eastern point, alert against *Princess*'s doubling back to escape into the Atlantic. Her chances were better in that direction, but it did not suit Gascoyne's plan.

There was a question, though, of clearing the western point. If they should be obliged to come about, the ship would lose way at the moment of coming into the wind before paying off on the new tack. At that moment of turning, her guns would be idled, while the ship would present an almost stationary target. It could mean disaster. Yet with Reilly at the wheel, if the wind did not fly around and catch them aback, there was every chance.

But the closer they came to the point, the more evident it became that *Princess* would not clear.

"We must get sea room!" Gascoyne exclaimed. "Hands by sheets and braces!"

Bulldog had not been firing. There was no use wasting ammunition, scarce on a foreign station, when the enemy was obligingly closing the range. But as the tacks lifted when the helm went down, making it plain that *Princess* was coming about, *Bulldog*'s guns opened fire again.

Princess, as nimble as ever came into the wind at the first touch of rudder. Never had she hung in stays, her head refusing to go through the wind and pay off. No one gave a thought to such a possibility. But at the critical moment, the headsails— inner and outer jib and fore-topmast staysail—came down with a run.

Gascoyne shouted, "I gave no orders to cast off halyards."

Metzger, leading some men to get the sails hoisted again, shouted back, "They wasn't cast off, sir—these halyards was cut."

And they knew, aft, that Pierre Duroc had done it, when they saw men grappling with him.

"We'll see to him later," Gascoyne said. "Now we must save our ship."

With headsails gone, crabbing off to leeward, it was clear they could not finish the maneuver until new halliards were rove off or the cut ones spliced. There wasn't time for that. They must turn away from the wind and run down toward *Growler*, making repairs in the short interval they would have.

"Up helm!" Gascoyne ordered.

To wear ship, turning away from the wind, meant swinging toward the land, too finely cut in the beginning, dangerously close now from their drift to leeward. But there was no choice.

Shadowed water warned of a shoal beneath the keel. How close? A jarring thud told them. Had she cleared? A shudder through her timbers from stem to stern answered that. *Princess* was hard aground. She lay over on her side.

The world of Thomas Potter seemed to be ending. *Princess* was dying. Clinging to a pin rail to keep from sliding down her steeply canted deck, Tommy saw her larboard guns pointing skyward! her starboard battery was submerged. She was defenseless. And he could not help her.

Bulldog eased in, firing unhurriedly. A near miss splashed water in Tommy's face without his feeling it. He could not move.

Gascoyne called, "Bring a white flag, Angel." His face was as white as the flag which Angel brought from the cuddy. The Spanish boy was sobbing, and his hands trembled so that he could not bend on the halyards. Reilly snatched it from him and bent the halyards on.

Where a cannon shot had not, this sight restored life to Tommy. "No!" he shouted. "No, Reilly! Don't!"

The tough old seaman looked to Gascoyne for instructions.

"*Mon ami,*" Gascoyne said, his voice vibrant with his passion, "we cannot watch our ship be smashed to galley firewood."

Reilly hauled the white flag of surrender to the masthead.

The field pieces were charging along the strand at a mad gallop. Ahead of them, at an even madder pace, rode the portly figure of Major Smith-Boulton. But Gascoyne did not see them. He stood, braced between the deckhouse and the high rail, looking forward along the deck he had so often trod. He seemed unaware of the excitement around him: men running back and forth, getting their sea bags and their prized trinkets. Pierre Lebecque came on deck carrying the *chapelle* with the Holy Virgin.

"Gascoyne," Tommy said, putting a hand on his captain's arm. "We'll get another ship."

"Another ship? Of course. But not this ship. Not this beauty we have sailed so well, and I have put ashore."

"You did not," Tommy said. "It was Pierre Duroc."

"True. Yet I could have sailed her without trouble into the

Atlantic. Only I wanted to lead them into the Caribbean, under our own fleet's guns. I tried to get too much, *mon ami.*"

"Don't forget that you saved Lady Milholme," Tommy reminded him.

"That Duroc!" Gascoyne exclaimed. "I will kill him!" He held his hands before him, staring at them as if seeing them squeeze out Duroc's life.

"It won't bring back our ship," Tommy said.

Some of the crew were quitting her, climbing over the rail into the small surf and wading shoreward. Others stood, looking aft, waiting the captain's orders.

"We'd better surrender to the major," Tommy suggested. "He will treat us as prisoners of war—not as rebels or pirates."

"I do not care," Gascoyne replied. "Do as you wish."

Tommy took a last look at *Princess,* her sails slatting idly, the low side of her main deck under water. He thought of going below to get a few belongings, but the mental vision of the cabin where he had spent so many hours, flooded, a shambles of disorder, was more than he could face.

Then he saw Reilly. His quadrant, for which the old seaman had fashioned a canvas cover when the mahogany case was given for the Virgin, swung from one hand; his sea chest balanced on one shoulder.

"Abandon ship!" Tommy ordered. The words almost choked him.

He left the ship last, except for Gascoyne, and, having climbed over the rail into the water, he did not look back.

CHAPTER TWENTY-TWO

THE ARTILLERY had unlimbered and the guns were trained on the stranded *Princess,* as if, by some miracle, she might right herself and get clear of the shoal, again in fighting trim. The infantry was slogging down the beach at double-time, a straggling horde.

Major Smith-Boulton sat his horse watching the shipwrecked men muster on the strand. There should have been forty of them. Tommy made it thirty-nine.

"One man is missing," he reported to Gascoyne.

"Duroc?" Gascoyne called. "Step out, Pierre Duroc!" But Duroc did not step out. "Where is he?" Gascoyne demanded of Pierre Lebecque.

"It is he who cut the halyards, *mon capitaine*," Lebecque replied. "He killed our ship."

"That I did not ask," Gascoyne flared. "I asked: where is Pierre Duroc?"

"*Mon capitaine*," Pierre Lebecque began, "in the compartment where we had our Holy Virgin the hull is bilged. Much water enters. By now it will be higher than a tall man's head. Pierre Duroc is short."

"Since when have you become captain that you pass judgment?" Gascoyne demanded. "And execute it also."

"He was a traitor, *mon capitaine*. He killed our ship."

"I am captain here, Pierre Lebecque," Gascoyne stormed, his fury almost uncontrolled. "I pass the judgments; I, only, have the right to execute them."

"It was the Judgment of Oléron, monsieur," Lebecque answered calmly, "which is above even captains. By the Judgment of Oléron he sinned; by them he died."

Major Smith-Boulton was becoming impatient. "Now see here, you men," he interrupted, "what's all the jabbering about?"

"We were making sure to see that all our men are safe ashore, monsieur," Gascoyne replied.

"And—"

"We are present, monsieur—all of mine."

The Major gave an order; they started back to town. Smith-Boulton rode slowly ahead; his militiamen, hot and winded from their double-time down the strand, plodded wearily beside the shipwrecked men. These walked dejectedly—sailors who had lost

their ship. All except Lebecque, who carried the statue of the
Holy Virgin. She seemed to give him courage. He walked
proudly, head erect.

When they reached the town, the whole populace had turned
out. Even the slaves from the cane fields and the sugar mill
had come down to see a sight that had never before come to
this coastal town. It was cause for holiday, this stranding of an
enemy ship and the capture of her crew. Yet the crowd did not
seem to be in a holiday mood. A few jeered, and there were
some jibes of "Pirate!" and "Corsair!" But there were friendly
greetings also. More than the catcalls and insults came "Bravo!"
and "Good lads, you Americans!" and "Come back some day and
trade with us!"

Until this war, there had been good trade between Nevis and
the American Colonies. The banning of this commercial interchange by English laws had caused great bitterness toward the
mother land, as it had on other British islands. Freedom-loving
themselves, these watchers caught a reflection of their own
future mirrored in the faces of these shipwrecked men.

When Pierre Lebecque passed, carrying the *chapelle*, men
removed their palm-thatch hats; women curtsied and crossed
themselves.

H.M.S. *Bulldog* had come to an anchor off the town, shun-
ning the water near *Princess* lest she get aground herself. Two
boats were coming in, sand-scrubbed oak blades flashing in the
bright sunlight, which sparkled on buckles and polished buttons. A naval lieutenant disembarked on the wharf and, with a
sergeant and a squad of marines, came double-timing toward
the village green, where Major Smith-Boulton had brought his
motley company to a halt.

The major sat his horse, looking apprehensive as the detachment from the warship approached. The lieutenant at once began
giving orders. "Two ranks now! Quick now! Search the prisoners,
sergeant."

"See here, sir," Major Smith-Boulton objected. "I'm in command here. There's no need to search these men."

"Not a firearm in the lot," Sergeant Busby growled, offended at this intrusion. "I'm not a big enough fool to miss that."

"Indeed?" the lieutenant observed with a cool stare.

But the marines stopped searching to await further orders. The lieutenant addressed Smith-Boulton with thinly veiled insolence. "I beg to disagree with your statement that you command here. Since, you might say, this is a joint expedition, and my captain is senior in rank, it is he who commands. His orders are to bring off the prisoners—every one of them." He transferred his drilling glance to Gascoyne. "This one above all."

"Well, now!" the major puffed. "I call this most outrageous. I'll not tolerate it for one moment."

"In that case," the lieutenant told him, "I suggest you go aboard and protest to Commander Ransom. His orders allow me no leeway. 'Bring the prisoners aboard,' he said. 'Aboard— dead or alive.' "

"Go see him I shall," Smith-Boulton fumed. "I'll have no whippersnapper naval leftenant giving orders in a town where I am magistrate and commander of militia."

"Do," the lieutenant replied icily. "One of the boats at the wharf will take you off." Then, completely ignoring the irate major, "Get on with it, sergeant of marines," he ordered. "Search these men."

As the marines resumed their searching, Major Smith-Boulton spurred his horse and rode off toward the wharf.

" 'Ere now!" the sergeant of marines exclaimed, noticing the *chapelle* which Lebecque held. "What's that yer 'oldin' in yer bloody 'and, proud like?"

The lieutenant, attracted by this remark, moved toward Lebecque to see for himself. "Blessed if it ain't a beautiful mahogany quadrant case," he observed. "Hand it over, my man."

But when he reached for it, Pierre Lebecque drew back. "*Jamais!*"

Gascoyne said, "In case you do not understand French, monsieur, Pierre Lebecque said, 'Never!' "

"I understood well enough," the lieutenant flared. "He'd better understand that I'll tolerate no impudence."

"He was not impudent, monsieur," Gascoyne persisted. "In the box is a statue of the Holy Virgin. She is not Pierre Lebecque's property to give. She is ours—all of us. She is our faith—our belief in God. Pierre Lebecque cannot give it. You cannot take it— while we live."

Hearing him, the crowd set up a cheer. Even the militiamen bristled with resentment at this threat of sacrilege. The sergeant of marines looked troubled: he had but a squad. "Best leave be, sir," he suggested.

"Very well," the lieutenant petulantly agreed. His eyes, searching for other game, fell upon Tommy's sea chest at Reilly's feet.

"Whose statue might be in that?" he asked bitingly and kicked the chest with his boot.

" 'Tis me officer's gear in ut," Reilly answered.

"Since he's no longer an officer," the lieutenant said, "he'll not be permitted a chest on board. Get rid of it."

"Rid of ut?" Reilly inquired amiably. "Will ye tell me how— wid your marines standin' guard all around?"

The lieutenant turned to the crowd. "Anyone care for an officer's sea chest?" he called.

A man reached quickly for it, but Reilly stamped on the grasping hand; and although the old sailor's feet were bare, they could hear the knuckle bones crack. The man reared back with an oath.

"Reilly!" Tommy cautioned.

" 'Tis outrageous plunder, sor. Would ye have that, now?"

Through the crowd, Tommy saw Denise, with Hawkins beside her elbowing her way through. "We want no trouble, Reilly," he said. "Give the chest up."

Reilly pushed the chest away from him toward the crowd with his foot. But no one else moved to take it.

The lieutenant now caught sight of the canvas bag in which Reilly was carrying Tommy's quadrant. "And what might this be?" he demanded.

"Me officer's quadrant."

"He'll not be shooting the sun very often, I expect," the lieutenant said. "Not in prisoners' hold. Hand it over."

"That I'll not," Reilly replied, tightening his grip on the bag.

The lieutenant moved to take it; Reilly moved away, swinging it in the manner of a truncheon. "I'll hand it over your skull, if ye move closer," he threatened.

"Sergeant of marines!" the lieutenant shouted.

But Tommy calmed the troubled waters. "Give it to him, Reilly. I can get another quadrant."

"*C'est ça*," Gascoyne agreed. "A quadrant can be replaced— but not a life."

The sergeant of marines moved toward Reilly. It was then that Denise broke through the circle, with Hawkins, white-faced and anxious, close behind. Denise planted herself squarely before the sergeant. Her hair, in the sunshine, seemed an angry flame; her eyes were the green of a stormy sea; her breasts heaved with the depth of her emotion.

"Don't you dare touch that quadrant," she ordered.

"Now see 'ere, miss!" the sergeant blustered. "See 'ere now! None o' yer sauce!"

He seized her arm and tried to force her aside. She kicked him hard, and while he was bending to rub his wounded shins, she gripped the haft of his cutlass and pulled it from its scabbard.

"Now then!" she invited.

The lieutenant seemed struck dumb. But his bulging eyes spoke feelingly. Gascoyne exclaimed, "But this *gamine* of yours has spirit, *mon ami!*"

"Reilly," Denise said, "I'll thank you for that quadrant."

"Aye, aye, Your Ladyship." Reilly handed it over.

"Now then," Denise told the sergeant, quadrant in one hand, cutlass in the other, "take it from me. But if you do—" she included the lieutenant in her glance—"if anyone does, you'll answer to my father, Captain the Lord Milholme, Royal Navy."

The crowd roared its delight. The sergeant of marines said, "Let's 'op it, sir."

"Prisoners 'tenshun!" the lieutenant shouted. "Two ranks now. Ready!"

"I'll thankee for me cutlass, miss," the chastened sergeant said.

Denise tossed the blade to him, haft up, point to the ground. He caught it deftly, and sent back, in return, a look of open admiration.

"March off the prisoners!" the lieutenant ordered sharply.

"Just a moment," Denise called. "In case you're leaving with any idea that civilians also plunder, I want you to know that I'll keep this until Ensign Potter comes for it. We're to be married one day."

Red-faced, the lieutenant ordered, "Forward march!" But the men still stood.

Hawkins shouldered Tommy's sea chest. "I'll keep this, too, sir, waitin' your return. The Lord bless an' keep you."

"*Mes enfants,*" Gascoyne said, "march on. We shall have our ship again one day. Our Tommy's lady will watch over her while we are gone."

The prisoners no longer wore a hangdog look. The saving of the *chapelle* and the sea chest and the quadrant seemed almost victory. They marched with their heads held high. "What beauty!" they said. "What courage!" "How our Tommy is a lucky man to have her for wife!"

The crowd cheered the prisoners, marching to the wharf. They jeered the British marines and shouted rude jibes. Denise walked beside Tommy, the quadrant swinging in one hand, the other tightly in his grip.

"We *shall* be married one day, shan't we, Tommy?" she asked.

How in God's name? Without a ship, now he surely would go home to France. "Of course," he answered.

"And I will look after your ship, Gascoyne," Denise went on. "Truly I will. I'll stand guard every day to see there'll be no looting."

"*Mon dieu,*" Gascoyne said, "I believe you, if you have a cutlass."

"At least," Tommy said, "she's got my quadrant."

"I'll practice using it while you're away, Tommy," she promised. "So I can take sights when I sail with you."

Gascoyne laughed. "Take care, *mon ami,* lest she become captain over you."

"I'll be captain of *Princess* while you're gone," she said. "I'll make Major Smith-Boulton keep sentries guarding her, and I'll stand watch myself while Hawkins stays with mother."

They talked as if, in a matter of days, they would be back, as if *Princess* would be theirs again. They could not believe they had lost her forever.

"Silence in the ranks, you prisoners!" the sergeant bellowed. It cast the dark shadow of defeat and imprisonment across them. They walked silently.

At the wharf, the sergeant ordered, "Into the boats now. 'Op it! Tumble aboard!"

Denise blinked away a tear, and then another. The drops glistened on her cheeks.

"Don't, darling," Tommy begged. "Everything is all right. Your mother is being cared for, you're in safe hands, and Hawkins is here to help you."

"You know it isn't that," she said.

"If it's me you're worrying about," Tommy said, "don't. I'll be exchanged shortly."

"But darling, you'll have no ship."

"She'll still be here," Tommy said. "This bay is sheltered from northers. She's beached on sand. She won't break up."

"Oh, Tommy," Denise sobbed. She could play the game no longer.

"You said you'd watch over her," he reminded, putting his arm around her waist.

" 'Ere now, 'ere!" the sergeant blustered, pulling Tommy's arm away. "When I say 'op it, I means 'op it!"

A marine private muttered, "They could saw me bloody arm off first!"

"Can't we even say good-by, sergeant?" Denise begged. "Please."

"Lady," the sergeant grumbled, "you're distructin' discipline." He turned angrily on Gascoyne, prodding him sharply between the shoulders with his cutlass point. "'Op it, you Frog! You 'eard what the lieutenant said: the old bulldog hisself wants a word with you."

Gascoyne smiled. "You have envy, *n'est-ce pas?* Truly she is charming." He disengaged her hand from Tommy's, bowed and pressed it to his lips. "*Au 'voir, ma'm'selle.* Our ship is in your hands."

Tommy took her in his arms and kissed her through her tears.

As the cutters pulled out to the ship, they passed *Bulldog's* gig pulling ashore. In the stern sheets sat Major Smith-Boulton. His face was a bright magenta, his manner dark and brooding. As the boats passed, the lieutenant saluted. Smith-Boulton only glared.

"'Tis an omen," Reilly said.

"What is?" Tommy demanded.

"The lieutenant should be dead, the look the major give him."

But the lieutenant was very much alive. "Silence in the boat," he ordered. "Any more grumbling and I'll skin your hides off with sand and canvas, once we get aboard."

The marines, when they had climbed aboard, herded the prisoners on the well-deck, forward near the manger, where pigs and sheep were sometimes kept to provide fresh meat for the captain's table; or a cow or goats to give fresh milk. The prisoners' wrists were bound with marling, and their ankles hobbled with a thick hemp rope. Gascoyne and Tommy received no different treatment, but they had not been long aboard before Commander Ransom sent for them to be brought to the poop where, the brig now being under way, he was conning.

"Well," he said jovially when they stood before him. "We're going to have a practice shoot. I thought you might do well as pilots."

The two said nothing.

"Ammunition is scarce on foreign stations—you must be well aware of that," Ransom went on. "I don't want to waste powder and ball, firing at long range."

Still Gascoyne and Tommy remained silent.

"You understand? I want to get close enough to be sure no shot will miss. Not a single shot." He was drooling with pleasure at the thought.

Gascoyne said, "Why do you shoot if ammunition is so scarce?"

"I must keep my gunners practiced," Ransom replied. "Yet I must not risk my ship by stranding. And of course I shan't, now that you are here. You know these waters well. And why not? You have just run your ship ashore."

"*Mon dieu!*" Gascoyne exclaimed. And a groan escaped Tommy at the monstrous thing that Ransom was about to do.

As they talked *Bulldog* had been slipping lazily across the roadstead, until now she was opposite *Princess,* seaward of her a safe distance. "You will warn me, pilot Gascoyne, if my ship is running into shoal water," Commander Ransom jibed. "I trust you."

"You are a swine," said Gascoyne.

"Ready, gunners?"

"Ready, sir," the first lieutenant answered.

"Shoot!" Ransom ordered.

They fired at *Princess,* one gun at a time. All fell short.

"We must get closer," Ransom said, elated at his new-found torture. He brought the brig about and stood back on the other tack, exercising the opposite battery. He brought her in quite close. "I have heard nothing contrary from the pilot," he told his first lieutenant. "We must be safe."

"Shall we fire again, sir?" the first lieutenant asked.

"Do, please."

The ball hid *Princess* for a moment in a cloud of spray. They could not tell whether it was a near miss short, or a hit along the waterline.

"I cannot watch this," Gascoyne said and crossed the deck, keeping his back turned. Tommy followed.

"You can't look, eh?" Ransom gloated. "Well, I say you will, by God. Marines!"

The marines seized them and were dragging them across the

deck to make them watch, when the first lieutenant sang out, "There's a frigate standing into the Narrows, sir."

Not one frigate but two had come into plain sight around the corner of Nevis, coming up from the direction of Charleston. Ransom put his long glass on them. "French, by God!" he exclaimed.

"Secure from drill, sir?" the first lieutenant queried.

"Aye. And set all sail. We'll clear out of here through the eastern entrance."

They tacked out through the channel, with *Growler* following astern, and headed northward along St. Kitts in the Atlantic in reverse of the course sailed by *Princess* earlier that day when discovered by *Growler*. The French frigates were no longer in sight when the screen of darkness fell across the two brigs.

Tommy and Gascoyne had been returned to the prisoners on the well-deck, where, with a marine sentry above them on the forecastlehead, and another between them and the officers' part of the ship, there was small comfort.

"Is that bandy-legged bastard aft there going to starve us?" Metzger grumbled. The crew had been piped to supper, but the prisoners had been given nothing, not even water.

"Marine!" Gascoyne called.

"What's the row?" the sentry demanded.

"My men are hungry," Gascoyne told him. "We have had nothing to eat since early morning. Nor drink."

"Happen you'd like some wine, bein' Frogs?"

"But of course," said Gascoyne.

"Corporal o' the guard!" the sentry called.

"What's all the bloody row?" the corporal demanded, hurrying up.

"Prisoners got a complaint about their food," the sentry said.

"Sweet Christ, ain't we all!" the corporal bawled and disappeared.

"He's gone to fetch yer wine," the sentry said.

The men now began to growl like hungry wolves and pound

on the deck until the sentry warned, "Here now. Any more o' that an' you'll get a good full meal o' gunpowder."

But the racket brought the sergeant, and with him came the first lieutenant. They stood in a pallid circle of light from a dip lanthorn carried by the master-at-arms who was making first lieutenant's rounds with him. The "first" was a competent-looking seaman, but he wore a harried expression.

"Any more of this unholy racket," he said, "and I'll have you on bread and water."

"Splendid," said Gascoyne. "It is what I was about to ask."

"Irons?" the harried-looking first lieutenant asked.

"Bread," said Gascoyne.

The first lieutenant laughed unpleasantly. "Bread? My man, there's no bread in the fleet, nor any flour. Yams from shore, when we can get them, must take the place of bread. But we have hand and leg irons. Be silent now, lest you wear them."

He turned away, throwing a last word to the sergeant. "Give them a bucket of water from the scuttle butt, marine."

The water a marine fetched to them was so green and slimy that, thirsty and hardened as they were, they could not get it down. The few who did could not keep it down. There was little sleep that night, empty bellies rumbling, and rain squalls flooding the deck where they must lie.

Turning the north end of St. Kitts, they had the last of a clouded moon. There were no ships in sight. *Growler* had disappeared, probably to resume her station in Deep Bay. And when they got down toward Brimstone Hill they found it quiet.

Tommy said, "It's true then. The English have surrendered."

"Without doubt," Gascoyne agreed.

But Admiral Hood's fleet was still off Basseterre. They could see the myriad riding lights spread along the roadstead.

Bulldog hove to, not risking a closer approach to the fleet's guns lest they be mistaken for a foe. The watch on deck snugged down comfortably wherever they could. The sound of straining cordage and the sough of wind in canvas, and the watchman's cry tolling the passing hours were all they heard. "Six bells and all's well," the cry came. At seven bells, still all was well; and at eight. But dawn, breaking with the suddenness of a lifted curtain, roused the ship in an uproar. There was shouting and pointing and men running aloft the better to see. The noise brought the first lieutenant on deck, rubbing sleep from his eyes, stamping and storming around demanding what all the unholy excitement was about.

Tommy, standing on tiptoe to see across the bulwarks, saw that the anchorage off Basseterre was empty. The wooden wall of ships that had barred M. de Grasse from giving aid to his colleague ashore was gone. Where Hood's fleet had been, only boats rode at anchor, left there with lanthorns lighted to give the appearance of ships still moored.

"Stole away," Booby softly brooded. "Like a thief in de night dem British stole away."

"Non!" Gascoyne exclaimed. "It is that M. de Bouillé has captured Brimstone Hill. What remains now for a British fleet to do here?"

"It's what the Marquis promised," Tommy recalled, choking on his excitement. "'I will take Brimstone Hill, monsieur, within the week M. de Grasse has allowed me,' the Marquis said. 'You will be good enough to inform His Excellency of that when you return.'"

Gascoyne shrugged. "You are not likely to return to give that message, mon ami, but the situation speaks for itself."

Commander Ransom, his long glass tucked beneath an arm, his hair blowing wildly in a wind that ballooned his pants' legs, climbed heavily into the main rigging. Soon he began shouting orders from the maintop. "Up helm! All hands make sail!" He pointed southward. "Sir Sam's gone downwind, chasing the Frenchies off."

But the forest of masts and spars they soon raised from deck were not those of Sir Sam Hood. It was the fleet of the Count de Grasse, lying off Nevis, near Charleston, the capital.

Commander Ransom slid down a backstay fast as any midshipman. "Head up the Narrows," he shouted, and men ran to brace round the yards with the same alacrity that had brought their captain to the deck. Three French sail of the line were beating up toward them, up toward Hood's deserted anchorage.

While *Bulldog* was tacking through the Narrows, off Newcastle, when it seemed they would get clean away into the Atlantic, the two French frigates that had chased the afternoon before stood out from behind Scotch Bonnet.

Quickly Ransom swung his ship about and stood back toward the Caribbean. But there the three French ships lay athwart his course. *Bulldog* was in the same snare that had caught *Princess*. But this was worse: two frigates and three line-of-battle ships had sprung this trap.

Princess's men, weary, wet, and hungry as they were, watched delightedly, and when they cheered, no sentry threatened a dose of gunpowder. In the desperateness of *Bulldog*'s situation, the prisoners had been forgotten.

"I think our bulldog has gone mad," Gascoyne observed.

Ransom was running from side to side, from taffrail to the break of the poop, fore and aft. He shouted orders, countermanded them. He headed *Bulldog* toward the rocky shore of St. Kitts, seemingly intent on wrecking her and escaping overland. But when the jagged rocks loomed close, he changed his mind. He brought the brig about and headed back toward midchannel, where, in deepest water, he ordered the carpenter to stand by sea cocks. He was going to scuttle her. But, in the end, he backed the topsails and lay to, awaiting the inevitable.

A French sail of the line was bearing down.

"It is *Pluton*," Gascoyne said. "D'Albert de Rions commands her. We fall into good hands."

What difference did it make, Tommy thought, good hands or bad? He was staring off toward Newcastle, where the waterfront was black with people. The militia was not assembling on the green, as it had been when *Princess* came in; nor had the mules been brought down to move artillery. Three great warships could not be driven off by a few field pieces. The people, knowing this, only watched; they would not attempt resistance.

Tommy was glad. Denise would be among that crowd. He could see her in his mind, swinging his quadrant in one hand, ready for anything. She would practice taking sights with it, she had said. To work navigation when she sailed with him. The memory brought a rueful smile. Sail with him! In what? He turned away; the sight of *Princess* lying on her side was more than he could bear.

Gascoyne spoke again: "Cheer up, *mon ami*. M. de Rions will send cutters and heavy anchors and all the men we need. Before dark we shall kedge our ship off and be afloat in her again."

Afloat in her! The wonderful sound of it shook Tommy out of his despair. "Will he really pull her clear? Without hurting her?"

"A heavy anchor down, perhaps two; a steady strain on a hawser to *Princess*—the rising tide will do the rest. She will slide off, you will see. A groan, perhaps, as she comes. But no damage."

"Will he help us to repair her, too?" Tommy asked.

"But of course. Have I not said M. de Rions is a good friend? His men will make her tight and shipshape again. We'll have our trading yet. The war marches, *mon ami*. M. de Grasse has taken St. Kitts and also Nevis. We'll soon be trading as we planned."

"I'm thinkin', sor," Reilly observed, "'tis tradin' ashore we'll be doin'—Mr. Midshipman Potter that was, an' me."

"*Bien*," said Gascoyne. "Since M. de Kerguenac will go to France, Midshipman Tommy can manage the plantation in my uncle's place. I will sail through the islands trading. Good partners, eh?"

Tommy said, "But you've always wanted a farm, Reilly— pigs and chicken."

"Ach, sor," Reilly answered shamelessly, "'tis all well an' good, a barnyard, only there's the smell of ut. I'd be happy wid fields o' sugar cane."

"And a *rhummerie, n'est-ce pas?*" Gascoyne joked.

Pluton came downwind to them under a towering pyramid of canvas. White water curled up from bows rimed with the salt of many seas. On the wind came the shrill of pipes, the roll of drums, the blare of trumpets. With man-of-war magic the canvas seemed to melt away.

" 'Tis a grand sight," Reilly said, aloud yet speaking to himself.

"More pretty than a sugar mill?" Gascoyne bantered.

" 'Tis not the same thing at all, sor," Reilly protested. He turned to Tommy. "Now if you was to command a grand ship like that . . ."

"I'd not trade her for our little *Princess*," Tommy said.

"Nor I," said Reilly. Then, seeing the devilment in Gascoyne's eyes, he added quickly, "Still an' all, what's one ship or anither? Wasn't we just afther sayin' we'd go to sea no more?"

Gascoyne laughed.

Pluton lay close aboard now, stripped of her canvas, except enough to give her steerage control. Her guns, two tiers of them, were run out; her cutters swung from the davits, loaded with marines. Her men stared from the bulwarks as M. de Rions hailed the *Bulldog*.

The English flag came down.

Gascoyne said, "More pretty than a sugar mill, eh, *mon ami?*"

Pretty? No. Now that she was close, Tommy saw that her storm-grayed canvas had shot-holes patched in many places. He saw the paint, stained and streaked, along her sides; the barnacles and sea grass fouling the hull between wind and water. Not pretty, but she was mighty—one of many ships in far-off seas, fighting under whatever flag to decide the Empire of the ocean. She was the work of men—and worked by men—who loved the sea sometimes, hated it often. Her guns were manned by men who fought for homeland, or because they had been conscripted, or simply because they knew no other way of life. Men like Reilly and Gascoyne; Lord Milholme, Ravenscroft, and Haskins.

Though Thomas Potter might not comprehend all this, he knew that he was one of them forever.

Caswell

To Chesapeake

Return from
Chesapeake

FLORIDA

BAHAMA

ISLANDS

CUBA

OLD CHANNEL

WINDWARD
PASSAGE

Ca

S T

JAMAICA

CARIBBEAN
SEA

St. Kitts

DIEPPE BAY

Growler
gives
chase

Brimstone
Hill

Basseterre

✕ WRECK

3rd Encounter
with H.M.S.
Bulldog

Hood's Fleet

Bulldog

THE NARROWS

Growler

Princess
stranded

Newcastle

Charleston

De Grasse

Nevis

Miles
0 1 2 3 4 5